DEEP WATERS

Chapters
Prologue

BUTCH
Janesville
Fire!
Lake Geneva
Great Lakes
NAS Glenview

JAPAN
Light
Darkness

SHARK
USS Indianapolis
The Philippine Sea

ISLAND
Evil
Love

JACK
California
Home?
Candy
Montana
Elvis
Lincoln

SADO
Lowlands
Highlands

JOKER
III
Tybee
Mark 15
A City Near You
700 years

Epilogue

Prologue

April 1, 2007

Blood dripped down the side of his mouth as he hung his head trying to buy some time between punches. Well, first came the questions and then came the punches. Questions that made no sense coming from two men dressed as ninjas—one young, amber-eyed and full of angry energy and the other an older, more settled, more patient, more calculating version of a ninja action figure. The angry one was the shorter of the two by several inches and jumped around the room like a wind-up toy, bouncing on his toes while he asked questions that seemed to float to him from above, but were definitely coming directly from his older compatriot who was feeding him suggestions by occasionally speaking into his sleeve. *Who did they think they were, the CIA?*

The older of the two, who was leaning against the kitchen stove casually taking in the inquisition, pushed off his perch and walked across the room. Chester Best, or Gerbil as he was known to his close navy pals, noted a barely perceivable limp as the man made his way to the doorway between the kitchen and the dining room. Chester sensed this man was much older than his wind-up partner, but could not distinguish much more through their dark fabric masks.

"Where are you going, Jiji?" the inquisitor asked as he let go a punch that sprayed more blood along the wall behind his captive.

Chester's head swung back to its original position, hanging forward, chin on his chest, before a sudden coughing fit caught him and he forcefully expelled blood droplets and chunks of congealed goo onto the bright white enamel of the refrigerator and aligning cabinetry. These loud, wet barks prevented Chester from observing the older man's response to his partner's query; it was a look that could have melted enamel—bloody or not.

It was not that the taller man felt disrespected by the title. After all, Jiji, or *Old Man,* was his given name these days, replacing the original Japanese name given to him in 1945. Umibozu was no more flattering than Jiji, but that was a story for another day. No, it was not the name-calling, but any reference to him at all. To anyone who knew the language of its origin, Jiji was likely to be taken as a derogatory term used in jest by the younger man. However, a smarter target might interpret details as small and seemingly insignificant as a name into useful facts that could be detrimental to their cause.

Rai, a name that meant *storm* in his native tongue, bowed his head to show respect for his indiscretion. Rai Mizushima, born at noon on May 26, 1983 during a 7.8 magnitude earthquake in the Sea of Japan, started life with a black cloud over his head and it became darker and darker with each passing year. The Nihonkai-chubu Earthquake itself only killed four people in Japan, but sent near-fifty-foot tsunami waves crashing into the northern shore of the Oga peninsula and the northeastern shore of Honshū, the main island of Japan, killing 100 people. This was Rai's namesake and the reason for his nickname, *Chīsana Jishin*, or *Little Quake.* He preferred Rai—dark clouds and all. In reality, there were no dark clouds on the day Rai was born. The sky had held no warning of the impending disaster and this was Rai's modus operandi: no warning, just an explosion of anger, hate and violence when his exterior crust cracked.

Jiji had a scar that gave him a permanent smirk, which was more a sign of the evil within than an expression of contentment. True happiness would only come when he finally found what he was looking for now that he had led Rai fully down the rabbit hole with promises of heartless revenge. Jiji was Rai's twisted Cheshire Cat and White Rabbit all rolled into one, whose promised revenge was more for him and less for Rai, but Rai would not likely live long enough to figure this out. Rai was just a tool, a cog, in Jiji's 60-year sojourn. Jiji knew he owed his freedom to Rai—feeding into his true-believer syndrome had been easier to execute than even plan—but now because of this deception, the journey toward their ultimate solution had truly begun. With today's *interview*, they were so close Jiji could taste it—and it tasted refined, like a rare wine. Eventually, Rai would have to pay for his family's transgressions—this was part of Jiji's ultimate solution—however, for now Rai would have to wait his turn because there were others who were way ahead of him in line.

"I do not believe this animal—what comes out of his mouth are lies."

"Take caution, *Little Quake*," Jiji said quietly enough not to be overheard by their detainee, but loud enough to get the barb across to his companion. "We have not achieved what we have come for, but may be on a trail of great fortune."

Jiji knew Rai got off on the thought of fortune and revenge, so he stoked the flame after each barb to reset him on their intended path.

Ding, Dong!

"Shit!"

Jiji grabbed Rai's arm as he started to walk to the front door.

"Are you crazy? Look at your pants and shoes."

Rai could see Chester's coughing fit had spayed more than the refrigerator and he kicked Chester hard in the shin for effect.

"What do we do?" Rai asked with some trepidation in his voice.

"Well, as I said, I believe we are done here." Jiji grabbed Chester by the hair, pulling his face to his, and asked, "Are we done here?"

"But we know nothing of the second bomb?" Rai questioned.

"Do not worry, my friend, we are one step closer to my—our dream now that I have *this*," Jiji said as he patted a square outlined in his clothes at his torso.

No expression came from the puffy, bloody mess Chester used to jokingly call his moneymaker. He just drooled out the side of his mouth, over a broken tooth and out through a tear in his lip. He had wanted to spit, but he could no longer control his jaw or lips and he had to settle for the natural river of bloody goo that his mouth could no longer contain. He knew Jiji had found his hidden address book and he racked his brain trying to think of who these monsters could want next. Chester began thinking of how he was going to warn them, then he closed his eyes in anguish, thinking, *How am I going to save anyone when I can't even save myself?* As hopelessness washed over him, he began to fade into unconsciousness.

Jiji pulled back harder on Chester's hair and bent to whisper in his ear, this time for only Chester to hear.

"Good night, my sweet . . . Gerbil. Sleep tight."

Jiji could not read an expression on Chester's excessively swollen face, but he knew referring to him as Gerbil set his mind racing. Well, it did not really matter now anyway. *Let his mind race—he is not going anywhere.* He released Chester's golden mane and let his head bob back to his chest before turning to Rai and saying, "Burn it! Burn it all!"

Rai lit the candle that sat in the middle of Chester's kitchen table. The flame of the candle reflected in Rai's amber eyes as he took one final look at the man he had tortured for the last four hours. Satisfied with his work, he turned to the stove and with a sharp twist of the knobs, turned on all four gas burners before following Jiji out the back door.

Thursday, October 12, 1307

It was a quiet night on the island of Cyprus. Clouds carpeted the sky, lending a deepened blackness to the night. A steady stream of men carrying crates from Kolossi castle to waiting wagons nodded their heads as they paraded past Aimo of Oiselay. Kolossi castle had been the headquarters of the Knights Templar for a year now, but it was abruptly evident it was time to find a safer place for that which they guarded with their lives.

In 1291, the Templars lost Acre—their last true stronghold in the Holy Land. During the siege, Acre, the current Templar headquarters since the fall of Jerusalem, was completely emptied of its treasure. With the fall of Tortosa, Atlit and the island of Arwad soon to follow, the Templars reluctantly relocated back to Nicosia castle in Limassol on the southern coast of Cyprus.

Cyprus had been in the Templars' history for 100 years at this point and the island housed many Templar fortresses. They had bought the island in 1191 from King Richard the Lionheart of England for a down payment of 40,000 gold bezants and the promise of 60,000 more to follow. Richard had taken the island in retaliation when some of his fleet and his betrothed, Berengaria of Navarre, were taken prisoner after their ships had either run aground or were too storm-battered to sail further.

Richard and Berengaria were later married on the island in May of that same year in Limassol castle, where they and their wedding party enjoyed Commandaria, the sweet wine unique to the island—a wine Richard declared to be the Wine of Kings.

Upon taking control of the island, the Templars initially set up base in Nicosia castle and left 14 Templar knights to administer the island as the bulk of the brotherhood continued to support the Third Crusade. Less than a year later, the Templars discovered Richard had taken the island nearly without bloodshed because the Cypriots hated oppressive rulers and did little to stop Richard from capturing Isaac Komnenos, the hated Byzantine Greek governor, who thought himself an emperor. In record time the Templars had become the new hated rulers and the revolt began, finally resulting in a siege upon the Templar castle. Then on Easter Sunday of 1192, the remaining Templars did what Templars do best: they massacred the Cypriots and put an end to the uprisings. However, this did not prevent the islanders from demolishing Nicosia castle while the Templars were away cutting down people in the countryside.

With grave realization, the Templars began to understand governing an island took more than brute force and they sought to have Richard buy back the island. Richard, now knee-deep in the Third Crusade, wanted no part of the island and resold the island to Guy de Lusignan, the prior King of Jerusalem. So, in the end, the Templars rented the island of Cyprus for less than a year for the price of 40,000 gold bezants. However, this did not end their presence in Cyprus—it was only the beginning. Hence, Cyprus was their landing site when Acre fell.

Aimo thumbed a parchment he held in his hand as if he were trying to wear a hole in it or rub out a word in the text. In truth, he would love to remove all the words of this secret communiqué from his Grand Master, Jacques "James" of Molay. Aimo could not believe the treachery of the French ruler, King Philip IV. He could not believe the world would turn on the Templars after all that they had offered, bled for, died for in the name of God. Still, orders were orders and he followed through like a good soldier, not knowing what was to come. Only time would tell if these words were truth, conjecture, or fable.

"We are ready, sir."

"Both ships are loaded?" Aimo queried.

"Yes, sir." The young man spoke with a dry rasp, his face marked with sweat and grim, evident even in the darkness.

"We must . . ." Aimo stopped, not wanting to make the final call to battle, though it felt more like a game of chess in this case—a move that could save the Templars or, by chance, help with their demise. He knew this was just as important as defending a siege—in truth, even more since fortresses lost could be recaptured, whereas treasures lost might be lost forever.

"Take these to the captain of each ship. One to sail east and one to sail west," Aimo said as he handed two envelopes to the young brother.

"With my life, sir," the young man said and turned to run back to the ships.

Aimo looked out over the endless horizon as a hint of light crept toward the island. He knew from James' correspondence that on this same day a fleet of Templar ships were leaving the harbor of La Rochelle in France laden with the bulk of the Templars' wealth in gold, silver, jewels and priceless treasures. The La Rochelle fleet would protect the Templar wealth, but he was charged with their history and their future, if there was to be one.

At 3:33 a.m., the *Warhorse* and the *Liberté*, true ocean galleons, left the shores of Cyprus, never to return: The *Warhorse* with secret orders to sail west to the land known as Greenland and the *Liberté* to sail east to the origin of the Silk Road. Two places on the other side of the world and far, far away from the turmoil of Europe and the Holy Land.

The next morning on Friday the 13th, the last Templar Grand Master, James de Molay, was arrested in France without a fight.

Seven years later, after a trial was held in France—ruthless torturers prompting a witness' willing involvement in the inquisitionary process—James, believing he was already absolved by the pope, was burned at the stake in Paris by the order of King Philip IV. James called to his God for Pope Clement V and King Philip IV to join him on the other side; within the year, they both did.

What had started as a ploy by King Philip IV to get out of his debts with the Templars, ended in false heresy, perpetuated hearsay and the eventual total destruction of the Knights Templar. Or did it?

BUTCH

Janesville

Fire!

Lake Geneva

Great Lakes

NAS Glenview

Janesville

April, 1945

A stiff Wisconsin wind rustled the leaves as it blew through the trees next to the two-story farmhouse. Foliaged applause resounded throughout the air as if a giant were rushing through a forest without a care in the world.

Butch sat atop a tractor revving the engine as his father, Jake, wrenched some settings.

"Punch it and then let it run!" Jake shouted over the noise.

Vroom!

Jake ducked his head under the engine compartment and smoothed the idle to his liking.

"We're good."

Butch took this as a sign to cut the engine. Once he did, the engine noise was immediately replaced by his father's booming voice.

"What the hell you doing, boy? I want you to plow the side field."

"What about Arthur?" Butch questioned.

"Arthur is working at the garage. Why the heck you think you're helping me tune the tractor rather than your older brother? You think I like telling my helper what every tool I need looks like? Life is too short to work with fools, but you're all I got."

Feeling more than a little deflated and dejected, Butch started up the John Deere and waited for his father to open the main barn doors so he could plow the side field to prepare it for planting. Butch hated driving the tractor and hated farm work in general. How could you enjoy being rattled to your bones for hours on end as dust flew at your face, eyes and teeth? Sometimes he would dislodge a speck of field grit from his teeth days after he had plowed a field.

Butch was from a large farm family and now that Arthur had found a good paying job outside the family farm, Butch was next in line to pull more than his weight, even though he was only 15. He much more enjoyed his part-time job at the local pharmacy during the winter months—brains over brawn would always be his choice, even though he had both.

Butch pulled the brim of his hat low over his brow and prepared for three hours of sinew-loosening tractor work. He wished he could listen to the radio while working the fields, but his father had forbidden it, going as far as removing the factory-installed radio. Plus, he would likely have to tape his little transistor radio directly over his ear to have any hopes of hearing over the loud roar of the tractor's engine. So, as usual, daydreams would need to be his entertainment as he plowed.

Butch, a healthy-looking dark-haired adolescent, had what could be referred to as an athletic body and was tall for his age. Maturing earlier than his other classmates made him fodder for jokes until high school football, where he took control in a time of depleted upper-classmen and was subsequently named the varsity quarterback in his sophomore year.

Partially due to the thin upper-class talent pool and partially to his natural given talent, he shined at quarterback and his team went on to win the Wisconsin state regionals, ultimately losing to Platteville in the finals. This had certainly turned the tables on his fellow students mocking him, but did nothing to help his father's over expectations of his current oldest child who he still controlled, yet did not seem to appreciate or even like.

Butch pulled the tractor into the barn and cut the

engine. He took off his sunglasses and the bandana he had tied around his mouth and nose as an attempt to filter out some of the windblown grit, but still felt some in his teeth. He spit out a gob of speck-filled saliva on the barn floor and scuffed it in the dirt with his boot, not wanting his father to have any more reasons to berate him.

As he was closing the barn door, he heard his mother calling.

"Dinner! Butch, you hear me? Dinner is on."

"Yes, mama. I'm coming in now."

"Well, shake off that field dirt and come in the back so you don't track that cloud following you into the house."

Butch just smiled. How was it that when his mother told him the obvious, he listened with a smile, with almost eager acceptance. Whereas, when his father barked out the same orders day after day—things he could now do in his sleep—an unknown emotion crept over his scalp and took refuge at the base of his neck.

Maria, Butch's mother, was a gift to the family and to the Janesville area at large. She worked the farm, fed the family, and participated in community, church and school committees. Everyone who knew her or met her for the first time, loved her more and more each day. She would have opened a restaurant long ago, but pushing out a child every 12 to 18 months does tend to take up your spare time, so she was content to play her part for the family.

After removing his overalls outside the back porch and banging them against a pole to release some of the dust, Butch came in through the back door and walked directly to the dining room. He grabbed the pewter pitcher from the middle of the table and immediately felt its warmth.

"Warm milk, again?" he questioned.

"That's how you know it's fresh, stupid," his father said, glaring at Butch as he spoke.

"Yep. That's how you know," Butch said as he poured a big glassful.

Butch sat around the table with his entire family, save his brother Arthur. His older sister, Rita, was helping Maria cook and set up the serving bowls. His little brothers, Bobby, Thomas and Owen, were eager to get started and Owen had his hand slapped back by his father when he tried to grab a roll before the family grace. The twins, Gina and Julie, were parked together on a piano bench at the far end of the table, directly across from their father.

Maria said the grace.

"Dear God, thank you for this bountiful feast you lay out before us. Please make us soldiers in your army of truth, justice and forgiveness. Amen."

At that moment hands shot out from under the table and even their father's glaring stare could not calm the hungry masses as they set out to satiate themselves on the beautiful bounty set before them.

After Butch finished his dinner, he gathered his plate and silverware and walked them into the kitchen. He knew since he had plowed the side field, he would not be asked to do any kitchen duties, which were almost always allotted to his sisters unless his father had a punishment in mind.

"Where are you off to so fast?" his mother asked.

"Candy and I are going to go for a ride since it's such a beautiful day."

"Well, you don't have a lot of daylight left, so don't be long."

"Yes, mama," Butch said as he kissed his mother on the cheek.

As Butch waited, he thought back to Homecoming last October and his first night with Candy. He had just executed an exciting comeback win in the last quarter of their high school Homecoming game, hurling himself into the end zone to put his team on top 31-28. He was 23 for 28 with 239 yards in the air and 123 on the ground. It was a great game against a tough opponent, but in the end, the Janesville Bluebirds beat Beloit for another year of bragging rights.

That was the night Candy, a senior and the head cheerleader, finally decided Butch was the real deal and gave into the tradition of small towns, and even big ones, where the head cheerleader and the football quarterback dated as a rule or a rite of passage.

She had led with, "So, sexy," and the craziest night he had ever been a part of started off with a bang, or a kiss more accurately, as Candy planted one on Butch's lips in case her *So, sexy* did not generate sufficient attention.

"Well, hello," Butch replied once he had use of his mouth again.

"Do you want to go to the Hill?" Candy asked.

"Sure, that would be swell. The Hill is always a good time," Butch responded, hoping not to sound anxious. He had been to the Hill many times, but never with the head cheerleader.

The *Hill* was the highest point in the woods behind the DuPree family farm. In addition to the hilltop clearing, Butch and Riff Dupree, his best friend, had carved out a clearing just off the dirt road that circled the farm so any parked cars would be hidden from view behind the mass of honeysuckle, huckleberry, dogwood and buckthorn that surrounded the woods. From the car park, it was a short walk up the path to the Hill where they would party with their friends. Most of the kids in Butch and Riff's circle knew about the Hill, but only a special few knew about the Rock. The Rock was a more distant place on the shore of the stream that ran along the base of the Hill and through the woods. The Hill is where you went to have a good time, but the Rock is where you went to have a better, more private, time.

"I can drive," Candy said with a smile.

"And I can't, so you're it," Butch returned.

When they arrived at the Hill, there was already a fair-sized group occupying the clearing at the crest of the Hill. Riff was there with his girlfriend, Laura, and Riff's sister, KK, was there with her boyfriend who Butch did not know. KK was a freshman, so it was not unusual to be unfamiliar with someone in her class, but still Butch felt he looked a bit out of place. A handful of football players and cheerleaders filled out the rest of the dance card for the group. Once they were amidst the crowd, Candy tugged on Butch's hand to pull him to a stop.

"So, soldier—you want to neck?"

"I cannot tell a lie," was all he could get out before Candy covered his mouth with hers.

That night there was kissing, drinking, dancing and an experience Butch had not yet encountered: second base. God, he was in love. Candy kissed like a goddess and her boobs were—*Christopher Columbus*, he was in love with boobs. He could not wait to get his mitts full of Candy again.

Butch lay against one of the many large fallen tree trunks placed throughout the clearing with Candy in his arms as one of the football players threw another log on the fire. Sparks exploded into the air and lazily circled back to the ground. As the night grew late, those who remained on the Hill were all a little sauced—some more than others.

Butch could feel Candy breathe, the slow repetition causing him to succumb to the rest he sorely needed. As he began to slip into his reward of sleep, he was suddenly snapped awake by a scream that echoed through the clearing. Butch attempted to guide Candy's body gently to the log as he stood, but she slipped from his hands and her head bounced off the log, waking her in a most unpleasant fashion.

"Ow," Candy cried and then sat up to rub her head.

"What was that?"

"Who was that?"

"Where did it come from?"

Questions shot across the clearing as the football players all jumped up ready to answer this call for help, but another scream never came.

"Riff, you go back to the cars and Joey, you go down the north side of the Hill. Todd and Jeremy, you cover the south side."

"Butch, what the heck. I have a bump on my head."

"Sorry, babe, someone is screaming for help."

Candy tried to complain more, but Butch disappeared into the thicket.

Once Butch cleared the thick brush, he stood on the path that led to the Rock. After waiting a moment for his eyes to adjust to a night sky without a fire in his peripheral vision, he continued down the path. He listened as he quickly traversed the path, but did not hear another scream or call for help. At about 50 yards from the Hill, he heard a muffled voice followed by a threatening whisper. He stopped and listened, again hoping to identify the direction he should take when he heard a louder cry that gave up the location.

"Ouch! What the heck, bitch," KK's boyfriend swore and lifted his hand to slap her.

Butch could see enough in the dark to tell the boy had had his hand over KK's mouth in an attempt to keep her quiet. From his reaction, KK, who had been struggling to talk through his hand, had made her statement silently by biting his palm. Butch made it to the pair just in time to grab the boy's wrist in midair. He then used the boy's own momentum to turn him right into his fist which landed squarely on the boy's nose. The boy fell like a thrown stone into the mud before he knew what hit him.

"Wha—" was all he could get out before KK stomped on his head with her boot.

"KK, what's going on? Are you hurt?"

"No. This king-sized asshole thinks just 'cause he can kiss me that he doesn't need to stop when I say to stop."

Butch could see KK's cardigan was unbuttoned or torn open and her blouse was muddy. Butch pressed his foot into the boy's back and asked, "So, you have a name?"

"His name is Derick. He's from Beloit."

Butch rolled the boy over and stared down into a sparsely bearded face that was not that of a freshman—more a fresh man.

Butch stared into Derick's eyes and spoke very slowly.

"I don't know how you get your kicks, Derick . . . but you can see KK plans to give you no more than the sole of her boot tonight, so I think you should take this opportunity to split and never come back. Got it?"

Derick nodded and once released ran into the night.

"It's a long walk back to Beloit, loser," KK yelled after him.

Butch just smiled and gave KK a hug. He then turned around so KK could straighten up her top.

"I know you had him where you wanted him. I was just helping."

"Thanks, Butch, honey. I didn't expect him to go ape on me. I was just lookin' for some fun."

"Well, you still have many nights of fun ahead of you,

but you have to be smart."

"Don't tell Riff. He'll snap a cap over this."

"Don't worry. We'll tell him you saw a snake."

KK smiled and started back toward the clearing with Butch.

When they got back to the Hill, Candy was gone.

The next afternoon while Butch was working in the barn to prepare for the fall harvest, Candy pulled up in her father's Mercury Club Coupe.

"Sorry I had to cut out last night, but I got a terrible headache after someone dropped my head on a log."

"Yeah—sorry about that."

"I'll forgive you if you come cruising with me," Candy expressed with a raised eyebrow.

"Give me 20 minutes and I'll take you up on that deal."

Butch ran into the house, told his mother he was off to run some errands, jumped into the shower and was back at Candy's car short of 14 minutes.

"Hop in," Candy called out the window as Butch approached her car.

"Candy, I was thinking we could take the Model T out for a quick ride before it gets dark."

"You don't just want to go up in the woods and neck?" she said with a smile.

"Yeah, we can do that too, but I really wanted to take out my brother's Model T before he gets back. I know he finished working on it and it should run like a rabbit with the new engine he put in it."

"Boys and cars . . . I just don't get it," she said as she pulled her car around to the far side of the smaller barn.

"Wait here," Butch told her as he threw his weight hard to the right to help leverage the door open and then slid it out of the way.

Within a minute, Butch emerged in a 1926 Model T

Runabout—top down, painted kelly green with yellow wheel spokes.

"Whoa—now this is a car," Candy exclaimed as she climbed into the passenger's seat.

"Let's see what this baby can do." Butch said before he stomped the gas pedal to the floor, sending both of their heads snapping back. They both exploded in laughter as the car slowed to a stop once Butch released the accelerator.

"Shit, what has my brother created? I bet this thing could rival your father's car."

"Well, let's not get too carried away—and no, we're not going to find out 'cause I'm not racing my father's car against anyone at any time."

"I know. I was just saying. Let's take it for a spin and see what more it has to offer."

Candy just smiled, not stating the obvious: that she likely had a lot more to offer than the car.

Butch pressed down on the gas pedal more judiciously this time, hoping to find a spot that was a little less punchy, then took the car down the back road to a gate that let out onto Avalon Road.

"This was a good choice, Butch," Candy said as she cuddled under his arm. "Open windows are one thing, but no windows is an entirely different experience."

"Yes, wind in your hair and bugs in your teeth. This is cooking with gas."

Butch and Candy leaned back in the seats with their sunglasses on and just enjoyed the fresh air that whipped around them.

The Ford Model T Runabout cost $365 brand new and had a top speed of 42 mph. Arthur picked it up as a trade for some tractor engine work he did for a nearby farmer who had the Model T just sitting in his barn. After Arthur was finished tinkering with the engine, replacing it with a V-6 and modifying various components with Ford motor parts he obtained for free from the junkyard behind the garage where he worked, he had a jalopy with unknown capabilities that he could call his own.

After making a wide circuit through the surrounding farmland, Butch turned down East Creek Road to start the trek homeward.

"This is a gas, Butch. I feel like I'm flying."

"Oh, you want to fly?" Butch answered and pressed the pedal down past the sweet spot he had found. The car lurched and almost bounced off the road, but Butch kept on it like a bucking bronco that he refused to let throw him.

"Whoa-wee," Candy screamed, holding tightly to Butch's arm and even tighter to her seat.

Butch kept the pedal to the floor as they rounded a bend and hit a bridge spanning a stream. Now there is a lesson here any Wisconsin driver should understand: Wisconsin roads cannot be trusted to be straight. You may go up a hill and then have to turn left at the peak to avoid hitting a tree growing where the road should be, or a seemingly straight road may turn ever so slightly to better line up with a bridge. Well, this was the case here for Butch—a fifteen-year-old who did not have his license and had not yet experienced these Wisconsin back road subtleties firsthand.

Butch hit the joint of the road and the bridge at a speed in excess of 60 miles per hour and the car bucked, then bucked again when the back wheels hit. This caused the car to literally bounce and shimmy across the bridge on shocks that were not built for such speeds. This would have been no more than a simple lesson in straight-on physics until he saw the road ahead took a slight left. Now he had to turn a bouncing car and he knew he was not going to make it. After the bridge, a combination of bouncing, momentum, loose gravel and a slight turn of the wheel caused the car to catch its front right tire and go airborne.

Butch and Candy flew through the air at nearly the same speed as the car and after what seemed to be a frozen moment in time, landed upside down in the roadside cornfield. The car continued to bounce and cartwheel along the road until it finally came to rest at their feet.

Butch and Candy, both dazed by the experience, looked out at the now upside-down world and started to laugh. Feeling no pain with the sudden expression of joy, they burst out even louder.

Butch was the first to right himself and he crawled across the flattened corn stalks to help Candy.

"You OK, babe?" he asked.

"I can't feel anything that really hurts. I think you hurt my head worse the other night than flying through the air did."

Candy then turned and looked at the car.

"You think the car is OK?"

All the momentary joy quickly drained from Butch's body and he felt like his skin was two sizes too small. *Jeez, I'm done for if Arthur's car is broken,* he thought to himself. Keeping a brave face, he answered, "Let's find out," and took her hand to help hoist her out of the corn.

Upon initial inspection, it looked as if the car had mostly bounced on its wheels as it flipped since all Butch could see as evident damage was the right front fender which was bent down to the wheel. Butch walked to the fender and pulled up hard; it budged begrudgingly, but did move enough to free the wheel.

"Let's see if she starts."

Candy crossed her fingers as Butch climbed into the driver's seat and cranked the engine. The engine zoomed to life without falter and an ocean of relief washed over Butch, returning his skin to its original size.

"You got moxie, Butch. I'll give you that," Candy said as she took the seat next to him. "I thought you were in the hot seat for sure, but you just kept your cool and carried on like it was nothing. Like a real soldier."

This was the moment where Butch had learned inward emotions and outward expressions should remain separated in their own part of his brain so he could look calm even when his brain was carrying on inside his head.

"Well, that was fun, but I think it's time to go home."

"Where are my cheaters?" Candy asked as she pawed her head looking for her sunglasses in the place they usually resided.

They both turned to look at the cornfield at the same moment. Knowing finding their sunglasses in a cornfield as the evening crept upon them was as likely as finding a needle in—they did not even need to finish their thought. Butch pressed down on the gas pedal and steered the car back onto East Creek Road to take the slow ride home.

Once they had the Model T back in the barn, Candy gave Butch a big smooch and said, "More to come," then left Butch to figure out what to do about the fender.

The next morning Arthur had a day off and planned to take his Model T down to the quarry to visit some of his friends. When he opened the side barn, he saw his car in the same spot he left it with a pile of boards on the barn floor next to the front right wheel.

"Dagnabbit," he cursed. "Who's the fool that piled these boards here?"

Arthur could see several boards remained stacked

against a support beam for the upper level, which told him something had caused them to fall on his car. He bent to observe the front of the car and after finding a slight dent on both sides of the fender where he surmised the boards hit, he cursed again.

"Jeez, I'm surrounded by stupid people."

Arthur took out his handkerchief to wipe the fender and after seeing it was likely he could pound out the dents without issue, he climbed in and headed for the quarry.

Arthur did not understand the boards could not have caused a dent on the *inside* of the fender and never knew that there was a stalk of corn, ear and all, wedged between the radiator and the engine block because the stalk fell out on his way to the quarry.

Butch's reverie of last fall was broken by Arthur as he passed on his way to the side barn.

"So, you gonna pluck that bird of yours? She's a stacked skirt if I've ever seen one."

Butch had learned to not give Arthur a reason to fight ever since Arthur almost busted Butch's cheekbone for no good reason, so he just let the comment slide, hoping he would just keep on moving on.

"You best hurry, son—able grables don't wait forever."

"Thanks for the advice," Butch responded as Arthur walked away snickering.

Moments later Candy pulled into the drive and circled to let Butch climb in. Not knowing Arthur had stopped to watch them, Butch leaned in to give Candy a kiss, which she eagerly returned.

"Thanks, soldier," she said.

Arthur continued to watch them from behind the barn as they drove off to start their date.

Their night started off well enough—time at the diner,

time at the movies and eventually time at the Rock—but Butch did not feel right. Arthur's comments continued to play in his head and he wondered if he was on the beam of his choosing. Sure, he was neat and now that he was a successful quarterback, the school loved him. But was he in control? Candy had chosen him and in most all choices—other than the cornfield flight night—she had been the controlling force. Now, tonight, she wanted to go the whole way and he did not know if *he* was ready or even willing for her to be his first. He always imagined his first time being with a cute, leggy blonde like the ones he saw in the magazines: a pinup girl or a Vargas girl. Candy was 5'3" with dark brown hair. Sure, she was a doll, but he thought they were just having fun, not anything more serious.

Candy played with Butch's hair as he lay with his head in her lap, both lying back to admire the spring sky.

"What you thinking about?" Candy asked.

"Nothing much," Butch replied, keeping his brain compartments as far apart as he could manage.

"Well, I was hoping tonight would be the night we could hit the hay," she said as she moved her other hand that had been wrapped around him down to the front of his jeans.

"Candy . . ." he started and then paused.

Candy pushed him off her lap and started yelling.

"Why are you always putting me off? You think all those tongue baths I gave you were free without any effort on your part. What's wrong . . ." she said, then started to cry, ". . . am I not pretty enough for you?"

"No, Candy—you are beautiful. I just don't know if it's the right thing to do. I mean, I'm just a sophomore and you're a senior. I don't know if I'm ready."

"What are you talking about? You act all doll dizzy in

public, but you're not willing to go the whole way with your girl?"

"I didn't say I wouldn't—I mean, I just—"

Candy cut him off there. "Well, I thought you were the man in this relationship. I thought you would take control to help a woman out, but it looks like you're going to have to take things into your own hands now . . ." she said as she kicked her feet free of their entanglement and stood over him as Butch stared up at her quizzically, ". . . and I mean literally," she finished and then marched off up the path to her car.

"What about the dance tomorrow?" he called after her.

"You can be-bop at the dance with someone else. And I'll be looking for another king for prom."

Butch's heart sank with a thud and he lay back down to stare at the deep blue and white sky through the leaves as they danced in the wind—the leaves probably dancing more than he would be doing anytime soon.

* * *

It was Saturday night and the high school quarterback was being dropped off at the Harvest Dance by his mother. Butch could not think of a more ideal situation to improve his status than being dumped by the head cheerleader and being dropped off by his mother, but this was his life at the moment and one side of his head told him it was nothing but up from here.

"You have fun, honey . . . and be a good boy," Maria said, then leaned in to kiss him on the cheek.

"Don't worry—I'm on the beam, mom."

"OK. I trust that means you will be good."

One side of Butch's brain said, "It means I'll be great, mom," while a voice inside shouted, *You fathead!*

Butch thanked his mom for the ride, then trotted over to where Riff was standing with a group of kids.

"What's buzzin', cousin?"

Riff looked up from his conversation and immediately pulled Butch aside.

"I heard about your break up."

"Already?" Butch was hoping to keep the news out of the public ear for a while at least.

"Yeah, she's saying you couldn't get it up and she's done with you."

Butch wanted to have a stern conversation with the hopeful side of his brain because it was certainly not looking better, but he did his best to turn the tide.

"Well, you know that's all gobbledygook. She's just mad we broke up. That girl is bonkers, so don't be busting my chops over her."

"So, give me the dope. Why did you break up?" Riff insisted.

"Time for a change, Riff. Time for a change," Butch said with unfelt confidence, then slapped Riff on the shoulder and led him toward the gym.

The dance was going surprisingly well. Butch was surrounded by cheerleaders and girls who never seemed to have noticed him before, then suddenly, the cheerleaders split like a flock of scared pigeons. Butch looked up to see Candy entering the dance and understood the others did not want Candy to catch them picking at her leftover carrion. Butch then watched with some appreciation as the scattered cheerleaders came together from different parts of the gym and swelled upon Candy, covering her with praise about her dress and her hair, trying to calm the beast they knew her to be when she was mad or upset.

"So, I see my ex-meatball is here."

"Yes, Candy. Do you want some punch? I know for a fact Jimmy Butler spiked it, so it should give you a buzz after just a few glasses. I think that's what you need, babe—a buzz. Right?"

"What I need is for everyone to know about what I said about his johnson. Got it, Rose?"

Rose swallowed hard and wished she could just go home. In another five years, she would have tried to click her heels, but that trick was yet to come and only worked in the movies.

"Rose," Candy said as she grabbed Rose's arm to pull her close so she could speak directly into her ear. "You know what I told you. I want you to go tell him in front of all those *fat Nancys*."

Rose tried to swallow again, but came up with so little saliva that she found it difficult and instead just nodded acknowledgment.

Rose then grabbed Carol by the arm in a likewise fashion and pulled her along with her on the way toward Butch and what was left of his female entourage.

Candy watched from the punch table across the room as Rose gave the group the news and was flooded with glee when she saw every girl in the group react in the same surprised manner. However, they also had a likewise uniform reaction when Butch answered Rose's statement with his own—they all laughed even harder and placed an endearing hand on Butch's arm, shoulder and back.

Candy exploded and walked toward the group a bit too fast for her high heels. She did not fall, but looked a bit like a duck as she hurried across the gym floor.

"What's so funny?" Candy yelled. "Rose?"

Rose, knowing she had nothing more to swallow, just stared back in silence. Butch wanted to repeat his comment, but one side of his brain was holding him back and before he finally decided to let it fly, he heard it come from behind him.

"He said, 'If there's a problem with my johnson, it's likely her problem and not mine.'"

"Whaaa," Candy screamed and then launched her drink into Butch's face before storming off, duck-like, out of the dance.

Butch used the sleeve of his suit coat to wipe the fruit punch from his eyes and turned to see KK laughing at him.

"Wow, girl. You sure pack a punch," he said smiling.

"Looks like you're the one packin' the punch," KK replied with a giggle.

"Would you like to dance?"

"If you promise not to get me sticky."

"I can only hope," he smirked.

Riff offered to drive Butch home after the dance, but Riff was a little too drunk, so Butch suggested now that he officially had his learner's permit, he would drive Riff's car and take Riff and KK home.

"Or, I can drive," KK said as they walked to the car.

"I don't think it's a good idea to have a 14-year-old girl driving her family car after drinking at the dance either."

"Well, first off, is that 'cause I'm a girl or 'cause I'm 14?"

"KK, you know being a girl doesn't matter much anymore. These are modern times."

"It's good to hear you say that, Butch, 'cause I just turned 15."

"When?"

"About an hour ago—officially, but today is my birthday."

"Happy birthday, KK," Butch followed up his felicitations with a big hug for the birthday girl. "We should celebrate."

"My idea exactly. How 'bout we drop off my brother

and go to the Rock?"

"A brainchild if I ever heard one."

After aiming Riff toward the front door, KK took the keys from Butch and drove them to the hidden clearing where they parked their car and started the long, dark walk to the Rock.

"Hey, KK, since it's an overcast night, maybe we should just take the simple way out and head to the Hill."

"Sounds OK to me. I've learned that it's not the place, but the person anyway."

Butch felt the back of his neck tingle in strange anticipation as he trekked up the hill after KK. As he followed he started to ponder if KK was what he was actually looking for in a girl. He could not actually see her clearly now in the darkness of the tree-covered path, but he envisioned her as he saw her at the dance: a blonde who took no prisoners. While Candy was 5'3" and likely to stay there, KK was 5'5" and still growing; while Candy was bossy, KK was confident; while Candy was prissy, KK was outgoing; while Candy was pretty and judgmental, KK was cute and kind. All this time she had been hiding in plain sight.

Once they were atop the Hill, Butch made a fire to light their conversation and keep them warm. After several minutes of small talk, KK reached into her bra exposing the top of her right breast and pulled out a cigarette.

"Do you want to smoke some?" she asked.

"I don't smoke, but thanks."

"This isn't a ciggy. This is Mary Jane."

"Where did you get weed from?"

"Have you ever heard of *Hemp for Victory*?"

Butch returned a vacant stare, so KK continued.

"Well, my friend's dad now grows hemp for the government. For the soldiers."

"They're sending weed to the soldiers?" Butch asked with some amazement, finally thinking he grasped the concept.

"No, they're growing *hemp* for the Army to make ropes and material, like parachutes. His father just works a little Mary Jane into the mix and then sells it for kicks."

"Aren't you afraid it will . . ."

"Will what? Show me a good time? Don't believe all that stuff they've been tellin' us in school. Just last year a medical school in New York reported that weed wasn't the Grim Reaper and that no one was goin' to go *mad* from smoking it."

"Where did you hear that?"

"I read it. I may be a girl, but I can still read." KK followed up her jest with a smile.

"So, how do you get it? Do you have to go to a . . . *pusher*?" Butch asked, uncertain of the term.

"Heck no. I steal it from the field before they harvest it. I ain't no *viper*."

"Wow! I don't know what to say."

"Just say yes."

"OK, KK," Butch said with dwindling hesitation.

They both lay back against a log and shared a smoke as the fire cracked in the quiet of the night. After catching more than a little buzz, they talked about things—their parents, their siblings, their dreams and disappointments. They cracked up over the littlest things—a mispronounced word or self-deprecating story. Then finally as the night grew cooler and the fire started to dwindle, they moved into each other's arms.

"You know, you ain't too shabby for a boy."

"And you aren't so bad for a dame."

"You really think I'm a dame—not just a girl."

"I think you're so much more than just a girl."

"Really?" KK smiled, then followed up with a tickle attack that sent them both rolling and laughing until they finally came to a stop with KK straddling Butch's torso and pinning his arms to the ground.

"So, you think you got me?"

"I hope so," KK answered and then lowered her face to kiss him.

They both fell into a maze of tangled legs and twisted clothes. They kissed and petted until KK finally came up for air and looked deeply into Butch's eyes. At that moment he knew what it was like to be in love and that he was about to lose his virginity on the Hill.

After it was all over, they continued to cuddle in each other's arms by the dying fire until they nodded off, both reliving their lovemaking in their dreams.

Crack!

Butch came awake with a start.

"What was that?"

They both sat up and looked around into the darkness, but did not see any movement. The evening air was silent; even the bugs and the fire had succumbed to the night.

"It could have been anything, but we should go."

"OK."

They both gathered their clothes and dressed in the darkness. They drove to Butch's house in silence and after a 15-second kiss that neither wanted to end, KK dropped Butch off at the top of his driveway.

Tomorrow was going to be an interesting day since he was going to have to tell Riff that he was dating his sister. Riff was his best friend, so he hoped this would not be a problem. He considered if Riff wanted to date one of his sisters that it would be OK with him, but then again, his sister Rita was eighteen and the twins were nine, so it was not likely this belief would ever be tested.

Yes, tomorrow will be an interesting day, he thought to himself, not knowing it was already tomorrow and it was going to be a lot worse than interesting. It was going to change his life forever.

Fire!

April, 1945

Butch started a slow walk down the dark, tree-covered drive toward his house. After about 50 yards, just past the gate to the horse training pen, he noted a flash to his left just within his peripheral vision. Thinking it was a firefly, he continued on his trek, then stopped abruptly as it came to him that it was early April and the fireflies were not due for another two months. His heart skipped a beat when he again saw the flash and realized it was a torch held high by the outstretched arm of a dark figure trying to open the rear door to the main barn.

Butch broke into a run, taking the most direct route through the horse pen, then jumped the back fence to follow the intruder into the main barn. When Butch came to the rear door, he took a deep breath before ducking into the barn, then immediately crouched down in case the unknown stranger heard him enter. In the darkness of the barn, Butch was at a huge advantage—not only did he know the barn with his eyes closed, but the stranger was wielding a torch that cast a glow everywhere he went.

The man—Butch assumed it was a man from his height and the way he walked—paused after passing the six animal stalls: horses on the right and the milk cow on the left. Butch watched from the shadows as the man looked back, not as if in search of someone following him, but as a momentary pause to consider the animals' role in what he was about to do. Seeming to have decided, the man turned and walked over to the muck stall that contained the mucking tools and a supply of straw to replenish the stalls once cleaned. He then lifted the torch.

Seeing his chance, Butch bolted for the man and tackled

him away from the straw he was about to set ablaze. Both men rolled across the barn floor and came to rest against the back right tractor wheel.

Not a bad tackle for a quarterback, Butch thought to himself as he popped to a knee and punched the man hard in the face.

The man, seeing the torch was still within reach, grabbed the handle and swung it hard toward Butch's head. Butch raised crossed forearms to block the blow, but still received a face full of hot embers that showered from the torch when it came to a painful stop against his arms. The intruder took this moment to better his situation and tossed a handful of barn floor dust into Butch's eyes, which blinded him even further. The man then tossed the torch aside, rolled away from Butch's blinded grasp and ran for the rear door.

Butch spit dust from his mouth as he pawed at his face trying to clear enough of the irritants away so he could chance opening his eyes again. His vision was impaired, but he could see clearly enough that the discarded torch had ignited a pile of barn sweepings and the flames were starting to spread. Butch immediately removed his suit coat and leapt to pat down the flames. Once he was certain he had extinguished every flicker, he left his badly singed suit coat on the barn floor and turned to grab the hose from the nearby muck stall to douse the area with water; he was taking no chances. However, what he saw behind him caught him off guard and he paused as his brain fought hard to comprehend his vision—the barn floor was on fire.

Shit, that must have started from the embers when he hit me with the torch, Butch reasoned, then ran for the hose to address his new problem. He grabbed the hose and started to spray the floor with water, but the flames just popped back to life when he stopped to evaluate his progress.

"Shit," he swore again as he saw the fire had established itself in the large oil stains on the barn floor and the flames were now running up a wall of hay bales near the two empty cow stalls. Butch dropped the hose and ran to the first cow stall to lead Betty, their milk cow, out of the barn. Once he had pushed her into the safety of the open field, he returned for the horses. He threw rope harnesses over their necks and led all three to the training pen, closing the gate behind them.

He collapsed against the horse training hut to catch his breath and looked back at the barn. A steady glow could now be seen through the windows all along the side facing the house. He felt water hit his face and looked to the sky for the only thing that was going to save the family barn now, but saw no clouds. Instead, he found Clifford, the big white stallion, sloppily lapping up water from the trough next to where Butch was sitting. Butch took this as a sign and used the trough water to further clean his face and eyes before heading into the house to alert his family and call the volunteer fire department. He knew the fire department to be very reliable, but dealing with a barn fire at this time of night did not give him too much hope anything other than the animals would actually be saved.

Just as he finished using his shirtsleeve to wipe his face free of water and dirt, he looked up to see Candy running from the barn wearing only her panties and an open blouse; she was carrying what looked to be the rest of her wardrobe. A male figure soon followed her out and hurried Candy to the backside of the barn where her car was parked.

Instantly, Butch thought of Arthur.

Hot damn, Arthur. You didn't even wait for me to tell

you I broke up with Candy before swooping in.

Butch then started to wonder if their little rendezvous was *not* a result of him and Candy breaking up, which made his blood boil just as if he were actually standing next to the burning barn. He pushed Clifford out of the way and headed for the pen gate to confront Candy and her new beau.

The male figure came back around the barn into the light of the flames and looked directly at Butch—they both froze. Seconds ago, Butch's blood was boiling and he was ready for a fight, but now his blood ran cold and he quickly darted back to the cover of the horse trough thinking, *What am I doing, I can't fight him*, and hoping it was too dark for the figure to see him as more than a shadow in the night.

Butch watched as if in a trance as the night progressed and the chaos grew. Within minutes of him hiding, his family poured out of the house and in an act of desperation tried to put out the fire with the yard hose—certainly an exercise in futility. Once the fire department arrived, everyone was in the yard watching the battle between fire and water, knowing deep in their hearts that fire had already won.

Butch became momentarily complacent from the shock of the night's events, until a sudden feeling of dread splashed over him with the subtly of a fire hose.

My suit coat is inside the barn.

Butch prayed there would be nothing left of it after the fire, but now he knew he had to cover his tracks if it proved otherwise. In an attempt to do just that, he left the pen gate open and headed for the back of the house. He prayed again no one would question how three horses had run from the barn into the safety of the training pen of their own accord. His shock allowed this fairytale and simultaneously blocked out the fact that the horses must have also put on their own rope harnesses before starting their journey.

Butch crawled in a back window and quickly showered to remove all evidence of his presence in the barn. After dressing, he walked to the living room window to watch the ongoing disaster now that he was again safely hidden from view. As the flames finally succumbed to the constant downpour of water, his family continued to mill about, waiting for the all clear from the firefighters.

Butch was contemplating what to do next when a firefighter emerged from the barn holding what looked to be a blanket. However, when he held it up for his family to see, Butch was gut-punched—it was his suit coat. It was at that moment he knew his life here in this house would never be the same. Butch needed to leave and needed to leave now. He immediately grabbed a duffle bag and stuffed it with clothes and other necessities, then crawled out the same back window and quietly walked into the night.

* * *

The next morning when Butch awoke, he found himself in the hayloft of the DuPree family barn. Not fully remembering or acknowledging the events of the night before, he seemed momentarily mystified about why he was there. He remembered making love to KK and then . . . then it all came flooding back and suddenly feeling morose was an understatement.

He climbed down out of the loft and made his way to the back of KK's house. He tossed pebbles at her bedroom window and raised a finger to his mouth to shush her when she came into view.

"Meet me in the barn," he called out as quietly as possible and then returned to the barn to wait.

"What is it?" KK asked as she closed the barn door behind her.

"Did your family hear about the fire?" he asked, wondering if news of the fire was on the radio and if the chain-reaction telephone calls had started throughout the town as usual.

"No. What fire?"

"Our barn burned down last night."

"What . . . how?"

"When I got home after I left you, I saw someone with a torch enter our barn."

"Do you know who it was?" KK queried.

"Yes—I'm certain. I saw his face when I punched him."

"Who—who was it?"

"Derick!"

"Derick? I'm so sorry. I knew that guy was trouble, but that didn't stop me. Sometimes I think any voice in my head is my mother and I wildly do the opposite just to be foolishly defiant or recklessly independent."

"I don't blame you. I'm the one who punched him last fall. The guy is bad news. I think he was stalking you, or me, and got mad when he saw us together on the Hill. Remember the twig snap we heard?"

"That could have been a deer," KK justified.

"Well, can you explain why Derick chose yesterday to get back at me then—almost six months after our fight? Regardless, you need to be careful. Understand?"

KK nodded her head in acknowledgment, then looked at Butch quizzically and finally asked, "But I don't understand. Why did you sleep here . . . in our barn?"

Butch crossed the short distance between them and hugged KK. He held her for a few short seconds and then whispered into her ear.

KK pushed him away and in an inadequately hushed voice said, "You gotta be kiddin' me."

"It's true. And to make it worse, I can't say I wasn't there to see them because the firefighters found my suit coat in the barn."

"Why was—"

"I used it to put out the flames. It worked for a while, but once the oil on the floor caught fire, it was pretty much over."

"What are you goin' to do?"

"Well, I have to admit to myself that my life here will never be the same."

"But you're one of the most popular kids in high school—you're the quarterback and you have a new girlfriend."

"High school popularity isn't going to make my father forgive me or make him treat me any better than he already does or doesn't. I only see it getting worse—a lot worse since he will certainly blame me for the fire. And, I don't even know if my family will forgive me. They know I was in the barn now, but I can't really say I was there without . . . I don't know if I can live like that. Wait, you said I have a new girlfriend."

"Yes . . . of course you do," KK said with a smile.

"Shit!"

"Don't worry. I don't feel like I'm long for this town either. Let's say you write me and tell me where you are so I know where to reach you when I've had enough of Janesville or Janesville has had enough of me."

"Will you tell my mom I'm sorry and I love her? I mean in secret."

"You can count on me. I'm a secret myself."

"Yes, you are—my little secret," Butch said and then

reached out to pull KK close for a kiss.

"KK, where are you? It's time for church," Riff shouted from the driveway.

"Coming," she said, then paused for one last kiss. Still in his embrace, she took one last look into his eyes before turning from his grasp and squeezing through the barn door.

"What were you doing in the barn?" her brother asked.

"Just talking with the chickens."

"And what were you talking about?"

"Just seein' if they had any ideas on how to egg you on."

"Funny girl."

"Yep, that's me," she said as she walked alongside her brother, chancing one last look over her shoulder at the barn.

Butch lay on his back staring at the barn ceiling with a piece of straw in his mouth. After a moment of quiet contemplation, he decided what he needed to do—not where he needed to go, that was still up to fate or luck or the weather, but what he needed to do right now. So, he rolled off the bale and headed for the Hill.

Once in the clearing of the Hill, Butch followed the path to the Rock and at the exact place that he had saved KK from Derick, he pulled out his knife and started to carve the bark of a large oak just off the path. When he was done, he stepped back to assess his handiwork. The carving was rudimentary at best, but got the point across. It read *Butch & KK*; no encompassing heart—just the names. Simple and to the point.

Now with that accomplished, the day became much more difficult. Where was he to go? Ultimately, he wanted to be far, far away from the corn belt of Wisconsin, but he had not decided much more beyond that. Eventually, he settled on Lake Geneva, which was still close, but was a good start. He bet he could get a job on the lake somewhere and he loved the water.

As a plan started to form in his head, he walked back toward his house without even seeing the road ahead. His plan included *borrowing* Arthur's Model T, which only seemed fair after everything that had happened. Butch was not going to hitchhike across America looking for a landing spot. He needed wheels and the Model T had been under a tarp for more than a month since Arthur had bought a used Ford Deuce. Butch bet Arthur would not even notice it was gone—for a while at least.

Butch knew his parents were still at church and would be for a while, so he did not have to do any sneaking around. However, he did take the time to prop up the tarp that had covered the Model T so it would appear the car was still there lying in wait. Again, he stepped back to appraise his work. He smiled and allowed a chuckle before he started up the Model T and left Janesville for what he thought would be the last time.

Butch left his family home and the mother who loved him without fully understanding what he was actually running from. Now that the firefighters had found his suit coat, he was convinced those in the barn would know he had seen them and he was concerned his family would blame him for the fire since they now knew he was there. As Butch walked away from the only family he had ever known, little did he know there was so much more that would be blamed on him because he chose to leave rather than fight.

Lake Geneva

April—May, 1945

Butch walked the docks and the streets of Lake Geneva looking for work. He was amazed at the grandeur of the Italianate-styled Riviera, the ornately beautiful recreation center and ballroom built to draw tourists to the small lake town—especially those from Chicago, which was just a 2-hour train ride away.

Lake Geneva, originally named Geneva but later changed to avoid confusion with a nearby town of the same name in Illinois, started its history in 1837 when Thomas McKaig laid out the city's plat design, which included streets, parks and a cemetery. Geneva, which sits on the shores of Geneva Lake, a lake name much less confusing when the town was Geneva, grew slowly along McKaig's design until 1871 when the Chicago Fire caused many Chicagoans to flee to Geneva, either to buy land or to move into their lake homes or mansions. This influx of population was made possible just three months prior when the railway from Chicago to Geneva was repaired after ceasing operation in 1859 due to track failure. Now there was a railway pipeline from Chicago and during this era, Geneva became the *Newport of the West* as it grew to become the chosen summer destination of the Chicago wealthy.

Butch was excited to see the great tour boats lined along the pier, freshly launched as the ice retreated for the season. He read off the names to himself—*Walworth, Marietta, Tilford, Louise* and *Polaris*. When he inquired about working on one of these grand boats, he was more than a little disappointed to learn all the positions were already filled. His hopes again perked up when he spotted a flyer about becoming a *Walworth* mail boat jumper.

> We are looking for the best of the best who want to become mail delivery "jumpers" this season on the *Walworth*. Applicants will be selected based on a grading of 50 percent for athletic skill, 50 percent for delivery accuracy, and 50 percent for enthusiasm.
> -Tryouts start June 13th.

Butch was crestfallen to see a that job he would certainly excel at—jumping on and off a moving boat—was still more than two months away. But he continued to walk and drive around the area trying to dig up whatever was available.

Around town he found few opportunities that were not already taken by women or other children his age. He ate one meal a day at the diner on Main Street and slept in the park at night. Each day he walked the shore path further and further from downtown hoping to find work until he finally decided to walk around the entire lake—a 26-mile trip. Along the way he admired the cottages and lake houses tucked away in the trees that surrounded the lake, but could not even fathom the riches needed to build or simply maintain the many mansions that dotted the lakeshore.

Among these mansions were Villa Hortensia, built in 1906 by Edward F. Swift of the Swift meat-packing family; Alta Vista, rebuilt in 1909 by Colonel William N. Pelouze of the Pelouze Scale and Balance family; the Maxwell Mansion, built in 1856 by a Chicago surgeon; Northwoodside, originally owned by General Henry Strong, president of the Santa Fe Railroad, then by O.N. Tevander who had become a multimillionaire at the age of 26 for inventing the sanitary disc stamped atop glass milk bottles;

The Stenning—now owned by Walden W. Shaw, co-founder of the Yellow Cab Company in Chicago—started out as Wadsworth Hall when built in 1906 by Norman W. Harris of the Harris Trust and Savings Bank, but would eventually come to be known as Glanworth Gardens; The House in the Woods, which was built under a tent borrowed from P.T. Barnum, whose headquarters for his three-ring circus were in nearby Delavan; the Schwinn Estate, built in 1928 by Ignatz Schwinn of the Schwinn Bicycle Company family; Jerseyhurst, built in 1879 by R.T. Crane of the Crane Plumbing Company family; Glenn Annie, built in 1895 and used by Freeman Gosden and Charles Corel, best known for their Amos and Andy radio show, which was broadcast from the front porch when the two vacationed here in the 1930s; and the Wrigley Mansions—Green Gables & Hillcroft—owned by the Wrigley family known for chewing gum and owners of the Chicago Cubs baseball team.

Another fascinating sight on the lake was Yerkes Observatory. Butch was not much on science—he was more a physical being—but he had read about Yerkes having the largest refracting-type telescope ever successfully used for astronomy. Owned by the University of Chicago since 1897 and nestled in the hills of Williams Bay, Yerkes was a gem along the banks of Geneva Lake. He had read that part of the mounting system—equatorial, or something like that, which allows the telescope to stay fixed on an object in the sky and not be affected by the earth's rotation—had been on display at the 1893 World's Fair while the observatory was being built. He also remembered reading that Albert Einstein said he wanted to visit just two places when he came to America for the first time: Niagara Falls and Yerkes Observatory. Butch had even seen a picture of Einstein in front of the big telescope with a crowd of similarly dressed unsmiling older people, but he could not comment on whether Albert made it to the Falls.

Continuing along the shore path out of Williams Bay, Butch came upon a huge granite rock the size of a car. He stood on the rock and looked out at the lake as a sailboat race was just beginning. He heard the *boom* of the starting gun and watched as the sailboats turned this way and that trying to make the most of the shifting wind. One boat seemed to be better at this task than the rest or at least luckier as it continued to lengthen its lead on the others. Knowing this could take a while, Butch sat on the rock in the shade to watch the rest of the race. Eventually, he lay back and fell asleep on the top of the rock. Another *boom* awoke him and he was surprised to see a different boat was first to cross the finish line.

Tortoise and the hare all over again, he thought to himself.

On his return home from his circuit of the lake, he came upon Younglands Manor, which was now a church camp and school for girls run by the Episcopal Order of St. Anne. He had seen it from across the lake, but figured it was a public building since it was so different from the other more sprawling mansions on the lake. Younglands had been the envisioned vacation cottage of Otto Young who began construction on the mansion in 1899. During construction, Otto made many additions and the original $15,000 price tag eventually grew to almost $2,000,000. The 40,000-square-foot limestone mansion sat on over 11 acres, had seven levels, 50 rooms and housed a dining room large enough to hold 100 diners, a nine-hole miniature golf course, a bowling alley and a roof garden. Nearly every light switch, outlet, fixture and doorknob was plated in 14-carat gold. It even had indoor plumbing—a luxury in those days—and a rudimentary air-conditioning system created by blowing air over large chunks of ice taken from the lake during winter and stored in the sub-basement.

Otto started his career by selling costume jewelry from a pushcart on the streets of New York. After the Chicago Fire of 1871, he moved west to take advantage of the great opportunity to rebuild Chicago and would eventually turn to real estate. Much of what is known today as the Loop in Chicago was purchased by Otto as he built his 25-million-dollar family fortune. Once the mansion was completed, Otto moved his family in and lived there for a short five years until his death from tuberculosis in 1906. The house stayed in the family for several more decades before it was eventually donated to the Episcopal Church in the 1940s and became a private school for girls. The mansion would continue to change hands throughout the decades, selling for as little as $75,000 dollars in an auction and as much as several million for a just a portion of the whole.

The Young family also owned a steam-powered yacht named the *Polaris*. Built in 1898 and decked out with mahogany and brass, the *Polaris* would go on to be a tour boat and the oldest remaining yacht on the lake. Butch remembered seeing it at the Riviera dock as they readied it for the upcoming season.

Butch decided to try his luck at Younglands before taking a dishwashing job at one of the lakeside diners he had stumbled upon, where he figured he might at least get some free food along with his wages. But serendipity was upon him and he was hired on the spot to replace the gardener who was just let go for drinking on the job, which also resulted in him cutting off two of his fingers. Butch was fairly certain the ex-gardener did not get fired for cutting off his fingers—it was probably the drinking, but he did not plan on doing either.

The next morning while receiving instructions from the head gardener, Marino Danielson, he saw a gaggle of young girls run down the expansive front lawn to the pier. As he listened and watched the girls, he caught the eye of a tall, thin middle-aged woman with dark drab hair walking behind the passing group of girls.

"If I were you, I would turn away," the head gardener said. "That is Miss Margaret. She is the camp administrator. You need to stay clear of her. She will burn a hole in you if she thinks you are even considering talking to one of her girls."

"We can't talk to the girls?" Butch asked with some surprise.

"God, no. If she catches you, you are as good as fired. Talk is going around that she cut off Tommy's fingers. Some even say that she just looked at him and he cut off his own fingers just to make her stop."

"Heck, that can't be true," Butch said as he continued to stare at the woman.

"Well, I am not finding out if it is true and it would be best if you did not either. And God help you if she hears you swear."

"Heck?" Butch questioned.

"Might as well be hell to her."

Butch held his breath and slowly moved his line of sight back to Marino. Once he saw in his peripheral vision that Miss Margaret had passed them, he snuck a glance at a tall, leggy brunette among a group of the shorter blondes. This was the first time he had been taken by a brunette and he was more than a little surprised.

She's striking, he thought to himself. *Wow, maybe I'm*

not stuck on blondes after all.

Butch continued to take quick and frequent glances at the girls without being caught by the gardener or the evil Miss Margaret. After finishing up his orientation, he was dismissed and asked to come back tomorrow at six in the morning to start his new job.

Having half a day to play, Butch decided to go into Lake Geneva.

Let's see what trouble I can stay away from, he thought to himself with a chuckle. He reached into his pocket and thumbed his remaining money, thanking God he had found something to sustain his future. He decided to have one last meal at the diner since going forward, he would be receiving his meals in the carriage house behind the mansion. He ordered a ham on rye with a coke and was opening his mouth to sink his teeth in for his first bite when a hand slapped him on the back and instead pushed his face into the sandwich.

"I thought that was you. Dang, what you doin' here, Butch?"

Butch grabbed a napkin to remove mustard from the tip of his nose and then looked up to see the beaming face of Robby Robart, a recent graduate of Janesville High School.

"Robby, how you been?" Butch returned, trying to change the subject so as not to have to explain his current situation or unforeseen journey thus far.

"Good, good—no, great. I'm a recruiter for the Navy now and serving my country as best I can."

Butch remembered Robby to be kind of a shy kid, which only got worse when he tipped the family tractor and crushed his leg. He could still walk, but he had a hitch that announced he was not entirely whole.

"Well, congratulations. So, where do you work?"

"I work out of the recruiting office on Broad Street. I'm

on break now, but you should come by some time so I can show you around."

"Jeez, that would be great."

The two continued catching up as Butch finished his meal and then walked outside where Robby immediately lit up a cigarette.

"You want one?" Robby motioned.

"No. I'm not 18 yet."

"Why would you let that stop you? You should give it a try. Doctors say so. And it makes you look tough, too."

Butch smothered a smile and said, "I'll think about it. I'll see you around Robby."

"Yep—and remember to come on by the office so I can show you around," Robby repeated, then turned to walk to the corner of Main and Broad Streets.

Butch took off the other way hoping to find a place to sleep that was a bit closer to the mansion, ultimately hoping to make enough to rent an apartment. As he made his way east, he heard raised voices behind him that caused him to look back over his shoulder.

"Look at this fool. Thinks he's a soldier all dressed up like a grandstander as he limps his way down the street."

"You're no soldier. Our soldiers are brave and strong."

"Yeah, they ain't no 4F gimps, like you."

Butch saw two young men spitting insults at Robby as they circled around him. Robby, trying to be brave and maintain eye contact with the larger of the two hooligans, only made things worse by continually demonstrating his ailment as he limped in a circle. Butch immediately ran to Robby's defense and chest bumped the smaller man off his feet as they crossed paths.

"Excuse me. Completely my fault. Let me help you up," Butch said to the man on the ground, then offered his hand.

"Damn right it's your fault, you clumsy crumb," the man swore at Butch, then reached out to grab his hand.

Just as the man was leveraging himself to stand, Butch released his hand and the man toppled back to the sidewalk like a sack of potatoes.

"What you doing to my buddy?" the bigger man bellowed.

"I was just helping him up. I didn't realize he was a gimp."

"I ain't no gimp," the man on the ground exclaimed, struggling to right himself.

"Oh, so then you're just a chucklehead like your buddy here," Butch claimed as he thumbed at the bigger man.

"Why you," the bigger man huffed as he took a swing at Butch.

The blow was meant to be a sucker punch, but Butch expected it and dipped out of the way, clipping the man's trailing foot as he passed. With no way to plant his foot to offset his weight change, the larger man fell like a tree directly on top of his companion.

"Looks like these two want to be alone," Butch said a little louder than necessary and the small crowd that had gathered to surround the scuffle burst out in laughter. Some even continued to mock the pair as Butch and Robby slipped away across Main Street.

"Thanks, Butch. That was real swell of you. If I can ever do you a favor, just let me know."

Butch aimed Robby toward the pharmacy on Broad Street so they would be out of sight when their two accosters cleared the crowd and started looking for them.

"Well . . . you could start by buying me some cigarettes," Butch blurted out to justify their diversion.

"I thought you didn't smoke?" Robby questioned with a puzzled look on his face.

"Naw, I smoke. All of us tough guys smoke," Butch said as he slapped Robby on the back.

"What do you smoke? I'm a Pall Mall man."

Butch was momentarily frozen by the obvious but unanticipated question. He quickly looked around for some visual help.

"Me . . . oh, I'm a . . . Chesterfield man," he finally spouted after seeing an ad featuring a sailor and a pack of Chesterfields—*In the Navy – It's Chesterfield.* He also observed an ad with Santa Claus, but skipped over that initially as being too juvenile. Now fully taking it in, he noted the Santa ad was for Pall Mall.

Well, to each their own, he thought as he waited for Robby to buy the cigarettes.

Outside the pharmacy, the two said their goodbyes and went on their separate ways after Butch promised to stop by the recruiting office so Robby could properly show him around. Butch did not know what more Robby could show him than posters and flyers, but he promised anyway.

* * *

Butch arrived at the Younglands carriage house at 5:50 the next morning.

"You look like you slept in the garden," Marino said as Butch walked in the door.

Marino was a stocky man of average height with kind eyes and hands as big as boxing gloves.

"I—"

"Did you sleep outside last night?" Marino interrupted, knowing when he was about to be lied to. "Listen here—if you are coming off a bender, you cannot be working here."

"A what?" Butch questioned.

"A toot," Marino continued bending his arm in animation as if he were drinking.

"What? No—no I . . ."

"Spit it out, son," Marino demanded.

"I slept outside because I don't have a place to stay yet," Butch said continually looking down at his feet as he kicked at the ground.

"What? How long have you been here?"

"About two weeks."

"Good God, young man," Marino exclaimed and then quickly lowered his voice so as not to be overheard swearing.

This was followed by a look that took Butch by surprise. He was expecting a hand around his neck to throw him out the door, but instead received a soft hand on his shoulder and a caring look from Marino's kind eyes.

"You poor boy. We have lodging here for you, son. You will not have to sleep outside anymore. There is a bath in the back," Marino added as he envisioned Butch cleaning up in the lake early in the morning or late at night, a vision that was completely accurate. "You can even park your car in the carriage house garage to keep it out of the rain."

"Thank you," was all Butch could mutter in response.

"Well, enough of this. Let us get started on the day. This is a big place."

Later in the day as Butch was turning over the garden soil in preparation for the spring annuals that were still a month or more from being planted and Marino was trimming the nearby hedges, Miss Margaret walked up to Marino. Thinking they were alone, she started her biblical diatribe about the new employee.

"I will not even ask you for the new gardener's name because I do not expect to talk with him ever and feel he will be gone soon enough once I speak with Mrs. Hardy."

"I do not understand." Marino responded.

"He is too young and presents a distraction to the young women of this school. Once the camp starts this spring, he will be the only boy on this entire property and I do not like the . . . possibilities." She finished with emphasis.

This caused Butch's ears to perk up even more.

The only boy around—am I still sleeping?

"Well, Miss Margaret, I can assure you Butch has no intention of any activities other than gardening. We have over 11 acres to maintain and I think that is more than enough room for him and 100 girls."

"There will be more than 100 girls here this spring, Mr. Danielson," she returned as if the underestimate was an attempted swipe at her and her school.

"Even so—he is here to work. As am I. Are we finished?"

"Yes, we are . . . and I would continue to interview applicants so we are not caught short-handed when Butch is let go."

Snip! Snip!

Marino returned to trimming the hedge without comment.

Once Miss Margaret was out of earshot, Marino said quietly, "That old battle-axe is as delightful as a face full of angry hornets."

"Thanks, Marino," Butch said through the hedges.

* * *

As the weeks went on, Butch tried as best he could to remain invisible to Miss Battle-axe while still enjoying the view of the many young girls on the manor grounds. He was especially bold to spy whenever the tall, leggy brunette was among the gaggle. During his second week there, he made eye contact with the brunette several times and found she was spying on him almost as much as he was spying on her. He enjoyed this attention, but fear of being caught made him more apprehensive than excited.

Several weeks into his gardening career, Butch and Marino sat talking at the kitchen table in the carriage house. Marino had made a habit of staying for dinner on Wednesdays even though he had a wife and three children waiting for him at home. Marino, a bountiful man with dark hair and a thick mustache, got up from the table and retrieved a coffee cup from the drying rack, then poured a tad of beer into the cup and handed it to Butch.

"Why a coffee cup, Marino?" Butch inquired.

"So if anyone sees you drinking, they will be none the wiser. Do you like it?" Marino asked, anticipating a sour-faced response.

"You know it," Butch replied, raising his mug as in a toast. "To beer, cigarettes and women . . . all you need in life."

"A job would be nice too . . . and maybe a family," Marino responded, knocking Butch off his high horse. "Plus, if the battle-axe hears you talk like that, you may have beer, cigarettes and a woman, but you will no longer have life—not *a life*, but *life*."

"I understand. No disrespect intended."

"None taken. I think you got it right. I just would not say it out loud," Marino responded, then followed up with a wink.

After dinner, Marino left for the night and Butch pretty much went straight to bed. This was early for him, but gardening all day, especially on these unseasonably warm spring days, hit his body like a double football practice and he needed his rest more than ever. He fell asleep quickly and almost immediately began to dream.

He was sitting on the pier watching the girls run and jump or dive into the water. The tall, leggy brunette came and sat beside him on the pier and looked into his eyes.

"You're cute," she said.

He did not even know her name and wanted to say something funny or clever, but nothing was coming to him.

"How old are you?" she asked as he failed to keep up his side of the conversation.

He tried to speak, but could not make his tongue work. To cover his momentary muteness, he held up his fingers to display his age.

"You're three-and-a-half?" she questioned.

He looked down at his right hand and saw he was missing his pinky and half of his ring finger. He tried to scream, but again found his tongue still frozen. He fought to make it move, thrashing around like a fish on the pier, but nothing seemed to work until he finally woke in a cold sweat. He sat up and looked around, almost surprised not to find himself on the pier, then realized it had all been a dream. Well, more like a nightmare, but the semantics were lost on his sweating forehead and rapid heart rate.

Thinking he could use a smoke to help him fall asleep again, he grabbed his coat and headed for the lakeshore; he knew better than to smoke in or even near the carriage house. Once at the lake, he sat on a rock by the shore, avoiding the pier altogether. He rationalized this was to remain out of view of the manor, then somewhat admitted to himself it was due to his recent dream as well.

He lit a match. The slight lake breeze made the flame dance, but was not enough to hinder lighting his cigarette. The breeze felt good after an unusually warm May day.

"Can I have one?" a voice called out from his right.

"Hello?" he said into the darkness.

He saw a figure lean forward from a tree trunk and say, "Or we could just share that one."

Butch swallowed and took another drag, momentarily looking at his hand as if verifying he still had all of his fingers before answering.

"It's the lady's prerogative."

"Well then . . ." the figure stood and continued as she came to sit on the rock beside Butch, ". . . let's share."

Butch held up the cigarette. The girl's slender hand took it from between his fingers and brought it to her lips, the glowing embers of tobacco illuminating her face.

"You're the brunette," Butch burst out without thinking.

"I'm not the *only* brunette here, but I like being called *the* brunette. It's kind of flattering. However, most people call me Katie."

"Katie? I've never heard that name before."

"Yes, I'm a Katherine, but that sounds so frumpy, so I made it cuter. What do you think?"

"Yes, but you would be cute even if your name were Mildred," Butch again blurted out without much thought, but felt as if this comment was a bit more of a winner.

Katie blew out a smoke ring and held up the shrinking cigarette. When Butch leaned over to grab the proffered smoke, Katie leaned in to kiss him on the check and said, "Thank you. That was nice."

Butch beamed brightly, happy that the darkness offered him cover, and then went to take another drag.

"But my mom's name is Mildred. Do you think my mom is frumpy or dowdy?"

Katie could see Butch's eyes get as big as saucers as he took in the comment mid drag and she broke out laughing.

Butch coughed several times before he could speak.

"What's so funny? I—I bet your mom is beautiful too. I

mean—"

"Hahaha," she continued. "My mom's name is Ellen and she's nothing much to look at . . . but thank you anyway."

Suddenly Butch felt as if he were a bit out of his league with this one and he hoped he could hold on long enough to claim the right to at least make a second impression in the future.

"So, what are you doing out here this late at night?" he inquired. "Aren't you scared Miss Margaret will catch you and send you home?"

"Miss Margaret is all puffy during the day, but when it's all lights out after curfew, she runs around the house like she's the Duchess of Younglands. Have you seen this place inside? Spiffy or swanky doesn't do it justice—gold-plated everything, bowling, miniature golf, icebergs in the basement. I have never seen anything like it. My house would fit in the dining room." She then looked back over her shoulder and said, "Maybe next time we should smoke on the roof garden. I bet it's real nice up there."

Still wondering what icebergs in the basement meant, Butch stated with some caution, "I think it would be prudent to keep a safe distance between the *duchess* and us."

"Well, she has nothing over me."

"So you're not scared she would send you home if she caught you smoking? I mean, I'm not even supposed to be talking with you right now."

"But you are."

"I know."

"And why?"

"Let's not discuss the obvious," Butch replied thinking that one was a hit as well.

Katie smiled, then continued. "As I said, the duchess has nothing over me. I don't even know if I'm going to stay here the whole time. I'm too young to be cooped up in this nunnery."

"So, do you have plans? Where would you go? What do you want to see?" Butch asked, hoping her answers would spawn ideas for his own possible future journeys.

"This world is not enough. If there's a house like this in Lake Geneva, imagine what there is in France or Italy or anywhere other than my small Wisconsin town."

Plop!

Butch and Katie both ducked down behind the rock they were sitting on when they heard what was likely a rock splash the water. Butch found his arm had naturally gone around her waist and felt their cheeks briefly brush as they hid in the moonlight.

"See, you don't sneed a bar to havsum . . . fun."

"Ok, Craig. Just keep walking."

"Why aren't these rocks skippin'?"

Plop!

"You have to throw them sidearm."

Plop!

"Nope. They're just duds. Stupid rocks."

"Ok, Craig. Just keep walking."

When the two drunks had passed, Katie and Butch both sat up on the rock again.

"I think that should be our night . . . until the next time then?"

"Yes, until the next time," Butch answered.

Katie took off running up the huge front lawn toward the manor, then abruptly turned and ran back.

"How about a kiss for two butts?" she said as she approached and then kissed Butch on the mouth before he could answer. She then held her hand out and Butch deposited three cigarettes and his book of matches without a word. Katie closed her hand around her new treasure and ran up the hill to the manor.

Butch—still a little bit in shock, but loving life more right now than in a long time—decided it was best for him to take a more leisurely and cautious walk back to the carriage house by way of the tree-covered northern edge of the property.

He had no problem falling asleep after his encounter with Katie and his dreams were actual dreams . . . the good kind.

The next day was just like the day before and the day before that, but this mattered little to Butch who thought of Katie and nothing else as he floated through the day with boundless energy. Even Marino was amazed at his stamina after the hard work they had put in the day before.

"Are you OK, son?" Marino queried. "You are not on the dope, are you?"

"What? No, where did that come from?"

"You are extra energized today and being a teenage boy, I expect you to start dragging this time of day . . . as you usually do."

"No, I'm not on *the dope*, but thanks for the concern. I'm just anxious for the day to be over so I can . . . well, let's just say *love is my drug*. Wow, that's kind of catchy. Like a song."

"I doubt we will ever hear songs about drugs on the radio, so I would put that thought out of your head. So, what is it that has you all *anxious* as you put it . . . or should I ask who?"

"You could say I might have a date tonight."

"Might have a date? Boy, you are never going to *have* a date if you think *might* have a date is good enough."

"Don't you worry about me. I have my plans all laid

out."

"OK. Suit yourself. What do I know about women anyway?"

"A lot I'm sure. It's just a little dated . . . that's all."

"A little dated? Well, at least I actually dated and did not fool around with *might*. But you are a good kid, so I bet you will figure it out," Marino said as he walked away, then mumbled internally, *Hopefully before you are 30*.

The rest of the day was uneventful and Marino went home to his family, leaving Butch alone with his dinner and his thoughts. After finishing the meal without even tasting much of anything, Butch paced around the carriage house waiting for dusk to fall. Once he felt it was dark enough, he retraced the north tree line and returned to the rock on the lakeshore.

Butch waited for the sun to set, then for darkness to claim the night and for the moon to rise, but still no sign of Katie. Then all at once the day's expended energy leapt from his body and he was left feeling dejected and completely drained. He took another look back over his shoulder and even got up to check out the tree Katie had been resting against the night before, but found nothing. Butch sat against the rock and decided to have a cigarette to try to calm his dismay.

Halfway through his smoke he chanced a glance over his shoulder and spotted a tall, lean figure coming his way. He almost stood to greet them, but did not want his silhouette to be broadcast to anyone who might be looking at the lake from the manor. His heart beat fast with anticipation as the figure approached the shoreline. As the person crept closer, his throat closed tight and he completely stopped breathing as he could see in the moonlight that it was Miss Margaret and not Katie.

"Hahaha!"

The laughter echoed down the manor lawn.

Miss Margaret, now just 30 feet from Butch who was crouched low behind the rock, turned like a hound dog and searched the hill behind her. After a long moment, she found what she was looking for and quickly reversed course. When Butch dared a peek over the rock, he found her halfway up the lawn.

"Huff!"

Butch's lungs let loose—air, smoke and spittle exploded from his mouth. After three quick breaths to maintain consciousness, he snuck another look at Miss Margaret and found she was already nearing the manor stairs. He then saw what she was after. A red cherry glowed in the night high atop the manor—someone was smoking on the roof garden. Once Miss Margaret entered the front door, the bright, burning cherry started to move back and forth in a slow wave and Butch soon realized Katie's impromptu laugh had just saved him from the battle-axe.

The next morning Marino and Butch decided to trim the bushes and trees by the lakeshore. This was Butch's idea since he hoped he could sneak a word or two with Katie to thank her for saving his skin last night, but when the girls came down, Katie was not among them. Butch continued to work, but was severely distracted as he glanced this way and that hoping to see Katie or at least understand why she was not with her usual Thursday group. Marino noted his distraction, but bit his lip. He did not need another discussion like the night before and even though Butch's effort was on the lighter side today—if Marino were being nice—he knew it all evened out when they were at this age.

Nope—not going to sucker me in this time, Marino thought to himself and then made his way to trim the bushes on the south side of the pier.

Butch watched the girls put suntan lotion on each other; some lay on the pier while others jumped from the diving board into the still chilly lake water. Butch's mind was so wound up that he could not even enjoy this up-close spectacle of feminine youth. Once the girls' time at the pier was up, they all gathered their belongings and started the long trek up the front lawn to the manor. Suddenly a beach ball bounded from the group in Butch's direction and a short blonde girl wrapped tightly in a towel jogged over to retrieve it. As she bent for the ball, she dropped a folded piece of paper next to the ball.

Shhh!

Butch was bright enough to understand the girl did not drop the paper by accident and made no acknowledgment of the act. He just continued to work as if the thought of the square piece of paper was *not* burning a hole in his brain. After he finally finished his side of the pier, he gathered his tools into the wheelbarrow to go help Marino. As he passed the paper, his rake, which he had placed most precariously over the edge of the wheelbarrow, fell onto the ground. As Butch leant over to pick up the wayward rake, he snatched the paper in the same movement. Now all he had to do was wait until he had some privacy.

Gosh, this day may prove to be even longer then yesterday, he huffed to himself.

Later that night, Butch sat at the carriage house kitchen table and read the note. It was much longer than he expected, but he was fairly certain it was in fact from Katie. She did not seem to be the type to sign her name with a heart to dot the *i*, but what did he know about girls—he had had only one and a half girlfriends thus far in his illustrious 15-year career.

Butch learned Katie had run from the rooftop garden and avoided Miss Margaret. However, that night Miss Margaret woke the dorms one by one and made all the girls do jumping jacks, telling them it was all an exercise to honor the troops across the ocean. When she made it to Katie's dorm, Miss Margaret's plan paid off: she smelled smoke on Katie's breath as she huffed and puffed through the exercise.

Now with all the evidence she needed, Miss Margaret grabbed Katie by the ear and pulled her toward the door. Katie knocked her hand away and stood defiant in the middle of the room, all eyes watching her. Miss Margaret then grabbed a handful of hair and pulled Katie even harder toward the door. Again, Katie fought to be released and when Miss Margaret had had enough of her squirming, she raised a hand and slapped Katie across the face. Katie went down like a ragdoll, hitting her head on a trunk at the end of one of the beds. Without even acknowledging Katie might be hurt, Miss Margaret again grabbed a handful of hair and dragged her from the room.

Katie was now isolated in one of the smaller bedrooms for breaking the no smoking on manor grounds rule. She had managed to slip Cindy, the short blonde messenger, the note Butch held in his hand when Cindy delivered Katie's morning meal. Butch was fuming. As he looked at the note again, a tear fell on the heart Katie had drawn in her name and the ink started to run. Butch wiped it away and then continued to read the postscript.

P.S. Butch, don't do anything stupid. I have a plan to get even with the battle-axe. And battle-axe, if you intercept this message . . .

Butch felt himself blush at the language. Yes, he had heard

all those words before, but never strung together to paint such a vivid picture. He allowed himself a chuckle and started to get cleaned up for the evening meal.

The next morning, Butch got dressed and waited for Marino to arrive to start their day. Butch paced back and forth in the kitchen as the minutes passed. It was unlike Marino to be this late. Butch frequently joked with him that he believed Marino had an internal clock since he seemed to know what time it was nearly anytime of the day.

Butch heard muffled shouting from the driveway in front of the house. He could hear Marino's voice, but could not make out the other. He made his way to the window where he saw Marino arguing with Miss Margaret and it did not look civil. Miss Margaret was not Marino's boss—Mrs. Hardy was—but she could make life difficult for him if he was not careful. It was hard to discern the exact subject they were discussing, with at the very least elevated voices, but it did not resemble any kind of *careful* Butch had ever seen. He was quickly becoming worried for Marino.

Marino suddenly burst in the door and slammed it closed behind him.

"That woman is the devil's spawn," he yelled, still in argument mode, then sat down hard on the sofa.

"Marino, what is it? What's wrong?"

"Apparently, Katie has run away."

"What? Why?" Butch asked, his head spinning.

"Miss Margaret caught her smoking late the night before and then threatened to call her parents to come and take her home. This morning Katie was gone."

"Do you know Miss Margaret hit Katie and gave her a black eye?" Butch did not know if Katie truly had a black eye, but assumed so because of the violent blow she described suffering in front of her bedmates.

"No, I did not know about that," Marino answered truthfully. "I guess you could call them even then," Marino said, obviously mulling over this new information.

"What do you mean . . . even?"

Marino gave Butch a little smile and then chuckled.

"Oh, I am sorry for laughing while Katie is missing, but before Katie left, she put glue into Miss Margaret's shoe polish."

"What? Why is that funny?" Butch asked, searching for a string to help him follow the conversation.

"Well, it was not the shoe polish she used on her shoes. It was the liquid shoe polish she used on her hair to cover the gray between her beauty appointments. She is incensed and wants to hang anyone she suspects might have helped Katie. She came looking for you, but I told her I gave you the day off."

"Shoe polish in her hair?"

"And glue. You should have seen it. It took all I had to keep yelling and not just break down and laugh at her with her hair all stiff and sticking out here and there."

Butch continued to look at Marino with widening eyes until his brain finally caught up with the visual and they both burst out in laughter.

"Oh my, what a sight," Marino cried, slapping his knee as he laughed.

Butch decided to lay low for the rest of the morning and then went for a nice long walk. He walked the back roads to Buttons Bay and sat at a picnic table under a tree at the park. *Yes, the park is what I need*, he thought to himself as he lay back on the bench to look at the sky and watch the soft cotton candy clouds float across the bright blue heavens.

Normally he would have enjoyed this moment, but the situation with Katie had him in unknown territory. He thought back to his life just a few short months ago and found it hard not to think that disappointment followed him like a stray dog, but he refused to give in and eventually fell asleep.

* * *

The girls played with a beach ball on the huge grass patio out in front of the main entry to the manor. Lake privileges had been suspended in an attempt to get one of the girls to snitch on Katie. Miss Margaret especially had her eye on Cindy and Lucy, two of Katie's closest companions over the last month or so.

Miss Margaret stood on the front steps watching the girls with eyes that burned with detestation. She was a child of the Depression and had grown bitter over her lack of the luxuries that flowed so bountifully throughout the Younglands Manor and all the mansions like it. She had started with nearly anything a child could want or need and ended homeless and wanting. Her father had been a second-generation railroad robber baron who became complacent over his investments in the 1920s. In 1929 when the stock market crashed, he was so leveraged—having bought much of his stocks on margin to maximize his profit—he lost everything. On the day the bank came to foreclose on their house, he committed suicide with his hunting rifle. Miss Margaret was a privileged woman suddenly thrown into a world that did not acknowledge her status and her discontent grew until it burned like a fire deep in her soul.

Marino walked up the side steps to the grass patio to deadhead the flowers planted along the house. When he saw Miss Margaret on the steps, he tried to reverse course without looking obvious, but Miss Margaret called out his name and he knew he could not ignore her after showing such disrespect this morning during their shouting match. As Marino approached, the beach ball the girls were playing with bounded over Cindy's head and she slowly walked over to retrieve it.

"So, I hope you have disciplined your temper from this morning," Miss Margaret spat out contemptuously.

Marino, not certain of what that actually meant, said, "Yes, ma'am."

"I am still looking for your boy," she said, holding out a closed fist in front of Marino's face. "Do not even deny you are covering for him by saying he has the day off. I know he has taken Katie and you will have to answer to the police for your role in this farce."

"What do you mean?" was Marino's agape response.

"This is what I mean," she said, then opened her fist to reveal a crumpled pack of Chesterfield cigarettes. "These were found in the carriage house kitchen and I know you are smart enough not to smoke in the manor, so they must be your boy's."

"So? There is no rule against smoking if he does not do it on the grounds. Did you find an ashtray in the carriage house?" Marino volleyed back.

"I don't care about ashtrays, you fool. I care that I also found this on the roof garden." She then held up a cigarette butt with a slight hint of lipstick on the filter.

"Unless your boy wears lipstick, we can assume this is the cigarette Katie was smoking two nights ago and I do not have to assume the police will come to the same conclusion that I have made. Your boy gave Katie the cigarettes, which also means they talked and thus he may have lulled her into trusting him . . . and now she is missing."

Marino could not prevent himself from bringing his hands to his face while thinking, *What have I done. I have set Butch up to be roped into this crazy woman's conspiracy.*

Cindy picked up the ball, ran back to Lucy and whispered in her ear. After a moment, the girls grouped into a smaller circle and kicked the ball between them. Then all of a sudden, Lucy broke from the group screaming.

"Beee!"

The whole group soon followed and what had been a quiet afternoon of kickball quickly turned into a mad run for the water. The girls continued full-tilt toward the pier and proceeded to jump into the water. Miss Margaret was torn from her dressing down of Marino to hurriedly waddle after the group.

"Stay out of the water. No swimming today," she shouted as she made her way down the huge lawn.

Marino watched in wonder and then out of the corner of his eye caught sight of Cindy who had hid behind the steps during the commotion.

Marino looked at her and asked quite honestly, "Are you not afraid of bees?"

"There was no bee, Mr. Danielson. I stayed back to warn Butch about Miss Margaret's plans."

"What girl? I don't see a girl," Marino said and then winked as he started down toward the lake so he could have an alibi if one were to be needed.

Cindy snuck around the north side of the manor and ran for the carriage house. This was no short jog, but she was determined to do this for Katie and for Butch. Once she was across the main road, she heard sirens and turned to see flashing lights as two cop cars passed the carriage house driveway and turned into the manor drive. Cindy flew the rest of the way and entered the carriage house with enough momentum to slam the door back against the wall. She quickly entered the kitchen and started opening drawers to locate a pen and paper. On her third attempt, she struck gold. Full of anxiety from the police arrival and the wrath of Miss Margaret, she wrote quickly and then folded the notepaper in half. She returned to the entryway, took a wad of gum out of her mouth and pushed the note and the gum against the backside of the door. Now all she had to do was to get back without being seen.

* * *

Butch returned to the carriage house and entered though the back door. He thought he heard the front door slam shut, but was still enjoying his relaxed afternoon, so he did not concern himself immediately. When he walked into the kitchen, he found several of the drawers not fully closed and wondered if Marino was looking for something. Again, he did not concern himself as his day off had almost completely drained away his worries. Nonetheless, deep in the back of his mind he still sensed some panic, but he was not about to let it flood out the peace he had found at the park. *Now I understand why old people take afternoon naps—wow, am I relaxed.*

Seeing the kitchen sink reminded Butch that he was parched, so he immediately filled a glass and drank voraciously. The park had been relaxing, but the water fountain was broken and he had not had a drink for over four hours.

"Ah! That is some good water."

He sat at the kitchen table and picked up a pen that was

left on the table. This was not unusual, but he did remember putting it away the last time he used it. He put the pen back down and took another drink. He seemed content to just look around the kitchen, so that is what he did until he heard what sounded like something dropping on the floor in the front room. *God, I hope another bird didn't get into the carriage house*—he was way too relaxed to ruin it by chasing a bird around the room while fretting about it breaking something. He took another drink and walked into the front room to look for the origin of the sound.

He did not see anything immediately, but as he made his way further into the room, he noticed a small dark circle on the front door. Once in the foyer, he saw the folded note on the floor and bent over to pick it up. It was a little heavier than it looked and he flipped it over to find a large circle of moist pink bubblegum stuck to the back of *the letter. He looked at the gum and then at the door and then back at the gum.

"Hmm," he said before opening the note.

The note contained only one word boldly printed at an angle across the full width of the paper.

RUN!

While he was attempting to comprehend the meaning of this simple, yet commanding message, he heard voices from the front lawn.

He pulled back the curtain slightly enough to see Miss Margaret and two police officers walking up the front drive. Butch's heart leaped into near arrhythmia as the uneasiness he had sufficiently penned up for the day all came flooding back. He ran for his room and quickly grabbed his duffle bag to throw in whatever he could before quietly opening the window to make a run for the garage. As he climbed down the back stairs, he could hear the police still banging on the front door.

At the garage, Butch unlocked the main doors and quickly slipped inside. He pulled off the new tarp that now covered the Model T and stuffed it in the passenger seat along with his duffle bag. He then started the engine and crept forward enough to just touch the doors so he could gently push them open with his bumper. When the doors were about halfway open, Butch could see Miss Margaret and the police running down the drive directly toward him. He had not been as stealthy as he had hoped, but he still had the advantage. He gunned the engine and the Model T leapt to life, sending the doors slamming back against the garage. By the time he had reached his pursuers, all they could do was leap out of the way. Butch watched in the rearview as Miss Margaret backpedaled awkwardly until she finally tripped and fell ass-first into a large mud puddle at the side of the drive. Butch looked around as he pulled out onto the Lake Shore Drive and did not see any cop cars, so he felt like he had enough of a lead to get lost before they made it back to their cars to follow him.

Butch followed the drive to West Main Street and quickly cut across to Mill Street so he could park in the back lot behind the Broad Street storefronts. Parking directly behind the recruiting station, Butch pulled his car into a niche behind a dumpster and carefully covered it with the tarp. He then snuck in the back door of the station and spied from the back room before entering.

"Hi-de-ho, Robby. You got time for a tour?"

"Wha—jeez, Butch, you nearly scared me to death. Why are you sneaking up on me like that?" Robby huffed out after clearly being startled.

"Sorry, Robby. I'm actually here to talk to you about

enlisting."

"But you aren't even 17 yet. You gotta be 17 to be in the Navy."

"Well, I'm going to be 16 any day now and I was hoping I could take you up on that favor you owed me."

"I thought buying you the cigarettes was the favor." Robby answered honestly.

"You think saving you from those thugs was only worth a pack of cigarettes? I'm hurt. I thought I was doing a friend a king-sized favor."

"Jeez, Butch. I don't know. I could get in trouble. I really like this job."

Butch decided the truth would be his best option, so he told Robby he was in trouble, real trouble, if he did not get out of town quick. He filled him in on the details that would help his story and none that Robby could later spill to anyone who might ask. In reality, he was scared Katie was gone for good and that he would be arrested and ultimately blamed for her disappearance without hope of her ever being found.

"You see. A future this unsure is in need of some redirection."

"Wow, I don't know what to say. I hear old lady Margaret is a real witch . . . and you knocked her into a mud puddle with your car. Oh, boy is she going to be mad at you."

If that's what Robby got from my story and is now sympathetic, who is to argue, Butch thought to himself.

"Well, what do you think?"

"I don't know. We don't have too much time before my boss comes back."

"So, what do we need to do? Do I need a medical exam or can you do that?"

"No, we have a doctor who does those, but to tell you

the truth, the guy is a souse and is three sheets to the wind most of the time after noon and sometimes before. Oh, crap—wait. I forgot about the stash of medical forms my boss has when the doc is *unavailable*."

Robby went into the back room and quickly returned with a form. With a slightly shaking hand, he held it up to hand to Butch.

"If we do this, you have to promise me you didn't get this from me," Robby said with a slight tremor in his voice as well.

"The secret dies with me," Butch responded with his hand over his heart.

"OK, this is already signed by the doctor and the recruiter. All you have to do is fill in your info and fake your father's signature, then get it back to me before we close today. There's a bus coming tomorrow morning at 9:00 a.m. that will take you and the rest of the new recruits to the Great Lakes Naval Station. Your paper work should not be scrutinized since my boss is rarely here before that on any morning and doesn't care to see the dopey faces of the men and boys he convinced to be sailors as they leave here on Saturday mornings."

Butch told Robby he would fill out the form and leave it in the front seat of his car that was parked just outside the back door. He also gave Robby his keys.

"Take care of her. I'll be back once we win the war," Butch said, then made a sharp salute.

Robby returned the salute and Butch slipped out the back. Butch was concerned his true age would eventually be discovered, so he would have to try to act older if there were such a thing. He was excited to be a 15 soon to be 16-year-old sailor. He wondered if he would be the youngest sailor ever. Little did he know he would join the ranks of many 16 and 17-year-old sailors who, unlike him, had their parent's consent, but there were many more like him who did not—the youngest being Calvin Graham who was 12 years old when he enlisted.

Great Lakes

May, 1945

Butch slipped in the back door of the recruiting station just before 9:00 a.m. and waited inside by the front windows. When he heard his full name read aloud, he stepped out the door and pushed through the crowd of onlookers that had gathered to see the new sailors off.

"Jack? I'm not going to say it thrice," the bus driver called.

"Here. I'm Jack," Butch said, finally squeezing between two women to stand in front of the bus driver.

"Well, get on the bus, son," the driver remarked with some irritation. "What part of 'get on the bus when I call your name' don't you understand?"

"Sorry, sir!" Butch replied before hopping on the bus.

"Now, that's better. Next is Mark Murry."

"Yes, sir!" Murry stepped forward and immediately jumped on the bus.

Butch sat on the bus, now content to be called Jack by his superiors. At home, his father was Jake and he was Jack, which quickly became Butch because even Jake and Jack were not different enough for Butch's father—Jake did not like being called to the phone to find one of Jack's friends on the other end. So, Jack became Butch on the insistence of his mother who wanted to call him *Junior*, but knew it was not an option put on the table by either of the involved parties. When Butch was young, he often felt his father did not truly like him. As he grew older, he found he was correct. Butch was the third child, but in his father's mind, he should have been the fifth. After Arthur and Rita, his mother had two miscarriages, which, again in his father's mind, put them behind on producing the eventual free labor needed to run the farm. Maria's lucky number was three and after two lost children and Butch being born on the third try as her third child, he quickly became her favorite and this too was not right in his father's mind.

The bus pulled out at 9:37 a.m. and headed toward Waukegan, Illinois. At the top of the big hill that led into Lake Geneva from the east, two police officers waved the bus through a roadblock. Butch tipped his head and turned his face from the window as the bus maneuvered around the police cruisers. He knew this roadblock was for him and now he knew unequivocally that running, again, was the right thing to do to survive.

The bus rolled through the gated entry of the *Great Lakes - U.S. Naval Training Station* before noon and Butch could feel the buzz of excitement flow like electricity through the bus. The recruits had not talked much on the bus as thoughts of what they were leaving behind monopolized their minds. However, now that they had arrived, they all felt the dawn of a new life, a new experience, a new duty and they were excited to start.

The Great Lakes Station was dedicated in 1911 and went on to train 125,000 sailors during World War I. After the attack on Pearl Harbor, the Station grew more than 10-fold to become a huge 1,600-acre Class A naval training center. During the US involvement in WWII, start to finish, there were four million active-duty sailors and one million of them came through Great Lakes. Among the most famous sailors to graduate from Great Lakes at the start of the war were "The Five Fighting Sullivans"—five brothers who were killed in action together when their light cruiser, the USS *Juneau*, was torpedoed. In 1944, classes began to integrate and in March of that year, the station graduated the Golden Thirteen: the first African American enlisted men to become commissioned and warrant officers in the U.S. Navy.

The new recruits were led by a petty officer to the registration office where a yeoman took their paper work and officially enrolled them in the Navy. Next, it was off to the barber, then the clinic where they were all checked out medically—this included a vision test, a dental exam and any needed vaccinations. Then the long line of recruits, now Seaman Recruits, or Boots, or Bluejackets, received their gear from the navy supply clerks. They received their sea bag, their whites, their blues, their shoes and their sleep gear. They would all soon learn how to roll and stow all these items in specific order according to regulations. All items were to be stenciled with the sailor's name. They were also issued their Navy Bible—the Bluejacket's Manual. Week one did not officially start until Monday, but they had their initial physical fitness assessment to pass and more than enough reading and fretting to do until then.

Week one of boot camp involved physical conditioning—calisthenics, military drill marching, swim classes and physical qualifications—along with rank and rate recognition, and learning Navy Core Values. Week one is where Butch met Darcy Lawson and Chester Best, or Joker and Gerbil. They were two boys from Kansas who grew up together and, as Butch would learn on more than a few occasions, had each other's backs. He also learned nicknames were a key identifier within the ranks and he would remain Butch to his fellow sailors regardless of what the brass called him.

"That company commander is a real hard-ass. I'm so tired I can barely fart without crying," Joker said, lying on his back on the bottom bunk, his arm stretched across his face at an attempt to block out any hint of light.

"Yeah, Chief Petty Officer Blowhard is a real pain in my ass," Gerbil groaned from the upper bunk.

"His name is Bowlen," Butch corrected.

"Like the knot?" Joker queried in jest.

"It's called a bowline, you idiot!" called a voice from several bunks over—the other recruits clearly not in tune with Joker's sense of humor and Gerbil's sometimes feeble attempts to mimic it.

"No, not like the knot," Butch reinforced. "And, Gerbil, I would be careful with your nicknames or you may find yourself marching until your legs fall off," Butch rebuked.

"Yeah . . . marching nude . . . in a thunderstorm . . . holding a flagpole . . . with your ass cheeks," Joker added, first laughing, then wincing in pain. "Why does the bad man hate us?"

"Because, you never shut up," came a voice from further down the barracks. "Just go to sleep, fat-head."

"Right-oh, captain," Joker answered and then quickly sailed off to sleep.

Week two of boot camp found the trio learning about the Navy chain of command, customs and courtesies as well as basic watchstanding or watchkeeping. But it was the testing that set this week apart; testing provided a hope for a more certain future. There were 49 trades in the Navy and doing well on these tests could give an enlisted sailor a leg up. As it turned out, all three had talents that would be discovered through testing and they were all quickly on their way toward their eventual trade. Butch would become a Hospital Apprentice with hopes of becoming a Pharmacist's Mate; Joker's father owned a plumbing, heating and cooling company where Joker worked during the summers and was thus set to become a Machinist's Mate specializing in refrigeration; and Gerbil would become a Baker because of the cooking knowledge he obtained by working at his family's bakery.

The following weeks held many adventures for the trio and continued their training with hands-on naval training, including knowledge of rules, routines and history as well as handgun and rifle training, continued physical fitness training and of course, marching. Every morning the recruits were up before 6:00 a.m. and marched or trained until at least dusk. There was little free time except at night and on weekends. Sailors mostly used this time for studying, or reading, or writing letters and of course some planned and unplanned recreation.

Then there were the Saturday reviews. Every Saturday the station officers reviewed each company and the winners were awarded flags denoting their weekly achievements. The "E" Flags, or *Efficiency Flags*—more commonly referred to as the Rooster Flags—were coveted prizes awarded to the company for overall excellence. Butch's company continuously scored high in the recruit training and barrack inspection, but persistently lost points for marching. Their marching deficiencies could be directly linked to Gerbil's rhythm, or lack thereof. His 5' 2 ¼" frame did not blend well with the average sailor's gait—this was most dramatically illustrated at the weekend dances, where Gerbil was often described as looking like a drunk duck who had had too much coffee—and he found it more than a little difficult to keep in step or even turn the correct way much of the time. Butch at 6' 2" did not help create a smooth horizon to the formation either, but he was a natural athlete and melded quite well otherwise. Gerbil tried as he could to make up for his total marching deficits by always testing at the top of the top tier and never having a less than stellar bunk rating, but as the company grew tired of him ruining their chances each week, dissent began to grow in the ranks. Joker, who was constantly defending Gerbil with his wit or his fists, found this job relentless as more and more of the other recruits started to bash or bad mouth Gerbil. Having Butch in their ranks prevented an all-out brawl, but tensions were high.

This is when Steven Mackenzie came into their lives. Mackenzie was three-fourths of an inch taller than Gerbil and had a full-blown Napoleon complex. History would show Napoleon was actually average height for his time, so this made Mackenzie three inches shorter than the emperor and he also lacked his confidence. This resulted in overly-aggressive domineering behavior which he only imparted upon those who were shorter than him. Unfortunately, this was a company of one: Gerbil. For several weeks in secret, Mackenzie made Gerbil's life a living hell until Butch and Joker caught him peeing on Gerbil in the shower. Butch punched Mackenzie square in the face and held him as instructed by Joker, who then proceeded to shove a full bar of soap up Mackenzie's ass. From that point forward, Mackenzie was referred to as *Bubble Butt* by all who had heard the story. Mackenzie being a narcissistic little prick, could not take losing face and quit within the week, swearing he would get even with every one of the trio.

The following weekend Joker came up with a brilliant plan to get everyone's minds off Gerbil and Mackenzie, and bring the company together to take the flag. That Saturday, they cleaned and prepped as usual and when they were inspected, all was right with the world. Then on the drill field, they shined—they were smooth as butter throughout the entire drill. Their company ended up taking the Rooster and their company commander was extremely proud, if not a little surprised. He could not even pick out Gerbil this Saturday and it usually was not difficult.

When the recruits returned to the barracks, everyone was looking for Gerbil to slap him on the back for really coming through this time.

"Where is Gerbil?"

"Yeah, that dopey guy really did swell."

"Darn right he did."

"Who marched next to him?"

"I wish it was me. What a memorable day."

"Where is he, Joker?"

"Boys, may I present to you the hero of the day . . . Gerbil," Joker said as he pulled on the ties of Gerbil's sea bag and Gerbil crawled out.

"Jeepers, guys. I don't know what to say," Gerbil said with a big grin.

The room immediately broke into a roar that could be heard across the field.

"Well, they seem happy to win," Master Chief Petty Officer Cooper remarked as he stood with Chief Petty Officer Marshall Bowlen, their company commander, at the edge of the drill field.

"Yes, sir. They are a tight bunch. Good sailors through and through," replied Bowlen.

"Good to hear. Keep it up, commander."

"Yes, sir. Thank you," Bowlen responded with a salute and then returned to his quarters to celebrate with a scotch.

* * *

As the weeks passed, Butch, Joker and Gerbil continued to foster their relationship and their bond became even stronger. This was not lost on the company commander who would make the final recommendations for placement. Great Lakes housed many Class A schools at the time and they all would have a chance to further their trade education at Great Lakes if this was the decision. The three sailors began to be seen as a unit within the company as they continued to surpass expectations and help elevate their company toward excellence. To outsiders they seemed greater than their sum. How could a farm boy jock, a comedic plumber and a rodent-like baker be such winners—but win they did.

Individually, they all made their marks as well. Butch ruled the play field on the weekends, no matter what the sport; Joker knew more about refrigeration than his instructor; and Gerbil excelled in class and baked cinnamon rolls on the weekends that were in higher demand than anything sold in the commissary. Then there were the extracurriculars—this is where Joker shined. He made a name for himself in every circle on the base. Between his three-card monte and the jokes he told or made up on the spot and those he played on targeted individuals—the powder box being his most famous—he was a hit and opened many doors for the trio.

In week six, the recruits learned about firefighting, damage control and how to wear a gas mask. By now they were all in top-notch shape and looking forward to week seven and the *Battle Stations* exercise—a 12-hour comprehensive test covering everything they had learned in boot camp.

On Thursday of week six, the trio was called to Company Commander Bowlen's office.

"Sir!" they all said as they saluted once inside the office.

"At ease, sailors . . . take a seat." Company Commander Bowlen gestured toward the chairs in front of his desk. "The reason I called you in this evening is because I owe my good friend Charles a debt and I think you three are the sailors that can set me straight with him."

"Wait—you're selling us to your friend Chuck?" Joker asked.

"Son, you are in the Navy and I can do with you anything that suits me, so let us cut the shit for just a minute here. Darcy, I know you are capable of such a feat, correct?"

"Yes, sir," Joker replied.

"What I am doing is moving you three out in the morning to join Captain Charles B. McVay III on the USS *Indianapolis* in San Francisco. You are all E-3 Seamen now and will be learning your trades on ship. Luckily for you, Captain McVay is in need of a baker, a refrigeration specialist's mate and a pharmacist's mate. You are not at these rankings yet, but you have impressed me more than I can put into words and I have to admit I am surprised and a bit flummoxed by your progress here at the station—together and individually. You have even acquired a name among the petty officers—*The Unfathomable Ones*. Sarcasm and truth rolled into one. But mostly you are called *The Trio*."

"Thank you?" Joker just had to say.

"I will warn you. Do not screw the pooch on this one or I will geld you myself."

"Geld?" Gerbil questioned.

Butch replied, "Don't ask."

"Be ready at 05:30 sharp. You are dismissed. Oh, and one additional piece of information—Captain McVay goes by *Charles*. If he hears you call him *Chuck*, there will be nothing left for me to geld. Enjoy your flight."

Gerbil scrunched up his face and looked at Butch.

"Don't worry," he whispered.

The trio stood and said, "Thank you, sir," in unison, matched with a sharp salute before leaving the office.

On Friday, July 13, Butch, Joker and Gerbil left Great Lakes behind. They would not participate in the Battle Stations exercise next week and would not get to parade for graduation—by that time they would already be off on a secret mission that would ultimately win the war and quite possibly cost them their lives.

NAS Glenview

July, 1945

Sleepy and jittery with anticipation at the same time, the three sat on the bus discussing what type of plane they might be flying in to San Francisco. Eventually, their bus pulled into Naval Air Station Glenview and they were astounded at the activity that seemed to flow all around them in this somewhat smallish airport. Then they saw planes taking off from and landing on the same airstrip at the same time.

"I swear, I just saw those planes fly through each other," Gerbil shouted as he whipped around in his seat to see the rest of the landing since the plane that had taken off was already lost in the clouds.

They all continued to take in the flares and lights, and the men seamlessly dancing between the jeeps and planes.

"This looks like a musical," Gerbil continued.

The other two did not disagree, but also did not commit to such vocalized praise. None of the three had seen a ship's crew during docking, or casting off, or even during a drill, so they really had little to compare. However, one thing they did not see was marching—and this was alright with them.

Curtis-Reynolds Field began as a small airfield in the village of Glenview. At its peak it was thought to be one of the finest airfields in the Midwest, as it housed the largest hangar built to date—Hangar One—and a one gigacandela electric light that was so bright it allowed most all airfield activity to continue even at night. In 1933, Charles Lindbergh attended the International Air Races hosted at the field.

In 1936, Great Lakes leased the airfield and then bought it outright after World War II started. The field soon grew from a 200-acre airfield to a fully functional air station. At that time, NRAB Chicago—eventually to be renamed NAS Glenview—became the Navy's largest primary training base. During the war, two commercial paddle steamer ships were retrofitted into aircraft carriers—the USS *Wolverine* and the USS *Sable*—and docked in Chicago at what would later be called Navy Pier. Afloat in Lake Michigan, these two comprised the Corn Belt Fleet and experienced thousands of successful takeoffs and landings, which helped to train countless navy pilots.

Two future U.S. Presidents, George H.W. Bush and Gerald Ford, trained here—Ford was currently serving as a training officer when the trio arrived—and not too distantly in the future, the first astronaut to walk on the moon, Neal Armstrong, would serve here as a navy aviator. Then there was Edward Henry O'Hare, who was credited with single-handedly shooting down five enemy bombers as their formation of nine heavy bombers approached his aircraft carrier, the USS *Lexington*. O'Hare was the first naval recipient of the Medal of Honor in World War II and went on to have a U.S. Navy destroyer and the major international airport in Chicago named after him.

The bus pulled up to a hangar that could only be described as the mouth of a monster and the three disembarked.

"Take your orders to the hangar commander," the bus driver said out the window before closing it and pulling away.

"I'm not sure I want to walk in there. It looks like it could just about eat us," Joker jested.

"Yeah, and I want to know how they keep the ceiling up

before I go in there," Gerbil stated emphatically.

"Don't know. Don't care," Butch replied and walked in front of the others leading the way, or to slaughter as far as Joker was concerned.

"Do you guys see that plane?" Butch asked as they approached the hangar office. Butch was pointing at a Beechcraft C-45, which served the Navy as a light, or VIP, transport plane.

"She's a beauty."

"Yeah—a real killer diller," Gerbil added.

"But I bet we'll be taking that one," Joker said as he popped his head toward a Budd Conestoga, a high-winged heavy transport.

Both planes had their engines running as if eager to take off and leave the hungry hangar behind.

"No way I'm getting on that thing. It looks like a pregnant tadpole with wings," Gerbil cried.

Joker looked at Gerbil as if to say, *Hey, I'm the funny one here*, but also with a little pride, thinking, *Gerbils can be trained*.

As the boys approached a glassed-in room full of desks, clipboards and clocks, a lanky petty officer padded over to intercept them.

"You're late! We cannot be idling our engines waiting on three simple seamen. Get on the bus," he said as he pointed to his right.

The only problem was his finger pointed in the direction of both the idling airplanes the trio had commented on during their saunter to the hangar office. Butch quickly decided he would be the one to ask the obvious question before the other two could make a stupid comment and piss off the petty officer any further.

"Which bus, sir?"

The petty officer looked up and said, "The pretty one.

Satisfied?"

"Yes, sir!"

The three saluted sharply. The petty officer returned the salute and walked back to his office.

The Beechcraft C-45 was a twin-engine, low-wing, double tail H-style aircraft utilized by the U.S. Navy, Air Force and Marines during World War II. Its shiny, tapered fuselage was highlighted by sleek rectangular windows. When the boys boarded, they found spacious seating for six. They were just getting settled when the cockpit door opened and a voice called out.

"Nice of you to join us. Now, buckle up, boys."

The cockpit door closed and then opened again.

"Sorry, no stewardess this trip, but there's water in the box at the back of the plane if you get thirsty."

The door closed again and within 30 seconds the plane jerked into motion and headed for the runway. Once in the air, the plane stormed into the clouds and leveled off at 15,000 feet. The three remained glued to their windows for the first hour or so of the flight until Joker got up to get some of the promised water. He soon returned with a bottle of scotch.

"This must be the *good* water," he said smiling as he went to open the bottle.

Butch grabbed his hand and said, "You can just put that back. Did he say we were welcome to *scotch* or *water* from the box in back?"

"How about scotch and water?"

"Hey, this is not the time. Remember we are The Unfathomable Ones and nothing less. We should respect the opportunity we've been given and not start our navy career with a court-martial."

"I know I'm the funny one, but I thought Gerbil was the smart one. Hey, Gerbil, he's taking your job," Joker said as he walked the bottle back to the box and brought back three waters.

Gerbil did not answer—he was already asleep in his seat—so the other two drank their water and stared out their window at the endless field of clouds, so comfortable and so content. Little did they know in just over two weeks they would see nothing but clouds, but would be neither comfortable nor content.

JAPAN

Light

Darkness

Light

光

Asa – Morning
Aika – Love Song
Fukushima – Blessed Island
Kumakichi – Fortunate Bear
Chiyo – Thousand Generations

April, 1308

Asa Fukushima walked beside the shallow stream that meandered down the mountainside to the sea. The day seemed eerily quiet, especially when compared to the last 18 hours when Asa's little village had held on for their dear lives as a typhoon pounded the island without remorse. She noted the salt in the morning air was certainly more prevalent than usual and stung her eyes as she approached the shore; nevertheless, she walked on undeterred, happy to still be alive and free. She really did not have anything to do at the shore, but was anxious to get out after being imprisoned by the storm as it stalled over their island for nearly a day.

Asa lived with her family on Sado Island in a village hidden high up the mountain along the bank of a stream. Sado, Japan's sixth largest island, was 20 miles off the west coast of Japan. It had a rich history even by the beginning of the fourteenth century and had been inhabited for over 10,000 years. The island's near future held the discovery of gold—which would bring the status of the island back into the Japanese fold—but at this time in history, Sado was an island of exile.

From the eighth century through the eighteenth, Sado was a place of banishment for troublesome Japanese leaders or subjects who could not be or were not dealt with by the most severe punishment—death. Sado became Japan's Australia—a problem-child island paradise—and would be the eventual home for a poet, an emperor, a Buddhist monk and so many more bothersome or inconvenient Japanese citizens.

Asa broke through the trees and walked onto the sandy shore of the inlet at the mouth of the stream. She picked up a deep onyx stone, smoothed by the sea, and tossed it side arm to skip it across the now glass-like water.

Tunk!

Asa looked up at the sound, but could not discern why totally calm water would make such a noise. She picked up another stone and flung it likewise at the water, but received no reward. As she walked out calf-deep in the water to look closer, she thought she saw something floating just beneath the surface. She returned to the beach and ran south around the shoreline to find a large plank of wood floating in the water just off the mouth of the inlet. She scanned the horizon for more and was astonished to see a huge wooden box floating in the open sea. She then saw many other items floating listlessly on the undisturbed water. She turned to pick up another stone, excited by what might be in such a box, and then saw something that caused her to fall backside first into the water. Not even 30 yards down the beach was a ship as big as a temple resting askew on the rocks and sand. *Liberté* was written across the ship's stern and Asa wondered what this strange word might mean.

Asa's heart was aflutter as she wondered what she should do. Should she go see this monster of a vessel for herself or should she run back to the village and tell her father or the elders? Life on Sado was no more challenging than most ocean islands; nonetheless, it did have a dark side that infused caution into her village: the banished. Asa's little village was remote and undisturbed by the larger population in the island lowlands and had been so for centuries. What little trade they made was directly with other trusted islanders or on the main island if they chanced the ocean journey. Few of the lowlanders even knew of their village, so this boat could be a blessing, bringing them items beyond their imaginations, or a curse, bringing knowledge of their remote village to the wider island. The decision was obvious. She took off running up the mountain to fetch her father.

Within the hour the small mountain village of Haru was electrified with the news. Even though work began immediately, it would take nearly three weeks to take apart the shipwrecked galleon piece by piece. Within the first week the villagers had taken off the voluminous cargo to lighten the ship, then patched the hull so they could pull the boat into the inlet where it would be hidden from passing boats, even if they came somewhat close to shore. By the second week, they had all but the hull moved further up the mountain. They selected a leveled off clearing deep in the trees northeast of the stream; when the stream hooked left, they went right. The third week completed the excavation as pieces of the hull were used to create a shelter in the clearing to cover the hundreds of boxes and other items retrieved from the galleon's cargo holds.

During the fourth week, the village as a whole finally had time to breathe and the village elders held a meeting to decide what to do about the mysterious cargo, remnants of the boat and one other very important unresolved issue. First, the elders inspected the cargo and found hundreds of boxes of papers with strange writing, extraordinary items and artifacts of the likes they had never seen—and then there was the treasure: boxes and boxes of gold and silver and jewels.

The elders decided to utilize much of the wood from the ship's cabins to build out the village. This would allow stronger wood shelters without removing trees that provided the canopy that helped isolate the village. Major pieces of the galleon—deck boards and pieces of the hull—for now would continue to be used to keep the ship's cargo safe from the elements.

Now, only one decision remained: what to do with the three sailors rescued from the *Liberté*. Asa had named the biggest of the three Kumakichi, or *Fortunate Bear*. The village cared for the sailors as best they could, but fate would only allow Fortunate Bear to survive. The elders ultimately decided Fortunate Bear would be taken in by Asa's family since she was the one who had saved his life. As time went on, Fortunate Bear would become a valued member of the mountain village and eventually fall in love with and marry Asa's older sister, Aika. Their first child—a girl with wavy jet-black hair and piercing jade eyes—was named *Chiyo*.

Over the years, Asa loved to retell the story of the day she found a sailing ship as big as a temple. Asa, Aika and Kumakichi would eventually help this tale come to fruition in the truest sense when they used the remaining parts of the ship to create an actual temple. The *Temple of Ai*, hidden in the remote mountainside of Sado, would become a traditional Japanese place of worship as well as a secret society that over the next centuries would promote love and equality among all people of the world—even if they had to help things along.

Darkness

闇

Kaminari – Thunder
Takeshi – Warrior
Mizushima – Water Island

October, 1242

Emperor Juntoku, the exiled 84th emperor of Japan—now known as Sado-no In after his banishment to Sado Island in 1221 for his involvement in the Jokyu War—lay on his deathbed. Profound sadness enveloped his family as they surrounded his bed awaiting Sado-no In's last breath. Undercurrents of what the ex-emperor's death might mean to the island of Sado spread throughout the lowlands of the island like a grass fire; anticipation and foreboding ran together like watercolors in the mist of uncertainty.

However, for Kaminari Mizushima this day brought glee, as she had grand ideas of what she and her amber-eyed son, Takeshi, might accomplish now that she would finally be permitted to spend the small fortune she was paid by the emperor's magistrate to keep their little secret. She planned to settle along the coast on the south side of the lowlands. Here she would build a palace and take over the fishing boats of the nearby settlement to control the inflow of seafood to *her* area of the island.

Yes, her spirit was full of big dreams; unfortunately, much of what she dreamt caused nightmares for those around her. She was black inside and no amount of money nor power or even respect would ever change this character that was encoded into her soul. This inherent darkness would be handed down from generation to generation and eventually grow darker and darker with each passing century. Lucky for many of Kaminari's descendants, this was a recessive trait. Through the years the family would learn this trait was tied to another: those children born with amber eyes would also likely be born with this darkness or thunder in their soul. For those who received this family distinction, the world was often not enough and darkness could easily overtake them even in the most mundane situations; such was the fate of Takeshi, Kaminari's first born son.

The following decades would prove prosperous for the Mizushima family as they built their fishing fleet into a flourishing fishing monopoly, often using unscrupulous tactics to fend off their competition. Their hands-on business plan was so successful that during their reign many of the other fishing companies in the area relocated to the north coast of the Sado lowlands while most of the independent fishing boats in the area were all but forced to join the Mizushima fleet.

Forty years after Sado-on In's death, Kaminari died—taking the secret of her family fortune with her.

SHARK

USS Indianapolis

The Philippine Sea

USS Indianapolis

July, 1945

Butch, Joker and Gerbil disembarked their VIP flight and were immediately waved to a waiting jeep.

"Pick it up, sailors. We don't have all day. How about some double-time," Seaman Merrill yelled as the trio walked to the jeep.

"What seems to be the rush? Do we have our orders?" Gerbil asked eagerly.

"No, we're still docked and cocked, but it's Friday night and you never know when you're going to hear the whistle, so you have to make the best of your liberty."

"This is the life. One day as seamen and we're already on liberty." Joker climbed aboard the jeep and folded his hands behind his head. "Yep, sea living is alright with me."

"Wait—you think you're going out on liberty tonight? Hahaha! I have strict orders to take you three directly to the ship. Something about advanced training or training in advance. I'm not certain, but all you will be seeing for a while are bulkheads and hatches. Be nice to them 'cause they are your friends. My favorite hatch is *Betty* and her dog, the hatch handle, is *Pudgy*."

"Then drive on to our prison, sailor," Joker said as he resolved to his fate, but still leaned back to enjoy the pleasant San Francisco weather.

"You name the hatches?" Gerbil questioned.

"Of course. How else you gonna get to know them?"

"Can you tell us anything else about our ship?" Gerbil asked, checking the man's uniform for his name, then added, "Seaman Merrill."

"Boys, you're fortunate enough to be serving on the USS *Indianapolis* under the command of Captain Charles B.

McVay, the third. He's a righteous commander and fair captain—he would never let the little guy down. Then there's the lady herself. The *Indy* is a Portland-class heavy cruiser, hull number 35, and has served as a flagship for nearly all her life. Commissioned in 1932, she served as a floating White House for FDR, she has seen action in Bougainville, Kiska, Amchitka, Attu, Tarawa, Kwajalein, Saipan and Lelilu, and was fortunate enough to be out on maneuvers when the Japs hit Pearl Harbor. Luck runs in her blood, or oil, I guess. She has sailed through the ice of the North and the ovens of the tropics. The *Indy* was there when the Marines raised the flag at Iwo Jima. I know you've seen that picture, unless you've been living under a rock."

"Wow, that's a lot of history," Butch interjected.

"Yep, and she will be there when we win the war."

Butch remembered joking about just that subject several weeks before, then unexpectedly felt some foreboding. He wrote it off to being estranged from his family and running for his life from the police, but something seemed to be gnawing at his subconscious nonetheless.

The jeep drove off to the Mare Island Naval Shipyard—a huge rolling complex of expansive piers, slips, docks and launches—where the *Indy* was completing needed repairs after suffering damage from a kamikaze attack during the invasion of Okinawa. The plane had missed the ship, but the pilot was able to release a bomb at close range that blew through the deck, the mess hall, and the berthing compartment until it finally hit the fuel tanks and left two gaping holes in the keel just below the drive shaft. In all, nine sailors were killed. After some initial attempts to repair the damage, the *Indianapolis* crossed the Pacific at a

17-degree list, but under her own power, to return to Mare Island.

The jeep pulled onto the dock that held the *Indianapolis* and they all got out to follow their driver up the gangplank.

"There she is, boys—11,500 tons with a top speed of 33 knots. She doesn't have the 13 inches of steel armor amidship like the newer battleships do, only four inches for her, but she's fast."

The trio went quiet. *How does that thing even stay afloat?* they all thought to themselves. Contemplating how a steel-plated boat longer than two football fields floated, much less moved around at any speed, had tied the boys' tongues.

At the top of the gangplank, Seaman Merrill saluted and said to the officer of the deck, "Request permission to come aboard, sir."

Seeing this, the three jumped in line and saluted, saying, "Sir," in unison.

It did not matter what rank the sailor on watch held, he represented the commander of the ship and was to be respected as such.

The sailor reached out his hand saying, "Papers, boys."

The three quickly retrieved their assignment documentation and handed it to the OOD.

After a quick appraisal, he turned and said to the petty officer standing on the quarterdeck, "Callahan, take these seamen to see the captain."

"Yes, sir," Callahan saluted and turned to the bow of the ship.

The three followed along, all the while rubbernecking to take in the structures of the ship. On their short walk along the main deck, they saw a folded seaplane in one of the hangars and several rows of guns that were bigger than any tank they had ever seen. As they entered the ship's superstructure, they all looked up to see towers of steel that seemed to touch the sky. When they arrived at the captain's quarters, Callahan knocked three times on the door. A muffled "Enter" was heard through the door which he then opened and led the three sailors into the small cabin.

All four sailors snapped to attention.

"Captain McVay, I present Seaman First Class Darcy Lawson, Seaman First Class Chester Best, and Seaman First Class Jack—"

"Yes, Petty Officer Callahan, thank you. That will be all. Please wait outside my quarters to take these men to their lockers and then deliver them to their duty officers of the day."

"Sir." Callahan saluted and exited, closing the door behind him.

At 46, McVay was a good-looking man who had been in the Navy since he was 20. He was well liked by the top brass as well as by his officers and enlisted men.

"So, my old friend Marshall Bowlen tells me you three are the ones to watch. What was it he called you . . . The Unfathomable Ones? Cute nickname. Since we are on a warship during a world war, let us all hope it is true. Just yesterday I was informed by naval command that we will be leaving port on the sixteenth. The call will be going out soon and when it does this ship will be inundated with hundreds of shiny new sailors. Let me make no bones about this, we are at war and these sailors will need to learn the ropes as we sail. You will as well. And I am counting on your complete commitment and full attention to this task. Marshall said you helped make your company greater than the sum of its parts. We will need some of that magic on our pending journey. So, do I have your complete commitment and full attention?"

"Yes, sir."

"And do you promise to keep your noses clean? I have heard you can be a handful if you decide to be."

Butch caught Joker start to move his hand to his face and slapped it back into place. This was not lost on McVay as he continued.

"Before you are dismissed, I do have one question. I can account for all of your nicknames except one. Butch is obvious, as is Joker, as just displayed."

Butch let out a *huff* that he hoped was not overtly evident in the small quarters.

"But for the life of me, I cannot figure out where Gerbil comes from. Yes, you are on the lower end of the navy height scale, but if that were the determining factor, we would certainly have more rodent-derived nicknames. Yes, we have had a *Ratface* and a *Gopher* and even a *Possum* on the ship—all were well deserved I might add—but none beyond this. So, can one of you please enlighten me?"

"It's how he eats, sir," Butch offered.

"Yes, like he has a tiny piece of corn in his hands," Joker added.

"Yes, sir, that's how I have eaten ever since I was a child," Gerbil confirmed and then put both hands up to his mouth as if he were holding a tiny piece of corn and rapidly nibbled away.

McVay chuckled and said, "Well, I look forward to your baking anyway, Seaman Best. You boys are dismissed and remember, you promised to keep your noses clean—especially you, Seaman Lawson."

"Yes, sir," Joker replied.

The three sailors exited the captain's quarters and Butch immediately punched Joker in the shoulder.

"What were you thinking? Or should I say you weren't

thinking?"

"I was only going to—"

"I know, you were only going to pick your nose in front of the captain."

"He said to keep our noses clean. I was just checking."

"You were going to pick your nose in front of the captain?" Gerbil chimed in. "Are you crazy? Not the time, Joker. Not the time," Gerbil chanted while shaking his head.

"See. If Gerbil agrees you're crazy, then you must be."

"Or stupid," Gerbil added.

"No, not crazy or stupid. Just a comic genius who isn't appreciated in his own time."

"Joker, there's a time for comedy and a time to be serious," Butch rebuked.

"You two can live your lives however you desire, but I'm here to be happy and enjoy every minute of each day. Every moment should be approached with a smile. We all take too much too seriously. When it's time to get serious, you will know it. Plus, have I ever let you down . . . well?"

"No."

"Nope."

"And have I ever made you laugh at what you thought was a serious moment?"

"Yes."

"Yep."

"Therein lies the lesson then."

Butch and Gerbil looked at each other and decided to give in to Joker's logic. Eventually, life would teach him the cruel truth, unless Joker taught life first—which seemed to be Joker's point and admittedly, knowing Joker as they did, was a possibility.

"You guys brothers or something?" Callahan asked, a bit confused by the dialogue that just took place.

"Nope, just shipmates like you," Joker answered.

Callahan took the three to their lockers and showed them which bunks they would have during off watch hours. He then introduced each to their duty officer so their training could begin.

Butch met Jack, Romeo, Harry and Homer. He was assigned to shadow Jack, a Pharmacist's Mate First Class, until he was officially at a PM3c rank. John Schmueck was their Chief.

Gerbil was introduced to Clarence and Salvador who would be on his shift. Since baking was not a necessary part of running or navigating the ship, it was not considered an official part of watchkeeping, but they still kept to the same schedule. Gerbil would train under Clarence.

Joker was thrown into a sea of faces in the engine room. The only name he remembered once he was through with all the introductions was Lucky, the engine room pigeon, who was there for CO detection. *If Lucky remained lucky, then so did you* read the plaque over his cage. Joker was eventually assigned to be John Muldoon's apprentice.

The *Indianapolis* was now ready to return to service. She had a new paint job—a camouflage stripe—and new guns as well. As the *Indy* lay in wait, a flurry of yard birds, or shipyard workers, abruptly started clearing the midship deck—removing a seaplane in the process—without giving any reason. It was all very hush-hush. Soon after this eruption of activity, the *Indy* left Mare Island and sailed to Hunters Point Naval Shipyard, a mere 30 miles south, located in the southeast corner of San Francisco. Once docked, hundreds of new sailors boarded her, replacing those who had finished their rotation after Okinawa. This was not ideal for any ship, especially during a world war, but it was what it was; training would need to happen during their journey back into action—there would be no honeymoon period for the new *Indy* crew.

Just prior to all this hush-hush business aboard the *Indy*, Rear Admiral William Purnell and Captain William Parsons had assigned Captain McVay and his crew a top-secret mission after their original choice, the USS *Pensacola*, had suffered engine failure during a rough-sea trial run. Now the *Indianapolis*' fate was cast: it was to travel to Tinian Island post haste with two pieces of secret cargo. That was if everything went according to plan.

July 16

The crew had prepared the ship and were awaiting orders to set sail. Earlier that morning, several trucks pulled up beside the *Indy* and the dock was a flourish of navy brass the likes of which the average sailor had never seen. Word spread quickly and every sailor who could spare an eye had one on the dock. Soon afterwards, the *Indy* crane lifted a large crate onto the deck and the Marines on watch secured it to the port hangar deck. At this same time and with a lot less fanfare, two artillery officers, Major Robert Furman and Captain James Nolan, carried two small canisters—each about the size of an old-fashioned ice cream maker—onto the ship. The bucket-like containers hung like lead bricks between the two officers on a simple pipe. Since the admiral's quarters were not currently occupied, the canisters were brought there and were spot-welded to the deck to keep them secure during transit. The crew, anxious to get underway, awaited the call to cast off, but none came. Questions arose about the delay, but no reason was offered.

Being a boat of mostly teenagers, speculation grew about the mysterious cargo and a pool was even started to bet on what was inside the giant crate now surrounded by marines. There were many guesses, some serious, some funny, some dirty, but none even close. The top vote getter when the boat sailed was 5,000 rolls of scented toilet paper for General MacArthur.

Finally, upon McVay's orders, the *Indianapolis* departed Hunters Point and made way for Pearl Harbor at a speed of 29 knots. This was faster than usual and caused several families to miss the ceremonial wave-off at the Golden Gate Bridge: a tradition where families of the sailors on board gathered on the bridge to wave goodbye as the ship passed beneath the bridge.

July 19

The *Indy* made it to Pearl Harbor in a record 74 ½ hours at an average speed of 29 knots, then wasted little time refueling before racing on to Tinian, again with record speed. McVay was warned by the engine room that maintaining a top speed for hours on end could burn out the engines. His answer: "Maintain full speed, sailor." He had faith in his crew and their abilities under stress, so why not the *Indy* herself?

It was breakfast time the first morning out of Hawaii when Gerbil overheard the cooks talking while he was baking bread for lunch with Clarence and Salvador.

"This batch is for the captain, so don't screw it up," Morgan told his crew.

"Aye aye, sir," Keith answered as he flipped a pancake high over the griddle.

"Hey, Morgan. You want to make those *special* for the captain?" Gerbil asked from across the galley.

"What are you suggesting, sailor?"

"Here, let me show you."

Gerbil took a bowl and dipped it into the huge mixing bowl of batter, then whisked in a few ingredients that were readily available on the counter.

"Here you go Keith. Flip these and see what we get," Gerbil said as he handed Keith the bowl of newly mixed batter.

"Hey, Gerbil, these are fluffy as a marshmallow. What did you do to these? The captain is going to flip his wig—in a good way, that is."

About 10 minutes after the pancakes were brought out to the captain's table, Captain McVay walked into the galley and asked who made his pancakes this morning. Keith shot a worried glance at Gerbil.

"I mixed the batter, sir. So I'm responsible if they didn't meet your expectations," Gerbil replied.

"What did you do differently?" McVay queried.

"I just folded in some extra baking powder, a dash more baking soda and added a touch of vanilla extract."

"Can you follow orders, sailor?" McVay asked.

"Yes, sir!" Gerbil responded, then held his breath, suddenly concerned for his future as a baker on the *Indy*.

"And the rest of you?"

"Yes, sir," the bakers and cooks said in near unison.

"Good. Then I order you to make this recipe for the entire crew every time pancakes are served."

"Aye aye, sir," Keith called out before anyone else could respond.

"Good," Captain McVay said, then left the galley.

"Phew!" Gerbil let out an audible breath.

"Good work, sailor," Morgan called to Gerbil from across the galley.

"Just helping the team, sir," Gerbil responded, happy his recipe did not go south like a deflated soufflé.

The next time pancakes were served in the mess hall, Butch and Joker could not help but tell everyone in earshot that this was their pal Gerbil's recipe.

"Good, ain't they?" Joker asked his fellow machinist mates, Gabe and John.

"Fluffy like my girl's fanny," one sailor called out from down the table while Gabe and John just made grunting sounds as they scooped more pancake into their pie holes.

Joker smiled at the comment, then caught sight of Leslie A. McConnell, the commissary steward, berating the mess attendants.

Joker slapped Butch on the shoulder and said, "That jackass is at it again."

"Yeah, it's never-ending with him," Butch responded, then took another big bite of pancake.

"Why is it that some people don't understand being someone's superior doesn't mean you are superior to them? He's such an ass."

"Can you say narcissist?" Butch said through a mouthful of pancake.

"Hey, Leslie," Joker called out at a near shout.

"Oh, shit," Butch said, not nearly quiet enough.

"So, Leslie. Remind me what your middle initial stands for—is the 'A' for Alice or Asshole?"

The whole mess erupted into a fit of laughing. An officer passing by in the hall ducked his head in to see what all the fuss was about, then ultimately started to laugh himself as if there were a cloud of nitrous oxide in the air; he just laughed, smiled, shook his head and went back into the passageway.

This only caused Leslie to increase his vitriolic monologue to the mess attendants. They all backed away which made Leslie feel like he imparted fear into the lot, not knowing they were just trying to keep out of range of the spittle that constantly sprayed from his mouth when he talked at most any volume; some people whistled or slurred when they spoke—Leslie sprayed. When he felt like he had control of the situation again, he shot a look at Joker, his eyes cold and dead. Joker just locked eyes and stared back with an especially dopey expression on his face. Leslie finally broke off the contest to glance at Butch, who did not think Leslie's eyes could get any colder, but they did.

July 26

Once at Tinian, the giant crate and the canisters were off-loaded onto a barge. The water surrounding the barge was teeming with whaleboats and other small vessels, again full of high-ranking navy brass. At the dock, a large number of military police awaited the cargo. Nolan and Furman disembarked with the canisters, as they were not artillery officers, but members of the Manhattan Project in disguise. Little did the crew know, but the *Indianapolis* had just delivered components of *Little Boy*—the atomic gun-type mechanism in the crate and half of the United States' enriched uranium in the canisters—the atomic bomb that would eventually help end the war. The components of *Fat Man*, the plutonium implosion nuclear bomb, were flown in from Kirtland Army Air Field in Albuquerque, New Mexico immediately after the components for *Little Boy* arrived safely in Tinian. In fact, the initial departure delay from Hunters Point was due to Nolan and Furman awaiting validation that the Trinity Test—the first successful detonation of a nuclear bomb, nicknamed *Gadget*—was successful.

With their top-secret mission successfully completed, the *Indianapolis* was sent on to Apra Harbor, Guam where again members of the crew who had completed their tours of duty were relieved by other sailors. The *Indy* took on fuel, stores and ammunition before receiving orders to follow Route Peddie on a direct line to the island of Leyte, where her crew would receive training before continuing on to Okinawa to join Vice Admiral Jesse B. Oldendorf's Task Force 95.

McVay had agreed to sail unaccompanied across the Pacific under a cloak of secrecy to deliver unknown cargo; however, now he requested a destroyer escort to cross the Philippine Sea—a navy standard of operations. The request was denied for unknown reasons and instead he was told to zigzag at his discretion in order to avoid being easy prey for enemy submarines. He was also not given the option to take a more *indirect* route to Leyte, which would have been the best option when traveling without an escort. What McVay was *not* told was that the Navy knew there were enemy submarines in the area because they had broken the Japanese code and were intercepting submarine transmissions. However, the Navy did not want the Japanese to discover their code had been broken, so this information remained a tightly guarded secret. Unfortunately, the fact that the USS *Underhill*, a destroyer that *could* detect submarines, was sunk just two days before sending the *Indianapolis*, a ship that *could not* detect submarines, unattended was lost on the navy command. So, the *Indianapolis* left unescorted for Leyte— the first heavy warship to do so—zigzagging at Captain

McVay's discretion, still under a cloak of secrecy, as few of the navy fleet even knew the *Indy* was in the area.

The Philippine Sea

July 28, 1945

The crew was looking forward to joining a fleet in training. They had repeated drills during much of their journey to Tinian, but running maneuvers with a fleet was something entirely different. Expectations ran high and the crew was wired with anticipation. During the *Indy*'s trip to Tinian, as usual, Joker had broken the ice with much of the crew and the trio was now held in high regard by most of the officers as well. It was a bit surreal how Joker could just be Joker and get away with all but the most blatant missteps, all in the name of humor. To some he was a mascot, to others a jester, but to most a friend and this was his real magic—he appealed to the masses.

There were always exceptions to this rule and each of the three had at least one sailor who did not get along with them. This was usually due to a miscommunication, a misconception or jealousy—Butch looked like the boy that stole your girls, or Joker got all the laughs, or you thought you heard Gerbil say something bad about you. All in all, it usually got hammered out since if you got caught fighting on the ship, even well-placed humor was not likely to get you out of trouble. Plus, on a ship you had to know who had your back and let them know in no uncertain terms that you had theirs.

About an hour out of Apra Harbor, Gerbil was in the galley baking a batch of his world-famous—well, at least navy-famous—cinnamon rolls.

"Gerbil, those rolls smell like heaven. You are probably one bite away from making Baker Third Class," Clarence, his ship mentor, said as he audibly sniffed the air.

"Maybe just one *sniff* if we could pipe the aroma into

the captain's quarters," Salvador agreed.

"Not the bridge though. We don't want them running the ship into a rock. Got to have their senses up there," Ray added as he continually tossed a large dough ball. Ray was from another watch, or shift, but came down early to start the dinner rolls for the next day so Gerbil could concentrate on baking his cinnamon rolls.

Several minutes later, Commissary Steward Leslie A. McConnell walked into the galley.

"What am I smelling? Those are not dinner rolls that I smell," he said, then walked directly up to Gerbil and continued. "On whose orders are you baking these pastries?" he asked forcefully, a spray of spittle washing over Gerbil's face with every word.

"They are in celebration of our record-breaking trip to deliver the mystery crate to Tinian, sir," Clarence answered.

"Was I speaking to you, sailor?"

"No, sir."

"And you, sailor, what are you doing?" Leslie called out, clearly not remembering Ray's name.

"Tossing dough, sir," Ray replied.

"Sailor, I am not stupid. Do you think I am stupid?"

Ray did not answer.

"Well!" Leslie yelled, turning red in the process.

"Oh—sorry, sir. I thought it was a rhetorical question, sir," Ray replied, but still did not offer a response.

"Why are you baking unauthorized pastries? What's next, croissants? Do you think you are in the French Navy?" Leslie continued to reprimand Gerbil.

"Hey, hey. What is all the yelling about," Joker called out as he entered the galley with Butch and three other sailors in tow.

"None of your business, Darcy," Leslie retorted, refusing

to call him by his nickname.

"What is that godawful sore on your lip? You been licking toilet seats again?"

"Again, that is none of your business, Darcy."

As the two bantered back and forth, Butch walked over to stand beside Gerbil and noticed his face glistening with more than sweat. He immediately shot a look over to Joker to convey his displeasure. Meanwhile, three of the cooks, Morgan, Earl and Keith, began to take notice of the conversation and took a break from their chores to walk over to the group forming around Leslie.

"None of my business, huh. Hey, Butch, do you remember a simpler life?" Joker said, changing the subject somewhat abruptly.

"Yes, I do, Joker," Butch answered.

"How about you, Gabe?"

"Yes, sir. I yearn for that simpler life."

"And you . . . John, Norm?"

"Yep," they both replied without hesitation.

"Did you ever blow Bubbles as a kid?" Joker asked as he gazed off into the galley.

Leslie immediately followed his glance, but saw only the ceiling.

"Well, Leslie. Did you ever blow Bubbles as a kid?"

"Cut the shit, Darcy. Everyone blew bubbles as a kid."

"Well, Bubbles is back in town and he would like to see you again."

The group around Leslie exploded in laughter. After a moment of hesitation, Leslie—red as a valentine heart—took a step toward Joker, but Butch stepped in his path.

"Asshole!" he yelled, pointing over Butch's shoulder.

"Funny thing about assholes, Leslie," Butch said as if continuing Joker's monologue. "If you meet one asshole a day, then you probably met an asshole or a poor soul who was having a very bad day. But if you meet assholes all day long, then most likely *you* are the asshole."

Again, the group erupted.

"What are you doing here, Leslie?" Butch asked in a non-threatening tone with his arms loosely folded on his chest.

"I said . . . none of your business. I outrank you, seaman, and do not answer to you," Leslie said with disdain.

"You don't outrank me," Clarence said, taking a step forward.

"Or me," Morgan said, doing likewise.

"Or me," John added and stepped forward with the others to further confine Leslie.

"Well, Leslie, we're just making sure it is in fact *your* business," Butch said, then added, "Are you the duty officer today?"

"No, but I—"

"'No, but I' is enough, Boner."

Butch had done it now. He used the nickname he had given Leslie in front of their entire berth when they had all been awoken for a drill and Leslie woke with visible night wood. Now this could happen to any sailor awoken at night and it had, but these sailors were not narcissistic assholes who deserved a derogatory nickname. So, Leslie was assigned a nickname and *Boner* it was. Up to now Butch had not used the name again since that night. Leslie had pretty much cooled down since then, leaving at least the trio's immediate shipmates out of his sights, but now, Butch unleashed the moniker with a fury after hearing Leslie berate the bakers and seeing the spittle on Gerbil's face.

While the group was challenging Leslie, it was Joker's turn to check out Gerbil, making Leslie uncertain of whom to watch. However, once Butch had made his remarks and dropped the nickname, Leslie forgot all about Joker and stared down Butch, looking as if he were about to flip his wig and go for Butch's throat.

Butch stared back intensely, then slightly shifted his glance to quickly look at Gerbil and Joker standing over by the counter and pantry cabinets. This caught Leslie's eye and he turned to look at the two and found Joker fiddling with something in a drawer. Leslie quickly stomped over to the counter.

"What do you have there?" Leslie demanded. "You have no right to come into my galley and take whatever you please. This galley should be off limits to non-commissary personnel and scuttle like yourself."

As he verbally accosted Joker, Leslie pushed his way through the other sailors who had gathered around to observe the heated discussion.

"Give me that," he said as he grabbed Joker's hand and struggled to open his fingers.

"No, this is mine," Joker yelled as he fought to keep his fingers wrapped around the item in question.

Few of the sailors understood what was happening, but this was, aided by Butch, another of Joker's webs and Leslie had thrown himself fully into it.

"No-No," Joker continued as he feigned reluctance to release his grip, but eventually allowed Leslie to win the battle and Leslie finally pulled the box free of Joker's grasp.

Leslie immediately stepped away from the group to assess his prize. He now held a small box slightly smaller than a pack of cigarettes. The top of the box was imprinted with the words **Do Not Open** and some smaller writing just below. This smaller writing was written in a font that could not be easily read upside-down, thus forcing Leslie to turn the box to finish the message. The smaller text simply stated, This side up.

"What do you have in here?" Leslie spat as he tried to open the box.

Joker did his best to look guilty while claiming his innocence. The box was no pushover to open and required the user to read the tiny instructions on its sides, directing them where to *hold* and where to *push*. Leslie looked closely at the sides of the box and did as instructed. With a flash the box burst open and several tablespoons of flour exploded into Leslie's face. Now, totally blinded, Leslie dropped the box and clawed at his face to remove the flour from his eyes. As Leslie pawed at his face, he wandered between the counter and the panty doors. As he approached the pantry side, Butch, who had just opened a cupboard door in Leslie's path, yelled, "Look out," and pretended to try to grab the door to close it, but instead *accidentally* gave the door a little push toward Leslie's head. The door bounced off Leslie's head and caused him to pop backwards, which in turn caused his feet to slip on the flour on the floor beneath him. He went down like a sea bag full of sand. He landed on his back and slammed the back of his head into the floor. Everyone immediately came to his aid.

"Leslie, are you OK?"

"Someone call the Doc," Butch yelled.

"I told you not to open that, sir. I don't know what more I could've done?" Joker claimed over the banter.

Everyone continued to call him *sir* as the bakers had and as did most anyone who was the same rank or lower than him. This appealed to his self-absorbed ego and helped to appease him, which could often redirect some of his wrath when he was in a bad mood, which was most of the time.

"Did I hear someone call for a doctor?" Lieutenant Commander Earl Henry Sr, the ship dentist, announced as he entered the galley. "What do we have here?"

"It's more than a toothache, doc. He's hit both sides of his head," Joker informed the dentist.

"Let me take a look at you, sailor. Oh, yeah, you are going to have a knot on your forehead . . ." he said, then, feeling around the back of Leslie's head, added, ". . . and one on the back as well. Get this man two bags of ice and take him to sick bay."

Several sailors helped pick Leslie up off the floor and slowly got him to his feet. His face was still white with flour, so Salvador gave him a wet towel to wipe his face, which helped clear his vision, but did little for his growing concussion. Two sailors with Gerbil's help wrapped Leslie's head in ice and then three sailors led him from the galley to deliver him to sick bay. The trailing sailor looked back to give Butch and the others a wink before continuing out the hatch. With all the excitement gone and the galley returned to normal, Gerbil immediately jumped to the oven to remove the rolls.

"So, can someone tell me what happened here?" Dr. Henry asked.

Joker started to wind a story while Butch and Salvador threw in random facts, but the dentist was having none of it. He had heard stories of both Joker and Leslie, so he did not need to assume more than what was obvious and did not need an earful of gobbledygook.

"OK. That will be enough. I assume this was an accident, correct?"

"Yes, sir," answered all the sailors left in the galley.

"Then on to more important matters. Have you seen the picture of my new baby boy? I have a son. I am a father."

"Congratulations, sir."

"He's a dashing boy, sir."

"Yes, he is."

Lieutenant Commander Earl Henry became Lieutenant Commander Earl Henry *Sr*, just two days after his leave ended and he had to rejoin the USS *Indianapolis* on their mission to Tinian. He received photographic proof of this miracle when they docked in Guam and he was making sure everyone who would listen heard the good news. Sailors loved family and good news, so this was not a hard sell. In addition to his dental skills, few sailors knew Henry was also a talented artist and taxidermist—and now a father.

"Wow. What is that wonderful smell?" Henry asked to change the subject.

"Cinnamon rolls, sir."

"Are they ready to sample?"

"Sir, this batch may be a little overdone due to our unwelcomed interruption, but you're welcome to try them anyway," Gerbil said as he finished icing the last of the rolls, then held up a knife.

Lieutenant Henry took the proffered knife and cut out a corner roll; icing strung from the roll as he lifted it from the pan. Lieutenant Henry used his tongue to wrap the hanging icing around the roll and then took a bite.

"Oh, my God. Gerbil, these are like heaven. I love the burnt caramelization of the cinnamon and sugar and butter and—oh," he said as he dove in for another bite. "I would get several of these up to the bridge so the captain can enjoy this sensation—oh," he said again as he walked out of the galley to head back to his bay.

Clarence and Gerbil removed the rest of the cinnamon rolls and placed them on a tray. Clarence then delivered them to the bridge.

Even before taking a bite, Captain McVay said to Clarence, "Please thank Chester. This will be a treat to enjoy before we are neck-deep in training maneuvers."

"Yes, sir," Clarence said and returned to the galley to complete his watch.

Gerbil, Clarence and Salvador exchanged the usual banter with Bert and Wyatt as they ended their shift and made way for some much-needed free time and some ever-precious sleep. They didn't need to mention the incident with Leslie since Ray remained behind to fill in his shipmates. Gerbil was certain no baker would be left disappointed this evening.

Word quickly spread around the ship. The officers heard Lieutenant Henry's official version that it was an *unfortunate* accident, while the average sailor was further enlightened to the whole story that it was a *well-deserved* accident.

Butch was doing his night shift in the pharmacy when he learned from Homer Orr, a hospital apprentice, that Leslie had a concussion and was not even talking. This was good and bad news all rolled into one. It was good Leslie was not blabbing his mouth on how Joker, Butch and other sailors had ganged up on him and bad news that he might be hurt worse than they had intended. They wanted to shock the dog, not maim him. Well, it was what it was, so the three continued to go about their duties with the usual rigor and not waste time reflecting on what might hit the fan when Leslie awoke. They all hoped for amnesia, but knew they were unlikely to be that lucky.

July 29

The next day passed just like the day before. This was the

routine on a ship—rotating watches or shifts. The rotation was set to 4-hour watches for two or three teams. There was also a dogged watch around the dinner hours which was basically a 4-hour watch broken down into two 2-hour sections so each team could eat more efficiently. This also caused the teams to fall on a different watch on the subsequent day so watch did not become too routine or monotonous.

Due to the extreme tropical heat—still 95 degrees at 10:00 p.m. at night—many of the crew received approval to sleep on the deck. To help cool those sailors in the lower decks, the *Indy* sailed in a Yoke-Modified state, which left many of the interior hatches open to encourage better airflow. The *Indy* was born to be an Atlantic ship and thus did not fare well below decks in the extreme tropical heat.

It was dark and cloudy with rough seas during the final watch of the night and Captain McVay, thinking the navy intelligence he was given—no known enemy subs in the area—was factual and understanding zigzagging could not effectively avoid a Kaiten torpedo anyway, gave the order to cease zigzagging just after 7:30 p.m. However, there was still yet another piece of the puzzle that Captain McVay did not have: the USS *Underhill* had been sunk by two Kaiten torpedoes. A Kaiten was the torpedo version of a Kamikaze plane. They were 2-man torpedoes that could chase a boat and be detonated at the will of the pilots. First developed as rideable torpedoes for sabotage missions, they quickly developed into what was their true translated name: *Return to Heaven*. They were the embodiment of a one-way ticket.

* * *

Shortly after 11:00 p.m. about 450 miles from Leyte, the Japanese submarine I-58 spotted what their captain, Lieutenant Commander Mochitsura Hashimoto—who had just returned to the bridge after saying a prayer at the Shinto shrine aboard his submarine—thought was an Idaho-class battleship since it was unescorted. His new target was in fact the *Indianapolis*—a heavy cruiser without the benefit of sonar or hydrophones to detect and thus avoid submarines—intermittently backlit by the moon and sailing straight away at just 12-17 knots.

"All-knowing One, please send us a great American ship. Please give us good hunting to sink her," he had prayed in Japanese and now saw his prayer being answered.

Commander Hashimoto had yet to sink, much less even hit, an American ship since the war began. Now on the bridge his throat went dry, knowing this was his chance at glory.

Two Kaiten pilots stood at attention by their commander's side repeating their mantra to be chosen for the glory of the empire, for the glory of the emperor, for a noble death—to return to heaven. Hashimoto did not acknowledge these chants, as he was busy maneuvering the sub to the most advantageous position and observing his prey through the periscope.

As the *Indianapolis* came into range, he addressed the Kaiten pilots.

"We will not be needing your sacrifice tonight."

At 11:39 p.m. the commander ordered six Type 95 torpedoes—powered by kerosene-oxygen wet-heater engines—to be loaded and ready. Less than 30 minutes later, just after midnight, he counted down the range and at 1,500 meters called out at two-second intervals firing an array of six torpedoes—the array would account for any attempted zigzag maneuvers without the need for Kaitens.

* * *

The first torpedo hit the *Indy*'s starboard bow, tearing off 60 plus feet directly in front of the forward gun mount—destroying sick bay and several sleeping berths, and igniting a tank of aviation fuel. The resulting explosion sent a pillar of fire several hundred feet into the night sky. The engines continued to drive the ship forward, forcing water into the gaping hole in the hull. Between intermittent explosions near the bow, bulkheads could be heard collapsing as the sea pressed further into the ship. The second torpedo hit midship at the forward boiler stack, setting off fuel tanks and powder magazines. A string of powerful explosions took out much of the electrical systems and intra-ship communications, and nearly ripped the *Indianapolis* in half.

Captain McVay was sleeping in the emergency cabin just aft of the bridge when he was rocked awake by the first blast. When the second torpedo hit, he was tossed around like a rag doll and found himself on the deck. While thick, acrid white smoke filled his cabin, he regained his feet and felt his way to the bridge. When he entered the bridge, he called for the conn and immediately ordered General Quarters. Captain McVay called for status reports, but with communications out, he needed eyes-on intelligence. As the ship continued to falter, some officers returned to report off to the captain, while others were never seen again.

Gerbil was just off his watch when the first torpedo hit. He called out to his shipmates Salvador and Clarence to grab their kapok life jackets. They were making their way to the main deck when the ship was hit by the second torpedo, sending all three crashing violently into the bulkhead.

"Remember to spit on a hatch before you grab the dog," Gerbil yelled over his shoulder to his companions, reminding them if the spit sizzles, don't grab the dog.

The three fought through a maze of smoke and blocked corridors, explosions coming from every direction along their path, until they finally emerged on the main deck. They stood at the rail with a group of very anxious sailors, all awaiting orders.

Joker was in the engine room when the first torpedo hit. After the explosion, he was immediately dispatched by the duty officer to retrieve kapoks for the engine room crew. When the second torpedo hit, Joker was chased down a corridor by a thick, furling cloud of black smoke and had to seal a hatch to prevent the smoke from filling the entire passageway. He knew there were other ways out of the engine room, but the smoke cloud did not bode well for the crew on watch. He then heard a string of explosions and felt the boat shudder. With his hand pressed against a bulkhead, he sensed a different hum. It was not the hum of electronics or air circulators and the water rushing *past* the hull; no, it was the hum of the screws pushing the hull *into* the water and the popping of bulkheads as they gave way to the pressure. With his path back to the engine room cut off and the boat starting to list, Joker made his way to the port side of the main deck with an arm full of kapok jackets to await orders. At the rail he could already see sailors in the water, but he waited. Back in the forward engine room, engines No. 1 and No. 4 were off line—casualties of the second torpedo. Lieutenant Richard B. Redmayne, the Chief Engineer, called the aft engine room and ordered faltering engine No. 2 shut down. Failing to reach the bridge and with no other orders to go on, the last order stood: engine No. 3 was left at full-speed-ahead.

Butch was just starting his watch in the pharmacy when a sailor threw up on his uniform while waiting for medication. He was in his berth cleaning up when the first torpedo hit and the blast tossed him to the deck where he was immediately trapped by an avalanche of collapsing bunks and falling sailors. Once free of his entanglement, the second torpedo hit and he decided he had no time to worry about his pants or his shoes; he grabbed his kapok and rushed for the main deck.

McVay sent word to the radio shack to send out an SOS. Chief Warrant Officer Leonard Woods sent everyone in communications to the main deck while he and Radio Technician 2nd Class Herbert J. Miner stayed to repeatedly send out the SOS call as the bow of the *Indy* continued to plow into the water. They saw the meter move with each transmission, so they were confident messages were sent.

Joseph A. Flynn returned from assessing below decks to report to McVay that the *Indy* had suffered extensive damage and was taking on water at an incredible rate. The listing was gradual, but noticeable and eventually unrecoverable. McVay called to abandon ship; his orders passed by word of mouth since intra-ship communications were out. McVay then made his way to the radio room to verify the SOS was sent and received. While on the ladder from the bridge, the *Indy* listed severely and he realized he was not going to make it anywhere but into the water.

Upon the abandon ship orders, kapok life jackets and emergency equipment were cut loose from the main deck and sailors snatched up whatever they could get their hands on before heading for the rail. Prior to this some sailors, thinking they had time and not wanting to wait for the cache of kapoks to be freed, returned below deck to grab their own jacket—some returned to the rail and some did not. A number of sailors were already in the water, having been tossed off the ship by an explosion or washed over the side by the ever-encroaching water as the bow dove further beneath the surface. Sailors ran to the rails waiting for their turn to jump. Many were selflessly handing out kapoks while others pushed and shoved their way to the rail, not wanting to wait their turn. As Gerbil placed a foot on the rail to prepare for his jump, a sailor behind him grabbed Gerbil's shirt collar and tossed him back into the waiting crowd. The sailor then jumped without looking and thus was not prepared for what greeted him when he hit the water—heavy oil and fuel had poured out of the gaping hole in the hull and completely coated the ocean surface on the starboard side of the ship. You could hardly prevent getting a faceful of oil, but you definitely wanted to prevent the oil from getting into your eyes or taking a big gulp of it when you hit the water or came up for air. This sailor did both and started his journey toward rescue blinded, coughing and vomiting.

    Gerbil quickly recovered and jumped into the soup with his kapok clutched tightly to his face and chest. Once he hit the water, he was not immediately pulled to the surface as he would have been if he had his kapok belted on. Now he had the time to push some fresh water to the surface and splash his arms so he could at least attempt to clear the surface of oil. It worked well enough and he could see he fared better than many of the other sailors who had jumped with their jackets on and were now covered in oil. Once in the water, swimming free of the surface oil was the primary focus of any sailor on the starboard side since many of these pools of oil were on fire, creating a whole different challenge for a swimming or jumping sailor. Gerbil quickly swam into the wind as taught in boot camp so he would be moving in the opposite direction of the burning pools of oil.

Some life rafts could not be cut loose, so men just jumped over the side without them. One stack of life rafts was being guarded by a Marine who was waiting for the official call to abandon ship and did not believe the many sailors who were spreading the order by word of mouth as directed. Several men attempting to free one of the 26-foot whaleboats were killed when the top-heavy *Indy* abruptly listed at an even greater angle, causing the whaleboat to crush them against the boathouse wall. In the end, only a dozen or so life rafts and half that many floater nets were released from the *Indianapolis* before she went down.

Joker clung to the rail as he watched sailors jump off the ship, some hitting the hull, some slipping and sliding down the deck toward the bow, eventually hitting something to send them into the water. He knew he had to go soon, but seemed to be caught up in the surreal scene unfolding before him.

"Hey, Joker, can I have a kapok?"

The question broke the spell and Joker handed the sailor two jackets.

"Find someone who doesn't have a jacket and then get into the water."

"You bet. Thanks!"

Joker held the remaining jackets tightly in his right hand, then grabbed the rail to climb over and stand on the hull. He took in a deep breath, then ran down the side of the severely listing ship and jumped into the water.

Butch looked over the side of the ship and saw a dark smear in the water. He knew what this was and was preparing himself for his jump. The *Indy* was well tipped forward and listing near 45 degrees when Butch placed a foot on the top rail. Now ready, he tossed his cache of kapok jackets into the water before preparing to dive in after them. In that moment of pause, an explosion rocked the dying ship and Butch was struck from the rail by a piece of shrapnel that shattered his right shoulder blade and propelled him into the water. With searing pain telling him to stop, he swam as hard as he could to avoid being sucked under by the ship when it finally slipped below the surface. Hoping he was far enough away from the sinking giant, he turned to steal a glace back and saw the screws— No. 3 still turning—disappear into the sea. The *Indianapolis* had sunk in only 12 minutes from the first torpedo strike and because the bow and mid hull were so badly damaged, the ship slipped beneath the surface with hardly a sound.

* * *

Lieutenant Commander Mochitsura Hashimoto ordered his crew to reposition the sub for another attack on the crippled ship, but when he made his next periscope check, the *Indy* was gone. He radioed Japan to report that he had just sunk a battleship and gave his current location.

* * *

Of the nearly 1,200 on board the *Indy*, about 900 sailors

made it into the water. They clung to kapok vests, life rafts, boxes and cargo nets to stay afloat, hoping the morning sun would bring more than light to their sudden darkness.

Of the three stations who received the *Indianapolis'* SOS, none responded. U.S. Navy protocol was to treat messages that could not be confirmed as attempts to mislead, but in all three cases, little to no effort was made to validate the message. A radio operator at Navy Command at Leyte woke Commodore Jacob Jacobsen—who had reportedly been drinking—to report the SOS, but nothing was done beyond that. The Officer of the Day at a second naval outpost responded by dispatching two fast navy tugboats to the reported site, but Commodore Norman Gillette recalled the tugs as soon as he was notified since they were sent without his authority and he believed the SOS to be a Japanese ruse to lure American rescue boats into an ambush. At a third station, the commanding officer, who gave prior *Do Not Disturb* orders, did not give any definitive orders upon hearing the report. In addition to this, the message from the Japanese submarine I-58 had been intercepted at Leyte after the sinking of the *Indianapolis*, but was discounted largely because of previous exaggerated claims of the Japanese sinking other vessels.

After the initial torpedo strike, the *Indy* continued to plow forward at 12 knots, spreading its crew over a large swath of ocean—miles of open ocean would eventually separate the sailors who were initially thrown from the ship and those who fell from the fantail like ants in the final moments before the *Indy* slipped beneath the surface. In those initial 12 minutes after the first torpedo hit, being covered in fuel oil was only the first concern since, due to the Navy's recruiting push during the final months of the war, many sailors did not know how to swim. Those lucky enough to abandon ship with a kapok survived and those who entered the water without a life jacket either quickly learned how to tread water or drowned.

As the midnight moon shone down upon the surviving *Indianapolis* crew, little did they know they were still, unintentionally, under a cloak of secrecy. It was a reality unknown to these hopeful souls that no one knew where they were or even that they were missing since no one responded to their SOS and their destination harbor had already removed them from the tracking board as an *expected* arrival.

July 30 – first 24 hours in the water

By the first morning, most of the badly burned or wounded sailors had perished, though some still clung to life in the hopes of rescue. As the sun emerged over the horizon, lone sailors found each other in the 12-foot swells and gradually smaller clumps of survivors became larger groups. Gerbil was soon in a group of 80 survivors who began stringing life rafts and cargo netting together to form makeshift flotillas. Officers in the various groups took charge to help organize these floating cities and also cared for the wounded in the rafts. Food and water were scarce—SPAM, malted milk balls and three ounces of water twice a day was a banquet in some groups, while others had nothing. Occasionally, a random rain cloud would bring rain, but it was difficult to catch raindrops with only your mouth without also getting a mouthful of saltwater.

Soon the groups began to notice sharks swimming far

below them in the crystal-clear ocean water. At first the sharks just seemed curious, but this would soon change. Attracted by the sound of the explosions and blood in the water, they congregated below the floating sailors and at times the school was so thick, the sailors could virtually walk on their backs.

There was an especially large shark circling Gerbil's group that the men named Charlie. Charlie seemed like a willing mascot until he ravenously attacked a SPAM can thrown overboard after it was emptied of its contents. This seemed to spark something in all the sharks and now they were more than just curious. Initially, the sharks only attacked the dead or wounded, but now were also drawn to the sailors without pants or shoes. To a curious shark, the flashing white feet and legs of a sailor treading water resembled a wounded fish. Now, without warning, any bleeding or lone sailor swimming or splashing could be pulled below to be replaced by a plume of crimson.

All morning, intermittent blood-curdling screams could be heard echoing across the water. Eventually, the sharks began to attack even the larger groups, picking off random sailors at the outskirts of a clump of men and pulling them below. Dorsal fins could be seen between the sailors as the sharks poked and prodded, trying to free a sailor from the group. Some sailors fought off the sharks and survived these attacks, while others just disappeared with a *swoosh* beneath the surface. After an attack, men flailed violently to put distance between themselves and the bloodied water; some were successful, while others only attracted more sharks and were violently attacked as well. Gerbil's group alone lost at least 20 men to shark attacks that first day.

In the early morning hours of the first day, Butch found a

group of Marines who had a single life raft and a large collection of kapok life jackets. He joined the group and gladly added his extra kapoks to the pile. The Marines pulled him aboard the raft and bandaged his shoulder as best they could, then continued to look for survivors. If they found a man without a life jacket, they would give him one and have him join their group. If they found a sailor who had succumbed to his injuries or had died from swallowing too much fuel oil, they removed his kapok to save for a survivor in need. Unfortunately, the *Indy* crew would soon discover these extra jackets were important to more than just those sailors without one.

The jackets were rated for three days in the water, but the fuel oil tended to weaken the seams and prolonged exposure to saltwater tended to saturate them so badly that eventually a sailor had to actually sit on the failing jacket to stay afloat. The jackets themselves were a mixed blessing as well since sailors covered in oil or baking in the hot sun soon found the canvas digging into their necks and underarms. This could be as annoying as a slight irritation or all-out destruction of skin and even muscle, especially if there were burns or other injuries involved.

Whether Captain McVay went down with the ship or was washed overboard by a wall of water is unknown. Rumors circulated that he did go down with the ship, but was carried to the surface in a large air bubble emitted from the hull of the *Indianapolis* as it dove for the ocean floor. Some said this was an act of love from a dying ship that was well-served by this brave crew and captain, while others claimed it was just good fortune. At first Captain McVay was alone and he thought he was the sole survivor. He soon found a lone life raft, but severe dread remained with him until morning brought sight of more survivors.

His group quickly grew to nine sailors clinging to three lashed together rafts. McVay, still worried this was all that was left of his men, did not know that more than two-thirds of the *Indy*'s crew was just out of sight all around him in the water.

From time to time throughout the day, sailors would hear the engines of a plane overhead. This livened up the survivors at first, but as they looked up to see a plane so high in the sky it looked small to them, they knew—even though flares were fired and mirrors were flashed—from the plane, a man's head or even a group of rafts in the water were even smaller to the pilot.

By midday Joker found himself in the middle of the largest concentration of survivors: a group several hundred strong. This group needed kapoks badly since many sailors had to abandon ship before they could claim one. Each kapok jacket was designed with a pass-through pocket sewn into the back of the jacket that could be used to support a sailor in the water or lift them from the water. Men with kapoks linked arms though these pockets to support those without jackets and soon these men formed little clusters within the giant group. In the calm seas this worked well, but as the swells grew larger, it was a burden not to have your hands available to help you stay afloat or keep the saltwater out of your face and mouth.

Joker's group also included Dr. Lewis Haynes, the *Indy*'s chief medical officer. While abandoning ship, Dr. Haynes badly burned his hands on a hot bulkhead before crawling out of a porthole to escape a fire consuming the passageway where he had been trapped. The doctor was quickly called to help various survivors: sailors who were vomiting from swallowing fuel oil; sailors who were badly burned in an explosion; sailors who burned their hands when attempting to turn a hot dog, or hatch wheel; and sailors who were bleeding from countless other injuries. Without medical supplies or any equipment and painful hands that were all but useless, Dr. Haynes was more a counselor or a coroner than a savior. As the hours of the first day rolled by, Dr. Haynes continued to swim among the hundreds of men, checking those that did not return his greeting and answering to those who called his name. If a sailor did not answer or awaken with a shake, he would check their eyes. If their pupils were dilated and did not respond to pressure, the sailor was pronounced dead and their life jacket was given to a sailor who was treading water or otherwise supported by sailors who had kapoks. Initially, Dr. Haynes also took the sailor's dog tags, but soon the growing number of tags became such a burden that they threatened to pull him under, so he released them to the sea.

Dusk brought increased shark attacks and many more sailors were lost from the various groups. When the sun set it gave the sailors a reprieve from the skin scorching heat, but the night also signaled shivers as the cool seawater seemed to creep deeper into the survivors' bodies as they began to break down due to the extreme conditions and lack of food and water.

At dusk that first night, Joker's group brought all the smaller groups together into one giant floating mass by everyone locking arms through the kapok jackets. This helped to stave off the sharks, as they seemed most interested in lone victims or smaller groups, and also seemed to help create a community heatsink that helped to fight off the nighttime chill.

July 31 – 24-48 hours in the water

The second morning had calmer seas and brought back the warmth of the sun—a welcome relief for the shivering sailors in the water, but soon would turn as scorching as the day before. Floating in the open ocean water was like having your head stuck through a mirror as the direct sunlight and 110-degree temps baked your head. As the day went on, those with fuel oil on their faces noted the fuel oil was an excellent sunscreen and protected their skin from the harsh rays of the sun—a definite benefit if the fuel oil did not initially kill you.

Gerbil's group spotted several ammunition cans as well as potato and orange crates floating in the water and devised a way to lash them together to make crude raft. The fruit gave these lucky sailors some much-needed sustenance. The potatoes were rotting on the outside, but if squeezed and peeled—some sailors used their fingernails, while other used their teeth—the rotting flesh could be removed leaving a reward sometimes no bigger than a carrot, but still a reward.

The hours in the water were taking their toll on more than just the sailors—kapoks were failing after becoming waterlogged and some mornings unfortunate sailors were found floating just below the surface in their water laden-jackets. Gerbil's newly formed raft was used to rotate out the waterlogged kapok jackets. After forcefully wringing out saturated kapoks, the sailors used this somewhat flat raft surface to dry the jackets in the sun, eventually exchanging them with kapoks in the water. Other groups were doing likewise to keep the kapoks, and the sailors inside them, afloat as the seemingly endless hours in the water continued to tick by.

Soon, the lack of water caused tongues to swell and lips to crack. The beating sun turned the briny ocean water to a crust that caked in eyes and on faces adding to the pain of already sunburned skin. Overwhelming thirst began to drive some sailors to drink the saltwater. Even though a shipmate would try to hold them back, yelling, "Don't do it, buddy," some would still dip their mouths below the surface and take a gulp. This initially satisfied them, but the resulting elevated sodium levels and failing red blood cells eventually only increased their thirst and drove them to drink again. Repeatedly drinking saltwater would lead to hypernatremia—too much salt or sodium in their blood—which eventually led to hallucinations. These hallucinations took on many forms of delusions.

> "Hey, Tommy. You smell that bread baking? Oh, them rolls got to be straight out of the oven. I'm going down to get a roll or two. I'll bring one back for you if I don't eat it first."

> "Bob, will you cover for me with the brass while I visit my girl in the berth? I smuggled her on and she's waiting for me. Can you smell the candles she has burning?"

> "Look! Over there! The *Indy* is waiting for us to climb back on board. Everyone, follow me."

> "Hey, everyone. There's fresh water and food in the galley just below us. You comin'?"

> "What are you doing? Hey, I found a Jap. Get back or

I'll stab you."

"Hey, do you see the spotlight? They found us. They're coming to rescue us."

"Wait! They could be Japs."

"Hey, I found a Jap too. I got him. I got him."

"Look! An island. Let's swim for it. Last one there is a chicken."

"My stomach hurts. I think I drank too much tomato juice on the island."

"Look at this—a whole store full of watermelons. Wow, are these delish."

Sailors drowned swimming to imaginary islands or by taking off their kapoks so they could swim below to see their girl, or get some fresh water, or any of a number of invented reasons. Fighting was worse in some groups than others, but took its toll nonetheless as sailors fought and even stabbed their companions, believing the other to be a fictitious enemy. Some sailors who swam off were never seen again, while others were seen being attacked and eaten by a group of sharks excited by the sailor's splashing. Those who drank sea water greedily bypassed the hallucinations and went directly to full madness as they roared in rage and pain, thrashing and writhing like a wounded animal until death took them, or they drowned or attracted a hungry shark. Though it was not an option for a hallucinating sailor, staying calm and still was the best way to avoid a shark attack. Many sailors who kept their cool even as huge 8- to 12-foot sharks swam between them and rubbed up against their legs or bumped their torsos lived to tell their tale. Others who panicked were not as fortunate.

As dusk approached, Gerbil's group prepared for the sharks to return. A nearby flotilla consisting of a cargo net surrounded by three rafts was frustrating circling sharks by hoisting the free-floating sailors out of the water each time a shark was spotted. Eventually the sharks stopped circling, but then came up baring their teeth from beneath the net with such force that the net was destroyed; lucky sailors were launched into the air, while others disappeared with the net.

By the third night, Joker's group had disbanded their community cluster as getting stabbed by a fellow survivor quickly became more dangerous than freezing in the ocean waters. At first sailors tried to calm their delusional shipmates, but after many of the hysterical sailors stabbed those that came to their aid, no one wanted to be within arm's length of anyone that had been drinking saltwater.

August 1 – 48-72 hours in the water

That next morning, there were a lot fewer sailors in Joker's group. Some hoped this was a result of the group disbanding, but knew in their hearts it was a result of continued shark attacks and the fighting brought on by the hallucinations.

Gerbil's group was now down to 17 sailors.

Thus far, shark attacks, dehydration and the hallucinations

of hypernatremia were the main killers, but now hypothermia made its debut. The ocean water was like bath water, but still well below a sailor's normal body temperature. So, for those in the ocean without access to a raft to occasionally get free of the water, their body temperatures continued to gradually fall even as their heads baked in the sun. Eventually, the effects of extreme exposure would begin to cause hallucinations as well and even more men would suffer from these crippling delusions. Photophobia from the unrelenting sun was also an issue and some sailors were all but blind during the day.

Shark attacks continued throughout the day with the usual peaks at dusk and dawn. Finding the torso of a half-eaten sailor floating among the groups was not uncommon and sharks continued to nibble at this easy prey.

Butch and his Marine shipmates had moved on again and now were handing out or exchanging jackets in another large group of survivors. Here they found Father Thomas Michael Conway tending to the group. From the first night, Father Conway—who knew very well there were no atheists on a sinking ship—had swum from group to group to pray with them, asking if there were any Catholics who would like to be given last sacraments. His energy was endless; his courage and devotion pressed him on constantly. He tended to the frightened and tried to reason with the maddened. He never stopped—comforting or encouraging countless sailors—until exhaustion finally took its toll and he followed the many who had gone before him into the deep.

August 2 – 72+ hours in the water

Four days in the water had taken its toll on every group of survivors, large or small. The large groups were somewhat more protected from shark attacks due to their numbers, but without fresh water or rations, they suffered from a different enemy. Drinking saltwater and the extreme conditions continued to lead to an array of hallucinations—sometimes pleasant, sometimes violent. Survivors had seen by now that any type of hallucination could kill you and many times take a shipmate with you. The smaller groups, if they had kapoks and a raft with rations, could manage fairly well, though most groups by now had either consumed their ration of SPAM or thrown it overboard when they discovered opening the can attracted sharks. Here, the elements—exposure to the sun or hypothermia from the ocean—took their greatest toll, especially on the groups of twos and threes who were often overcome with hopelessness, which could evolve into deep depression; some sailors would eventually just give up.

The morning, again, met the men with another dose of the blazing hot sun and more exposure after the night before caused most to suffer from chattering teeth and shivers so severe, they bordered on rigors. Sharks still circled the groups, but most sailors were too exhausted to move enough to encourage an attack.

Gerbil's group was now in the single digits—many of them floating like pillows in the water.

Joker's group was still the largest, but its numbers were a shadow of the several hundred-strong after the sinking.

Butch's group was the liveliest. Banter was the dish of the day and they continued as best they could to talk and tease each other, trying to keep positive or at the very least keep their minds off the obvious.

Aug 2, 11:00 AM - 83 hours in the water

"Sir, we have nothing but static," the aviation ordnanceman reported.

"Warren, take the yoke—the antenna is tangled again."

"Got it, Chuck."

Lieutenant Wilbur "Chuck" Gwinn and his crew were in a Lockheed PV-1 Ventura bomber on a routine anti-submarine patrol testing out a new antenna when the sock used to weigh it down fell off and the antenna became tangled for a third time. Lieutenant Gwinn walked to the glass blister at the back of the plane to help with the untangling process and was rewarded with a crick in his neck. Once he had finished, he stayed in the blister and rubbed his sore neck while watching the water fly by beneath him. The plane was cruising at 3,000 feet—an altitude high enough that he could see 20 square miles of ocean at a glance, but low enough that he could see large details on the water. As he lay in the blister beneath the plane, he saw a flash of light and then noticed a deep dark pool on the water.

"We have an oil spill," Gwinn called out as he made his way back to the cockpit. "Taking over the controls."

The copilot called out the heading, then asked, "What's going on, Chuck?"

"Look for yourself. We are diving. Get ready to drop."

Lieutenant Gwinn circled around and readied for an attack on what he thought was an oil spill from an enemy sub, but as he got closer, he saw groups of men in the water; some splashing and waving while others floated like mannequins. He did not know of any US ships in this part of the Philippine Sea, so he did not know if they were American or Japanese seamen. All he knew was there were boys in the water and that is all that mattered—a ship you fired on, while helpless sailors in the water you rescued.

The crew immediately dropped water canisters, life jackets and a life raft with a radio transmitter, but at their current altitude, the water canisters exploded on impact and the raft landed too far for the exhausted sailors to reach. Gwinn could tell many of those in the water were on their last leg, if not already dead, and immediately called for help.

"We have boys in the water. Send all you have and send it quick."

"They saw us. They saw us," sailors yelled, slapping the water and thanking God.

After the Navy wasted time debating how sailors in the water at that location was even possible, the squadron commander at Peleliu dispatched an amphibious PBY-5A Catalina or *Dumbo* to observe and report.

Now low on fuel, Gwinn and his crew made one last circle around the groups of *Indy* survivors and dipped his wing before heading back to base. Gwinn's plane was soon replaced by another Ventura crew who would keep track of the survivors until help arrived. More rafts were dropped and the sailors climbed in or clung to their sides, hoping to survive now that rescue was so close. In the face of severe dehydration, it was hard to produce actual tears, but crying in relief and prayers of thankfulness were abounding throughout every group.

Upon arriving at the stated location, Lieutenant Commander Robert Adrian Marks and his crew, at a much lower altitude, took in a sight they could not believe with their own eyes—hundreds of sailors bobbing listlessly in the open ocean. They too began to drop water canisters and life rafts to the weary sailors. Marks had standing orders to observe and report, but upon seeing a white tip shark savagely attack and devour a screaming sailor in the water below him, he and his crew made a decision that most would consider insane. Against strict orders, he was going to land his seaplane on 12-foot swells of open ocean water.

"Get set boys—we're setting down."

Marks hit the crest of the first wave and bounced 15 feet into the air only to crash down on the next crest. Rivets popped from the sheer force of the plane being bent by the cresting water. After finally settling in a swell, he headed for the big group he had seen from the air, but then remembering the shark attack, rerouted to pick up the lone sailors in the area since they were clearly the most at risk.

As they taxied up to the first survivor, Ensign Morgan F. Hensley, an ex-wrestler and a bull of a man, asked as he hoisted the sailor into the plane via the port blister, "What ship are you from, sailor?" He almost fell into the water when he heard the response.

"The *Indianapolis*, sir. God bless you."

Marks immediately made the call. "We need surface ships here. There are hundreds of sailors from the *Indianapolis* in the water. I repeat hundreds of *our* boys are in the water."

"She crashed. I know she crashed. We're lost," a sailor cried as he saw the PBY bounce off a second wave crest, then disappear.

"They must have radioed our location. It doesn't matter. We're saved," another sailor consoled.

"Look! He landed it. He actually landed it," a third sailor shouted as he pointed to the plane now taxiing toward them.

The men cheered for the brave pilot. Rescue was certain now, but many of the survivors would not be reached until well into the next day. Unfortunately, many of these men would not make it another 24 hours and would die before it was their turn to be pulled from the water.

* * *

During the trip back to base, Lieutenant Gwinn was contacted by Lieutenant Commander W. Graham Claytor of the destroyer escort USS *Cecil J. Doyle* inquiring about the situation they were hearing over the radio. Upon learning the details straight from an eyewitness and unencumbered by navy rhetoric, Lieutenant Claytor decided to sail at full speed toward the survivors; he would let the orders come while en route, if they came at all.

* * *

Lieutenant Marks continued to taxi from sailor to sailor and group to group. By the time he reached all he could, his plane was at full capacity, but he could see many more that he needed to get out of the water, so he cut his engines and began to put sailors on his wings. In the end he had 56 sailors in his plane and on his wings with many, many more holding on to the plane and rafts surrounding the plane. At times Marks had to ask a sailor to stay in the water if able so he could place a more critical sailor in the plane. He never received an argument. When they passed a keg of water around the plane, Marks told the survivors they had to make it last, so only to take one sip and then pass it on. Not only did they follow his order to the letter, taking a single sip and then passing the keg on to the next sailor, some sailors admitted they had already had their sip when errantly offered another.

Shortly after dusk, the *Cecil J. Doyle* came on the scene and immediately scanned the area with searchlights. Whaleboats were launched and men were plucked from the sea to be taken back aboard the *Doyle*. As the men came aboard, the *Doyle* crew could see men suffering from blindness, pneumonia, dehydration and severe exposure. Many were covered with ulcers, burns, shark bites and other wounds. Some wounds were so bad that the flesh just peeled away when touched. With miles of vast ocean separating the survivors, it was obvious more help was needed and six additional rescue vessels were dispatched to aid in the recovery.

August 3 – 96 - 108 hours in the water

The searchlights of the arriving ships reminded many sailors of the illusions that caused some of their shipmates to swim to the light and drown or swim away thinking it was a Japanese boat coming to kill them. These hallucinations continued throughout the night and rescuers sometimes had to fight off attacks from delusional survivors or spend precious time convincing them to be taken into the rescue boat.

"Thank you."

"You're not taking me alive, Jap!"

"You're an angel. Bless you."

"You got any good drinking water aboard? If not, then get lost and just leave us be."

"No, I don't need a ride. I'm just waiting for my girl to pick me up."

Sailors thought to be dead miraculously came back to life and those clinging to life held on with seemingly endless willpower. The USS *Ringness* pulled the last survivor from the water 108 hours after his feet left the *Indianapolis*. From the late hours of the second night of searching through August 8, flotsam and bodies were recovered, but no more living survivors were rescued. After almost 900 sailors were tossed or jumped into the sea to escape the sinking *Indianapolis*, only 318 survived; soon that number would fall to 316 after two sailors succumbed to their injuries and died in the hospital.

When all the survivors were removed from the PBY, it was obvious to Lieutenant Marks that she would never fly again. Orders were given for the *Doyle* to prevent the Japanese from finding her, so the *Doyle* pointed her guns at the broken plane and opened fire, sending her to the bottom of the ocean.

Of the 880 sailors who died, it was estimated at least 150 had been killed by sharks. This was clearly the worst shark attack in history and the worst U.S. naval disaster ever.

Charles Butler McVay III, CAPT – survived
  Of the 13 men on the bridge – 10 perished
Lewis Leavitt Haynes, LCDR (Dr.) – survived
Thomas Michael Conway, LT (Rev.) – perished
Earl O'Dell Henry, LCDR (Dr.) – perished
Herbert J. Miner, RT2 – survived
Leonard Woods, CWO – perished
Richard Banks Redmayne, LT – survived
Machinist Mates (41 on board): Darcy, John, Norm, Gabe and 6 others – survived
  All others – perished
Bakers (6 on board): Chester, Clarence, Salvador and all others – survived
Cooks (12 on board): Morgan, Keith and 3 others – survived
  Earl and 6 others – perished
Pharmacist's and Hospital Mates (16 on board): Butch and John Alton Schmueck, CPHMP – survived
  Jack, Romeo, Harry, Homer and 14 others – perished

* * *

The Japanese submarine I-58 had left Kure Harbor on the island of Honshu with orders to harass enemy communications on the same day the *Indianapolis* left San Francisco to sail to Tinian. Upon completing his mission and in need of fuel and supplies, Commander Hashimoto arrived back in Japan to learn he had sunk the *Indianapolis*, the flagship of the Fifth Fleet. However, there was no time for celebration as he also learned his country had already surrendered to the Allies.

* * *

Three days after the last sailor was rescued from the ocean, the B-29 bomber *Enola Gay* dropped *Little Boy* on Hiroshima, Japan. This was the first true clue to the surviving members of the *Indianapolis* crew of just how important their secret mission had been. Three days after that, the B-29 bomber *Bockscar* dropped *Fat Man* on Nagasaki, Japan. These were the first atomic weapons used during wartime. Less than a week later, on August 15, Japan surrendered to the Allies. However, it was not until August 17 when the newspapers announced the war was over and the Allies celebrated V-J Day that the rest of the world learned, from an article tucked at the bottom of the front page, about the sinking of the *Indianapolis*. The *Indy* disaster was such a tightly-held secret until the end of the war was announced that letters home from the *Indy* crew were censored so as not to disclose the event prior to the overshadowing V-J Day announcement.

Public outcry, after what appeared to be the Navy trying to bury the story of losing sight of 1,196 men, caused the inquiry already launched by Admiral Chester Nimitz to turn into a search for a scapegoat. In addition to giving Captain McVay no escort and faulty or incomplete intelligence about the waters he needed to sail through to complete his orders, the Navy denied that any SOS messages were ever received. The Navy could not be at fault and even though no captain had ever been court-martialed for losing a ship in the history of the U.S. Navy— over 700 vessels were lost during WWII—a trial was called. Admiral Nimitz strongly disagreed with this course of action and instead tried to issue a letter of reprimand, but Admiral Ernest King overturned this decision with the support of Secretary of the Navy James Forrestal, who insisted on a trial to satisfy the public.

Captain Charles Butler McVay III was charged with

failure to zigzag in enemy waters and failure to order abandon ship in a timely fashion. When Lieutenant Commander Mochitsura Hashimoto of the submarine I-58 that sunk the *Indianapolis* was remarkably called to testify at the trial, he claimed visibility was fair at best and that zigzagging would not have saved the doomed vessel, but his testimony was mistranslated or ignored and the Navy plodded on with the charges. Eventually, the documented visibility became *good* and zigzagging, even though not supported by American submarine experts either, became *necessary*. Captain McVay was found not guilty for failing to call abandon ship, but guilty for failing to zigzag, even though he had followed his given orders to the letter—*zigzag at your discretion, weather permitting*.

It later came out that Admiral King may have had a grudge against McVay's father who, while an admiral, had issued a letter of reprimand to the then junior officer King for sneaking girls aboard a ship.

Although the sentence was eventually overturned after the spectacle of the court-martial had dimmed and Captain McVay would eventually become a rear admiral, he never forgave himself for losing his ship. Now, this could be said of every captain who had ever lost a ship, but due to the media circus of the trial and the Navy choosing him over the many other more probable options to blame, the public now also blamed him. Captain McVay eventually retired from the Navy in 1949, but after the loss of his wife to cancer, the unrelenting abusive phone calls and vitriolic letters ceaselessly blaming him for the loss of loved ones sent him deeper into depression. On November 6, 1968, Charles McVay took his own life. He was found by his gardener clutching a toy sailor in one hand and his service revolver in the other.

Many of his crew believe McVay was unfairly blamed

for the sinking and worked endlessly to exonerate him. This effort involved the captain of the USS *Indianapolis* (SSN-697)—a fast attack nuclear submarine—and countless politicians. In 1975 President Ford, himself a World War II naval officer, refused to honor Captain McVay with a Presidential Unit Citation. It was not until a sixth-grade student, Hunter Scott, from Pensacola, Florida did a National History Day project on the sinking of the *Indianapolis*—after watching the movie *Jaws* with his father—that any real progress was made. A new Congressional Investigation was initiated, and Scott and many of the *Indy* survivors testified in support of Captain McVay. More than three decades after his suicide, Congress and President Bill Clinton posthumously exonerated Captain Charles Butler McVay III and cleared his name on October 30, 2000.

ISLAND

Evil

Love

Evil

悪

Kohaku – Amber
Namiyo – Brave Man
Atsushi - Kind

August, 1945

The Mizushima Fishing and Exploration Company was thriving on the island of Sado. The company had been owned by the Mizushima family for centuries and seen growth beyond their wildest expectations. They now had operations in the Sea of Japan, the Yellow Sea, the East Sea of China and the Philippine Sea as well as reaching far into the vast Pacific Ocean. From merchant fishing and whaling to deep-sea exploration, they had their fingers in everything that floated near and far from the islands of Japan. Centuries after the company's formation there was still a painting of Kaminari Mizushima in the executive boardroom, but no one knew why. It was well known that Takeshi Mizushima was the first president of the company, so why a picture of his mother would be honored in such a way as to keep her picture on the wall that celebrates all the past and present greats of the company was a question often asked in private. One legend was that she was the one who designed the company logo, which appeared to be a Japanese line drawing of a boat at sea. No one still living knew the truth—well, almost no one. She had in fact drawn the symbol, but in truth it was nothing more than the Japanese symbol for *evil* with waves beneath it. Evil or darkness were the standards by which she worked, so nothing ever stood in her way.

Atsushi Mizushima was the second-born son of Kohaku Mizushima, the current president of the company, who was known for his amber eyes and his lightning-quick temper. Atsushi's big brother, Namiyo—a mirror image of their father and his favorite—was given all the best opportunities in the company. Currently, his brother was exploring a shipwreck to scavenge whatever could be taken off the bottom of the sea, while Atsushi was on his way into the warmer waters of the Philippine Sea to hunt whales. Hunting whales was highly profitable, but was not easy work, especially during wartime. Most whaling operations were either halted or restricted to the Sea of Japan or nearby Pacific Ocean, but this only caused Kohaku to whale more since he would then hold a bigger piece of the pie.

"If you cannot find gray whales off our shores, you must go to the warmer waters to find rights or humpbacks. We are of but only a few of the bravest to persist in this endeavor. The people need whale meat and oil, and we must provide it. Think of how the emperor will look upon us if we can provide in this time of need."

"Father, this is dangerous work," Atsushi said.

"Do you wish me to call your brother back from his important duties to help you like a wet nurse?"

"No, Father."

"Then go and make a noble journey our ancestors will speak of for generations to come."

"Yes, Father."

"And do not lose our boat."

As the whaling boat pulled away from the dock, Atsushi remembered his father's words. Not, *good luck*, or *be careful*, or *may the all-mighty One shine upon you on this journey*, but instead, *do not lose our boat*.

As Atsushi sailed along the coast of Japan, he recalled seeing the bright explosions above the cities of Tokyo, Nagoya, Osaka and Kobe. He was told by his emperor that these explosions were the Foreign Devils dying in the skies above our heavenly cities. He could not see the bombs dropping on the ground and the devastation left behind, so like so many loyal Japanese, he thought Japan was winning the war. That night while sailing past the southern islands of Japan, the sky lit up like nothing Atsushi and his crew had ever seen. Some of them had been momentarily blinded by the bright flash. Soon a cloud could be seen coming up from the ground and reaching for the heavens. Was this another Foreign Devil dying in the sky? Atsushi assumed since the cloud was coming up from the island and not down from the sky that this might be something entirely different. Unaware of the gravity of what they had witnessed, they continued on their journey to the Philippine Sea.

Several days after leaving Japanese waters, a crewmember spotted a pod of whales off the port bow and they gave chase. When the whaler caught up to the pod, Atsushi was visibly disappointed when he discovered they had been chasing a pod of Bryde's or anchovy whales. This was not the hunt he had hoped for as these whales were much smaller than the more respectable sei whale they resembled.

"Take them anyway," Atsushi called over the spray of the ocean.

He was frustrated over the catch, but did not want to come home empty handed. Small was not useless and was always better than nothing. Harpoons were fired and several of the small giants of the sea were pulled aboard.

"Captain Mizushima, we have spotted something off the port bow."

"Well, what is it?" Atsushi snapped, showing his disappointment in their catch, preparing for his father's disappointment in him.

"We do not know. It could be refuse from a boat," the sailor answered reluctantly.

"You want us to pick up refuse now? Is that it? We cannot catch real whales so now we are a garbage barge for the Philippine Sea?"

The sailor did not answer, but took the insults without faltering.

"Well?" Atsushi asked.

"I am sorry to disappoint you, captain. I thought something was better than nothing."

Atsushi took a deep breath and looked at the sailor with hard eyes before saying, *"Let us hope you are correct. Change course as indicated."*

"Yes, sir."

Twenty minutes later the boat pulled alongside what appeared to be several crates that were tied together with cargo netting.

"Hoist it from the water," Atsushi ordered.

The jumble of crates was pulled from the water much like a lifeless whale and dropped on the deck at Atsushi's feet.

"Let us see what we have. A treasure I am sure."

A sailor holding a crowbar and a knife approached the crates and cut the netting away so he could pry open one of the crates. When he finally pulled away the lid, he dropped both of his tools and fell back screaming.

"Kaiju! Kaiju!"

Sailors quickly fell in line in front of Atsushi to protect him from the beast in the crates, but Atsushi was having nothing of it and bravely walked forward to see the monster for himself. What he saw tangled in the netting behind the open crate was number 317—the last surviving crew member of the USS *Indianapolis*.

Love

爱

Saki – Blossom of New Hope
Mirai - Future

August, 1945

The Temple of Ai, or *Love*, was a twentieth century stronghold of universal virtue and kindness. Asa and Aika Fukushima, along with Kumakichi, or *Fortunate Bear*, had not only built a temple, they had started a movement that had lasted for centuries. It certainly appeared as if their first child, Chiyo, or *Thousand Generations*, was aptly named. The Society of Ai was now spread throughout the Far East. Ai temples were now on the outskirts of many of the larger Japanese cities, including Niigata, Sapporo, Tokyo, Kobe, Hiroshima and Oita, and stretched from South Korea to the isles of the Java Sea. Temples were never located directly in an urban environment, but instead were nestled on the outskirts of a nearby mountain town, usually beside a river, much like the original on Sado. This was by design—while the *public* Temple was a constant reminder of the nature of the movement, which helped to promote peace and social justice throughout the world, the *private* Society helped to make it happen. An Ai Temple was there to watch over the city from on high and the Ai Society was there to battle the demons below.

    The symbol of the Temple of Ai was simply the Japanese word for *love*, but with one key alteration. This subtle change went unnoticed by all but the keen of eye and could then be explained away by stating it represented the Japanese number ten as was preached in the temple, for *Give back love ten times what you receive* was their mantra. Only those in the family of Ai knew its true meaning: it was a cross that represented the religion of Fortunate Bear—the Knights Templar who had been shipwrecked on the island of Sado over six centuries earlier. Together, Fortunate Bear, Aika and Asa helped to transform the best of what Christianity and Buddhism had to offer the world into the Temple of Ai and its secret sisterhood society.

Like all Japanese temples, the Temple of Ai only had male priests and only allowed males to enter. However, this temple was slightly different from most and contained a secret room with a secret outdoor entrance that only allowed women. From the beginning Asa, Aika and Fortunate Bear agreed it was a man's world, but women ruled it. So, unlike many powerful families that only placed honor and esteem upon their first-born son, the Society of Ai anointed the first and second-born daughters, as were Asa and Aika, and the lineage grew from there. In addition, any son of the first two daughters who felt the calling of priesthood was invited into the temple. This kept their desire high and the bond between the two sides of Ai strong.

Saki Fukushima called her only child into her bedroom. Mirai, red faced from crying already, could not hold back her emotions and burst into tears as soon as she saw her mother, now frail and sallow from late-stage ovarian cancer.

"Please, my little bird. Do not cry," Saki whispered with a notable rasp.

"No, Mother. Please do not leave me," Mirai cried and fell to her knees at Saki's bedside.

"You know it is not my choice. I would be with you for a thousand generations like our ancestors if I had my way. But who is to know what God wants? He has left you as the only chance to continue our heritage. You are our future. You must be brave."

"I know," Mirai whispered, lowering her head to kiss her mother's hand and then pressing it close to her face. Tears ran down her cheeks and pooled on her mother's skin. Not wanting to let go, she raised her head and spoke once more.

"I do not have your strength. You are a castle and I am but a little grain of sand still growing."

She waited for more wisdom from her mother, but none was to come—Saki had passed on to heaven. Now Mirai, the only child of the only daughter and the last generation of Fukushimas was left alone to unfold her future and the future of the Society of Ai.

JACK

California

Home?

Candy

Montana

Elvis

Lincoln

California

August, 1949

After the war ended, Butch spent several weeks in the hospital and then in rehab to mend his shoulder. He was never going to be good as new—physically, or as many sailors would eventually discover, mentally—but he had survived and was grateful for another chance at life. He finished his time in the Navy as a Pharmacist's Mate First Class on the USS *Repose*, a Haven-class hospital ship. When he hit the street as a free man that spring, he had time for some reflection. His life had not gone as he had planned, but being in the Navy had taught him that your desired path may not always be made available to you and you should not carry the burden of poor decisions or unattainable goals into your future, but instead make the best of what paths are still accessible.

Butch decided going by *Jack* was a decision still left to him and it might help put a shine on this new chapter of his life that *he* intended on writing. His second decision was to stay in San Francisco and learn how to surf because when he was on the water, he felt a freedom he could not explain. He wanted this feeling every day and surfing gave it to him in spades. He was not scared of or even concerned about sharks while surfing. It was when he was sleeping that these imagined monsters occupied his dreams. While surfing he might see one shark, but when he closed his eyes there were hundreds. Jack was sure these same issues still handicapped many of his shipmates, but he found if he distracted his mind and didn't let it go there that he could live and sleep—both of which depended deeply upon the other.

For the remaining days of spring and summer, Jack got a

job in a local pharmacy and rented an apartment north of Sunset Village, just off Golden Gate Park and within walking distance of Ocean Beach. He surfed and tanned for several months before he embarked on his next big decision—to enroll in the College of Pharmacy of the University of California at San Francisco.

As it turned out, Jack's navy experience had earned him a real leg up and trimmed the required four-year pharmacy program to a more manageable three. During his first week of classes, he admitted to himself that he had to do something about his commute. Even though the Parnassus Heights campus was a straight shot down Judah Street, he was having an issue with work-school-life balance due to the time eaten up by commuting back and forth between the three. He knew this was not sustainable and looked for an alternative. This was when he saw a flyer for Rush Week.

Jack thought he had found an alternate reality—nothing but food, alcohol and women filled his time during rush. Though he was older than most of the rushees, it was not by much and he found this gave him a leg up since he already had several life-changing experiences to help him deal with any situation he was likely to come upon in fraternity life. He rushed several houses and finally found he had but one choice, as it was the clear stand-out. After formally pledging and preparing to enjoy the spoils of fraternity life, he soon found out it was about to get real— Hell Week was upon him.

During Hell Week Jack found he was to suffer as many demeaning activities as his half-sober, half-witted big brothers could bestow upon him; however, he had experience being a plebe, so this was not as challenging for him as it was for his fellow pledges. For a week straight pledges were awoken most every morning by having ice-cold water tossed on their cot or slowly dripped on their faces. On the mornings they were not abruptly awoken, most found it almost unbearable fretting about what might be coming. One night they were led naked down a hallway while candle wax was dripped on their bodies, after which they were sprayed with beer, forced to eat liver and then sent to class the next morning without showering. Early in the exercise, Jack noted some pledges were being singled out more than others and he admired one pledge who stood up to the big brothers more than was probably prudent. As disparaging as this might be, he found he was forming a stronger bond, if not a friendship, with each of his pledge brothers.

On Thursday of Hell Week, his big brother caught up with him after class.

"Hey, Jack. How's it going."

"Fine, Mike. What are you up to?"

"I was just checking on how you're surviving Hell Week. I know Gottfried and Barnaby can be asses sometimes, but once you make it through this week, you don't have to take any more of their shit."

"I know. I'll be fine. It's just they're really picking on Jimmy and it sometimes takes me to the edge. I want to speak up like John does, but I'm gauging myself for the war, not the battle."

"Smart, but it would be even smarter to distance yourself from John Ratz. He may not be long for this world, if you know what I mean. I gotta go—got class, but stay buckled down and you got this," Mike said, then made his way toward the engineering building.

On the way to his next class, Jack wondered what Mike meant by *Not long for this world*, but the phrase was all but forgotten when he entered the lecture hall and took his seat.

* * *

Jack's pledge class was coming around the bend of Hell Week. All that was left was the Friday night dinner and the Saturday night party before they officially became brothers. They had less than 48 hours to go, so hope and determination overruled whatever embarrassment they might have normally felt as they lined up in nothing but their skivvies and waited for the night to begin.

"Do you know what's up, Jack?" Glenn asked as the group stood in the house foyer waiting to be called into the great room.

"You know, I was in the Navy and if there's one thing a sailor knows, it's the smell of baked beans and I smell baked beans—a shitload of baked beans," Jack said, matter-of-factly.

"You know, now I smell it too," Jay said, actively sniffing the air.

"That's 'cause he said they was beans. That's why you smell them. It's psychologic," Mark claimed.

"Look, Rufus smells them too," Glenn said as he pointed to the fraternity hound dog who was scratching at the door.

Just then Gottfried opened the double door and said, "Come on in, plebes."

The eight pledges looked out into the great room and saw just what Jack had predicted: a giant vat of baked beans in the center of the room, with even more in big pots on the side.

"Whaaa" Jimmy and Dennis said in unison.

"Welcome to hell, plebes," Justin said, then waved his hand at the vat and added, "Please, gather 'round the poison."

A few of the pledges looked at each other before moving, but they all eventually gathered around the big vat of beans.

"As you see, plebes, we have a problem. Our fireplace is on fire and we do not have any water to put it out, so we are going to have to use these beans. Unfortunately, my brothers and I are dressed too nicely to reduce ourselves to such a chore, so we are going to need you plebes to take the beans to the fire to save us and the house."

Being so fixated on the beans, not one pledge noticed all the big brothers were dressed in black tuxedos.

"But isn't the fire supposed to be in the fireplace?" Mark asked, somewhat confused by the problem.

"No, you idiot. The fire is a metaphor for the fire," Gottfried chided.

"So, the fire represents fire," Jack said with a deadpan demeanor, hoping the mocking statement would go undiscovered.

Before Gottfried could compose a response, John asked in a sarcastic tone, "So, you want us to dump the beans into the fireplace?" He then added, "Seems like men's work to me," to cast another barb at the big brothers.

"Shut up, fool," Barnaby growled.

Justin continued, "No, this is work for babies, because you will have to pick up a mouthful of beans from the vat and then crawl on your hands and knees to the fireplace, where you will then spit the beans onto the fire until it is completely extinguished and we are saved."

"Save our brothers. Save our house," the big brothers chanted.

"Well? What are you waiting for, plebes?" Barnaby spat out at the pledges.

"Oh, and there is one more thing. The beans have been poisoned, so you should not swallow too many or have them in your mouth for too long. So, I would hurry."

"Hurry—save our brothers; hurry—save our house," the chant continued.

Jack saw his fellow pledges hesitate, so he took the initiative and got on his hands and knees and took a big mouthful of beans. He then turned and crawled on all fours to the fire where he let out a burst of beans and as much spit as he could muster. He then turned and crawled back to do it all again. By the time he made it back to the vat, he had to wait in line to get more beans. The first few trips were easy, but as time went on, the floor began to get slippery—first from the beans falling off the faces after they were dipped into the baked mess and then later on as more and more of the pledges coughed up their mouthful on their trip to the fireplace. Jack could hear slurping and spitting and coughing and even vomiting as some of the pledges could no longer tolerate the taste of the beans. Now the trip to the fireplace was slippery with beans and vomit, and he found himself praying no one would actually vomit in the vat itself. All and all this was soon becoming the second worst experience of his life—though a very distant second.

"So, what is the poison this year?" Mike asked.

"Ex-lax," Gottfried said. "I put in a bunch. They may shit for a week if they swallow too much."

"What do you mean, you?" Barnaby asked. "I was in charge of the poison this year."

"Yes, I told you to buy it, but Gottfried insisted you dropped the ball, so I asked him to do it instead," Justin said to Barnaby.

"Well, I bought it and I added it as I was instructed," Barnaby said defiantly.

"And I bought it since I thought you forgot as usual and then I added it."

"So, you *both* added Ex-lax to the beans?" Mike asked.

"I guess so," Gottfried answered.

"You guess so? You guess so?" Mike said with building volume while stepping toward the two.

Justin stepped forward and placed a hand in front of Mike.

"The pledges are looking at us. Let's take this up at the meeting later tonight."

"Shit, they're just plebes," Barnaby said, then returned to the edge of the crawling bean relay.

Soon big brothers were on either side of the big brown smear running from the vat to the fireplace and screaming at the plebes to crawl faster. Jimmy slipped flat on the hardwood floor and Barnaby walked into the river of beans to put his foot on Jimmy's back.

"Get up, plebe."

Jimmy attempted to get back up on all fours, but Barnaby easily pushed him back down. The sound of Jimmy splatting against the floor seemed to be entertaining to Barnaby and he demanded Jimmy get up again. John, who was crawling back the other way, feigned to slip himself and knocked out Barnaby's foot, which caused him to topple like the sack of shit he was and then *he* went *splat*.

"Sorry, sir," John said as he got up and continued to crawl to get more beans like a good pledge.

'Why you," Gottfried said, then stepped forward and kicked John in the ribs.

John fell to his side clutching his abdomen and gasping for breath. As Gottfried wound up to kick John again, this time in the face, Jack reached out to push on Gottfried's foot and like Barnaby he fell hard into the river of beans.

Now there was full-blown chaos as the two big brothers squirmed and slipped on the river of smashed beans while those around them tried to get out for their way—for the most part, anyway.

Then Stewart yelled, "It's out! It's out! I put the fire out!"

All the brothers and pledges, whether standing or lying in the bean river, turned to look at the fireplace.

"What a fucking mess," Mike said aloud, even though it seemed more of a private thought.

"You are going to fucking die," Barnaby said, pointing at John. Then Gottfried said the same to Jack.

"Tempers, boys. Tempers," Justin said, then told all the plebes to go get cleaned up. Once the pledges were gone, he said, "As I said before, we can discuss this all at our meeting tonight."

The rest of Friday passed without incident, as did all of Saturday until the party. Barnaby and Gottfried seemed overly nice at the party and it put Jack a bit on edge as he had seen too many times how smiling people can come back at you when you least expect it.

Jack and John were assigned to big brothers Eric and Jason who were bartending in the sunroom that was just behind the fireplace. The night was going well, so Jack relaxed a bit and John continued to be oblivious to his surroundings as usual. Throughout the night John continually drank and talked with girls he knew were already claimed by big brothers. He was reprimanded several times during the party—he was a plebe and should act accordingly—but John would be John, regardless. Eventually, Jason told the two to take the garbage out from behind the bar.

"Take the garbage out *during* the party. It's not even full and how would we even get it out of here?" Jack asked, a bit confused by the request.

"Take it out through the great room to the back stairs," Jason answered, then continued talking with the girl he was trying to pick up for the evening.

"This seems wrong," Jack said to John.

"Yeah. So, let's make it right. Take a side and we'll go out the window."

Jack grabbed a handle of the large trash can and they both lifted. The can was heavier than they estimated and initially seemed stuck to the floor, but they got it into the air and hoisted it up onto the windowsill behind the bar. They then jumped out the adjoining window and grabbed the handles from the other side. As they brought the can to the ground, Jack noticed a trail of liquid running down the side of the house. He looked inside and saw the same trail running from the bar to the window. Obviously there was a leak in the can and he was certainly happy they had selected this option, rather than trailing a stale beer river across the dance floor in the great room during a party.

As they were walking the can down the sidewalk to the back of the house, they saw a police cruiser parked at the end of the fraternity driveway.

"What you got there, boys? You stealing something?" Officer Mike Lee asked.

"No," John answered. "This is ours."

"So, this is your property?" Officer Lance Brown asked.

The hairs on the back of Jack's neck went stiff, but before he could respond, John answered for them.

"Yep," John said without hesitation.

"I see alcohol in here. I assume you're both 21 then," Officer Brown queried.

"Yep," John answered again, feigning confidence.

Shit, Jack thought to himself.

"We are going to need proof of that, son," Officer Lee said, then reached out his hand.

"My wallet is in my room at the dorm," John answered.

"You don't live here?" Officer Lee continued.

"No," John said emphatically. "I don't even know which frat house this is."

Jack could see where John was going with this, but also knew it would not work.

"So, where did you get this trash can and why are you carrying it down the sidewalk?" Brown queried again. "And, if you don't have your wallet, what is the bulge in your back pocket?" he added as he pointed.

"Here, let me show you."

John bent down as if retrieving something off the ground and when he stood back up, he tipped the trash can over onto Officer Lee's shoes, then ran in the opposite direction.

Jack thought, *Shit*, again, then stepped back from the expanding puddle and sat on the lawn.

The next morning Mike and Jack were talking by a big bay window in the great room. Jack could see brothers tossing a football around and playing horseshoes out on the front lawn.

"I told you to stay away from John Ratz," Mike said quietly.

"I didn't have much of a choice since I was paired up with him for the party," Jack responded.

"Yeah, I know and I blame myself. I had you paired with Stewart at the other bar, but Gottfried changed the teams behind my back. Barnaby really had it out for John and said if John made it through Hell Week that he would take his daddy's money to a different frat where they respected their legacies."

"So, it was a setup?"

"Yes. Barnaby's plan was to have John and another

pledge either ruin the party by dragging the trash can through the great room or be stopped by the police with alcohol. The can was rigged to leak once it was removed from its spot in the sunroom and Barnaby called the cops just before Jason told John to take out the trash, so he was doomed regardless. Though the window was a nice touch."

"Thanks . . . and?"

"John is out since he was arrested for assaulting a police officer."

"And the pledge with him?"

"This was to be John's last strike and the other pledge was going to be Jimmy who Barnaby dislikes as well."

"Isn't Jimmy a legacy?"

"Yes, but not a rich one."

"So, I'm Jimmy now and I'm out as well?"

"Yes, you're Jimmy now. Sorry, little brother, but it has to be this way. I've been in this frat for two years and I can tell you it's like playing your favorite sport knee-deep in shit. I think they may have done you a favor since you're not one to take kindly to the bigotry and chauvinism that Barnaby and Gottfried exude each day."

Later that day, Jack was called to the Dean of Students' office and told he was being expelled after being charged with underage drinking. Even though the charges were likely to be dropped, the school maintained its hard stance against student drinking and Jack decided his best option was to cut ties and give up on pharmacy school altogether. He then thought of KK for the first time in a long while and decided returning home to Janesville would be his next decision. After all, he missed his mother and felt he could find a life there again if he tried hard enough. However, he had no idea of just how hard he would have to try.

The evening after Jack left California for good, the fraternity burned to the ground.

Home?

October, 1949

Jack was not fully packed and ready to leave until the next afternoon. His 1940 Ford Woody, which was more like a wooden boat with wheels than a modern 1940s automobile, was packed to the gills—with a surfboard on top, of course. The Woody had a metal hood, fenders and bumpers, but that was it; the sides and back were all wood—shiny lacquered wood. He had bought the car so he could drive up and down the coast chasing the waves, but now the Woody was taking him home, away from the ocean. Because of his late start, he decided to stop in Nevada for the night rather than drive through the mountains in the dark.

Humboldt Wells was originally a railroad town famous for nothing more than burning down and being rebuilt as *Wells*. Apparently, *Humboldt* was lost in the fire, or maybe it was just left off because Wells was in fact not in Humboldt County.

Jack pulled into the Gates Motel, just off Highway 40.

"Welcome to the Gates Motel. My name is Diana. How may I help you this afternoon?"

"Well, Diane, I—"

"Diane—ah. My name is Diana. Like Deb—rah.'"

"So, is your name Debbie, Diane or Dianrah? I'm confused now," Jack asked with mock sincerity.

"Now you're just being smart. Or maybe you're just that dumb," Diana retorted.

"Do I look that dumb?" Jack asked, tipping his head and raising an eyebrow.

"Well, you do have a surfboard on your Woody. That's usually a pretty clear sign."

"Oh, so you don't like surfers."

"I'm uncertain if that's a conjecture on your part or a question to me, but I can honestly say I do not like one single surfer in this whole town."

"Do you have a lot of surfers here in Nevada this far from the ocean?"

"Nope, not a one," Diana answered straight-faced.

Jack chuckled and said, "Well, Diana, I would like a room for the night."

"Just one night?"

"Just one night. Unless there's so much to see here that I need to stay longer."

"Did you have your eyes open when you drove through town?" Diana queried.

"For the most part."

"Then you've seen it all. Thank you for visiting Wells. Please come back and see us when you have nothing better to do. That will be $4.50, unless you're a veteran, then you get a discount."

"I am a vet."

"I knew it. I can tell an army man every time."

"Navy, actually."

"Oh, I'm sorry. I didn't mean to insult you," she said with a smirk.

"Call us even, Dian—ah."

"What ship were you on?" Diana asked as she took Jack's five-dollar bill and handed him 75 cents change.

"The *Indy*," Jack said, quieter than he intended.

"Isn't that the one that—"

"Yep, that's the one. Here, take this for all your troubles," Jack said as he handed her a quarter.

"My troubles? You're a war hero, sir."

This was not the first time Jack had heard this, but he was still not used to it and really did not want to be reminded of his historic 18 days at sea—four of which were spent in the water waiting to die.

"Please, call me Jack or even Jack—ah if you wish."

"Welcome to Wells, Jack. I hope you have a wonderful night's sleep. Room 3 is just down the hall on the right," Diana said as she handed Jack his room key.

Jack thanked her and took the proffered key.

"Oh, sir—Jack, your receipt."

"You can keep it," Jack said, then turned to open the door to the hallway.

"Jack, I think you should take it . . . as a souvenir of your time in Wells . . . and in case you're ever in the area again, there's a coupon on the back."

Jack returned to the desk to grab the receipt and gave Diana a big smile. "Thank you, ma'am."

Diana put her hands on her hips and asked, "Was that for calling you sir?"

"Yep. Good night, Diana."

"Good night, Jack."

The next morning Jack got up early and Diana's little brother, Norman, checked him out.

"Were your accommodations satisfactory?" Norman asked.

"They were exceptional, Norman. Thank you. And, please thank your sister when she comes in this evening. She was very helpful last night."

"I will do, sir."

Jack got in his Woody and honked the horn as he was driving off. Norman took this as a friendly gesture and waved back, not knowing the honk was for Diana who was still sleeping in Room 3. Before pulling out onto the highway, Jack took the receipt out of his front pocket and looked it over. He had been uncertain why Diana was so adamant about him taking the receipt, then he turned it over and saw the *coupon* was a circled phone number on the back.

Jack made it to Lincoln, Nebraska before stopping for the second night. The next day he got an early start and made it into Janesville just after dinnertime. Even though he missed his mother dearly, he was not ready to stare down his father after leaving without a word—especially after the barn fire, when his family probably needed him the most. He still felt he had no choice but to leave when he did, but was not ready to dive back into that pool of drama just yet.

Jack pulled into the back road of the DuPree family farm and parked under the tree canopy near the path that led to the Hill. He then walked back to the farmhouse to toss pebbles at Riff's window and when he received no response, he crept around the front of the house to peer in through the big bay window. The DuPrees were still at the dinner table having what looked like dessert after a late evening meal. Riff was facing the window and his parents were at either end of the table; KK was not at the table. Jack stood and waved his hands trying to get Riff's attention, then ducked down quickly so as not to be seen if Riff's mom or dad looked his way.

"Mom, this pie is great," Riff said as he quickly shoveled four bites of pie into his mouth, adding more pie before he had fully chewed and swallowed the prior forkful.

"Clifford, slow down or you will choke yourself," his mother said with some concern. His father continued reading the evening paper, unaffected by the lively dessert conversation.

"Don't worry, Mom, this is so good I can't help myself," Riff said through a mouth full of pie, then waved Jack toward the barn while his mother took her own bite of pie.

"Oh, Clifford. Sometimes—"

"Thanks, Mom. Gotta go. Got homework."

"And chores," his dad added without looking up from his paper.

"And chores," Riff agreed, then kissed his mother's forehead, leaving a tiny bit of cherry behind.

Riff headed for the back door and then ran to the barn.

"My God. If not for the article about the USS *Indianapolis*, this whole town thought you were gone for good or dead," Riff said, then stepped up to give his best friend a big bear hug.

"So, the town knows I was on the *Indy*?"

"Knows? That was all we talked about for months after we got the news. The high school even had a cookie sale in your honor. I'm not sure why other than to support you . . ."

Jack noticed Riff trail off and thought it deserved a question.

"What do you mean . . . to support me?"

"It's a long story."

"I've got the time," Jack returned with a bit of annoyance in his voice.

"Then here, let me show you."

Riff walked over to a row of shelves along the barn wall and pulled a manila folder from under a stack of blankets.

"KK used to save newspaper articles about you—baseball, football, anything that even mentioned you. She's been your biggest fan ever since she was in grade school."

Jack was a bit confused by the direction of the conversation and why Riff was speaking in the past tense.

"This was the last article she saved before she was sent off to boarding school."

"What?! Why did your parents send KK to boarding

school?"

"I don't know. My parents never explained it and didn't even tell me which school she was at. One morning she was just gone. If it wasn't for her occasional letters home, I would've thought they killed her. I miss her dearly. More than I would have thought. You know when she was a toddler learning to speak, she could not pronounce my name, so Clifford came out as *Riff* and I've been Riff ever since. In effect, she made me who I am. Now she lives in Lincoln, Nebraska. I know we have relatives down there, so she does have family for Thanksgiving and Christmas, but she has never come home. She only wrote to me a few times, but I got the distinct feeling she was so mad at Mom and Dad for sending her away that she may never come back."

"Wow. That's a lot to take in."

"Well, it gets worse. You better sit down," Riff said, then motioned toward a bale of straw with his hand.

Jack sat on the bale and awaited more bad news.

"This first article is from the Gazette the week after you left," Riff said as he handed the clipping to Jack.

Local Boy Suspected in Burning of Family Barn

Late last Saturday night . . . family barn burned to the ground . . . three horses and a milk cow saved . . . son's jacket found in the barn . . . Jack, who goes by Butch, disappeared the same night and suspected of arson.
-GG

"KK saved this? Why?" Jack asked.

"She liked you and she did not like the way the paper framed these stories. Apparently, there's more to it than just local reporting."

"What do you mean?"

"Do you remember Guilford Gromley?"

"Yeah. The odd bookish kid that got beat up all the time."

"Yep—that's the guy. You know his dad owns the Gazette and Guilford is currently working as a writer—a writer with a kind of newsprint vendetta against you."

"What? He was three years ahead of us in school. He wasn't even in school when I left."

"It goes a little deeper than school. It's all about Candy."

"Candy?"

"Yep. Apparently, he's had a serious thing for her since the sixth grade and he really lost it when she, as a senior, decided to go out with a sophomore."

"Tough shit, Guilford. Where is Candy now?"

"Well, that's where it gets complicated," Riff said as he handed Jack another clipping.

Local Boy leaves Town after Impregnating Girlfriend

Jack read the headline, then immediately asked, "Candy was pregnant when I left?"

"Yes, and the story doesn't end there. As you will see from the story, Candy knew Guilford had a thing for her and when you left town, leaving her pregnant, she got Guilford to marry her."

"Guilford married Candy when she was carrying another man's baby?"

"No, this is the complicated part. She did not tell him and when the baby was born seven and a half months later, he became suspicious and once he determined you were the father, he demanded a divorce. That's when his articles took on an even more vindictive edge and when he wrote the missing girl article." Riff handed Jack the article in question.

Janesville Boy Wanted for Questioning in Lake Geneva Missing Girl Case

Katherine "Katie" Summerville is still missing from the Episcopal Order of St. Anne School for Girls . . . the old Younglands estate . . . Last seen in the company . . . young gardener, Butch . . . Miss Margaret . . . boy couldn't be trusted . . . he was suspicious . . . Marino Danielson, the head groundskeeper . . . Butch was a good worker . . . ran from police before he could be questioned and is now also missing. -GG

"Note the date . . . it's well after the girl went missing in May. That's why I continued to save the articles after KK left just in case you returned . . . or *when* you returned so you would be prepared."

Jack was tempted to tell Riff he had never actually slept with Candy, but even Candy might not believe that anymore. And what could he say about Katie other than he did not do it—whatever *it* was. He was relieved when he was prompted to ask a new question.

"Prepared for what?"

"Guilford has spread his poison throughout this town. You still have friends here, but most who don't know you may not receive you too warmly."

"Because I *supposedly* got a girl pregnant?"

"Finish reading the article."

Local Boy Leaves Town after Impregnating Girlfriend

Guilford Gromley is requesting an annulment from Candy Langdon after wife's improprieties with a local boy prior to their marriage . . . as previously reported here . . . Jack "Butch" . . . knowingly left town . . .

responsible for family barn fire . . . pregnant girlfriend . . . did not disclose to groom . . . now wanted for possible statutory rape charges. -GG

"Rape?!"

"And then there's this," Riff said as he handed Jack yet another article.

Dark Cloud Follows Local Boy onto the Doomed U.S.S. *Indianapolis*

Jack "Butch" . . . local boy who ran away after burning down the family barn . . . leaving girlfriend pregnant . . . also wanted in questioning of missing Lake Geneva girl . . . runs away again to join the Navy . . . on the ship for just over two weeks before tragedy befalls the entire crew as the boat sinks and hundreds die. Shipmates described him as a bad seed. -GG

"He's trying to blame me for the sinking of the *Indy*?"

"Not only trying—some in town believe you're cursed and have even taken it out on your family."

"Shit, I should go to my house and make this right."

"Jack, you need to know something first."

"What more could there be? I left this town as the first-string quarterback and have returned, not as a war hero, but as a cursed *local boy* because of the twisted lies Guilford has spread. I need to let my family know I'm OK and I did none of these things he's accusing me of."

Riff simply handed Jack the last article in the folder.

Obituaries

Maria . . . mother of eight—five boys and three girls—succumbed to breast cancer over the weekend . . . long fought three-year battle. . . surrounded at the end by her loving husband and seven of her children . . . only missing child was well-known troublemaker wanted in several local incidents. -GG

"I'm going to kill him. How could he print these lies in my mother's obituary?" Jack said leaping to his feet before the fact that his mother was gone fully hit him. "Shit, she's gone . . . my mother is gone." Jack flopped back onto the straw bale like a wet scarecrow, saddened beyond repair.

"Do you want to know what I think?" Riff asked after giving Jack a moment to take it all in.

"Right now I only have one option—to kill that little rat, so, yes, please expand my selection."

"I think your best option, maybe your only option if you want to live anywhere near Janesville ever again, is to go to the police and give them your story."

Jack seemed to be mulling this over as a viable choice.

"This type of news or rumor infiltrates society at every level," Riff continued. "It has already affected public opinion and even though you may not be officially wanted by the police, you're going to eventually be taken in for questioning . . . even if it's just to satisfy public opinion. So, what I'm saying is—"

"Head it off at the pass," Jack said, still staring blankly at the barn ceiling.

"Yes—exactly," Riff said with some excitement.

An hour later, Jack walked up to the sergeant's desk at the Janesville police station.

"Hello," the sergeant said without looking up from his papers.

"Hello, I'm here to answer some questions."

"Name, please," the sergeant said and then looked up to see Jack.

"Jack—"

"Butch? Oh, just take a seat over there. Officer Willard will be with you shortly," the sergeant said as he picked up the phone and dialed.

After about 15 minutes, Officer Conrad Willard walked over to Jack.

"Butch?"

"Yes, but it's *Jack* now."

"OK, Jack. Follow me."

They walked down a short hallway and entered a little room that contained a rectangular table with two chairs on either side.

"Take a seat." Officer Willard motioned to the right side of the table with his hand.

When Jack sat down he could see a mirror that he knew was a one-way viewing window from an observation room. He kept his cool since he had nothing to hide, but he could not prevent his heart from racing just a little. After all, he was about to be questioned by the police about several crimes—crimes he was not guilty of, but crimes nonetheless.

"So, you said you would like to make a statement?" Officer Willard asked as he sat across from Jack and opened a file filled with reports, memos and pictures.

Jack pulled out a folder of his own, then said, "Let's start here," as he pushed the first article along the tabletop toward Officer Willard.

Local Boy Suspected in Burning of Family Barn

"This article is partly true. I was in the barn the night it burned down. I tried to put out the flames with my suit coat, but the fire spread too quickly."

"So, are you admitting you started the fire?"

"I said the article was partly true. Derick Mahoney from Beloit started the fire. He was probably getting even with me for punching him when he was assaulting KK DuPree or maybe just jealous of me and KK—who knows."

"Was this incident ever reported to the police?"

"No."

"Will KK substantiate your claim?" Willard asked, still paging through his file, occasionally jotting something in the margin of a report or memo, then sliding it to the bottom of the pile.

"She will certainly corroborate the fact that I hit Derick in the face after pulling him off her, but she wasn't in the barn, so she has no knowledge of Derick being there."

"Where can we find KK?"

"That I don't know. I just returned from the war and heard she was sent off to a boarding school not long after I left."

"And, why did you leave again . . . I mean the barn just burned down, so why would you leave?"

"That really has to do more with this," Jack said as he pushed the next article toward the officer.

Local Boy Leaves Town after Impregnating Girlfriend

"I can honestly say I never slept with Candy Langdon. We were going to do it that night, but we broke up just prior to the dance."

"That doesn't answer the question of why you left," Officer Willard stated more than asked.

"That night I fought with Derick in the barn, but he managed to get away. I tried to put out the flames with my coat, but when I turned around and saw the whole floor was on fire, I knew it was a losing battle, so I let the milk cow out of the barn and led the horses to the training pen."

Officer Willard made another note, then asked, "And . . ."

"And, that's when I saw Candy and another person leave the barn. They had been in the hay loft the whole time."

"Did they see you?"

"I can't be certain. I think the man saw me, but I don't believe he knew who I was. Regardless, when they found my suit coat, I knew I could not deny being in the barn. At that point I felt life for me had changed and it was never going to be the same."

"But you had broken up with Candy, so what was the big deal?"

Tap! Tap!

"Just a second," Officer Willard said, then left the room.

Jack just sat there rolling options around in his mind, none of which seemed to help his cause. There were just too many fronts to this war, but Riff was right: starting with the police and the truth was his best opener.

Moments later Officer Willard reentered the room and sat down.

"I am still waiting to hear why you left."

Jack did not answer immediately, but instead took his time deciding on the least worst answer.

"Let me help you. Who was in the barn with Candy?"

"I can't say."

"Butch, I mean Jack, telling us this information will certainly absolve you of any wrongdoing if they saw your fight with Derick in the barn."

"I don't think they did and even if they did, I doubt they would admit to being there. I think you have to ask Candy these questions. I may not have seen the man clearly."

"So, it was a man and not another boy?"

"Like I said, I may not have seen him clearly enough to be certain."

"Then is that all you have to tell us today?"

"Not even close," Jack said as he pushed another article toward the officer.

Janesville Boy Wanted for Questioning in Lake Geneva Missing Girl Case

"I talked to this girl only once and she told me she was leaving because she wanted so much more out of life than a girl's school could give her. She also felt like she was being bullied by Miss Margaret who also had her knickers in a knot about me working there. I was a good employee and a hard worker and I never—"

"Jack, you can rest easy on this one. Katherine Summerville is living in a commune in California. She was found just a few weeks after she went missing."

"Then Guilford's article was published after the police already knew she was OK," Jack pressed.

"Yes, we are aware."

"So, you're aware he's publishing false stories about me to affect public opinion?" Jack's irritation growing.

"They certainly are misleading stories, but there is nothing concrete that we can say was an overstep on his part."

"Was I ever wanted for statutory rape?" Jack asked aggressively.

"Hmm . . . you might have something there," Officer Willard said then glanced back at the mirror for a second. "Let us investigate that possibility."

Jack was confused and for a second thought his outburst had led the officer to think they could charge Jack with statutory rape.

Officer Willard sensed Jack's dismay and added, "He did state *possible* charges, but you may still have enough of a case for a libel suit or at least a cease-and-desist order."

"Well, then maybe these two may help the case." Jack pushed the last two articles across the table.

Dark Cloud Follows Local Boy onto the Doomed U.S.S. *Indianapolis*

"This article about my time on the *Indy* and my shipmates is pure bullshit. And, what he said about me in my mother's obituary is beyond vindictive."

"I do not disagree. I will discuss this with my commander and I . . . well, we here at the station would like to thank you and the crew of the *Indy* for what you all did to help end the war. I know you and your shipmates suffered greatly . . ." Officer Willard paused to swallow and take a breath before continuing, ". . . and the folks in Janesville should be calling you the war hero that you are since they have you to thank for helping to end the war and bringing their boys, fathers and husbands home in one piece."

Jack was a little taken aback by this old familiar sentiment coming in the middle of a police interrogation, but he was thankful to be believed if that is what was happening.

"Thank you. Is that all then?"

"Well, we have just one more item for you to comment on. What do you know about the fraternity fire at UCSF last week?"

"What fraternity fire?" Jack said with obvious surprise.

"The fraternity you were pledging burned down the night after you were expelled. No one was hurt, but the fraternity dog died of smoke inhalation."

"Wait. I left just after noon on that day, so I wasn't even in town," Jack stated with some visible relief.

"Do you have anyone who can corroborate that you were out of town that night?"

Jack thought for only a moment, then pulled out his wallet to remove a folded receipt.

"Here is the receipt from my stay that same night."

Officer Willard took the receipt, then asked if he called the desk, would they remember him.

"If you flip it over and call that number, I can bet Diana will remember me."

"So, if we call this Diana, she can verify the date on the receipt with the motel log?"

"Yes, and tell her it's about Jack, the guy who called her Dian-rah. She should remember that."

Officer Willard left the room and returned about 15 minutes later.

"Diana verified you were at the Gates Motel on the night in question, so you are free to go."

"Free to go?"

"Yes, you have answered all of our questions and we have no reason to suspect you are involved in any of the incidents with which your name has been associated."

"What about Guilford?"

"These articles are more folklore now than actual current news, so we cannot justify a press conference, but my commander agreed we could pay Mr. Gromley a visit. We will *request* a full retraction of all accusations and make it clear you may be forced to file a libel suit if there is not something printed in the next paper."

"You can request this from Guilford? I don't need a lawyer?"

"Yes, these issues are usually carried out by a lawyer, but the station generally agrees Gromley is a disease—you are not his only target—and we would like to do this for you to say thank you for your service to our country," Officer Willard said, then extended his hand.

Jack reached out to shake Willard's hand and said, "I appreciate your help."

* * *

Jack stayed in Riff's barn until the retraction was printed. Riff brought several copies of the paper to the barn later that morning.

"Funny how his articles about you were always on the front page, but the retraction is on page 17. Still, it sounds pretty complete. I think Guilford felt he was too far out on a limb and was concerned what might happen to his career if he were to be sued for libel," Riff said as he handed over the papers to Jack.

After giving Jack a minute to read the retraction, Riff asked, "So, what are you going to do now?"

Jack had a look in his eyes that Riff had never seen before and it scared him a little more than he was willing to admit.

"Now that I have proof of my vindication, I'm going to go see my family . . . and then I'm going to make Guilford regret he was ever born."

Jack then walked out of the barn without a goodbye or even a thank you to Riff.

Candy

October, 1949

Candy now lived in Footville, a small town just west of Janesville proper. She had taken the first job available outside of Janesville after the divorce—suddenly a single mother forced to support her son, Joey, who was now almost four and growing like a weed. It was late afternoon when Jack pulled up to the address he was given by Riff. He took a piece of paper out of his front pocket to double check the house number, then walked up and knocked on the door.

"Hello," he called after knocking, then craned his neck to look through the front window.

The front door opened and a girl about high school age peered through the screen door.

"Can I help you?" she said, still holding the front door in front of her.

"Hi, I'm an old friend of Candy's. Is she home?"

"No, she works down at the diner during evening shift."

"Oh, thank you. I'll see if I can catch her there."

"It shouldn't be a problem. She should be there till they close at midnight tonight."

"Thank you for your help."

Before Jack could turn to step off the stoop, a young child's voice called from the living room, "Stacy, who is that?"

"Just a friend of your mama's," Stacy answered.

The child came to the door and clung to Stacy's leg before asking, "You know my mama?"

Jack bent down to get eye level with the child and even through the screen, he could see the family resemblance. He knew it would be a hard road back from becoming a public pariah, but now that he saw what amounted to a flesh and bone advertisement of his lies and misdeeds to all uninformed Janesvillians, he could see his choices were narrower than he assumed.

"Yes, I do. I'm an old friend of your mama's. So, what's your name?" Jack asked the boy.

"Joey . . . and I'm . . . three," the boy answered as he struggled to hold up three fingers, finally using his other hand to pull down his pinky finger.

"Joey is a great name."

"I know," Joey said, then ran off back to a pile of toys on the living room floor.

"Thank you for your help, Stacy. I hope to see you around."

"You're welcome, mister," Stacy said before she closed the door.

Jack pulled into a parking spot on the street in front of the diner. The diner was nearly full and he could see Candy inside running between tables. A bell rang as he opened the diner door, but not a soul looked up, as it was a very loud and busy place at the moment. Jack waited by the hostess desk. It took several minutes before Candy finally walked up to the desk and grabbed a menu.

"Just one, sir?"

"Yes, I'm alone."

Hearing the response caused Candy to look up at Jack's face. Her eyes beamed as her mouth spread in wonder, then she immediately burst into tears and fell into Jack's arms. After only a short moment, she released him and backed away.

"I'm so sorry. That's not very professional of me."

"Actually, it's just what I needed. I haven't been hugged in a long time. Candy, we need to talk. I need to know how you're doing. You know I care for you."

Jack's response almost sent Candy into another crying fit; her lip quivered, but she held her composure.

"Well, if you're asking about how I'm doing right now—we're down a waitress and our dishwasher is passed out drunk in the back, so our cook is cooking and washing dishes on one of our busiest nights. However, if you're asking about anything beyond that, then it will be a much longer answer and I just don't have the will or the time right now."

Jack rolled up his shirtsleeves and said, "I know how to wash dishes and had a close friend who taught me a bunch about cooking as well."

"Jack, I couldn't ask you to do that."

"Who said you asked? I'm offering and I'm not taking no for an answer."

"OK," Candy said, then gave Jack a big hug again. "The door to the kitchen is over there."

"See you at midnight."

Just after 7:30 p.m. a middle-aged man walked into the diner and headed for the kitchen. Jack was elbow-deep in greasy suds when he heard someone call his name.

"Butch? Well, I'll be damned—it is true. We have a real war hero washing our dishes. Do you remember me, son? You and my boy, Craig, played baseball together."

"Of course, I do, Mr. Parrish."

"A war hero can call me Brian," he said and then held out his hand to shake Jack's hand.

"Thank you, Brian. I'll have to take a rain check on that hand shake though," Jack said as he held up his hands that were virtual soapsuds mittens.

"You bet. I want to thank you for pitching in, but now I want you to get cleaned up and go find yourself an empty booth, 'cause tonight's meal is on the diner."

"Thank you, Brian. It was really nothing. I needed the distraction."

"Well, if you call hard work a distraction, then you are a better man than I," Brian said, then handed Jack a large dishtowel.

"So, do you own the diner?" Jack asked as he dried his hands.

"Yep . . . and my son Craig is the cook during the morning shift. He loves to cook breakfast. A fact that is obvious when you see him—looks like he's wearing a barrel, but still solid as ever."

"Yes, I remember he was a great first baseman back in the day."

"Yep . . . and now he coaches. You should think about coaching. You were a great athlete before the war interrupted your life."

"It did a little more than interrupt my life, but I know what you mean. If I stick around, I'll look into coaching. It's a good way of giving back."

"Certainly is. Now, go sit down and tell Candy what you want from the menu. Anything you want, but you must have dessert. Craig takes pride in his baked goods and I know you would love his cherry pie."

"Thank you. I'm sure I would."

Jack found a booth in the corner and waited for Candy to come by. He ordered meatloaf, mashed potatoes, green bean casserole and finished it off with a root beer. Once he was finished, Candy brought him a piece of cherry pie and he audibly moaned as he ate it. It was fantastic and took him back to his friend Gerbil's cinnamon rolls. Then a thought struck him and he asked Candy for a pen and two pieces of paper. Once he was finished writing, he called Candy over again.

"I know how tired you're going to be after your shift tonight, so I'm not going to hang around and force you to stay up to talk with me."

"You wouldn't be forcing me."

"I know, but I bet Joey gets up at the crack of dawn, so you're going to need your sleep."

"You met Joey," Candy said, looking down at the ground to avoid making eye contact with Jack.

"Yes, I did. And he looks like a handful," Jack added, then slid a piece of paper across the table to Candy. "This is Riff DuPree's phone number. If you want to get ahold of me, call his house and ask for Riff. He will give me any message you leave. I'm currently living in his barn."

"You aren't living at your house?"

"No, I'm not ready to tell them I'm back just yet. That's kind of what I wanted to talk to you about. We've both been beaten up by this town," Jack said, then realizing they were actually in Footville, pointed his finger east to correct himself, "I mean *that* town . . . and I have a proposition for you that might just lift us both up out of the hole we are in."

"Sounds intriguing." Candy added, her old flair flashing for a brief moment, reminding Jack of the woman he thought she could have been and hopefully the woman that Jack would help her become. "I'm off this Thursday, so I'll call in the morning."

"Great. See you then."

Jack got up, took her hand and gave it a squeeze before he leaned in to give her a kiss on the cheek.

"See you Thursday," Jack said, sensing the beginning of a blush as he left for the cash register.

"Thank you for dinner, Brian," Jack said as he approached the register.

"Thank you for pitching in to keep us afloat tonight,"

Brian returned.

"It was my pleasure and I have a little parting gift for Craig." Jack handed over the second piece of paper Candy had given him. "This is a good friend's cinnamon roll recipe and I believe it will complement Craig's delicious baked desserts—say, as a breakfast option."

"That's funny. Craig gave up on baking donuts since there are two donut shops in town—one close enough to throw a rock at—but this might give us a chance to get some of that business back. Thank you."

"I can honestly say these are so good that the donut shop employees may become customers as well."

Brian chuckled and shook Jack's hand before he left.

* * *

Jack woke with the rooster crow at dawn Thursday morning. He showered in the barn and put on clean clothes. He did not think the DuPrees knew he was living in their barn, but he still needed to find a real place to live so he was not immediately covered in dust after showering.

Just after 9:00 a.m., Riff entered the barn and told Jack that Candy would be there shortly. As he waited, Jack did not like how his mouth had gone dry at the thought of the pending conversation with Candy. This reminded him of his time in the water and he did not need *Indy* flashbacks to overwhelm him now as he was trying to get his life back on track—or at least the only reasonable track he could see at the time.

Candy entered the barn wearing a tight quarter-sleeved sweater top with a sailor's knot bow at the neck and a poodle skirt adorned with a clown holding a string of balloons. Her long curly hair fell below her shoulders and framed her face perfectly. Jack took a moment to appreciate her beauty before speaking.

"We can talk here or we can go to a café," Jack offered.

"I thought you didn't want to be seen yet," Candy asked.

"Well, it would be best if my family didn't know I was back until we've talked and come up with a plan."

"Then lay it on me, Jack. I'm dying to know what you have cooking in that devious mind of yours."

Jack knew this was not an insult, but more a compliment or even encouragement in her anticipation of his reveal. Jack went on to explain his thought process and the solutions, or options, left to them that would hopefully help shape a better future for them both. Candy listened, sitting on the same bale of straw that Jack had when he read the articles saved for him by KK and Riff.

"You're honestly offering this as a solution?" Candy asked, not quite aghast, but certainly surprised.

"I think it's our best option. It's not perfect—both of us will have some growing to do and we may have to or will have to rewrite history a bit—but I think we can make it work."

"OK. If you say so, then I will," Candy said with a smile.

Jack smiled back and said, "Then I'll go to the paper today and get the story in for the Friday edition."

"When do we celebrate?" Candy asked as she stood, then walked over to Jack to look into his eyes and place a hand on his chest.

"How about I pick you up tomorrow afternoon after the paper is out and we will go talk to my family, then we can think about celebrating."

"Deal," Candy said, then stood on her tiptoes to kiss Jack on the cheek. "See you tomorrow. I'll have to trade for the day shift or ask for my shift off, but it will be worth it."

"Yes, let's hope so."

"Bye," Candy said, blowing Jack a kiss as she went out the barn door.

Less than an hour later Jack walked up to Guilford Gromley's desk and handed him a handwritten note.

"Hey, Guile. I would like to have this published in tomorrow's social section."

Guilford grabbed the note, annoyed at Jack's use of his grade school nickname. After reading the text, he crumpled the note and tossed it into his trashcan.

"I am not printing this bullshit. She would never agree to this."

"Oh, she did more than agree," Jack answered, then baited Guilford with a wry smile. "No matter. It doesn't change anything, unless it gets out that you refused to print something I paid to have published in your paper. The lawyers may have something to say about that."

Guilford started to turn a bit crimson, but refused to comment.

"Suit yourself," Jack said, then walked out of the press room.

Once Jack was gone, Guilford reached into the trashcan and retrieved the note. He then walked it over to the customer service window and flattened it out on the counter.

"I would like to have this added to our social announcements for tomorrow," he said as he pushed the note under the window divider.

Melvin, who had worked in the paper's customer service department for 35 years, was a Don Knotts lookalike and had no love for Guilford, the entitled, moody brat of the paper's owner. Melvin took the proffered paper and read it aloud. Guilford began to turn crimson again.

"You do not have to read it out loud, you moron. I know what is on it."

"You do?"

"Of course. Just put it in the paper."

"I can't."

Guilford perked up, hoping this might be a way to officially refuse Jack. "Why not?"

"Well, some guy just submitted this exact article. Except for the spelling errors on your copy, they're virtually the same."

Guilford cringed. "I did not write that note."

"OK—if you say so, but I will use the one the guy gave me since it doesn't have spelling errors. Here is yours back."

Guilford could feel his head getting hot and his vision starting to blur. He wanted to explode, but noted every eye in the room was on him, so instead he bit his lip, which drew a gush of blood, then simply grabbed the note and stomped back to his desk.

* * *

Friday afternoon came quickly, and Jack and Candy prepared for their debut at Jack's family farm.

"You ready?" Candy asked.

"Yep. Let's do it."

Jack pulled into the familiar front drive of his family's farm and parked his car by the training pen. Jack had not been home since the barn fire and could not help but reminisce about his life here as a young boy and the mother who raised him, but he still had a hill to climb, so he did not let himself be pulled too deeply into any sentimental moodiness.

Jack and Candy got out of the car and walked to the front door, but before they had made the front stoop, the door flew open.

"Butch!" the twins ran at Jack and Candy screaming.

Jack opened his arms and his sisters hit his chest, almost knocking him off his feet. The two clung to him as if he might disappear if they ever let go. He buried his face in their hair, kissing each head one after the other.

"Hey, Gina. Hey, Julie," Jack said, then eased his hug so they could fall back to the ground.

"We missed you so much," Gina said.

"Thank you for coming home," Julie added, then they both burst into tears.

"Come on, girls. You know I would never leave you."

"But you did?" Julie questioned.

"Never again," Jack reinforced.

"Promise?" they both asked in near perfect unison.

"Of course. So, how have you been? How is school? Do you have boyfriends yet?"

"We missed you. School is boring and only Gina has a boyfriend. Boys are gross, so I don't care," Julie answered for the pair.

"Don't worry, Julie. Boys will get *un-gross* soon. Especially for a pretty girl like you," Candy added.

"Thanks, Candy," Julie replied somewhat shyly.

"So, you know about mom then, right?" Gina asked with a pout.

"Yes . . . and I'm sorry I wasn't here."

"It's OK. It was bad and we didn't want to be here either," Gina added.

"Let's talk about something else," Julie suggested with some excitement in her voice. "Dad was all quiet this morning at breakfast when we came down. He was reading the paper and then tossed it in the trash on his way to the barn. Did you see the new barn? It's red, isn't it?"

"It certainly is," Jack replied. "So, what upset dad so much this morning?"

"We thought you might want to tell us yourself," Gina said with a raised eyebrow.

"Well, maybe it had to do with—"

"We know! We know!" they both screamed jumping up and down, then moving forward to hug Jack again, this time pulling Candy in with them.

"So, you're happy about it?"

"Of course we are. You got a lot of crap from people for leaving the family to fight in the war, but this will shut them up," Gina stated as if it were a well-known fact.

Jack could not believe how perceptive two 13-year-old girls could be.

"I hope you're right. So, how are our brothers and sister?"

"We don't see Rita and Arthur much anymore. Arthur moved to Detroit to work for Ford and Rita got married and moved to Denver. Bobby, Thomas and Owen are in high school. Bobby is in trouble all the time, Thomas is the quarterback just like you, Owen is a straight A student and dad is . . ."

"Angry all the time," Gina said, finishing for her sister.

"Sorry to hear that," Jack said with some concern.

"Are you staying for dinner, Butch?" Gina asked.

"I go by *Jack* now and, yes, *we* will be staying for dinner."

"Hmm," Julie said. "You will always be Butch to us, but we can call you Jack if you wish. What does Candy call you?"

"Never later for dinner," Jack said.

"That's funny," Gina laughed.

"So, let's go make dinner."

The group all went inside to start preparing Jack's welcome home dinner.

Dinner—consisting of barbequed chicken, mashed potatoes and sweet corn with an apple pie for dessert—was served at 7:00 p.m. sharp.

"No way you two did this all yourself," Bobby said as he was scooping out enough mashed potatoes to feed a small family for a week.

"And why are you not sitting in your usual seats?" Jake, the girls' father, said in his usual grumpy tone.

"That's because we did have help from some very special guests," Gina said, trying as hard as she could to fend off her father's usual foul mood.

"You can come out now," Julie called to the kitchen.

"What the—" Bobby said as his jaw dropped open.

"Butch?" Thomas called and all three boys jumped to their feet to welcome their big brother.

"Why did you leave?"

"How was the war?"

"Did you really kill a shark to save a shipmate?"

"Do you have any medals?"

Jack was glad Guilford's toxic renditions of Jack's life had not seeped too deeply into the minds of his family. He knew they had to deal with those who believed the guile Guilford was peddling, but they had remained strong and true to family—a chore which he appreciated.

"I did stab a shark in the eye to keep it away from a dying sailor, but I don't know if I killed it. And, I left because I felt I had to support my country at a time of war. I never meant for the family to suffer because I left . . ." Jack then looked directly at his father and continued, "and now that I know, I regret leaving to enlist the afternoon before the barn burned down, but I'm back now to make things right."

"How did your jacket get in the barn then?" Bobby asked, speaking through a mouthful of mashed potatoes.

"I took my jacket off earlier that day while I did some chores in the barn and must have left it there. The police know all about it and, as was printed in the paper earlier this week, I'm no longer a suspect in any of the incidents Guildford accused me of in his newspaper articles. And, Owen, I do have a Purple Heart and a pretty neat scar I can show you one day."

"Neat."

"And now I would like to tell you all why we're here tonight," Jack said as he put out his hand for Candy to stand beside him. "Candy and I are getting married."

"Really?" Thomas asked.

"Yep," Julie answered before Jack or Candy could respond.

"Yes, we are. And we're going to live in Footville for a while until we get everything figured out."

"Footville? Doesn't Footville—"

"No, Bobby, Footville doesn't smell like feet. Any other questions?" Jack asked, looking directly at his father who would not meet his gaze. "Good, then let's eat."

The next afternoon, Jack and Candy went to City Hall to get a marriage license. Gina, Julie and Thomas tagged along to serve as witnesses for the Justice of the Peace ceremony. For the most part the process was quick and painless. After it was all over, only Thomas was allowed to sign the marriage certificate since Gina and Julie were not yet 16. However, Candy promised the girls they could sign the official copy once they received it in the mail. This excited the girls, but their enthusiasm went over the top when Jack offered to buy everyone ice cream to celebrate.

Later that day, Jack and Candy returned to the house Candy was renting and officially started their life together. That night after they made love, they laid in each other's arms as Candy tenderly stroked Jack's shoulder scar with her finger tips. After Jack had drifted off to sleep, Candy whispered into his ear before shutting her eyes for the night.

"My hero."

The 1950s were spent trying to reclaim past glamour, but the war had changed the world and this subtle over-coating scarcely hid a country filled with racial discrimination, Red Scare hysteria and the fear of a potential nuclear attack. McCarthyism grew out of the post-war era, where loyalty oaths and blacklisting became common practice in the country. Lawsuits and Supreme Court rulings ultimately helped to curb and eventually halt these extreme anti-extremist practices. During this time the country experienced greater economic growth than ever before—the population boomed, construction of new interstate highways was initiated and capitalism had its golden age. The country emerged from the war as one of the two dominant superpowers in the world. And there was so much more to come that would continue to change the country.

Jack and Candy fell into a routine. At first, they enjoyed each other's company and that soon grew into a relationship that most on the outside would call a marriage. The truth was they were not in love and lightning was not likely to ever strike to change this. Jack started working in a hardware store in Footville, but when they had their second—well, really their first—child, he needed to find work that paid more than the minimum wage. He tried to get a job at the local pharmacy, but there were no positions open and he could offer no more than being a well-trained pharmacy technician since he was not able to go to college to become a pharmacist. He thought about going back—community college first, then transfer to a UW school—but he did not have the time nor the money. As luck would have it, the Oscar Mayer plant in Madison was expanding and they needed long-haul truck drivers.

Jeannie was born on August 4, 1953, a week earlier than expected. She was a healthy child with brunette hair and a little turned up button nose just like her mother. Jack, who had taken the Oscar Mayer job in June, was out of town and missed Jeannie's first five days of life; Candy never let him forget his untimely absence. Jack had planned his routes to be home for the due date, but if there was anything Jack had learned in his 23 years of life, it was that plans are just as real as dreams when life decides otherwise.

Montana

October, 1962

The 60s were a time of cultural change and discovery—a revolution in social norms and technology. This decade took America through the Cold War, the Bay of Pigs and the Cuban Missile Crisis; from the Vietnam War to the birth of the counterculture; from an LSD trip to a trip to the moon; and continued the civil rights journey started by Rosa Parks and so many others—now led by Dr. Martin Luther King Jr and so many others. The 60s are probably best known for assassinations that tore at the very foundation of America and the counterculture movement that sparked changes in clothing, music, sexuality and just about everything else. But why did this movement take hold? There were certainly indications that this cultural shift was at least a ripple in the fabric of the country, but what helped turn it into a wave?

Under the codename MK-Ultra, run by chemist Sidney Gottlieb, the CIA bought 10 kilograms—every drop on the planet—of LSD-25 from Sandoz Pharmaceutical in Switzerland over concerns the Russians would get to it first and thus discover its mind control properties before the US. Lysergic Acid Diethylamide, or LSD, is synthesized from ergot fungus, which over the centuries has caused thousands of deaths through food contamination and has been attributed to countless events, big and small, such as the Salem Witch Trials in America and the Dancing Plague in Germany. When taken in a small enough dose, LSD and ergot are psychedelic drugs which can cause changes in perception ranging from intense euphoria to extreme dysphoria. However, when taken at a higher dose, the symptoms, also referred to as *St. Anthony's Fire*, can include seizures and death.

During the 1950s and 60s, the CIA experimented with LSD and other agents to see if they could control a subject's mind. The idea was to clear the mind with LSD and then replace it with a mind that could be manipulated. At first, subjects had full knowledge of the experiments. Many of these willing volunteers found the experience so pleasurable that they told their friends about it. People like Ken Kesey, author of *One Flew Over the Cuckoo's Nest*; Robert Hunter, the lyricist for the Grateful Dead; and the poet Allen Ginsberg, all got their first LSD trip from MK-Ultra. The organized crime boss, Whitey Bulger, volunteered as a prisoner for what he thought was an experiment to find a cure for schizophrenia, but was none other than an MK-Ultra experiment. Soon, experiments were happening all over the globe, from the Philippines to Europe as well as at home in America. LSD was used in many CIA interrogations during this time and there was also a sub-operation—Operation Midnight Climax—that filmed Johns as they were unknowingly given an LSD-laced martini by their ladies of the evening.

Numerous deaths occurred—some possibly intentional—but the full extent of the operation is hard to fathom since many of the records were purposely destroyed when MK-Ultra ultimately closed shop or went further underground. In the end, the LSD experiments led to nothing the CIA could usefully wield as a mind control weapon. However, while MK-Ultra did well to hide its own existence from the public, it could not hide LSD from the world; like a giant game of hippie telephone, word of mouth spread and LSD soon became a choice drug of the counterculture. The acid tri p was most loudly supported by Dr. Timothy Leary, a Harvard researcher, when he told America to "Turn on, tune in, drop out."

Jack was on a long-haul trip to one of Oscar Mayer's newly opened distribution centers. Vacuum packing and preservatives had extended the freshness date to such an extent that Oscar Mayer's reach was well beyond what was possible just a decade before. The Oscar Mayer Empire now produced over 200 varieties of meat products and Jack was busier than ever moving their sausage across America.

Back home things were rocky at best. Candy had started drinking more and was withdrawn or aloof whenever Jack was home. This caused Jack to want to drive more and be at home less. He used to plan a trip out and back followed by several days at home, but now he took several trips hauling loads back-to-back before finally returning home. It was during one of these trips out west that he planned to visit Joker.

Joker lived near Zig-Zag Lake in Montana. Zig-Zag Lake was not on the map and was named after Zig-Zag Road, which was not the actual name of the road, but the pattern of the road—the confusion was intended. US Highway 2—which travels 666.6 miles through northern Montana—has a seldom-used turn-off between Summit and Snowslip which was the gateway—as Jack would soon learn—to more than Joker's cabin. Joker had friends in both towns who were on alert for anyone who might be asking around about a Darcy Lawson or Joker from the Navy. Some would call these precautions overly cautious or even paranoid, but Joker claimed he was just being thorough; Joker had functional paranoia.

Joker told Jack he would need to drop his 18-wheeler at the Bear Creek Trading Post and have Lucile give him a ride to the lake. He should then wait at the pier. It was near dusk when Jack arrived at the pier and there was no one in sight. He sat down hard on a very weathered picnic table bench underneath a small shelter and waited.

"What have I gotten myself into here?" Jack asked himself aloud.

"Well, if I had to calculate it out for you, you're about to have the time of your life."

Jack turned, but saw no one. "Joker?"

Joker stepped forward into the light of the park shelter.

"Let's get going before it gets so dark you can't see your hand. They don't call this Big Sky Country for nothin'," Joker said as he walked over to give Jack a big bear hug.

"Do you live on this lake?"

"Nope, my cabin is up the river overlooking a small feeder pond. This is way too exposed for me."

Jack looked around the smallish lake with no homes or people in sight and wondered how someone could feel exposed in such a remote area.

Joker pulled his jeep up to a true log cabin. The cabin was set on a hill overlooking a large pond and was well hidden by a vast canopy of trees. Jack grabbed his bag from the back of the jeep and followed Joker through the front door. As Jack crossed the threshold, he immediately felt out of place. It was not because he was uncomfortable in a remote cabin, but rather because the remote cabin was only remote on the outside. The inside of the cabin was as modern a home as Jack had ever seen. The cabin had smooth walls with modern fixtures, furniture and appliances.

"I don't know what to say. I was expecting deer heads and a dirt floor," Jack said with some dismay.

"I know. It's all for looks. You can't even see in the windows from the outside, but take a look at this," Joker said as he walked to the huge bay window at the back of the main room.

"Wow. It's beautiful," Jack said as he took in the downhill view of the pond. "What is that little house down there?"

"I call that my guest house. It's actually just a storage shed to rest in when I'm fishing, but it does have its own outhouse."

"Nice—I guess."

"So, tequila or gin?"

"Tequila," Jack said without hesitation.

Joker went to a nearby bar that was filled with glass bottles full of every kind of alcohol you could imagine and returned with two glasses and a bottle of tequila.

"Pull up a chair, my friend," Joker said, then poured Jack a glassful of tequila.

The friends drank and talked deep into the night, finally passing out after 3:00 a.m. The next morning came much too early and Jack found the subtle sounds of nature coming from outside the cabin penetrating his skull like angry woodpeckers. Only the smell of coffee made him finally open his eyes.

"Morning, Sunshine," Joker said mockingly.

"Err," was all Jack could get out.

"Come on and get some breakfast—well, brunch at this point—so we can get out and enjoy this day."

Suddenly the smell of bacon permeated Jack's senses and his world started to come back into focus.

"I'll come eat if you promise to shoot the woodpecker making all that racket outside," Jack said as he struggled to free himself from the couch.

"Jack, there's no woodpecker outside. I only hear birds chirping and a hawk cry."

"Oh, God, I'm so glad I'm not in the city right now."

"You and me both," Joker said as he slid an omelet the size of a baseball glove and six strips of bacon onto Jack's plate.

Jack looked up at Joker through bloodshot eyes and said, "Trying to kill me?"

"Just trying to beef you up for our hike this afternoon."

"Hmm."

"Come on—eat!"

"OK. OK."

Within the hour Joker had Jack hiking through the woods of northern Montana, talking about their lives after the Navy.

"So, I hear you have two kids now," Joker said.

"Yes. Joey is 17 and a handful. I wasn't at home when I was 17, so it's hard to know if he's normal or worse than I would've been."

"Hard to say."

"And, Jeannie is nine and cute as a button. Totally takes after her mother. I guess being a princess is hereditary."

Joker laughed, then asked, "How are you and Candy doing? I know it's not ideal, but if you had another child, then you must at least be getting along," Joker asked as he ducked under a low-hanging branch.

Jack followed suit, then said, "We're . . . OK, but no better. We get along best when I'm on the road and not so much if I stay home for too long. Now that I'm making good money, we can afford the better vodka which makes her happy since, unfortunately, it is easier to drink."

"Sorry to hear that."

"It is what it is. Life just does what it wants and you hang on for the ride."

"I may have a remedy for that."

"For life?" Jack laughed.

"Well, at least a break from all the bullshit," Joker added.

"Sign me up."

"Let's head back and we can talk about it then. So, do you ever think of the *Indy*?" Joker asked, changing to a more somber tone.

"All the time, but I try to concentrate on the good times we had rather than the obvious. I have become so good at it that I can remember almost every day in Boot Camp and on the *Indy* before the sinking. I just don't let my mind go there, so I've actually forgotten much of the time in the water and even some of my four years in the Navy afterwards."

"You ever have nightmares?"

"Sure. I'm sure we all do. But I try not to let it get inside my head, to direct my thoughts and emotions. I have this feeling that if I let it take hold of me, I'll become my father—bitter and emotionally distant."

"Does it work? Can you do it?" Joker asked sincerely.

"Most of the time. Why? Are you having trouble?"

"No, not me. Sharks, lions, tigers and bears are all out to get us all. I just keep learning to keep living, but if I do have troubles, I just take this new drug to help me get away and reset."

"Do tell me more."

"We can talk about it when we get back to the cabin. Sad thing about Marilyn, huh," Joker said, awkwardly changing the subject.

"Yes. What a waste. You know she died on my little girl's 9th birthday," Jack responded.

"So, who do you think killed her?"

"I thought it was a suicide or an accident."

"That's what they want you to think. It's all about mind control these days."

"If you say so," Jack said, not wanting to follow Joker into another conspiracy wormhole.

Back at the cabin Joker turned on the radio and Elvis' "Girls! Girls! Girls!" broke the silence. "I'm just a red-blooded boy and I can't stop thinking about girls, girls, girls," Joker sang over the radio.

"I think you're in the wrong key—well, several wrong keys," Jack added with a chuckle.

"It's not about the notes. It's about the joy . . . and the girls of course," Joker said as he turned up the volume. "Elvis is like a James Dean that can sing and even more popular. Did you hear they stopped playing his movies in Mexico after there was a near-riot at a showing of *GI Blues*? It just happened a week ago."

"No, I didn't hear that," Jack replied, then added, "How do you stay so informed out here in the middle of nowhere?"

"I got a pipeline. Don't you worry about me. I'm hooked into the pulse."

Jack smiled, wondering, *The pulse of what?* then sat in a chair to rest and look out the window while he enjoyed the music. Outside a hawk circled high in the sky above the pond, then in the blink of an eye fell from the sky like a meteor, only to swoop at the grass along the edge of the pond at the last possible moment. When the hawk returned to a nearby tree with a frog in its talons, Jack thought, *If only my life were that easy*, then laughed at himself since watching a hawk for three minutes did not relay the whole of its life and struggles. Not wanting to fill his head with images of frog guts being stretched like red ribbons from the deceased amphibian, Jack looked down at the coffee table and grabbed a *Life* magazine. He flipped through the huge pages and stopped to peruse a story about Howard Hughes while he waited for Joker to return to the living room. Soon after, Joker came in from the kitchen with several baked potato skins smothered in cheese, sour cream and bacon.

"So, you ready to relax a bit?" Joker asked through a mouthful of potato.

"You know, Joker, I'm pretty sure vitamin B doesn't stand for *bacon*. Is that all you eat out here?"

"What are you, some kind of commie who doesn't like bacon?" Joker said in response, then immediately followed with, "Sorry, man. I didn't mean that. I shouldn't even joke like that."

"Don't worry. I'm no more a commie than you and I don't think anyone is close enough to overhear us out here even if we yelled from the rooftop," Jack responded as Joker returned to the kitchen.

"Sure. Yeah. Thanks. Have a potato skin and then we can talk about this," Joker said as he walked up to the coffee table and set down a silver tray containing a tiny tea set.

Jack picked up a stuffed potato skin and ate half of it in one bite.

"We going to have tea now?" Jack asked half-mockingly, then added, "Don't we need some dolls if the tea cups are that small?"

"You may joke now, but you will be laughing later."

"You usually have better retorts . . . and retorts that actually make sense. Are you feeling OK?"

"It will all become clear with time. As for the tiny tea set, it's my homage to *Alice in Wonderland*. We're going to drink a tiny bit of tea and open up a world of possibilities," Joker said, then poured tea into two of the cups.

Jack reached for one of the cups, but Joker waved him off.

"Not yet, my friend."

Joker then opened a small carved box that Jack had not

seen earlier and pulled out a sugar cube with a tweezer.

"If you say so," Jack said, then sat back to let Joker continue his ritual.

"Here you go. Sit back, drink up and let yourself be free."

"No tequila tonight?" Jack joked.

"You will not need the evil worm this night, my friend."

Jack thought Joker was sounding a little too poetic even for Joker, but he let it slide. He was exhausted after a day of fresh mountain air, so he gave in and just lay back in his chair with his eyes closed. He had been high plenty of times before and from what he could tell, this stuff was a dud as he only felt a bit lightheaded before falling into a deep sleep.

Jack awoke to a knock on the cabin door. Joker was out cold on the couch, one arm over the back and a leg on the floor. Jack opened the door to find Lucile bundled in a coat like she was in the middle of a winter storm.

"Hi, Jack. You seem smaller than I remember."

"Really?" Jack answered with more humor than annoyance.

"Well, anyway . . . I was wondering, could I borrow you or your truck for the night? We have kind of a situation down at the trading post that we need to remedy before the storm hits."

Jack tilted his head a bit to look out the door at the sky which was a bit gray and seemed to be swirling.

"Sure, just let me leave a note for Joker."

"Oh, don't worry. He'll know where you are."

Jack thought that to be a bit presumptuous, but did not see any paper near the door, so he grabbed his coat and followed Lucile to her jeep.

"We get a lot of storms up here in Montana," Lucile

said, trying to make small talk. "They come over the mountains and swallow us whole or just disappear like a good mood."

"Really," was all Jack could mumble in response.

"Yeah, half the time I want to cut off the damn weatherman's head. Wish I had a job where I could just make believe I knew what I was doing. I could just sit around and make up impossible things even before breakfast and then take the rest of the day at tea."

"I bet you would do a better job by just guessing," Jack said, thinking he should participate in the small talk rather than just sit back and mumble. "So, why do you need my truck again?" Jack asked, changing the subject back to the original theme since he was in fact, wondering why she needed his truck.

"We need to get some supplies to The Comp—to some campers before the storm hits."

Jack took another Pavlovian look outside, tilting his head again so he could see the sky. Black strands of mist twisted into the gray billowing clouds as they circled above.

At the trading post, Lucile introduced Jack to Mr. Lewis.

"Mr. Lewis drives the truck that makes deliveries to the . . . campsite, but the truck doesn't want to start tonight—stubborn as a mule she is."

"Nice to meet you, Jack. Is Jack short for anything or is that your name?" Mr. Lewis asked.

"No, just Jack," Jack said, then half-expected Mr. Lewis to call him *Just Jack*.

"Ok, Jack, we need to load this into your truck and get it up the mountain to the camp," Mr. Lewis said as he threw back the flap that covered the rear of his delivery truck.

Now it was Jack's turn to be the one to comment on the storm. He looked up and saw black and silver clouds undulating over their heads.

"It kind of looks like we may have already missed the window."

"Oh, don't you pay no mind to the weather. That weatherman don't know a cloud from a splash in the face."

Jack looked at Mr. Lewis for a response to Lucile's claim and he said, "Yep, we should be fine if we get going now and don't delay."

Jack followed Mr. Lewis to his truck and they used a dolly to move the bigger boxes first, then loaded the smaller ones by hand.

Jack swung the back doors of his semi closed and locked the latch.

"We're ready. So, where are we going?"

"We need to travel along Skyland Road just like we're going to Joker's house, but we're not turning off onto Zig-Zag Road. Instead, we're staying on Skyland until we're on the backside between Square Mountain and Slippery Bill Mountain. That's where the campsite is—about six miles down Skyland Road.

"Sounds kind of secluded," Jack said as they all climbed into the cab.

"Nope. Anyone can take Skyland Road. This is a free country after all," Lucile answered as if reading off a script.

Jack was puzzled by her response as he turned onto Skyland Road—apparently like any free American could—and eventually drove past the zig-zag turnoff on their way to the back side of Square Mountain.

The south side of Square Mountain was awash in past landslides, making it look a bit more like Mount Baldy than the stronger name suggested. However, the valley between Square and Slippery Bill was something to talk about. The land was lush with trees and meadows, and it even had a creek running along the road. About a half mile up the valley there was a turnoff clearly marked as a dead end.

"Take this one here," Lucile said, pointing with her left hand from the passenger's seat.

Jack took the turn and found he was on another zig-zagging road. Zig-zagging roads were clearly common in this mountainous country when climbing to higher altitudes, but this—and Joker's turnoff for that fact—seemed not to require such a back-and-forth design for the slight incline he was experiencing. He took the first cut back, then continued until he saw a clearing with a rocky tire-worn surface.

"This is it here," Lucile said, pointing again.

Jack pulled the truck into a big turn and aimed it back down the road from where he had come.

"This good?" Jack asked.

"Perfect," Mr. Lewis answered before Lucile could criticize Jack's maneuver.

"Yes, just fine," Lucile muttered in a monotone.

After the two exited the truck, Mr. Lewis came round to the driver's side window to speak to Jack.

"So, you wait here in the truck and we will radio the group to send some all-terrain vehicles down to pick up the supplies."

"You got it, Mr. Lewis. This is me staying put," Jack replied, then kicked his feet up onto the seat and leaned against the door.

"Thank you, Jack. We shouldn't be long."

Lucile and Mr. Lewis walked to the front of the truck and disappeared behind Jack. Jack grabbed a toothpick out of a little box on his dash and stuck it in his mouth. This was a typical trick for truckers to concentrate on chewing and flipping a toothpick in their mouth to pass the time.

Jack took up the practice after meeting a trucker who soaked his toothpicks in cinnamon oil, making the act more of a treat than a chore. Jack was leaning in to grab his second toothpick when he chanced a glance over his shoulder and saw Lucile and Mr. Lewis still waiting at the elbow in the road speaking into a large walkie-talkie. Lucile grabbed the talkie out of Mr. Lewis' hand and slapped the side of it hard; the antenna swayed back and forth for several seconds as it recovered from the violent hit. They were obviously having issues with communications and seemed to be discussing their options when Lucile just took off walking. Mr. Lewis fell in line behind her and the two were soon out of sight.

Jack took a moment to chuckle to himself and then resumed his toothpick mouth gymnastics until he saw a flash of white in his peripheral vision. He looked up to see a sight that he needed to rub his eyes to believe. It was a huge white bear.

"A polar bear?" Jack said aloud to himself.

Jack quickly shifted in his seat and watched the bear walk across the rocky clearing and take the same road Lucile and Mr. Lewis had just walked down.

"Shit!" Jack shouted in the cab of his truck.

The bear stopped in the road and took a moment to look back at the truck, then, seemingly uninterested, continued down the road.

I've got to warn them, Jack thought as he grabbed the door handle and jumped from the truck.

He immediately ran into the trees alongside the rocky road and tried to stay hidden from the bear as he quickly moved forward, hoping to catch up to Lucile and Mr. Lewis. Luckily, he was downwind which enabled him to move more quickly since the bear would not be aware of his scent. Finally catching up to the pair, he started to move from the hilly tree line toward them, but stopped when he saw the bear approaching from the rear. The bear also stopped, then stood on his back legs as if getting a better view of the pair in the road. Jack could see the bear's nose curl and twitch as if it were sniffing the air for the scent of the pair in front of him. Jack stood motionless taking this all in when the bear bounced back onto all fours and abruptly raced down the road toward Lucile and Mr. Lewis. Jack, fearing for their lives, decided he needed to do something and do something fast. Without really thinking, Jack screamed and clapped his hands trying to get the bear's attention. He saw the bear slow, and Lucile and Mr. Lewis turn to see both him and the bear, then the bear suddenly darted up the incline toward Jack.

Jack nearly shit his pants as he now was at a loss of what to do. He had saved Lucile and Mr. Lewis for the moment, but what was he going to do to keep the bear from devouring *him*? Jack turned and ran for the trees dodging between branches and bushes as he looked for someplace to hide or climb. Then he remembered, *bears can climb too*, so now he was just trying to outpace the bear. He chanced a glance behind him to gauge the distance and could sense the bear was making ground. *Of course he is. We are on his home field after all,* Jack thought as he huffed up the hill and through the trees. Jack looked forward and saw an unbroken row of thick bushes. He quickly looked for a spot that might give him entry into the hedge and dove head first into the greenery, praying he would make it through. He fought for what seemed like several feet before emerging on the other side. He was breathing hard and wanted to stop and rest, but a rustling bulge of hedge directly behind him made him turn and run.

He made it about three strides before he tripped and

fell forward. When he landed, he bounced off the ground like it was a trampoline and then flew through the air onto his back, slamming his head into the ground. Everything went black. As his vision slowly returned, everything looked as if he were peering through a pair of binoculars. He saw the big bright sky speckled with clouds and the sun dancing behind those clouds, then he saw a nose and whiskers appear over his forehead. He was still stunned enough that he could not move nor react, so when he saw the mouth open to reveal sharp white teeth that looked even more deadly through binoculars, all he could do was close his eyes. When he did not feel the expected pain of having his skull crushed in the giant jaws of a polar bear, he chanced another peek and saw the drooling jaws paused just above his face.

Maybe he thinks I'm dead. I heard that's what you're supposed to do—act dead.

Once again Jack squeezed his eyes shut to fully exploit the ruse, but then felt a thick, scratchy tongue begin to lick his forehead, followed by Mr. Lewis' voice calling from somewhere further down the tunnel.

"Rabbit! Get off him."

Then Jack passed out for good.

Jack awoke inside a hospital room, complete with bright lights, stainless steel fixtures and taupe paint.

"Hello? Anyone here?" Jack called.

"Just a minute, sir."

Jack waited the minute and as promised a red-headed girl stepped into his room and walked over to his bed.

"Well, it appears Mister Sleepyhead is finally getting up. I'm Jenny. I was your nurse for the night. Enjoy my company because nurse Florence is on the evening shift and she ain't no Nightingale—if you know what I mean."

Jack thought this was a strange introduction, but went with it anyway.

"So, what hospital is this?"

"Oh, this ain't no hospital. This is the medical wing for The Compound."

"Which compound?"

"*The* Compound, honey. Don't be silly."

"So, I see our patient is alive. That is good for our numbers. Good morning, I am Doctor Lorac. Let me put this out."

Dr. Lorac took one last puff of his cigarette and snuffed it out in an ashtray that was quickly whisked away to be cleaned by Jenny. Dr. Lorac then reached out his hand and Jack shook it, still wondering where he was.

"So, Jenny told me that I'm in The Compound, but that doesn't really give me any clue where I actually am."

"Did she now. Well, you are in our excellent care. What more do you really need to know? So, your chart says you are 6'1" and 175 pounds."

"In reality, I'm a bit bigger than that and two inches taller as well."

"I'm sure you are. So, I also see a large contusion to the back of your head and signs of a concussion. Is that true?"

"Aren't you the doctor?"

"I am. Yes, I am. And who are you and why are you here?"

"I think you just told me? Didn't you?"

"Yes, indeed. Just testing your concussion symptoms. So, can you stand?"

"I believe so," Jack said, then swung his legs around and placed them on the floor.

"Now, take it slow. You should stand and count to ten before taking a step. Being in a hospital bed is like taking too many tequila shots . . . 1 . . . 2 . . . 3 . . . floor," he said and motioned taking shots with each number.

Jack stood, counted a quick ten and then stepped out into the room. He walked over to the sink and looked in the mirror. He looked like the Sheik of Paleville with a large head bandage wrapped around his head and his face nearly as white as the bandage.

"So, can I walk around now?"

"I don't see why not. Just wait until we check with Mr. Lewis."

Just then the nurse returned with a totally different ashtray and placed it near the sink. Jack seemed to sense the nurse was different as well, but could not put a finger on it.

"I can show him around if you want," she said.

"Didn't you have red hair before?" he asked, half-guessing.

"Must be your head injury. The mind can be a tricky thing—especially when you slam it into a rock," Dr. Lorac said, then excused himself to go look for Mr. Lewis.

"Don't you love Dr. Lorac? He's a pillar of The Compound medical staff. I don't know where or who we would be without him. Certainly not who we are now. Good morning, I'm Ginny, Jenny's twin sister."

Jack looked at her and exclaimed, "So, I'm not crazy!"

"Yes, he was just joking with you. Then again that wasn't the crazy test, so I wouldn't get too over confident," Ginny said, then gave him a wink.

"Let's go to the cafeteria. That's always a great place to see the compoundists or the compoundies."

"Compoundists?"

"Yes, the people of The Compound. That's why we don't call this a commune, silly."

Ginny then took off walking and Jack had to hustle to keep up; each step sent lancing pain into his head and caused his eyes to flash with light. *Maybe staying in bed was a better choice*, he thought between jolts.

Once at the cafeteria, Jack saw several groups of compoundists finishing breakfast. Just then there was a flourish of activity behind him as a large entourage stepped into the cafeteria entryway beside Jack and Ginny. Jack looked over to see men in suits and white jackets, and women in fancy dresses and uniforms all surrounding a single man dressed in a leather jacket and blue jeans.

"Is that who I think it is?" Jack whispered to Ginny.

"Yep. I heard he was visiting today. Most of the big ones do—in case they ever need us."

"What is this place—a famous people retirement home?"

"Nope. It's The Compound."

Jack was about to say something sarcastic since this was the only answer he seemed to be getting from anyone, but then Ginny continued.

"It's the last stop . . . the last hope for people who are being chased by the devil."

Jack looked at her oddly, but could sense she had let her guard down and was now speaking somewhat frankly.

"Who else is here?" he asked.

She looked up as if pulled from a trance and said, "Oh, I'm not sure I'm supposed to tell you."

"But Jenny told me a bunch already. All about the history and how it was built," Jack said, lying through his teeth to try to get more information out of Ginny.

"Oh! Well, that's Marilyn's table over there. She came to us a couple of months back. Terrible how she was treated, but she will be safe here. Safe from the evil that was after her. Safe for the rest of her life. And that guy over by the ice cream machine . . . that's James Dean. Do you want to meet him? He's super nice. He was a bit angry when he first came, so I'm told since I was in high school back then, but he has mellowed and is my favorite compoundist to talk with now. Do you want me to introduce you?"

"To James Dean?"

"Yes, of course. Just don't say anything silly, like you liked him in *Giant* since he has done a lot to get away from his past life and didn't plan to have to stay here the whole time."

"OK?"

"Mr. Dean?"

A young man turned with an ice cream cone in his hand and said, "Please. My father is Mr. Dean. I'm James and you know it, Ginny."

Ginny blushed a bit, then turned to introduce Jack, forgetting his name in the process.

"This is um . . . he had an accident and I'm helping him get better."

"Nice to meet you, Um. How long have you been here?" James asked.

"Nice to meet you as well. It's Jack—just visiting. I was delivering supplies when I ran into a polar bear." This sounded a bit funny when he said it aloud, so he added, "I think."

"Oh, you must be talking about Rabbit, the albino bear owned by Mr. Hughes. He's the owner of this place. He's harmless unless you've got honey on you—then he might just lick you to death. I'm talking about Rabbit of course, not Mr. Hughes, for the honey part at least. I'm not even sure if Mr. Hughes likes honey."

Jack, glad to have part of his trauma validated as not totally insane, looked at Ginny who looked a bit upset.

"Something wrong, Ginny?" James asked before Jack could get the words out of his mouth.

"Oh, I think I've made a big mistake. I'll be right back," she said, then ran off.

"Speaking of licking, I would really like to get some ice cream if you two darlings would move over just a bit. But not too far."

"Hey, Marilyn. This is Jack Just Visiting."

"So, Jack, would a big strong man such as yourself like to fill my cone . . . for me?"

Jack swallowed hard, then managed to get a reply out of his mouth without sounding like a teenager at his first dance.

"It would be my pleasure, Ms. Monroe."

"So perceptive of you—knowing I was a single woman when I . . . disappeared," she said, saying the last word as a whisper in Jack's ear. "Please, call me Marilyn."

Jack smiled and filled a cone for Marilyn.

"Here you go, Marilyn," Jack said, holding up the newly filled cone.

Marilyn took the cone, making sure to touch Jack's hand in the process, then said, "Well, I'm off now. I have a pottery class. Going to throw some clay and see what sticks." She then stepped closer to Jack and said, "I sure hope to see you around, honey. I'll be thinking . . ." she paused to take a big lick of her ice cream cone and then continued. ". . . of you."

"Fun times, huh?" James said, then extended his hand. "Nice to meet you, Jack. Maybe we'll see you around before you get better."

"Thanks, and the honor was mine."

Jack watched as James walked away and wondered what he should do next. Then it became obvious—he was hungry. However, at the moment nothing was being served, so ice cream would have to be his sustenance. He topped off another cone and decided to take a walk to get a better feel for this place they called The Compound. Even after his first impression, which had led to a concussion, this place seemed more like Neverland than a camp in the hills of Montana.

Jack walked back out the cafeteria entrance and turned away from the medical wing to see a new part of the building. He passed elevators with numbers that were descending rather than ascending. There were eight floors in all. At the end of the hall, he walked into a huge great room with a vaulted timber ceiling—filled with stuffed leather chairs, couches, tables and a coffee shop—that easily covered an acre or more. From the entryway, he could see rooms off the giant room in each direction, including a bar, a dance floor, a bowling alley and a game room for cards. He also saw light streaming in from windows and doors directly across the floor from where he stood, so he made his way toward the light, licking his melting ice cream cone as he went.

Once at what he assumed were the front doors, he walked out into the light of the day and found he was under a vast semitransparent sheet of material that seemed to cover the entire compound; stretched taut and suspended on giant poles. Behind him, he could see acres of lawn with three golf holes, hills for dirt bikes, tennis and basketball courts and more.

Hmm, that covering must be what I bounced off so elegantly the other day. This is a strange place.

Just then Mr. Lewis walked up to Jack and said, "I hear you have recovered."

"I'm guessing I am since I can walk without my head threatening to explode and I'm getting hungry."

"Good to hear. We should get going then. It's been over a day since you left and I'm certain Joker may be getting impatient."

"Yes, seems likely if he didn't know where I went," Jack said, feeling good enough to throw a barb at Mr. Lewis, even though he was not the one who insisted on leaving before Jack could leave a message for Joker.

"Well, the storm last night really shut things down around here. We would have had to stay the night anyway. You're lucky—you slept right through it."

Jack felt like a concussion-induced 24-hour nap was not entirely lucky and wondered what the storm had been like if he was so fortunate to have missed it.

Jack, Lucile and Mr. Lewis all exited Jack's cab. Lucile handed Jack a prescription bottle from Dr. Lorac before quickly walking to her jeep.

"Remember to feed your head," Lucile said through her jeep window before she drove off, leaving them at the trading post.

Jack looked to Mr. Lewis, expecting some more words of wisdom, but none came.

"Lucile sure is a strange bird," Jack finally said, half to Mr. Lewis and half to himself.

"Lucile is not a bird," Mr. Lewis stated plainly.

"No, I guess she's not."

Mr. Lewis dropped Jack off back at Joker's cabin just before dinnertime and Jack could smell meat cooking on the outdoor grill.

"Glad you're back, buddy. Let's eat."

The rest of the night consisted of Jack and Joker eating elk meat with baked potatoes and drinking more tequila.

The next morning, Jack awoke naked on the bathroom floor with a knot on the back of his head the size of Rhode Island. He found he was laying in water, then looked above him and saw the source: a small trickle of water was running over the edge of the sink. Once he stood, he saw that the sink was full and overflowing. *Hmm, maybe I slipped while I was washing up*, he thought, then climbed into the shower as he likely intended when he entered the room the night before.

Refreshed, Jack came back into the living room and found Joker, still laid out on the couch—one arm over the back and a leg on the floor.

"Hey, Joker, I gotta get back."

"What?" Joker said, then realized what was happening. "But it's barely been two days."

"Joker, it's Monday. I need to go. Thank you for a great time. We will have to do this again," Jack said, understanding so many friends said these same words knowing very well they would likely never see each other again. But Jack wanted his friendship with Joker to be different and felt these words were true.

Jack stopped at the Bear Creek Trading Post on his way out of town to buy a paper. Lucile's daughter, Ingrid, was at the counter and took Jack's money.

"Hey, please tell your mom thanks again for the ride on Friday and I hope you all have a great holiday season."

"I sure will. Happy holidays to you too, mister."

Jack sat back in his truck and pulled open the paper, only then noting it was the Sunday edition. He sighed and said aloud, "Boy, I can't wait to get back to civilization where tomorrow is not today and today is not yesterday."

Elvis

August 16, 1977

Jack reacted to the news of Guilford Gromley's death differently than he expected. He was not elated by the taste of final revenge, but more dulled as if he had been running a marathon and it was finally over. It had been 28 years since he had dropped his marriage announcement on Guilford's desk and he had tried hard to drive Guilford and all the damage he had caused while Jack was away at war out of his mind. In all he was mostly unmoved at Guilford's early departure—dying before his 50th birthday. Guilford had been broken by what Candy had done to him and time had not been kind to him after that, but mostly it was the alcohol. Jack understood he shared a distant kinship with Guilford due to Candy's betrayals, but it ended there.

Wow, I've been married to Candy for 28 years, he thought.

He could honestly say the first decade or so was not unbearable, but the last 15 years had changed him. Ever since he returned from Joker's cabin, something felt off. He felt as if he was not seeing the whole picture anymore and it was slowly driving him mad. To that point he had perfected thought misdirection to avoid thinking about and thus reliving his time in the water, or Guilford's deceits to him and the public, or Candy's initial betrayal. He had to say *initial* now because when he returned from visiting Joker, he emptied an ashtray full of cigarette butts to find only half had lipstick on the filter. Now this was not enough to send her to the chair, but it was an indication that her loving demeanor when he was away and her indifference when he was home might be best explained by her not remaining totally faithful.

Jack knew he was partially to blame. In truth, they had remained in the marriage to raise their daughter, Jeannie. However, their marriage was further complicated when Candy became pregnant for a third time and eventually gave birth to their son, John, when Jeannie was 15 and already in high school. It was as if a giant escape portal was opening up as Jeannie got closer to graduating and then just slammed shut when Jack got the news of Candy's pregnancy. The sad thing was that he had tried to be a good father to Jeannie, and Joey before her, even though he was often away traveling around the map, but now he had to do this all over again for a child he was not even certain was his. The year was 1968 and as America continued to be shaped by assassinations and civil unrest, Jack felt his reality was finally floating away and would never be rescued.

Jack knew he had changed over the last 15 years. He did not feel his life was any worse than anyone else's, but now he could no longer stop his past from haunting him. At times he could not sleep at night due to recurring nightmares. He soon discovered Jack Daniels was a good partner to help him work things out. The issue was, you did not know how much you could drink until you had too much on at least one occasion. Frequent experimentation led him to understand there were four levels to his intoxication. The first level was relief from the day-to-day drama that encircled his life—again, really no different than your average bloke. The second level was a deeper understanding of the world and the ability to talk about the war. This is what Jack yearned for and made him a centerpiece of any bar he visited. He was considered by most to be a local war hero and thus enjoyed some level of celebrity, which occasionally included free drinks or at least people to talk with while he drank. However, the third level—which he had to travel through to get to the promised land of eventually passing out and earning the sweet reward of at least a few hours of unbroken, unblemished sleep—opened his mind even more and this is when he got into trouble. This was when he would gab endlessly about his time in Montana meeting James Dean, Marilyn Monroe, Elvis and Howard Hughes' albino bear. He repeated this story frequently when at level three intoxication and it soon became a game for the locals to get Jack drunk enough to tell his fairytale. No one at the bar believed these stories, but rumors spread and those who heard the story from others outside the bar had a different take on the story's authenticity. Of course, there were two camps for the outsiders: those who believed the story and rationalized some kind of government cover-up or conspiracy and those who thought Jack was just bat-shit crazy. Neither camp helped Jack's public persona and eventually they both breathed new life into the old rumors that Guilford had started so many years ago.

After years of fighting back to maintain some control of his life, Jack was now lost more than ever. The only bright light in his journey over the last nine years was his son, John. It was John's birthday today and Jack planned to take him to the batting cages after school to work on his swing. Jack had done well enough in life with his broken-up shoulder from the war and was able to teach his son to throw, catch and even swing the bat, but pitching overhand in any consistent manner was out of the question, so the batting cages were the answer. Jack decided to bide his time at his favorite watering hole while he waited for school to let out. This is when Jack saw the obituary for Guilford. Jack finished his drink and was walking to the door when two patrons entered the bar.

"Hey, Jack, you hear about Elvis? Died in the bathroom.

Sounds like he's on his way to Wyoming to that special place in the mountains."

"It's Montana, you dumbass. How many times does he have to tell that story for you to remember it?"

"Give me a break. I'm too drunk when he's telling it to remember much of anything. What are you doing? Taking notes like a schoolboy?" the bigger man said, then shoved the other.

"Nope. I can just remember stuff. Don't have to write down my phone number or nothing."

"Why—" the bigger man said, reaching for the other.

"Nope. Not going to happen," the smaller man said as he swatted the bigger man's hand away. "Just get us some beers while I hit the can. Have a nice afternoon, Jack."

"Yeah—bye, Jack. Say hey to Elvis."

"You still don't understand the story, do you?"

"What?"

Jack stepped out into the afternoon light and stumbled a bit, but it was not the drink—it was the birthdays. Marilyn Monroe died on Jeannie's ninth birthday and now Elvis died on John's. He was not a superstitious man, but something was at work here and he did not like this feeling of not being in control. He ached for another drink which over the last decade had given him some semblance of control, but knew better. One, he needed to pick up his son and take him to the batting cages; and two, he was not in the mood to go back into the bar and be ridiculed over an experience that was so real in his mind that it had caused him to question reality as he searched for the meaning of it all over the last 15 years.

Jack pulled up to the school at 4:25 p.m. as planned, but not a soul was around. He parked his truck next to the gym entrance and after finding the main doors locked, finally entered through an open door on the side of the building.

Inside he still saw no one until he walked down the stairs to the boys' locker room, where he found a janitor mopping the shower floor.

"This is almost a dream job. No pubes in the drains. No zits on the mirrors. No attitudes. Thank God, we got out of that high school when we did—damn pubes everywhere, even in my dreams."

"Excuse me," Jack called, interrupting the janitor's monologue.

"Yep. What can I help you with?" the man asked, still sweeping his mop from side to side.

"I was wondering where everyone was. I was supposed to pick up my son after an after-school activity today, but I don't see anyone around."

"There's no one to see. Everybody went home when we got the news."

"What news was that?" Jack asked, sensing he might have missed something important.

The man stopped mopping and turned to look at Jack, leaning slightly on the mop handle that he held next to his ear as if he were listening to it whisper to him.

"You didn't hear? Elvis is dead."

"I didn't think the kids really listened to Elvis these days."

"It's not for the kids. It's for the teachers. Some were so broke up they couldn't stop crying."

"Sorry to hear that."

"Yep. Everyone went home on the bus today. Not even a mouse left."

"Thanks for your time."

"Makes no difference to us—our chores ain't goin' nowhere. Right, Bessy?"

Jack had already turned to leave, so he did not hear the janitor refer to his mop as *Bessy*.

Jack needed to decide what to do and as much as he wanted a drink to hopefully help bring some clarity to this day, he knew there was only one place to be right now. When he pulled into his driveway, he could tell no one was home. Candy must have taken John out for dinner or an ice cream. Now Jack was free to decide for himself and again his next destination was obvious since the bar was still not an option. Jack drove up to the DuPree house near dusk. He knocked on the door and Mrs. DuPree answered, her eyes puffy and slightly red.

"Hello, Jack. Let me get Riff for you. Riff! You have a guest," she called back up the stairs behind her.

"Thank you, Mrs. DuPree. You look lovely tonight."

"Oh, please. My lovely days are far behind me, but I thank you for the compliment."

"Hey, Jack. What's up?"

"It looks like your mother has been crying. Is she upset about Elvis?"

"What about Elvis?"

"He died. Today on my son's birthday."

"Wow, that makes three people just today."

"Three? I know about Guilford, but who else?"

"KK's husband fell into a thrasher this morning. That's why my mom was crying and my dad is in his room. They haven't forgiven KK for never returning home after she had the baby, but they still love her and know she must be hurting."

"Baby?"

"Yeah. Turns out that's why they sent her to a boarding school in Kansas—she was pregnant."

Jack's world ripped open and the floor seemed to drop away when he heard those words. He reached out for the door frame to steady himself before speaking.

"She was pregnant?"

"Apparently. My parents looked for Derick, her boyfriend at the time, but they didn't know his last name, so they were never able to find him."

"Derick Mahoney. Actually, Frederick Mahoney."

"Really? How do you know that?"

"Because, I pulled him off your sister on the path to the Rock and punched him in the face the fall before I left. He was the one who burned down our barn the night of the dance."

"He's the one who burnt down your barn?"

"Yes. I fought with him in the barn that night . . . and that was also the night . . . I slept with your sister."

"You what?" Riff took a moment to process the new information.

Jack was expecting a punch in the face, but instead received a big bear hug.

"Oh, my God. Thank God. That Derick is a total tool and my parents hated the idea he was the father of their grandson. I'm not going to tell them you're the actual father, but maybe eventually. I don't know."

"You're not mad?"

"Are you kidding me? She's had a huge crush on you ever since the third grade. I'm surprised it took you so long to realize it."

Jack was still a little detached and Riff's unreal reaction did not do much to re-center him, but eventually he grasped that this day had turned his reality upside down. Suddenly, everything had changed and, if he dared say, finally made sense.

"I just realized I married Candy when I knew I wasn't the father of her child just to save face in a town that hated me and now I have a chance to finally make things right."

"I'm not sure what you're getting at."

"Do you have KK's address?"

"Yes. I stole it off one of the letters she sent to my mom and I write her every once in a while. Why?"

"Because, I now see the whole picture."

Lincoln

August, 1977

Jack asked Riff for some paper so he could write a note to his son, John, then made his way home. It was already late in the evening, so everyone was in bed when Jack entered through the front door. He took out the letter he had written to John and had his hand on the doorknob of his son's bedroom when the master bedroom door flew open and Candy came pounding down the hall toward him.

"What the fuck is wrong with you? You were supposed to take your son to the cages today. Instead, he came home and cried."

"School got out early. How was I supposed to know?"

"You're his father. You should know everything. Where were you—at the bar? At the bar while your son is crying?"

"Candy. I had no way of knowing he took the bus home. I was there when I was supposed to be there and if the plans changed and you had to get off your ass and do something, then I can't be blamed for it."

Candy came at him with fire in her eyes. She slashed at his face with her nails, but missed entirely, which caused her to lose balance and topple into the wall. Jack retreated to the living room and after Candy righted herself, she grabbed an ashtray full of cigarette butts off the kitchen counter and threw it at his head. This time she connected and the glass ashtray glanced off Jack's forehead, leaving a gash that started to gush blood, before it shattered into pieces against the fireplace.

"What has gotten into you?" Jack yelled.

"Shut up. You're going to wake up your son."

"Is he?" Jack asked, with more anger than he felt.

"Is he what?"

"Is he *my* son?"

Candy didn't answer immediately, then exploded. "Of course he's your son. Don't be a fool. You're raising him, aren't you?"

Jack could tell Candy had been drinking, which was not a good sign for thoughtful conversation since if he was a confident, almost chatty, drunk, she was just plain mean.

Candy's drinking had been a problem far longer than his and he knew it had probably started well before he returned from the war, so he did not feel *fully* responsible. After all, he knew what demons he was drinking away, but could only guess at the demons chasing her. Then suddenly, Jack realized she was doing it to him again. She was controlling the narrative by getting mad at him for something completely out of his control. He had come here with new clarity, even a new purpose in life, and she was putting him right back in the middle of what had become a 28-year-old whirlpool that they called a marriage.

"Candy, I came here to tell you I'm leaving."

"Oh, what big news. You're always leaving—never around when I need you even when you're here. Big deal."

"It's different this time."

"What, you will be gone for seven days instead of five? Or, this time you're going to try harder to be a good husband. I'm sick of it."

"No, Candy. This time I'm not coming back," Jack said, then walked out the door.

* * *

Jack slept at Riff's that night. He knew he could have gone home to his family in Janesville and would have been welcome, but they had their own problems and Jack did not want to impart his lifelong drama into an already stirred pot. Their father had died a few years back and Jack could remember the family, together for the first time in over a decade, all agreed that Julie should give the eulogy since she, as Gina blatantly stated, would be the least likely to go off script and actually tell the truth. It had been a solemn day, but everyone seemed happy to be together again. Now that their father was gone, Thomas ran the farm. He had planned to go to college, but after tearing his ACL in the Homecoming game of his junior year, the scholarship offers dried up and so did his chances for college. Owen was off in California working for a computer company and the twins were gone as well, though Julie still lived in town with a family of her own while Gina was in Hollywood trying to become an actress. Arthur was single and still living in Detroit, and Rita had recently moved to Boulder with her husband and their five children. Then there was Bobby who was still Bobby—at home and nothing but trouble.

After sleeping in KK's room for the night, Jack awoke to the smell of bacon thick in the air.

Knock! Knock!

"Jack, breakfast," Mrs. DuPree called through the door.

"Be right down."

Jack got out of bed and dressed for breakfast, but took a moment to look around the room. This was KK's room and contained the same things she owned and loved the night she left. The room was like a time capsule and Jack enjoyed reminiscing, but needed to get downstairs, so he decided he would take a good look around after breakfast and possibly slip some of the items he thought KK might like into his suitcase before leaving for Lincoln.

Jack had not experienced a real farm breakfast for

several decades. The table was covered with crispy bacon, thick-cut ham, scrambled eggs made with fresh cheese and peppers, orange juice and of course warm milk fresh out of the cow.

"Thank you for your hospitality, Mr. and Mrs. DuPree."

"You know any lifelong friend of Riff's is family," Mrs. DuPree said with a smile.

"Thank you. I appreciate that. So, Mr. DuPree, how is Riff doing taking care of the farm?"

"He's all we got, but better than most, so we consider ourselves lucky."

Jack recognized the roundabout compliment and the reference to KK being gone, but also sensed an appreciation for Riff that was not there while he was in high school.

Jack hoped the voyage he was about to set upon could eventually lead to bringing this family back together, but much more he hoped it would finally give him a family he could fully call his own. Jack took one last look at the address Riff had given him . . .

PO box 314
Lincoln, Nebraska

. . . then stuck the note in his front pocket, saying a silent prayer for whatever God thought was best for him and no more.

Jack left for Lincoln, Nebraska just after breakfast and arrived ten hours later. Riff had only given him a PO box, but he was hoping he could eventually turn it into an actual address. Regardless, it would all have to wait until the post office opened again in the morning, so Jack found a motel and checked in for the night. The next morning,

Jack treated himself to a black coffee and two donuts, then walked to the post office.

"Excuse me."

"Yes, sir, how may I help you?"

"I was wondering if you could give me the address of the person that owns this PO box," Jack asked, then showed the postman the crumpled piece of paper.

"Sorry, sir, we're not able to give out even the identity of the person who owns a PO box. I would suggest you send the person a letter to tell them you're in town and how they can get ahold of you."

"Thank you for your help."

"You're welcome."

Jack was disappointed, but not deflated. He was determined to find KK and nothing was going to stop him. He returned to the motel and wrote a letter, then drove back to drop it in the box at the post office. In a moment of serendipity, after Jack let the letter drop down the chute, he looked through the front window of the post office to see someone unlocking box 314. Jack rushed in the front door and walked up to find a boy about 16 or 17 stooping to peer into the empty box.

"Excuse me."

The boy turned to acknowledge Jack, his hand still on the open door. "Yes?"

"I was wondering if you're a member of KK's family. I'm an old friend in town for a while and I wanted to give her a call. I heard about her husband. A terrible thing. Was he your father?"

"No, my grandfather. I'm Edward. Nice to meet you."

"Nice to meet you. I'm Jack. I was wondering if I could follow you home so I could give my condolences."

"I'm sure grandma would love to have the company. I have the blue truck out front. You can follow me. She lives on a farm in Geneva about 70 miles from here."

"Thanks. I'm just down the street."

The fact that KK had a PO box 70 miles from her home specifically so her family could not trace the letters they exchanged to her actual address was beyond young Edward, who never understood this weekly 140-mile round trip chore, but did it out of love for his Grams. Jack followed Edward to a two-story farm house surrounded by a white picket fence, two big red barns, a stable and a big silo. Jack was used to the rolling hills of Wisconsin, but here the fields that surrounded the house were flat as a griddle and seemed to go on forever. Jack followed Edward up the short drive and parked under a tree at the side of the house. It was a beautiful piece of property and Jack was humored by the coincidence that she lived in Geneva since Lake Geneva had been his safe harbor when he left home.

"She should be in the kitchen," Edward said as he opened the front door. "Grams, someone is here to see you."

KK, who had suffered through the loss of her husband followed by a steady stream of family and friends constantly dropping by to see if she was OK, was not up to another day of visits.

Why can't they just leave me alone? she thought, then knew the answer immediately. *Because they love me and they're worried about me. So, maybe it's time to show them how well I'm doing. Maybe then it will all stop so I can finally get some rest.*

"Well, who is it this time, Edward?" KK said from the kitchen before stepping into the living room where Jack and Edward were waiting.

"Thank you for coming b—" KK froze when she saw Jack's face.

"Hello, KK. It's me, Jack."

"I . . ."

The tears came so quickly, they caused her voice to falter; they were tears of sorrow that she had not had time to cry after losing her husband, tears of joy for seeing her first love, and tears of exhaustion.

"Grams?"

"I'm OK, Edward. Jack, my dear. How have you been?"

"Better now," Jack said and followed it with a warm smile.

"Please sit. Let me get you some coffee."

"No, I'm fine."

"Well, I'm going to need it and I don't drink alone," KK said, then returned to the kitchen.

As she started to pour two cups of coffee, Edward walked in to see if she needed help.

"Who is that man, Grams?"

Twenty-seven years ago, KK, a single mother, married Dennis, the owner of a large farm in Geneva, Nebraska. They tried for years, but were never able to have children of their own. KK's five-year-old son, Johnny, knew Dennis was not his father, but Dennis raised Johnny like he was his own as he did for Johnny's son, Edward. KK, always an honest parent and too tired to play games, placed her hand on Edward's shoulder, then pulled him close for a hug before speaking.

"He's your grandfather."

Jack moved into KK's home as an honored guest that same day and moved into her bedroom as a treasured lover before Halloween. At first things were a bit awkward with John—losing a father and gaining a father within the same fortnight could be considered unusual—but then Jack met Jessica and Jennifer, John's twin daughters, and his confidence grew knowing twins were in his family. Now, there was no doubt in his mind that he was John's father and he could see from Edward's age that John had taken after him and KK by having a child at a very young age. Jack wondered how KK handled that news, but assumed it was with love and honesty—things Jack needed more of in his life. Then on Thanksgiving, when the grandchildren asked Jack to carve the turkey, he knew he was where he should be.

Jack liked KK's idea about the PO box and used it as the address when he wrote to his family. For the first time in his life, Jack wrote letters to Arthur and Rita, and all his younger brothers and sisters as well as his older children Joey and Jeannie. He only wrote once to Candy when he asked her for a divorce, but he did write every week to his son, John, and every week the letter came back. Candy could have very easily thrown out the letters and Jack would have never known. This would have been the smarter thing to do, but the vengefulness in her soul forced her to rub each and every letter Jack sent back in his face.

Jack also wrote to the DuPrees and the next year arranged to come home for Thanksgiving. He did not tell them he would be bringing KK, their grandson and their great-grandchildren with him, but when he did, all was forgiven and the DuPrees family was whole again.

The day Elvis died, Jack had an epiphany, but only after having his days filled with love and honesty did he uncover what the epiphany truly meant—he had discovered true happiness for the first time in his life. He had discovered happiness was family, the people you loved and those who loved you. It was not about saving face with strangers and critics, but instead feeling content with friends and loved ones.

After leaving Janesville 32 years earlier, Jack finally felt like he was part of a family again and knew he was now home to stay.

SADO

Lowlands

Highlands

Lowlands

悪

Atsushi – Kind
Daisake – Great Helper
Daichi – First Great Son
Yuji – Courageous Second Son
Rai – Thunder
Kaiju – Sea Monster
Jiji – Old Man

March, 2007

Now, seven centuries after the creation of the Mizushima Fishing and Exploration Company, it was one of the main industries on the island of Sado and controlled much of the politicking in the southern lowlands. Sado itself was now famous beyond its history of being an island of exile. In 1601, Sado experienced a gold rush and the mine flourished for over three centuries. Later in the seventeenth century, Sado became a major port for the Japanese Navy when traveling in the Sea of Japan. Then in the twentieth century, Sado had an event that would eventually be made into two separate movies when a British Douglas Dakota airplane, the *Sister Ann*, made an emergency landing on the island. The story tells of how the island people, just a few months after the end of World War II, aided the crew and even built a runway so the plane could take off after being repaired. Now in the twenty-first century, Sado was an island with a rich and generous history that had become a miniature Japan all its own.

Atsushi Mizushima sat in his chair, a hollow shell of his former self. He had outlived his only son and had watched his family's company devolve into something he could no longer be proud of. He was his father's second son, but when his older brother, Namiyo, died of leukemia just a year after the war, Atsushi became the family hope and was forced to marry a bride of his father's choosing. Atsushi and his new wife soon produced a son to make his father proud. Daisake was a good son and eventually was also assigned a wife by his grandfather. Daisake and his appointed wife went on to produce three sons. Because his bride was, of course, a somewhat-distant cousin, their third son, Rai, born during an earthquake, was a fiery child—with amber eyes like his great-grandfather—and the only child the young mother never lived to hold. Daisake, who truly loved his assigned wife, never recovered from her loss and just dwindled away until his early death.

Atsushi sat and wondered, *Is the Mizushima family now cursed? Did this happen when I brought the Kaiju home to present to Father? Father was so proud of me then, but did I open the gates of hell upon our descendants?*

Atsushi was now nothing more than a figurehead, barely able to lift his hand to feed himself, but he had not given up and knew he needed to do something before his company was gone. His first grandson was now also gone and the next in line was not named appropriately. Yuji, or *Courageous Second Son*, was neither courageous nor likely to produce offspring due to his proclivity for men. He was such a disappointment to the family and the company, and now that Atsushi was physically limited, Rai was controlling Yuji and, therefore, the company.

Rai had always been a rebel—a wild child who lived outside all lines, rules and traditions. He often intimidated his brothers with his sudden fury and violent outbursts. He also took a different tack with Kaiju and eventually befriended him. As a child, Rai spent hours each day talking and playing with the servant prisoner who eventually won his freedom to roam within the family compound—no more a servant, but still a prisoner. Rai now called him Jiji, or *old man*, replacing his original moniker, Kaiju—meaning *Strange Creature* or *Huge Monster*, but taken as *Sea Monster* since he came from the sea—since Rai's new friend and servant was more an old man than a monster these days anyway.

The Mizushima family kept Kaiju as a slave for over 60 years as atonement for the killing of their relatives. Kohaku had kept him in shackles for nearly three years, blaming his beloved son's leukemia on the bombs that this monster had dropped on the heavenly cities of Hiroshima and Nagasaki. Rai had never known his uncle, but he saw him as his closest amber-eyed relative—a true descendant of the Mizushima chosen ones. Eventually, Rai would make Jiji his primary advisor, as Jiji told him of a second nuclear bomb still on the shipwrecked USS *Indianapolis*. What better weapon would there be to help Rai punish those *truly* responsible for his uncle's death; Rai was elated by the thought of such karma.

"Think of it, my master and friend. The *Indianapolis* sailed to Tinian Island with no escort to deliver the bomb that destroyed your ancestors, then left again with no escort. Is this not a sure sign there was a second bomb? Does this not exude the karma you desire?"

Now Rai was pouring the company's money into his and Jiji's crusade to avenge the lives of people Rai had not even known. Atsushi knew Jiji was filling Rai's mind with lies and conspiracies that served only one purpose—to give Jiji power and freedom—but he was struck down as a feeble old man with delusions whenever he broached the subject. Finally, Atsushi decided to take a trip to the highlands to pray for absolution of his sins and those about to be committed by his grandson and his monster.

Highlands

爱

Mirai - Future
Sakiko – Child of Hope
Yumato – Great Harmony
Benjiro – Enjoys Peace
Kaida – Little Dragon
Keiko – Shadow Reflection

March, 2007

Mirai had been the family matriarch since the age of thirteen. She was now 76 and still bright and quick-minded as ever. She was not involved in the day to day running of the sisterhood anymore, but was a beloved elder who was included in every major decision. This is what brought her to the secret room this night and she listened intently as her 23-year-old twin granddaughters, Kaida and Keiko, made their case.

"*We have known of the Mizushima prisoner man for many decades, but have never felt he was a primary to monitor in the Mizushima family. However, now that the youngest son, Rai, has inserted himself as the family leader and has formed a bond with this man, we now believe the pair together present a clear danger,*" Kaida said.

"A danger to Sado?" Mirai asked.

"No, Gran. A danger to the world—specifically America."

"I see. Please present the evidence." Mirai beckoned Kaida to continue.

Keiko continued for her sister and laid out the

intelligence she had uncovered working in the shadows as the sisterhood had for so many centuries.

"Through some subliminal grooming, we have arranged for Atsushi Mizushima to visit the Ai Temple here on Sado. We know he is discouraged by what he sees in his grandson and believe he may give us information that we cannot obtain from looking in from the outside. I have been able to infiltrate the elder's inner circle by becoming a part-time caretaker in his household, but Rai has his own team and they are dumbstruck with allegiance to him."

Mirai was so proud of her granddaughters and her grandsons as well. Her only daughter, Sakiko, had given birth to two boys, Yamato and Benjiro, and then twin daughters, Kaida and Keiko. Sakiko was still alive, but greatly limited after suffering a stroke when the girls were still young. Because of this, Mirai, or *Gran*, raised the girls and cared for her own daughter as well. Now her grandchildren ran the temple and the society, and she could not be prouder—though she always fretted when Keiko was out being a little shadow.

"So, when do we expect Atsushi's visit?" Mirai asked.

"Within the week. He is not limited to weekend travel, so it could be any time. I should have the final itinerary soon and will forward the details to Kaida."

"Let us make our plans then."

The meeting went on for several more hours as every aspect of the expected visit was fleshed out. It was now time to meet secretly with the temple to share the society's expectations. As Keiko was the shadow that discovered hidden secrets, Kaida was the dragon that protected and steered the sisterhood. Here, meeting with Yamato, Head Priest of Sado's Ai Temple, the two siblings had different callings, but were equal and never at odds.

JOKER

III

Tybee

Mark 15

A City Near You

700 years

III

April 6, 2007

Jack sat with Gerbil and Kaida in a car parked under a huge elm tree on a street lined with two-flats and three-flats.

"Are we going to go in?" Gerbil said with nervous energy, still showing signs of his recent beating.

"Listen . . . to the quiet speaking," Kaida said with an outstretched index finger in the air between her and Gerbil. "Let Jack-san have a moment. I am sure he is plotting a clever strategy."

"Kaida, please call me Jack or Mr. Jack if you must, but Jack-san makes me sound like a noble figure, which I'm anything but . . . and as for clever, I'm 77 and my clever days are pretty much over."

"You are too hard on yourself, Mr. Jack. I know what I see even if you cannot."

"She always this nice?"

"Like I said, she saved my ass . . . I mean butt . . . I mean me." Gerbil flushed a bit as he stammered his well-meant words, then fell silent again.

* * *

A couple sat intertwined on a couch watching *Friday Night Lights* on the VCR when a knock came from the front door.

"I've got it," the man said.

"No, you already have a job. Now get to it before I change my mind."

"That might be a winning strategy since I don't know if I can do this."

"Then I may have to get even with you and you would not want that hanging over your head," the woman said, then threw a pillow from the couch at the man as he made his way through the dining room to the kitchen.

Knock! Knock! Knock!

"I'm coming! I'm coming!" the woman called. As she walked to the door, she flipped her head to toss her jet-black hair in the air, then pulled an afghan tightly around her before her hair settled around her shoulders.

She opened the door to a trio of faces—two smiling and one very serious. She decided to speak to the serious face since he was also the tallest of the bunch.

"Hello," she said brightly, then offered, "How may I help you?"

"I'm here—we're here to see John."

"Jonathan is here. Who may I say is visiting?"

"Tell him it's Jack."

"And tell him they got Joker," Gerbil added, then immediately went slack when Kaida placed her hand on the back of his neck.

The woman called back to the kitchen to her husband, "Jonathan, Jack and two of his friends are here to see you."

Jonathan walked to the front door holding a sundae he had made for his wife and nearly dropped it when he saw the man, only two inches shorter than himself, standing on his front stoop.

"Dad?"

"Junior."

"Dad? Junior?" Bo reacted as well, then immediately pulled the door fully opened and said to the group, "Please come in."

Jack looked down at the sundae and asked, "Are those pickles?"

Jonathan could not fully justify why he was holding a pickle split, so his wife, Bo, did it for him.

"Yes," she said with her hands on her hips holding back the afghan to clearly display her pregnant belly. "Do you want some?"

"Congratulations," Jack said as he entered the foyer followed by Gerbil and Kaida.

"So, you are JD's father. It is an honor to finally meet you."

"I'm not sure your husband feels the same, but we're in a pickle . . . sorry. We need your help. Joker is missing and we know he's in trouble."

"Come sit down and let's go through what you have," JD said as he waved everyone into the living room.

"By the way, this is Chester Best, or Gerbil, and this is Kaida Fukushima from the island of Sado, Japan."

"Nice to meet you both," Bo said, then immediately asked, "So, JD is a junior?"

"Actually, the third. My dad and me and JD are all named Jonathan Edward Dearfield. But no one ever went by Jonathan to save on the confusion, which I never much understood since we all had so many names like Senior, Junior, Jake, Jack, Butch and now JD that at times I'm a bit confused which one I am."

"Jonathan *Edward* Dearfield III. That means you are actually JED like Jethro's father and not JD," Bo said, smiling at JD.

"Maybe you should finish that sundae before it starts to melt, dear," JD suggested nicely.

Bo did not answer, but instead took a big scoop, which included a chunk of pickle, and just said, "Yum."

Everyone else in the room flinched a bit before Jack said, "I can see you have your hands full here, but we really need to talk this over."

"I apologize. It must be the hormones. It is just a lot to process. Please continue," Bo said, then took another scoop.

"So, how do you know someone has Joker and do you know who?"

"Kaida, I think you should start. Is that OK, Gerbil?" Jack asked.

"Yeah," Gerbil said without much enthusiasm.

Kaida went on to tell the story of the prisoner held by the Mizushima Fishing and Exploration Company for decades. She then explained how the youngest Mizushima, Rai, had taken over the company and was now plotting with the prisoner, who he calls Jiji, to find a lost nuclear bomb to finally retaliate for Japan losing the war.

"Jiji has made Rai believe there was another bomb on the USS *Indianapolis* when it sunk. He has also made Rai believe Joker and Jack hold the key to this secret."

"Hogwash," Jack said in disgust.

"I don't understand. How did you get wrapped up into this?" JD asked Kaida.

"I am from Sado and learned of the plot from Rai's grandfather. I have been trailing Rai ever since. I lost them when I saved Chester."

"Let me tell this part," Gerbil interjected.

Jack and Kaida both nodded their acknowledgment.

Gerbil went on to tell how Rai and Jiji had been dressed up as ninjas and had tortured him in his kitchen, asking him about the second bomb and trying to get Joker's and Jack's locations.

"I didn't tell them nothing, but then Jiji found my secret address book, which is probably how they found Joker. Before they left, Rai lit a candle and turned on the gas, then left me there to die. I was saying my prayers when Kaida came in and untied me. We couldn't go outside since they were still watching the house, so she carried me to the bathtub and covered us with blankets and a mattress from my guestroom. After the whole house exploded, she carried me to her car and nursed me back to health at her motel room. I can't thank her enough. She saved my life and now she's here to help us save Joker's."

"And how do you know these same people have Joker?"

"'Cause we went to his house and found a chair with bloody ropes and blood all over the place just like at my place. They got him alright and they're probably torturing him every day trying to find the second *Indy* nuke."

"Was there a second nuke on the *Indy* when she went down?" JD asked Gerbil.

"How am I supposed to know stuff like that? I'm a baker, for God's sake. Joker would know if any of us would." Gerbil retorted.

JD looked over at his dad, who nodded his head in agreement.

"So, you can see this is more than just a missing friend. We came to you because you're in the FBI and this may be a national security issue."

"How did you know I was in the FBI?" JD asked his dad.

"I may have left your mother, but I never intended to leave you. I kept tabs on you as best I could and have followed your career ever since you graduated college."

"OK, let me look in the FBI database for Joker to see what info we have on him," JD said, not knowing how to fully digest his father's revelation.

"I don't think you'll find much," Gerbil said a bit sheepishly.

"Why not?"

"He kinda worked for the CIA, so his info is limited, if not altogether misleading . . . like he never ran a dude ranch in Wyoming or worked for a fishing company off the coast of Seattle."

"Joker was CIA. I'll be damned," Jack said with some

pride in his voice.

"That certainly isn't going to make this any easier. What is Joker's full name? I'll see what I can find anyway."

"Darcy Lawson," Gerbil answered.

"OK, let me see what I can find out. Are you staying in town?"

"Yes, we're staying at a motel up on Belmont in Room 9."

"OK. I'll be in touch."

After Jack, Chester and Kaida left, Bo and JD sat back on the couch, but were not in the mood to finish their TV show.

"So, that was your dad. Is he the man you remember?"

"He disappeared from my life on my ninth birthday, so I don't remember much. Most of what I know of him is from my mother, who hated him for leaving us. She never had a nice word to say after that. Then there were the rumors all over town that seemed to flourish once he was gone. My mother repeated and believed every one of them and I guess I came to believe them too. I can't really say I ever loved him or missed him after he was gone and all that was left were the stories of how he burned down his own family's barn and how he got my mom pregnant then ran off to the Navy. They say he was even a suspect in a missing girl case, but I never heard anything more than the story. I think the worst parts were the stories of his drinking and the stuff he would make up. He told a story about meeting Elvis."

"Why is that so unbelievable?"

"Because, he says James Dean and Marilyn Monroe were there too."

"Oh. Well, I don't see that man in your father now. Maybe it's time to hear the stories from him?"

"It's hard to believe something isn't true once you've heard it preached as Gospel so many times."

"I still think you should give him a chance. He has a good friend in Chester and seems to stand by his friends, so he can't be all bad."

"I just wish he did the same for his family."

Bo let the conversation slide after that.

Tybee

April 11, 2007

After being released from the thick ropes that usually bound his hands, Joker rubbed his wrists before he grabbed the spoon and dug into his rice mush. He was certain it was not more than condensed soup mixed with rice, but at least he was being fed. Prior to each meal he could smell sumptuous aromas coming from the kitchen and he was certain what he was eating was not on the menu elsewhere on the boat—a kind of torture of its own.

They had come for Joker at night, right after he had fallen asleep. He heard one of the proximity alarms go off and groggily got out of bed to check it out, but the closed-circuit camera displayed only a black blur which was likely just a deer bounding through the area. While checking the other cameras, Joker saw a man approaching the front porch and ran to the front door to look through the peep hole. He saw a lone figure standing ready to kick in the door. He immediately unlocked the door and pulled it open at the precise moment the man's foot came forward to make contact. The man toppled inside and Joker fell upon him, swiftly handcuffing him in the process.

"Who are you?" Joker demanded.

"I'm your ride," the man replied.

As Joker was trying to figure out just what the man meant, a hood whooshed over his head and he was punched repeatedly until he blacked out. When he awoke he found himself tied to a chair facing toward two figures completely clothed in black, including black pullover masks.

Joker immediately assessed his situation and by the feel of his bindings, there was little he could do other than wait out this phase of the interrogation. If they did not kill him, then maybe he would have a chance further down the line. He could clearly see he was dealing with a shorter man who was no more than 30, if that, and an older man who was likely 60 or more. He could tell this by their posture, their mannerisms and their diction. He also sensed the younger captor, who the older one referred to as Rai, was a very angry young man, but could not get a good gauge of the older man's temperament. He remembered the interrogation vividly.

"So, Mr. Joker. Not too clever, are you—falling for my decoy as Jiji snuck up behind you?" Rai spat.

"I didn't know we were having a contest. If you had told me, I might have prepared better," Joker responded.

"Stupid American. Will you be stupid just like your friend Gerbil or will you choose to live?"

Joker had heard about the gas explosion at Gerbil's home and taken it as a warning—this paranoia was the entire reason he turned on his exterior alarm system after being unused for nearly a decade. He mourned his old friend and now that he knew these were the ones responsible for his demise, he bided his time, not taking the bait, but keeping his cool and further frustrating Rai.

"We have but one question. Was there another bomb on the *Indianapolis* when it went down?"

"There were tons of bombs on the *Indy* when she went down. That's kind of an easy one. You got anything harder?" Joker answered, trying to further inflame Rai.

Rai turned a throwing star in his left hand, drawing Joker's eyes, then swiftly blindsided him with a right hook.

Joker felt a crack and hoped it was a tooth and not his jaw. Blood dripped from his slack mouth as he lifted his head and said, "Is that all you got? Questions, I mean."

Rai was about to hit Joker again, but the older man who he had called Jiji quietly said, "No, Rai," then walked over to look down on Joker.

"It is a simple question. Was there another nuclear bomb on the *Indy* when it went down?"

"Oh, a *nuclear* bomb. Hey, Rai, this guy seems to know what questions to ask. I'm sure he could give you some tips."

This time Joker saw the punch coming and Jiji did nothing to stop it. Joker spit blood at Rai's feet, but this time kept his head down to give him some time to think.

Think, Joker, think. They will never find the Indy even if you tell them there was a second bomb. And what chance do you have at escape on a boat in the middle of the Philippine Sea. No, I need . . . got it.

Working for the CIA, Joker had extensive knowledge of many of the nation's secrets and missing nuclear bombs was on this list. In all he knew of nine bombs that had been lost and never recovered. Two in the Mediterranean, two on a sub that disappeared in the Atlantic, two in a swamp in North Carolina, two in the Pacific—one near Alaska and one near Japan—and one off Tybee Island on the Georgia coast. He knew from reports the Tybee bomb did not have a nuclear core or capsule, which was required to start the nuclear reaction, so this was his ticket.

"You're wasting your time with the *Indy* bomb. It's

old and weak—only 15 kilotons. There's a bomb just off the Georgia shore that's at least 100 times that. I'm talking *Megatons*."

Joker could see Rai's pupils dilate as he took in the new information. Now he had him.

"The Tybee bomb is in relatively shallow water too, when compared to the *Indy* that's probably at least three miles down."

"How do you know this?" Rai demanded.

"I was involved in the mission that found it." Joker said, leaving the bait out to be taken.

"Then why is it still lost?"

"Because the president thought it was best to leave it buried in the sandy soot rather than risk bringing it out. I believe it was the wrong decision, but we're a country ruled by our president and must accept his decisions." Joker was lying through his teeth now. He knew he had Rai, but he still could not read Jiji.

"This does sound more promising," Jiji said to Rai.

"Yes, but it is not the same karma as using a bomb from the *Indy* like the one that killed my uncle."

"But it is karma all the same and it is here for the taking. Powerful karma. Megatons of karma."

Jiji opened several kitchen drawers before he found a pad of paper and a pen, which he placed in front of Joker.

"I am going to untie your hands and you are going to write down everything we need to know about this bomb. If you try anything, Rai will drive his dagger into your brainstem. Do we understand each other?"

Joker looked to his left at Rai who was standing with a dagger that looked like it might hurt if driven into his brain, but he needed to barter.

"How do I know you're not going to kill me once you have this information?" Joker asked defiantly.

"Because you are coming with us," Rai answered.

"Why?"

"Because you are going to help us find the bomb."

"And, then?"

"Then we are going to strap you to it so you can be the first to feel its powerful karma."

Joker swallowed another ball of rice and chased it down with a big gulp of rust-flavored water. He tried to make small talk with his Japanese guard, but knew it was futile after his first guard was beaten publicly on the main deck by Rai for even acknowledging Joker's existence beyond feeding him like an animal. From what Joker could tell, they were on day five of their excursion and he had yet to see the sky other than the first day when he helped chart out where to search. He knew the ship was a Japanese vessel, but no one other than those on board would ever have guessed. Gone were the proud Japanese and Mizushima flags that usually adorned the control tower, replaced by a Union Jack. Also gone was the Japanese name, replaced by a very English name painted boldly on her stern.

Betty Mae
Tybee Island

Day after day as Joker lay in the bed he was tied to, he could feel the boat bob and roll with the ocean waves, then turn and retrace a path in the opposite direction—a standard search pattern aided by GPS and a sonar buoy with a specialized Geiger counter attachment. Joker gave Rai and his crew a match in a windstorm's chance of finding the nuke, but now during his early morning meal he felt the boat quickly decelerate and turn sharply. He feared luck was about to get fucked by karma and he was right. Excited calls echoed throughout the ship and Joker could hear heavy footsteps pounding above and below the main deck as the crew took up their stations.

"Shit. Looks like they found something," Joker said to no one.

Soon Joker's cabin door was opened and Rai strode through to stand over him.

"So, you are not a lying dog after all. We have found your lost bomb in just eight days. You Americans are useless. We should have the bomb on board and off to—"

"Rai, let's not give Joker any more information than he needs," Jiji said as he stepped into the cabin beside Rai.

"No matter. The bomb's final destination will be Joker's as well."

"Yes, and karma will be fulfilled."

"Come, Joker. Come see us pluck your bomb from the ocean floor."

Joker's guard leaned down to untie his hands, but Jiji stopped him when he knelt to untie his feet.

"No. He should remain shackled like a criminal until his ultimate punishment."

Jiji, who had taken off his black mask and now wore a scarf across his face, knew the boat would immediately be searched if on the off-chance someone saw a man on the deck with his wrists tied. *But they cannot see what is not seeable*, he thought and thus decided to keep Joker's feet shackled together so he would have enough movement to keep his balance on board, but not enough to kick or swim; even Joker thought jumping into the water to escape this far from shore without full use of his legs was a certain death sentence, even if he could disappear without being noticed. What Jiji did not know was that he was correct. Not about the ropes or Joker's imagined escape, but someone was watching and had been watching for quite a while.

Mark 15

April 11, 2007

Joker was brought to the aft working deck to watch as the crew readied the winch. The bomb, at nearly three feet in diameter and more than 11 feet in length, had been easy to locate by sonar once the specialized Geiger counter had determined the general location. Now, a giant claw with retractable fingers was being lowered to the ocean floor and, aided by two submersibles, would eventually bring the nearly 50-year-old behemoth to the surface.

Joker waddled to the gunwale to steady himself as the deck rolled beneath his feet. No one was paying any particular attention to him since he had his feet bound, and even he did not think he could slip away and swim to shore from their current location; however, this did not eliminate this strategy once they travelled closer to shore. He had positioned himself near the tool locker and at one point feigned a loss of balance to snatch a putty knife from the top drawer. Anyone watching this would have laughed at the foolishness of grabbing the dullest tool from a drawer full of knives, box cutters, scissors and awls, but they did not know Joker.

Joker leaned against the gunwale again, smiling mindlessly as the sun shone down from the cloudless three o'clock sky. Behind him he flicked his wrist at precise intervals to catch the sun's rays and reflect them back across the ocean surface toward shore. This was difficult if not impossible to do behind his back without looking, but he had been in dire straits on the water before, where only his wits and ingenuity brought him through. He did not see a boat in that direction and could not even see the shore, but he knew this might be his only chance and he had to try something.

Beside him, further down the deck, two sailors were mindlessly tossing a fishing net into the ocean and pulling it out at various intervals.

Well before the morning was over, Joker was relegated back to his cabin below deck for not wiping the smirk off his face when Rai commanded it.

* * *

JD sat in his office in the FBI building on Roosevelt Road. He looked out his window and could see the iconic Route 66 that stretched from Chicago all the way to Los Angeles and the Pacific Ocean. He wanted to take a Route 66 road trip with Bo one of these days, but now it would have to wait until their unborn child was old enough to appreciate the history. He only hoped the road was still there when that day finally came.

JD had been recruited by the Chicago branch of the FBI after he and Ken solved the *Patriotic Killer* case while working in the Chicago Special Investigations Unit. It was all over the news for weeks after the story broke and now filming was even underway for a movie about the case. After talking the offer over with Bo—the half Irish, half Venezuelan woman he had met during the *PK* case and eventually married—JD decided to enroll in the 20-week training program at Quantico. He was 39 at the time—two years over the age limit for new recruits—but by threading some loopholes, the FBI admitted him without any issues. He had hoped Ken would join him at the bureau, but Ken said he was comfortable on the CSIU and did not want to upset his current family dynamic, which had recently taken a hit because of the PK case. JD could not blame Ken, but would miss working with him. He knew their paths would still cross in Chicago, but not on a daily basis as they had for more than a decade.

It had been several days since the visit from his father and JD had nothing to show for all the digging he had done. He was frustrated, to say the least. He did not want to appear as a failure to his father, even though the man had only been an actual father to him for less than a quarter of his life. JD was planning to meet Ken Griffen for lunch today, so maybe they could throw some ideas at the wall to see what stuck. However, JD held little hope since Joker had been off the grid for so long before he vanished that there was not much of a trail to follow.

JD was about to step out for lunch when his phone rang.

"Hello, Special Officer Dearfield. How may I assist you?"

"Hello, this is Captain Jack. I run a shrimper out of Tybee, Georgia and I have an odd story to report."

"Go on."

"Well, yesterday we were coming back from a shrimp run and my first mate saw some blinking lights. I thought it was just a boat window catching the sun as it bobbed in the water, but my first mate was in the Navy and he said it was Morse code, so he grabbed a pad and started to write out the message. He didn't get the entire message, but did write down this number."

"So, what did the message say—the part that he did get," JD questioned, trying to hide his anticipation.

"Let me read it to you, '. . . taken captive S O S call 3 1 2 5 5 5 1 9 4 5 John D nuke . . .' was all he could get."

"Thank you, Captain Jack. I have your number if we need anything further."

"You're welcome. I just hope this is a hoax. That's my livelihood out there."

"We will look into this immediately. Thank you, again."

JD called Ken and cancelled their lunch, then dialed his partner, Gabriel Rodgers.

"Gabby, we need to get to Georgia. We have a missing person case that may just have gone nuclear. Meet me in the Unit Chief's office."

Unit Chief Marcus Tillman sat back in his chair and listened to JD report off all he knew about the Darcy Lawson missing person case he was following.

"So, the call this morning was not connected to anything you had investigated thus far?" Tillman questioned.

"I don't believe so. We have a BOLO out with Joker's description, but the call did not identify Darcy. It only gave other information involved in his case. I believe Darcy was the one sending the signal. He may be a captive on the boat, but somehow managed to find a mirror or piece of metal to send the Morse code signal."

"Do you believe they have a nuke already and if they do, why are they in Tybee? The Georgia coast seems like an unlikely target for Japanese retaliation."

"I believe I can answer that, but first I would not term this presumed plot as *Japanese* retaliation. This is a misguided and unilateral plot of only two men, not Japan, and should not be taken to represent anything other than the facts we have to date."

"I am sorry, I was only speaking in generalities," Tillman added.

"I know you meant no ill intent, but a misquote could cause a chain reaction of international issues that we must avoid at all costs. Remember the Spanish Flu of 1918? The first case was actually reported in Kansas, but with the media lock-down during World War I, Spain, a neutral country during the war, was one of the only countries to freely report the reality of the pandemic. When the Spanish King, Alfonso XIII, contracted the virus, the entire world from then on referred to the disease as the Spanish Flu. The US was lucky twice here since the first case was in the US and President Woodrow Wilson also contracted the flu in 1919 during the Treaty of Versailles talks. He suffered for five days with a 103-degree fever, though his doctor spun it to the press as only a bad cold."

"So, what about Tybee?" Tillman asked, already used to Gabby's long-winded history lessons.

"We believe they're searching for a missing nuclear bomb."

"A missing nuke?" Tillman exclaimed.

"Yes. In 1958 an F-86 fighter collided with a B-47 bomber in midair over Wassaw Sound just east of Tybee Island, which is near Savannah. The bomber pilot jettisoned the 7,600-pound bomb to decrease his payload so he could better control the faltering plane. The plane managed to land, but the bomb was never recovered. There are conflicting reports stating whether the bomb was fully functional with an active nuclear capsule, so there is nothing conclusive as to its actual destructive ability, but it would be somewhere between quite large and gigantic. We also know for a fact that Rai Mizushima's company has the capacity and technology for deep-sea exploration and may be attempting to retrieve the nuke. We also believe if the housing and mechanism are still intact that it could be used to create a nuclear explosion within the US."

"OK, enough talking. I sanction this case and want you to follow up every lead. I will reach out to the Atlanta Field Office and the Savannah Resident Agency to tell them you will be in the area, but until we have a better feel for the actual capabilities of this so-called two-man enterprise, we will keep this as a missing person case to all outsiders."

JD and Gabby shook hands with Marcus and left to prepare for their trip to Tybee.

* * *

JD held Bo in his arms for a long moment before speaking.

"I don't know how long I'll be gone, but like I told my dad, we have a line on Darcy now that seems promising."

"I'll be OK. I have Ken and Maggie to look after me," Bo said, giving JD a kiss and a hug, then followed him out to send Gabby a friendly wave before stepping back inside.

"We have a 2:30 p.m. flight to Savannah/Hilton Head International Airport and then it's a 30-mile drive from there."

Gabriel was a 5'6" black woman who JD had befriended at Quantico. She was his main competition and he finished less than a percentage point ahead of her in their class—he was only second to Steffen Riggins who was a self-serving know-it-all that no one liked. It seemed amusing to JD that Gabriel was called Gabby by her friends more for her endless chatter than for the contraction of her name. However, her chatter was never a blind monologue, but conversation that always seemed to engage those around her. She never spoke down and was often able to challenge your beliefs without you even realizing it. She could make the same points as Riggins, but did it with well-spoken fluidity that involved the listener rather than taking aim at them or belittling them.

* * *

JD and Gabby met agent Wheeler on a dock on the backside of Tybee Island along Tybee Creek.

"Agent Wheeler?"

"Yes. Tom Wheeler."

"I'm Agent Dearfield and this is Agent Rodgers, but please call us JD and Gabby."

"Gabby, huh. Is that short for Gabriel?" Tom queried.

"Sort of," JD answered for Gabby, then asked, "So, we think the person we're looking for is on a working boat out near Wassaw Sound."

"I can take you out there, but if you want to board a boat, we will need to involve the Coast Guard."

"No, this is purely observational. We want to confirm without giving away our presence. We would like to track rather than confront."

"Got it. Life preservers are under the back seat."

The trio sat in the three-engine, 39-foot, center console Bertram, each scanning the ocean with a pair of binoculars. They had moved twice after seeing nothing but pleasure boats and fishing trawlers.

"I've got another bikini-covered cabin cruiser," Tom reported from the port side.

"And I have another fishing vessel—just two guys tossing a net over the side," Gabby stated matter-of-factly from the bow.

"Let me take a look," JD said as he edged his way toward Gabby.

"JD, it concerns me that you chose to verify the fishing boat rather than checking out the bikini party," Gabby said, taking a deadpan jab at her partner.

"Seen one bikini, you've seen them all," JD responded as he brought his binoculars up and focused in on the boat in question.

"JD, I believe you need to see more bikinis if that's your life conclusion," Tom said, joining in on the fun.

"They certainly are fishing," JD said, then noted an obvious difference. "But they are tossing the net free-hand over the side—it's not hanging from the hoist or crane."

"Sometimes these working vessels fish with nets to catch enough to feed the crew and no more."

"Indeed, but if they are fishing to feed the crew, then what is their purpose to be out on the ocean? We're at the wrong angle to get the numbers off the bow, but can you check on the registration for a . . . *Betty Mae* out of Tybee?"

Tom walked back to the aft deck and called in the boat name and port, then waited for his office to run a check while Gabby and JD continued their surveillance.

"This is certainly not a fishing vessel since there are no drum winches for the nets. This is clearly meant for exploration—you see," JD pointed, "they have something in the water . . . there are a series of cables running from the aft arch hoist."

"Yes, I see. It looks as if they may be scanning the ocean floor, but they are not moving, so maybe they are exploring the bottom?" Gabby guessed.

"Like they already found what they were looking for?" JD noted more than asked.

Gabby simply replied, "Yes."

Tom returned to the front of the boat after hanging up with his office.

"My office tells me there are two *Betty Mae*s registered in this three-state area. One on Marco Island and one on Key West, but nothing in South Carolina or here in Georgia. So, she's not from Tybee Island as her stern paint claims."

"Looks like we have a winner," JD exclaimed, then added, "and I believe we spotted our person of interest," to further their story.

"Great. So, we still sit and wait?" Tom asked.

"Yes—for now that's the plan."

"It is hard to tell their nationality from this far away since most sailors have darkened weathered faces," Gabby observed.

"So, you're telling me all sailors look the same?" JD said with a chuckle.

"From this distance, yes, but we dare not get any closer."

"Agreed. Let's take shifts watching the crew while the other two sit and talk like it's just another day out on the ocean."

"Then this will come in handy if we want to appear somewhat normal to an observer," Tom said as he opened a built-in cooler and revealed a mix of lagers and pale ales.

"Gabby, you're on first shift while Tom and I give you cover. Tom, grab the church key and let's get started."

"Brother," Gabby said, not quite under her breath.

"And Gabby—"

"I know—watch for the watcher."

"It's like you two are married," Tom said as he handed JD a Stone Pale Ale.

Nearing dusk it was plain to see the *Betty Mae* was having issues with whatever they were trying to accomplish. JD could not see on the ocean side of the vessel, but he could tell the captain was clearly speaking with someone over the starboard side and guessed it was likely a submersible. It was looking more and more like it was going to be an overnighter, but they were prepared since Tom had brought a sleeping bag for each of them.

After the sun set, JD suggested a watch schedule going forward.

"OK, from here on out we will maintain four-hour shifts

so we can log some rest when we are off watch."

"I can take the first shift," Tom offered.

"OK, but wake us both if there's anything suspicious."

"Roger. Oh, I mean Roger, not Rodger," Tom said to Gabby.

"I got it. Don't worry."

In the early hours of the next morning, JD watched as the *Betty Mae*'s main crane pulled a soot-covered pod from the water and secured it to the working deck. Two submersibles were then lifted from the water by the aft crane before the *Betty Mae* was underway.

"OK, looks like we're going ashore—wherever that might be," JD said as he watched the water behind the *Betty Mae* start to foam.

"We will keep our distance. She shouldn't be able to outrun us and doesn't look to be concerned with doing so," Tom said as he pressed the throttle forward to edge the motors into action, then picked up his phone to call his partner on shore.

Tom followed the *Betty Mae* back around the north side of Tybee Island all the way to Lazaretto Creek where her captain docked her at a boat yard pier. Feigning engine trouble, Tom settled into the next dock over so they could keep an eye on her crew. There were only a few other boats on the creek, one zipping by as they docked, but otherwise it was quiet. Tom continued to talk with his partner who was already in the area.

"You were right, Mike. They came to Lazaretto Boat Yard. I believe the captain is calling his land team as we speak. From the looks of it we have a while, but we cannot miss this one."

"No sweat, Tom. I'm parked in the back watching them now. No one can come in or out without me seeing.

Remember, we have a chopper available, if needed."

"Got it. Thanks, Mike. I'll stay on the line."

JD casually watched the captain arguing with a shorter man and from this distance he could tell they were all Japanese.

"Looks like they're discussing if the dock can handle the weight of the—their discovery," JD said to Gabby, not wanting *bomb* to be overheard by Tom.

"At almost four tons, they better be certain."

"I guess we will find out."

Just then Tom called out, "Mike says a truck came in the back and is backing into place. He says it's a big one, but not an 18-wheeler. Do you see it there coming round the bushes?" Tom pointed toward a side building east of the main complex.

The three watched the truck flatten several bushes as it backed as close as possible to the pier. Then a three-man team rolled open the back lift gate and pulled a cable from a winch on the truck bed toward the pier.

"Looks like they're taking no chances," JD remarked.

The three men from the truck were met on the pier by four men from the boat and they all waited for the cranes to finish their business. First the aft crane lifted one of the subs off its rolling cradle and set the sub gently on the deck. Next the empty cradle was lifted to the pier and then the bomb was laid in the cradle by the main crane. Finally, the cable was attached and the cradle was pulled ever so slowly along the pier. At one point a pier board snapped and everyone watching thought the pier was going to collapse under the weight, but the winch slowly pulled the now-bent cradle up from the hole and its journey continued until a wheel snapped, causing the weight of the bomb to bend the cradle further. Now all that could be done was to pull the cradle along the remainder of the pier, deeply scoring the boards, until it was on solid ground. From there the winch continued to do its job, leaving a path of tilled earth and etched concrete in its wake.

While the team was monitoring the progress of their prize, a girl in a Chinese straw hat rode her bike directly into the side of the truck as if it were not there.

"Did you see that?" Tom asked.

"Yes," JD replied. "Seemed a bit odd."

"Maybe she did not see the cable until it was too late, then lost control," Gabby added.

"Seems plausible," JD responded without fully committing to the explanation, then decided, before things got too out of hand that it was a good time to come clean with Tom.

"So, Tom, we have something to admit to you. We did come down here on a missing person case, but we believe what they have found is—"

"The Tybee nuclear bomb lost in 1958," Tom interrupted.

"So, you knew all along?"

"No, not completely, but we have the area under surveillance anyway for the obvious reasons and when I saw your person of interest was on a deep exploration vessel with a fake name, bells went off. We now have several agents in the field to monitor the situation."

"Are you going to seize the bomb once it's in the truck?"

"No, we're going to wait until they relocate to a warehouse so we can capture as many involved in the plot as possible."

"I have to admit we haven't seen the man we're looking for yet, but assume he's below deck or possibly dead."

"Well, let's hope for below deck then," Tom finished,

then continued to talk with Mike. "Mike, since you may have been seen already, stay back and give the three of us a ride. We can follow at a safe distance and join the arrest once they have stopped."

"What if they drive it directly to a city?"

"We have orders to stop the truck at our discretion if it goes directly toward a large metropolitan area, but we believe the bomb needs some work before it's usable, so we likely have some time."

"I heard the Tybee bomb did not have a nuclear core or capsule," Gabby interjected from her perch watching the boatyard pier.

"That may be the case. There was a Strategic Air Command order to remove the nuclear capsules of older Mark 15 devices the same month the bomb went missing. But even if this was done, there could still be a nuclear core and, if not, the device still has a shitload of conventional explosives, so either way it's deadly."

"Agreed," JD said, while nodding his head.

"I think we have Darcy," Gabby called out as she peered through her binoculars. "Yeah, that has to be him—same height, same age. Looks like he's rubbing his wrist as if he were tied up below."

"So, now we do have a hostage situation as well," JD said to stress this could no longer be a guns blazing type of arrest.

"So we do," Tom said, expecting this development, but not happy with how it would curb his team's choices.

Pursuit vehicle A, driven by a young college-age couple, followed the truck west along Highway 80, occasionally passing their mark, then falling behind. Vehicle B, a rusty old truck driven by a man with a full beard and a *CAT* hat that was so stained it looked as if it were used as a spittoon when not being worn, puttered along behind. There were also two additional pursuit vehicles traveling ahead of the pack that could be swapped in if needed. JD and his team, now a foursome taking directions from the radio, followed well behind.

"They're crossing McQueen's Island and taking the bridge to Talahi Island," vehicle B called over the radio.

"Planning to pass after they cross the bridge," vehicle A informed the group. "Passing now . . . oh! They're pulling off the road into a boatyard. We will stop at the bar just up the road."

Vehicle B responded, "I'm stopping. Put a smoker under my hood to appear overheated, but I'm past the entry and my direct view is blocked by trees and bushes. I know there's a group of storage units on the other side of this tree line. Someone may get a better angle from there or we can call the chopper if there's a significant delay."

Mike drove past the smoking truck and pulled into the bar parking lot.

"Looks like we sit and wait."

"This is vehicle C . . . we're approaching the storage facility now. Wait, here comes the truck pulling around the trees. He's driving through a back yard to get here. We're pulling between the buildings to appear to be visiting a unit and will set up there if they stop as well. Nope, they're driving through . . . should be coming into the bar lot within a minute."

"We see them," vehicle A answered. "Do you think they made one of us?"

"I don't know. They could have stopped to pick up tools or personnel," vehicle B responded. "I will wrap up here and join up again after they pull out and see me stalled on the side of the road."

JD listened in, but was not fully convinced. He watched

with the others from their car as the truck pulled out of the storage complex and continued around behind the bar. When the truck appeared again and moved up to pull back onto the highway, JD saw a flash of green light. He pulled up his binoculars and watched as the truck drove away. He still could not shake the bad feeling brewing in his gut, so he spoke up.

"I don't like this. Should we check the lot where they stopped?" JD asked Tom from the back seat.

"We can have vehicle D circle back to check out the spot."

Still, something bothered JD and it troubled him that he could not put a finger on it. He closed his eyes and after a moment of silence saw a green flash again.

"The bumper!" JD called out to the car.

"What?" Tom asked, a bit confused by JD's outburst.

"The bumper of that truck wasn't bent."

"So . . .?"

"So, it's not the same truck. When we saw the Chinese girl ride her bike into the side of the truck, I noticed the right rear end of the iron bumper had a slight twist. The truck that just pulled out onto the highway did not."

"How can you be certain at such a distance?"

"I checked it with my field glasses," JD confirmed while holding up his binoculars. I think we need to check the field they drove through."

"OK, you take this car and we'll have vehicle D pick us up instead of circling back to the field. I hate you missing out on this arrest, but we can't stay too far back."

"I understand—thank you for the car."

JD climbed into the front seat and drove the car to the backside of the bar.

"Let's talk this out. How do you want to go about this?" he asked Gabby.

"Well, if they are still there and we happen upon them, it could be trouble—we are severely outnumbered."

"And, if they have already made the pursuit team, then they're probably on heightened alert."

"We could take a drive down the frontage road that runs along the parking lot down to the boat dock."

"Yes, I was thinking that same option. At the very least we can have eyes on the portion of the boatyard that's obstructed from the highway. Let's give it a try."

JD drove the car around the bar and pulled onto the highway using the same outlet the truck used several minutes earlier. He drove northeast, back toward the bridge, then turned off at the boatyard entrance, taking a right on what turned out to be Old Tybee Road. Using his mirrors to glance back at the far corner of the boatyard, JD did not see anything that alarmed him.

JD pointed to Mike's cooler and said, "Let's park in the lot looking back toward the corner and eat some lunch."

Gabby opened the cooler and peered in. "Looks as if they came prepared for a long sit. All the better for us, but there is nothing in here that will not eventually kill us. If we are in for a long haul, we will need to get some sustenance that is less offensive."

JD smirked as he grabbed a Slim Jim.

They spent the next several minutes having their mock lunch and discussing what to do next.

"I think we have to sneak some peeks at that corner and if we do not see anything, then we need to drive to the corner of the lot to have a cigarette while we walk amongst the old abandoned boats," Gabby suggested.

"You have cigarettes?" JD asked.

Gabby popped open the glove compartment and pulled out a pack of Marlboros.

"Do you not smell the smoke-soaked upholstery in this

beast?"

"Now I can," JD admitted.

After a few more minutes of eating and pretending to talk, JD snuck a peak at the far corner of the lot with his binoculars.

"Nothing."

A moment later, Gabby did the same. "Nothing."

On JD's next look he saw a flash of green light that made him look closer at a group of trees and thought he saw white among the branches and leaves.

"I think I see white through the branches of the tree near the blue boat, but it could just be a building."

JD looked at the property at the end of the lot and saw a house with a garage and a shed and a fenced-in back yard.

"If it's a shed, I don't think it belongs to the property over there since it's well outside the fence line. Seems like a strange place to have an outbuilding. Maybe it's a tool shack or a pumping station."

"Yeah. I think I see shingles up above. Wait!"

"What is it?"

"I think I saw movement. Yes, it is a building, but there is something white moving beside it."

JD pulled up his binoculars just in time to see green grass flash between two white surfaces as a white truck pulled out from behind the outbuilding.

"Shit. I think that's the truck. We have to be careful since we are the only tailing vehicle this time."

"I guess we have been promoted to car #1," Gabby said, watching through her binoculars as the truck pulled out onto the highway. "And, JD, you are correct—the right end of the rear iron bumper is slightly twisted."

JD followed at a safe distance while Gabby called Tom.

"Tom, I believe we are following the original truck with

the twisted bumper. This doesn't mean they didn't switch the cargo, but we both know it is unlikely they could have moved four tons in such a short time period."

"Gabby, there is a tracking device in the glove compartment."

"Next to your cigarettes?"

"Yes, next to Mike's cigarettes. Try to place it when they stop for gas since you don't have back up. Our truck is leading us toward the airport. We may have to close in on them there if there are no other developments."

"Roger," Gabby said before she hung up.

JD followed the truck through the historical district of Savannah until it finally turned onto Interstate 16 which eventually turned into I-75. Over the next several hours they followed the truck until it eventually stopped for gas in Chattanooga.

"This is our chance," JD said as he pulled into a pump several aisles over.

"I will create a distraction while you place the tracker. When I kick my foot, you are good to go," Gabby said as she jumped out of the car with a baseball cap in hand.

Gabby circled around by the store and came out in front of the truck with her pants rolled up to appear as shorts and her socks pulled to their limit, almost making her knees. She was not wearing her coat and her blouse was unbuttoned to the middle of her chest. She had also pulled her hair out of its tight bun. This left pigtails sticking out from her cap, which she had pulled down to hide her face. With all this in place, she slowly walked in front of the truck eating a Slim Jim and skipping every other step.

JD grabbed the window washer squeegee and walked to the aisle where the truck was pumping gas. He kept an eye on Gabby and when Gabby kicked her foot, he slipped behind the truck and knelt to place the tracker. This is when he saw there was another tracker already in place. Momentarily confused, he set the device and slipped away after grabbing a handful of towels from the pump island and uttering swear words as if he were bothered to have to come to another dispenser to get a simple paper towel.

Gabby climbed back into the car after the truck pulled away to get back on the highway.

"What are you smiling at?" Gabby asked, yet knowing full well.

"You just reminded me of an old colleague that I haven't thought about for a while. Her name is Ellie and she had your problem-solving skills as well."

"Yeah, the knee socks and the pig tails may have been enough for a car full of Japanese sailors, but I did not want to take any chances."

"Well done. However, there's a new issue."

"What is that?"

"There are now two trackers on that truck."

"Two? Someone from our team already placed a tracker and Tom didn't know?"

"Or . . . it's not an FBI tracker."

* * *

Tom and his team sat at various locations around the hangar complex and waited. The truck they were following had turned into an open hangar several hours before and was still idling inside.

"I still don't see any movement and I can't see the driver anymore," Mike said, then pulled the binoculars away from his face and rubbed his eyes. "What do you think they're doing? Are they waiting for someone to come or are they working on the bomb in the back of the truck?"

Tom sat back in his seat with his head against the head rest.

"I honestly don't know any more. We are wasting precious time if we're truly following the wrong truck, but if we play our cards now, we may not set a wide enough net and we could miss some players—possibly important players," Tom replied with his eyes closed.

"Mike, we have someone at the truck," came a voice over the radio.

Tom sat up to listen as Mike replied. "What are they doing?"

"Looks like he's just sniffing around. He walked around it once and—and now he's opening up the driver's door."

"Go! Go now!" Tom yelled and moments later the hangar echoed with screeching tires as four sedans converged upon the truck.

A Mexican man sat in the truck's driver seat wide-eyed with most of the blood drained from his face.

"I wasn't stealing it. I was just turning it off. Here—here, take the keys," he said as he tossed the keys at Agent Wheeler's feet.

"Nothing in the back," Mike called from the rear of the truck. "Just a couple of candy wrappers."

Then Freddie, a thin agent with a caterpillar mustache, standing next to Mike at the back of the truck said, "I'm not getting a reading either, Tom. I don't think the bomb was ever in this truck."

"Bomb?" the Mexican man yelled then jumped out of the truck.

"Hold up . . . Miguel," Tom said after seeing the man's name on his work shirt. "We still have some questions for you and you heard the man—there is no bomb. There is no bomb . . ." Tom said again aloud, making it register that his team had followed the wrong truck and now the truck with the bomb had only one vehicle in pursuit, which did not include any members of his team.

"Should I contact JD and Gabby?" Mike asked.

"No, you interview Miguel and I'll swallow that pill."

"Thanks, partner!"

"So, Miguel, how long have you worked here?" Mike asked as Tom walked away to call JD and Gabby.

* * *

JD and Gabby drove in silence for a while, then resumed the small talk they had enjoyed on the first leg of the journey. At Chattanooga they had swapped seats to let Gabby drive for a while and give JD a chance to rest and think. JD sensed where the truck was going, but could not fully commit to the reasoning.

Just then JD's phone rang.

"Special Agent Dearfield."

"JD, you have the potato," Tom said matter-of-factly.

JD quickly placed his hand over his phone and whispered to Gabby, "We were right."

"We have an empty truck and no suspects. The driver must have exited the passenger's side door and slipped out the building or into a basement tunnel before we set up a perimeter. Please tell me you're still in pursuit," Tom continued.

"Yes, we have them in sight and we were able to place a tracker," JD confirmed.

"Thank God. I really thought we actually *shot* the pooch on this one. What's your 20?"

"We're on I-24 just northwest of Chattanooga."

"Great. Give me the tracker info and we'll follow in the helicopter. Where do you think they're headed?"

"My best guess is Indianapolis, but I haven't fully talked

myself into it yet. Indy could certainly be considered an emotional enough target, but I feel something is missing."

"Indy seems like a reasonable enough target. That's where the USS *Indianapolis* National Memorial is located—on Canal Walk in the heart of the city."

"I'm still not convinced. Indy does make some sense, but there are so many other options. This act is an act of vengeance, rife with emotion. Indy seems more tit-for-tat. Why not San Francisco, the *Indy*'s home port, or New York, the symbol of American freedom and success."

"Let's be glad these guys are picking a smaller city. A bomb in a city the size of New York would be a disaster. Any city or place in America is bad, but God help us if this does go off, we want it as far away from a densely populated area as possible. We still don't have confirmation from the Air Force, but even if the bomb doesn't contain fissionable material, it can still cause major damage if ignited."

"Then why are we not arresting them now?"

"We have orders to not engage until we know they're not meeting with further contacts."

"Seems like a gamble."

"Yes, it is, but again, this is likely a non-nuke and we have an unknown organization that brought what they thought was a viable nuclear device onto US soil. Washington wants to know who helped these guys, so they can sleep at night knowing this group is finished and not going to linger on like so many other terrorist groups that are constantly biting at our ankles."

"I'll call our office to get them researching probable locations beyond the memorial. We'll keep you updated."

"Thanks. We're right behind you."

"Just stay low and at a distance. We don't need them freaking because they see a chopper constantly in the sky behind them."

"No worries. We're going to grasshopper it. Talk to you soon."

"Indy does seem logical," Gabby added once JD was off the phone.

"Yes, logical. But emotional? I'm still not buying it. Something is mis—"

Ring! Ring!

"Special Agent Dearfield."

"JD, I just talked to Joker."

A City Near You

April 12, 2007

"Dad?"

"Yeah. We've been calling him ever since he disappeared, but he never picked up until now. He says he's in a truck heading northwest. He got his phone back when they left it in a duffle in the back of the truck. He says they have the bomb. They have the bomb!"

"Whoa, slow down, Dad," JD said, taking a moment to think. "Does it sound like he's under duress?"

"No, he said he's in a cage at the front of the compartment and was able to get his phone through the bars. He can only call when they have the music playing and they're working on the bomb. The music sounds Japanese to me. What are we going to do?"

"Calm down, Dad. *We* are not going to do anything. I am going—"

"If you think after the life I have led that I'm going to sit on my hands and watch my friend die, you don't know me at all. I'm either coming with you or I'm going it alone with Gerbil and Kaida. There are no other options."

"Sounds like he's calmed down now," Gabby commented without taking her eyes off the road.

JD put his hand over the phone and sighed, then said, "We will figure something out, Dad. Just, please, don't do anything until we can talk this through. If we had known about Joker's phone, we may have been able to locate him via GPS."

"Joker would never leave his location on—he's too paranoid."

"Well, if you talk again, have him switch it on and send me his number."

"Got it."

JD and Gabby followed the truck through Nashville onto I-65 to Louisville. At the outskirts of Indianapolis, the truck stopped for gas and Gabby casually followed them, stopping at a gas station across the road to watch from a distance.

After fueling, JD took his time and went into the store to stock up on some healthier snack alternatives. Upon returning he settled back into the driver's seat again.

"Seems like they're in no rush to get back on the road," Gabby commented as JD was fastening his seat belt.

"Nope. Maybe setting up a meet or getting directions."

"Or going to the bathroom," Gabby said with the binoculars to her face. "Looks like they have a honey pot in the back for the workers. They are emptying it now."

"Bet it smells like a rose in the cargo compartment of that truck. A 7,600-pound bomb lost at the bottom of the ocean for nearly 50 years must have a unique scent all its own."

"Yes, I feel fortunate to only have to deal with smoke infused car seats and not dying algae, human sweat and excrement. What a lucky girl I am."

"Looks like they're pulling out."

JD followed the truck again at a safe distance, but close enough to see the truck if it exited the highway. The truck took I-65 through the city, but on the west leg where JD expected them to exit, they continued north out of the city.

"Maybe they are going to a meet first?" Gabby suggested as they watched the truck continue on through the city, then they both had chills as they saw the sign over the highway directly ahead of them—North I-65 to Chicago.

"Why Chicago?" JD said aloud.

"If they need help repairing the bomb, maybe Chicago makes sense."

"But with all the planning they did to recover this nuke, I would have to believe they have someone capable of repairing it already on their team. Plus, Joker said they were working on it in the truck already. Though, working on a bomb, nuclear or not, while bouncing down the highway is either nuts or crazy to begin with, but mad does what mad wants, so we could very well be going to Chicago."

"Maybe they decided they need a lab?"

"That might be the golden ticket right there. Wasn't Chicago the birthplace of the bomb—at least in the public's eye? That might be the tie we're looking for."

"Argonne National Laboratory is the obvious choice," Gabby added. "It was originally the Metallurgical Laboratory, operated by the University of Chicago and was the first national laboratory in the US—an integral player in the Manhattan Project. I'll call the office to research other likely options."

"I'll call Tom and catch him up."

JD continued to follow the truck up I-65. They drove for miles seeing nothing but flat farm fields with an occasional hill as a poor attempt to break the monotony.

"There are plenty of universities in this part of the country. Maybe they're going to Purdue or U of I—Illinois was involved in the Manhattan Project, was it not?" JD asked Gabby.

"Yes, there are several of the twenty or so sites involved with the project in the Midwest, but none on the scale of the Chicago lab."

"But this still doesn't make sense to me. Do they have

some disgruntled physicist involved in this plot? I know many of the scientists involved in the Manhattan Project formed a coalition to educate the world about atomic weapons and even tried to establish an international atomic development authority as an attempt to curb the anticipated arms race. They ultimately failed, but it seems unlikely that a physicist would be involved in actually setting off a bomb in protest of the bomb. Or am I naive to think every scientist approaches regret as Alfred Nobel did?"

"Do you know Nobel decided on creating the Nobel Prize after his brother died in France and a paper published Alfred's obituary instead. It was titled *The Merchant of Death is Dead* and claimed Alfred Nobel had become rich by finding ways to kill more people faster than ever before. The article condemned him for his invention of military explosives, which was of course the exploitation of his actual invention, dynamite, which he created for civilian applications."

"Strange how the world works sometimes."

"Yes. So, I think you are correct. A physicist would not think of a *weapon* as a tool of protest, but it could just as well be a disgruntled professor or student," Gabby surmised.

"So, have we decided they're going to Chicago to blow up the Manhattan Project lab in retaliation or contact a disgruntled professor or student?"

"Or maybe a sleeper."

"Oh, we are way down the rabbit hole now. Let's take a break and look at the corn."

"Funny."

The truck turned onto I-90 at Gary and continued toward Chicago. Even though Tom was simultaneously tracking the truck's progress via the GPS tracker, JD called him again to discuss the truck's likely destination and go over their options.

"Tom, they're heading right for Chicago. I think we should consider stopping them before we have a situation we can't control on our hands."

"I hear what you're saying, but Washington wants their associates," Tom returned, stating the company line again.

"OK. We will continue to follow at a safe distance," JD replied, then hung up. "Gabby?"

"I know."

"What I know is that we may be following *their* bomb, but we're entering *our* city, so we should have a say in how this goes down. Can you call Unit Chief Tillman to get his take on this?"

"Already dialing."

Gabby spoke to Marcus Tillman on the phone for only a moment before hanging up and turning to JD.

"Washington wants their associates. Period."

"They're really betting this bomb isn't viable."

"That is the line, but no one from the Air Force has verified this since the files are not online and no one is around from when the bomb originally disappeared. All they really know is what was told to the public, not what was actually known by the Air Force."

"Shit. We are knee deep in shit."

After talking it over, Tom decided to fly ahead to the University of Chicago and prepare their team for the truck's likely arrival. JD called his office and two cars were dispatched into the city to be available if needed. The truck continued on I-90, then exited onto South Indianapolis Avenue before eventually turning north onto South Ewing Avenue. JD was happy to be back in the city again, back to ground he knew, but feared the uncertainty of this current homecoming. South Ewing wound through the south side of Chicago before meeting up with South Lake Shore Drive in Jackson Park. South Lake Shore Drive was a tour of historical and cultural Chicago. Jackson Park, at its southernmost end, was the site of the 1893 World's Fair—the Columbian Exposition—and still contained the Statue of the Republic and the only remaining main-site fair building, which now housed the Museum of Science and Industry. This is also where the Midway Plaisance—the carnival experience at the exposition and the likely seed for future boardwalks and theme parks, such as Coney Island in New York—stretched out into the city and onto the University of Chicago campus.

The truck meandered through the park and continued north into the center of the city at the expected turnoff.

"Where is he going?" Gabby asked.

"I wish I knew. Call Tom and tell him he may be sitting on another dud."

Lake Shore Drive, which had started as a two-lane highway, soon expanded into a busy five-lane expressway which was further complicated by numerous stop lights along the way. The truck continued past McCormick Place Convention Center, Soldier Field football stadium, Field Museum of Natural History, Adler Planetarium, Shedd Aquarium, Buckingham Fountain and Millennium Park. Soon, JD found he was a full two lights behind the truck.

"I'm glad we have the tracker in place—this is getting a little dicey. Can you call the two cars we have on standby and have one shadow us on the Inner Drive and the other on Michigan Avenue?"

Gabby, who was tracking the truck GPS on her laptop and watching it in traffic through her binoculars, said, "We still have her. They are not lost yet," then relayed JD's message to the other Chicago chase cars.

"They are getting off at Navy Pier," Gabby informed JD as they sat caught by the light at Monroe.

"OK. Tell me where they turn," JD said as he started to accelerate through the S-curve before taking the Navy Pier exit.

"They are on Grand at Michigan Avenue. They must be stopped at the light. Oh, here they go and—wait, they disappeared?"

"What do you mean they disappeared?"

"They must have turned onto Lower Michigan Avenue and we lost the signal."

"Shit. I had a feeling something like this was coming our way. It has just been too easy up to this point."

"What do we do?"

"Where are our other cars?"

"One is on Michigan right above them, but can't get there any sooner than we can and the other is circling around Grant Park to get back on the Drive."

"Keep a car on Michigan and Upper Wacker. They may have better luck with the signal if they are directly above them. Send the other to follow us."

"Got it."

JD drove down Lower Wacker Drive, but with so many turnoff options he knew if they did not have some old-fashioned luck that the search was futile.

"You still can't pick up the GPS?" JD asked with some desperation.

"No. It is like a Faraday cage down here. Our own GPS says we are on Michigan Avenue half of the time."

"Well, let's get back up top and try to figure this out. I have a feeling there's no actual bigger conspiracy here and we just let two nut jobs loose with a bomb in Chicago."

* * *

The truck turned left off Grand Avenue onto Lower Michigan Avenue and drove for several blocks in the eerie combination of artificial light mixed with sunlight and intermittent darkness. They eventually turned right onto Lower North Water Street, which turned into Kinzie Street, then followed it to a loading dock on Lower Wabash Avenue. The gang of eight in the truck included the driver and his shotgun co-pilot, three scientists, two bodyguards and Joker.

"Hey, you can't park there. Don't you see the sign? It says *No vehicle parking on the yellow stripes*," shouted Elmer, the weather-worn dock traffic flagman, then pointed at the ground and continued. "You see there? Those are yellow stripes."

"We are here delivering the hyperbolic chamber for Mr. Mizushima's new condo in this illustrious skyscraper."

"What seems to be the problem here?" Ralph, Elmer's dock manager, asked as he walked John Wayne-like toward the truck.

"We are here to deliver the hyperbolic chamber to the condo of Mr. Mizushima on floor 88," the driver restated.

"Let's take a look," Ralph said as he continued to the back of the truck.

"But they're parked on the yellow stripes and even came in the exit," Elmer chirped.

"We will deal with that in a moment, Elmer. So, what you got here?"

The driver opened the lift gate of the truck to reveal a 12-foot by 4-foot wooden crate wrapped in chains.

Ralph was immediately hit by a wall of stale malodorous air and took three steps back. "What else did you have back here?" he said coughing and waving his hand, then looked up again and asked, "What is behind the curtain?"

At the front end of the cargo compartment a curtain was drawn to hide the cage, which now contained Joker, the tools used to prepare the bomb and the five men who inhabited the compartment since leaving Georgia. Joker sat in a back corner with his mouth gagged and a pistol pointed at his temple.

"Earlier the truck contained a pair of toy donkeys that we delivered to Mr. Mizushima's niece in Lake Forest. Their cage with straw and their droppings is behind the curtain. Would you like to inspect them?"

Ralph stood expressionless for a moment and then continued as if it were just another day. Elmer, on the other hand, looked wide-eyed at Ralph and the driver, then walked away mumbling.

After refocusing on the crate, Ralph asked, "How much does the crate weigh?"

"We believe less than 8,000 pounds," the driver replied.

"Less than 8,000 pounds?! You mean this thing weighs almost four tons?" Ralph said, now finally alarmed by something.

"Yes. This chamber is very important to Mr. Mizushima and must be moved into his unit at once."

"As important as this is to Mr. Mizushima, he will not be moving into his unit for over a year, so the crate will have to wait its turn on the schedule. If it were storable, I would offer to keep it in storage here until it was time to move it into his unit, but at four tons, we do not have the capacity or the means to move this into the building's storage area from the dock. I'm sorry, you will need to make an appointment at the crane loading dock when we are ready to lift it to Mr. Mizushima's unit."

"But the owner of this glorious tower promised it would

be moved into position today."

"Well, I'm not sure if you spoke with him or one of his sons, but the 88th floor will likely remain open to the weather for at least a few more months, so it is unwise to move a piece of electronics into the space at this time."

"So, you are familiar with hyperbaric chambers?"

"Of course I am. We have installed three of them already, but only at time of floor closure and none of them weighed four tons. We will have to verify with our engineers where a chamber of this weight can be placed well before we can move it into position."

"We have our promises. Mr. Mizushima feels it would cause him bad karma to delay. Do you intend to bet your job on this?"

"Promises from this company are mostly rainbows. They are meant to look nice, but are usually only illusion. I do my job right and trust the engineers will do the same no matter what is promised. As for karma, I don't much know about that."

"Very well," the driver said while closing and relocking the lift gate. He then bowed his head and walked out of the loading dock, leaving his truck behind.

"Well, I'll be darned," Ralph said, then watched the man in the passenger's seat exit the truck cabin and follow his companion out. Ralph looked at the truck parked on the yellow stripes and said, "Something new every day with this crazy building."

* * *

Rai and Jiji sat in a brand-new Cadillac Escalade on Kinzie Street awaiting a call from their driver when someone knocked on the driver's side window. Rai rolled down the window to find he was looking into the faces of his truck driver, Kogen, and his bodyguard, Banzan.

"What are you doing here, you fools?"

"We came to inform you they will not move your crate today," Kogen said.

"Then when?"

"They said maybe in a few months."

"Lies," Rai shouted and moved his left hand inside his coat.

Jiji reacted immediately and pinned Rai's hand to his side. Rai's amber eyes flared like fire, but Jiji calmed him.

"Master, you can dispatch this fool at any time you wish, but here in the middle of the city your desire to punish may not be the best timing. Remember karma. If they will not move the bomb for use on the 88th floor, then we will move it. Why don't we drive the truck into the highest parking level and prepare it there?"

"Brilliant idea," Rai exclaimed, praising Jiji.

"Master, I believe this to be the answer, but the truck will not be able to enter the garage as it is too tall," Kogen said with some trepidation.

Again, Rai's left hand twitched toward his coat, but he stopped himself this time.

"Master, we do have the second SUV to serve as our back-up plan," Jiji noted.

Rai gave a big broad smile and said, "Let us meet in the bowels of this beast of a city and move the crate into the other Cadillac. America's truck will now aid us in our journey. Kogen and Banzan, retrieve the trucks and follow us."

"Yes, master."

* * *

"I can't take this anymore. JD isn't updating us and we're

just sitting here doing nothing," Jack said, clearly frustrated.

"But what can we do knowing nothing?" Kaida asked.

"We can do plenty. Joker told us during his last call that the men holding him were talking about Chicago. He doesn't know much Japanese, but it's hard to miss *Chicago* no matter what the language."

"So, what do you suggest?" Gerbil asked.

"Let's get ourselves into the city and be ready."

* * *

When Kogen returned to retrieve the truck, he seemed unaffected by the evil-eye he received from Elmer as he watched his every move. After finding a blind alley several blocks away, Rai watched as Kogen and Banzan backed the trucks together and then used a rolling ramp to help move the giant crate into the Escalade. Even with the beefed-up suspension, the weight of the bomb was redlining every system of the SUV. Rai chose not to drive the Escalade into the garage since if it failed, he wanted someone to blame. Kogen gratefully accepted the challenge knowing if he was successful, he would win the praise of his master. Kogen slowly drove the Escalade though the streets of Chicago to come around to Wabash Avenue and up to the parking garage entrance, where he was blindly waved through as just another truck with a crate by the construction parking attendant. The rest of the team followed in Rai's Escalade.

* * *

JD's hairs went stiff on the back of his neck when he heard the message come across the radio.

"JD, we found the truck."

"Where is it?" JD asked quickly, readying himself to turn.

"It's in a canyon alley west of Wabash between Hubbard and Illinois. We really got lucky on this one. The GPS only beeped once as we drove by."

"Have you looked inside yet?"

"Nope. My partner is going up now."

JD could hardly contain his anxiety over the reveal.

"Looks like we have an empty truck. Sorry, JD. We will keep patrolling to see if we can spot anything suspicious."

JD was near devastation and held no hopes for finding anything suspicious, but had no better ideas.

"OK. Thanks, Sam."

"What do we do now?"

"I don't know just yet, Gabby. Let me think."

* * *

Jack, who had been checking Joker's GPS on his phone called out excitedly to the group. "I have a signal!"

"Where is he?" Gerbil asked, just as excited.

"I don't know. This just gives coordinates. We will need to drive to these coordinates to find his location."

The group continued through the streets of Chicago, fighting the one-way streets and the lower-only access until they arrived directly in front of the location—401 N Wabash Avenue. The trio looked up to see the name of the building in question.

Trump International Hotel & Tower

"Looks like they're in there somewhere?" Jack said, a little deflated.

"How are we going to search a gigantic building all by ourselves?" Gerbil said, likewise discouraged.

"I believe we search for where the bomb could go," Kaida suggested. "Maybe we should start with the parking garage?"

"I don't disagree, but how do we get in there with a guard at the entrance?" Gerbil asked, still a bit down.

"We distract and go around," Kaida said plainly. "Let us park to begin."

After parking further down Wabash, Kaida walked into a convenience store and emerged a few moments later.

"Are we ready?" she asked the two men.

Jack and Gerbil nodded yes and followed Kaida as she crossed the street and walked toward Trump Tower. As the group approached the hotel's circular drive, Jack and Gerbil casually sat on the garden wall at the garage entrance having a smoke as Kaida continued on to the hotel entrance. A moment later there was a raging fire in the city garbage can in front of the hotel. The garage attendant did not immediately see the fire, so Gerbil pointed it out to him.

"Looks like that fire might just catch those trees on fire," he called to the attendant.

"Huh . . . oh, shit!" the attendant yelled and then ran to help put out the fire. Seconds later, all three were on the ramp winding up toward the parking garage.

* * *

After their disappointment over finding the original truck empty, JD and Gabby resumed patrolling Lower Wacker with the other two Chicago cars.

"Do you have anything on Joker's phone?" JD asked Gabby.

"Nope. Quiet as a church mouse."

JD called all the teams, his and Tom's, for reports, but

received nothing positive. He considered calling his father, but could not bear to disappoint him further. He had to find something—anything.

* * *

Jack, Gerbil and Kaida roamed the massive garage structure, but found it mostly abandoned at this time of night. Sure, there were teams working at night, but nothing like the manpower displayed during the daytime hours. It was nearing midnight when the trio approached two ominous-looking black SUVs.

"Thank you for coming," a voice called from behind them.

They all turned in tandem to see Rai and Jiji standing with three other men, all dressed as masked ninja. Gerbil's first reaction was to look back toward the SUVs for a lane of escape, but instead found another group of four likewise dressed men holding Joker.

"Joker!" Gerbil called.

Jack and Kaida also turned to see Joker.

"Yep. I am the guest of this fine group of ant people. Glad to see you're alive, little buddy."

The man farthest to the right of the group stepped in front of Joker and punched him in the stomach. Gerbil took a step forward, but Kaida place an arm gently on his arm to stop him.

"Now is not our time," she said softly.

"You have all been led here to be a part of history as we explode the world's tallest building," Rai ceremoniously told the group.

Jack and Gerbil looked at each other while Joker just plain broke down and laughed, earning him another punch to his gut.

"You ant people don't have your facts right. Have you been living in a hole? Oh, I guess that makes sense," Joker jested. "This isn't the tallest building in the world. It's not even the tallest building in Chicago."

"Lies," Rai spat, then swung his arm to indicate Joker was due another blow.

Joker took the punch in stride and continued, "Look it up if you don't believe me. Trump planned for this to be the tallest building in the world, but then 9/11 crushed his dream and he had to settle for second best in the birthplace of the skyscraper. Plus, I'm not one for counting the spires, so I think it's really number three in Chicago."

Rai glanced at Jiji with a look of uncertainty, then yelled, "Grab them and bring them to the trucks . . . and take their phones."

Just then there was a flash of green light and several of the garage lights went dark.

* * *

"I think you should call your dad," Gabby said. "I am sure he's worried sick and you want him to trust you."

"You're right. My brain tells me that's the right thing to do, but my gut is still on absent father mode and it's a hard feeling to kick."

"You may never kick it, but you are more than just an agent on this case. You have to feel that."

"I do. I just don't know what to tell him."

"When you were nine, you wanted the truth, so give him the truth. Truth always wins."

JD picked up his phone and dialed his father, but there was no answer. He thought it was a bit weird he would not be waiting for his call, but then again, he did not know his father all that well and for all JD knew his dad could be drunk at a bar somewhere.

"Not answering. Let me see if he has his location on?"

JD plugged his dad's number into his laptop and waited for his GPS to register on the screen. A pulsating blue circle eventually appeared and JD was a bit surprised to see his father was not at one of the many college bars in JD's neighborhood.

"He's just a few streets down—just over the Wabash Bridge. From the looks of it, he's in the Trump Hotel?"

Gabby and JD glanced at each other and knew this was not a sure bet, but did breathe life into what was turning out to be more of a postmortem than an active investigation.

"Should we tell the team?" Gabby asked.

"Let's tell Sam we're looking into a possible lead, but keep it at that. I don't want to let everyone know we called the whole team in because I found my dad at the Trump International Bar and Grill."

"The hotel is not even open yet," Gabby laughed.

"I know. I was just making a point."

* * *

"Gentlemen and my little mountain nymph, let me show you the agent of your destruction," Rai said to the group as he walked over to stand above the men attempting to bring the bomb out of the SUV.

The fact that the rolling ramp—a ramp with rows of wheels to easily move items out of a truck—had worked well when laid flat between two truck beds, gave the group encouragement it could be used as intended, to slide the crate down from the bed of the truck to the floor of the garage. As they pushed the crate further out onto the ramp, the ramp began to bend. However, the men pushing in the truck could not see this and continued to push until the crate was extended enough that the weight snapped the ramp like a twig. When the extended end of the crate hit the ground, the crate exploded into pieces and the bomb rolled out and continued to roll due to the slope of the garage floor. The men standing above the ramp were shoved backwards by flying pieces of wood from the crate, while those working below were likewise sprayed with shards of wood, but also had the rolling bomb to deal with. As the men scattered for their lives, one unfortunate man was virtually steamrolled to death by the runaway four-ton bomb.

Every soul in the garage stared at the man who was now nothing more than a pulp spot on the concrete floor and then with extreme trepidation followed the bomb until it slammed against the inner garage wall just within the remaining light.

Physics never loses, Joker thought to himself.

* * *

JD parked his sedan in front of the Trump Hotel and walked with Gabby to the parking garage entrance. As they climbed the driveway to the garage entrance, JD saw several lights flash off in his peripheral vision.

"Did you see that?" JD asked Gabby.

"The lights going out?"

"Yes. We may have our location and I think that gives us probable cause since there's no night watchman to grant us admission."

"Agreed. Safeties off," Gabby said as she pulled her gun and followed JD to the pedestrian entrance of the garage. Within no time at all, JD had picked the lock and they were on their way up the ramp.

* * *

Rai stood beside the tailgate of the SUV and addressed his captives who were now sitting with their hands tied, huddled along the inner wall just a few yards away from the giant bomb.

"It is no matter. America will still pay for its unholy cruelty. I am but the tool."

"Got that right," Joker remarked, now sitting with the group to the left of Gerbil, Jack and Kaida.

"Enough," Jiji yelled. "You all will learn your place. And you too, Kaida. Do you think us heathens, unwise to your manipulation? Your temple is but a joke on Sado. Poor and in the highlands like so many other sheep. You have no power here, but you will pay for your betrayal, as will these others."

"I cannot betray one who I do not respect and who does not respect me," Kaida answered without emotion.

"Enough of this petulance. Tie Joker to the bomb," Rai announced to his team.

"No, tie that one," Jiji countered as he pointed directly at Jack. "I originally thought it too cliché, but now it does seem to speak to me."

JD and Gabby crept up in the darkness to hide behind a pillar just as the bomb hit the floor, crushed a man and rolled toward them. They held their breath and were ready to bolt when the bomb came to rest just a few parking spaces away. They continued to observe the group and were ready to jump in if needed before backup could arrive.

"Not the Joker?" Rai questioned. "He has insulted me too

many times. He must be the one."

"No. This is not about Joker, though he will die—melted with Gerbil by the nuclear blast. This is about that man. The one who left me to die and America who left me as a slave in Sado. This is about revenge for a life ruined."

The taller Jiji then stepped forward and pulled off his mask. Gerbil made an audible grunt, but Joker and Jack just stared—Joker used to controlling his emotions and Jack in shock.

Finally, Jack said what the other two were thinking: "Leslie?"

Rai followed the response with his own, saying, "Leslie? No man named Leslie is telling me what to do."

"Oh, shut up," Leslie said, then pulled out a pistol and shot Rai in the leg.

Kogen stepped forward to retaliate against Leslie, but was stabbed through the back of his neck with a dagger that exited through his mouth like a snake's tongue before being withdrawn. Kogen and Rai both dropped to the concrete—Rai badly injured and Kogen dead as a stone. Rai looked back at his other bodyguards, but no one would make eye contact with him. After watching Banzan wipe off his dagger on Kogen's pant leg, Rai bowed his head. He now understood he was at the mercy of Jiji, whom he had freed from servitude, but still treated as less than a man.

"So, Jack, you are the one who will feel the blast firsthand. Maybe you can tell the others in hell what it was like."

"Leslie, I don't understand. We all thought you were dead," Jack said with repressed emotion as adrenaline pumped through his veins.

"What do you not understand about constantly making a fool of me in front of my shipmates? What do you not understand about putting me in sick bay to be nearly blown to pieces in the torpedo attack? All of you are guilty," Leslie said as he pointed at the trio.

Just then Leslie removed his shirt to reveal a badly scarred torso.

"These are not scars I carry with pride of service. After being left to die by you and my country, I was taken as a slave for over 60 years and beaten and whipped by this inbred's family." Leslie then kicked Rai in the leg wound, causing him to cry out in pain. "Shut up, you little dog."

"Great plan, Leslie. Except for one little issue—there's no nuclear material in this bomb of yours."

"Do you think this was about the bomb? How slow are you, Joker? This was never about the bomb. This was about finding you three so I could execute you. Nuclear melting or gunshot, it is all the same to me. So, any last words before you die?"

Joker said, "I would like to say something."

"Very good then—spit it out."

"I would like to make a confession."

"Excellent. What do you confess, Joker?"

"I would like to confess to Jack. Jack, I gave you LSD when you were in Montana. I'm sorry, but it was my job at the time."

"Joker, what are you taking about? We certainly got drunk, but I definitely don't remember seeing dancing colors or chasing psychedelic butterflies. We had a barbeque and a hike and I visited The Compound. It was a great four-day visit, Joker. Nothing else."

"It was only three days, but regardless, what is The Compound?" Joker asked.

"The place Lucile and Mr. Lewis took me to so we could deliver supplies. You were still sleeping when Lucile came by to ask me to help out with the delivery since Mr. Lewis' truck was on the fritz."

"I know Lucile, but who is Mr. Lewis?"

"He said he was Mr. Hughes' personal assistant and ran the supply chain for The Compound."

"And where is this compound?" Joker asked calmly.

"Off Skyland Road in the valley between Square and Slippery Bill mountains."

"Jack, there ain't nothing but trees and scree in that valley."

"What are you talking about? I delivered at least 12 crates of supplies that night."

"What else did you see at this Compound?" Joker asked cautiously.

Jack took a moment before answering since the answer had caused years of confusion, sleepless nights and ridicule. "Are you telling me it was all an LSD trip?" Jack looked at Joker, then at Gerbil sitting directly next to him. Gerbil just shrugged.

"What else did you see? I would bet it had a lot to do with what was on your mind that night. LSD seems to work that way—it either frees you from your thoughts or folds them into your trip."

"Shit, Joker. It took me 15 years to shake off the stigma of telling and retelling that story to my bar mates. And what do you mean it was your job?"

"That cabin I lived in was actually a safe house for the CIA and at that time was used by MK-Ultra to tape high-profile targets."

"And I was a high-profile target?"

"No, you were a best friend who I thought I was helping. Like many of us, I thought you were having trouble escaping your time in the water."

Gerbil subtly shifted his eyes to stare at the ground with the mention of *time in the water.*

"I kind of remember that part of the discussion now."

"Me too. You talked about Marilyn Monroe dying on your daughter's birthday and you not being there . . . and there was a Howard Hughes article in *Life* magazine you were reading while waiting for tea . . . and I said Elvis was like James Dean."

"The sausage guy is like Elvis?" Gerbil asked, trying to fit all the names together.

"No, *James* Dean the actor," Jack corrected, then continued. "And you gave me a sugar cube in a tiny tea cup, which you said was an homage to *Alice in Wonderland*. Shit. That explains the giant albino bear named Rabbit. What the hell, Joker. You almost ruined my life."

"Jack, you really have to tell us the whole story one day—sounds like you really got your money's worth," Gerbil added, not fully hearing Jack's last comment.

Suddenly, Jack thought back to a day before the galley event when Leslie had come to the pharmacy for penicillin to treat a probable syphilis infection. He wondered if his current mental instability was due to tertiary syphilis on top of 60 years of captivity. If so, it was not his fault Leslie did not receive his full treatment; he could blame that on the Japanese. Then again, Leslie had always been an ass—now he was just a crazy one—and it was hard to blame that on anything other than Leslie being Leslie.

"Enough. As I do much enjoy how you have tortured each other while I was away, I believe we have reached an end to the confession portion of the evening and, with no bomb, all that is left is to determine who will be first. Maybe I will shoot Gerbil, then Joker, so you can watch them die before I shoot yo—."

"I would like to confess that I am sorry," Jack blurted out, interrupting Leslie.

"Sorry for what, Jack? Not that it will make a difference

60 years too late."

"I would like to say I'm sorry you're still an ass."

"Thanks, Jack. Now you have moved to the front of the line," Leslie said, then raised his pistol and pointed it at Jack's chest.

JD tapped Gabby's thigh as a sign it was time to go and they both jumped out from behind the pillar shouting, "FBI. FBI. Drop your weapon."

JD was along the inner wall near the bomb and Gabby had taken up position closer to the outer wall. Leslie held up an open palm indicating he heard the message and started to lower his weapon, then quietly said to his team, "Now."

Leslie's team of five remaining men jumped in all directions and a spray of throwing stars shot toward JD and Gabby. JD was hit in the chest and the shoulder, while Gabby was hit directly in the forehead and knocked flat on her back. JD's vest prevented the star embedded in his chest from doing any real damage, but his right shoulder was slashed and bleeding profusely. He looked over at Gabby with hopeful anticipation, but then saw the embedded star and the steadily expanding pool of blood beneath her head. Believing she was dead, he returned his focus to Leslie and raised his now bloodied pistol.

"No, no, no, Mr. FBI," Leslie said as he aimed his pistol point-blank at Jack's chest. "I think you must drop your weapon before more people die."

JD knew even if he took out Leslie that he probably would not survive another onslaught of throwing stars and then would never be able to save his father and the other prisoners. As he contemplated his next move, his hand began to go numb and his wrist began to droop. With regret and more than just a little double guessing, he lowered his weapon and dropped it to the concrete, hoping he would live to fight another day.

"Very smart choice," Leslie said, then motioned for the man next to him to gather the weapon. "Check him for an ankle holster and get his dead partner's gun as well."

The man brought back the three guns and handed Leslie JD's primary pistol.

"Very nice. An official FBI weapon," he said as he looked at it more closely, turning it from side to side and testing its weight in his hand. "I assume you have a round chambered. Let's find out," Leslie said, then pointed the gun at Jack's chest again and pulled the trigger.

"No!" JD screamed. He had just watched his partner die and now his father, no matter how estranged, shot in front of him with his own weapon. He knew he was still losing blood and starting to feel a little dizzy, but Leslie's viciousness caused an emotional surge of adrenaline that he prayed would see him through to act if given the chance.

Before the echo of the gunshot had fully subsided, four throwing stars came flying out of the darkness behind JD and struck four of Leslie's remaining soldiers. Three of them dropped like bricks, grabbing their throats as blood oozed between their fingers, while the fourth screamed as he fell to the ground with a star pushed deep into his left eye socket. Now, all that remained of Leslie's team were Banzan, Leslie and a badly injured Rai.

Leslie ducked behind the Escalade and yelled, "Grab her," pointing to Kaida.

Banzan ran then rolled as four more stars flew over his head and slammed into the back panel of the Escalade, one puncturing the rear tire.

With a dagger in his hand, Banzan grabbed Kaida to pull

her to her feet. Gerbil reached across Jack's slumped body and grabbed at Banzan's arm in an attempt to free Kaida. Banzan's blade slashed across Gerbil's forearm and he recoiled in pain as blood poured from the wound. Banzan then pulled Kaida up by her hair and yanked her in front of him, holding the blade to her throat as he backpedaled to his master.

"Give her to me," Leslie said, then pulled her violently to his chest.

Banzan then moved behind Leslie, both men partially protected by the rear of the Escalade.

"I demand you show yourself or the girl gets her head blown off. I am giving you three seconds: one, two, thr—"

A slight Japanese girl ran up to the light, but remained just in the shadows.

JD feigned fright and crawled away toward Gabby. The girl was just a few feet away, but even in the limited light he could see she was the mirror image of Kaida.

"Ah, so it is true. The virgin has a twin," Leslie called out to the girl standing at the edge of the darkness. "Come into the light so you can watch your sister die."

As Leslie took a step forward from behind the car, Rai chose this moment to have his revenge and pulled out his dagger to stab at Leslie's thigh. Leslie screamed in pain and lowered his gun from Kaida's throat, but still kept her pinned tightly to his chest. In retaliation, Banzan flashed his own dagger and sliced off Rai's right ear. Rai likewise screamed in agony and held his ear as his body rolled unevenly down the parking ramp until he came to rest just feet from JD and Gabby. Even though JD was fighting to stay conscious and now seeing double, he cursed under his breath that he did not act after Leslie was stabbed. He knew opportunities like that were rare.

Keiko stepped forward into the light, then turned to look at JD, her jade eyes flashing in the ceiling light now directly above her head giving JD a moment of déjà vu.

Leslie, having suffered only a flesh wound and not the deep penetrating stab wound Rai had intended, refocused his attention on Kaida's twin sister. As soon as their eyes met, Keiko cartwheeled to her left beyond JD and threw two stars toward Leslie. The stars both missed wide, glancing off the SUV's rear window.

"Ha! I guess you have used up all your tricks. And a poor shot at that," Leslie called out to the girl.

Thump!

Leslie turned at the sound and found Banzan lying on the ground with two stars buried in his face.

Twang!

Leslie heard this sound too, but before he could turn to locate its source, he felt an arrow slam into the side of his neck.

Thud!

JD watched as Leslie let Kaida slide from his grasp. She fell to the floor and with the grace of a gymnast, rolled and leapt to take cover in front of the SUV.

Leslie pawed at the arrow stuck in his neck, then, deciding it was not a fatal blow, lowered his gun toward Keiko.

"Goodbye, my little green-eyed virgin," he managed to croak out of his throat, but before he leveled off his gun to take aim, his elbow exploded and his gun tumbled to the ground.

Every eye in the garage turned to see JD pointing Gabby's leg at Leslie, the end of her pants still smoking. After seeing he hit his target, JD, weak from blood loss, lay back to see an old woman standing with a crossbow at the edge of the darkness as the girl had before. He then heard voices yelling, "FBI. Hands up. Everyone, hands up." As he began to black out, he watched the old woman melt into the darkness.

700 years

April 13, 2007

JD awoke in an ambulance under the Trump Hotel porte-cochere to learn Gabby, Jack, Leslie and Rai had all been taken to the hospital, and that Joker and Gerbil were likewise being attended to on the premises by the ambulance crew. He would also come to understand through questions met with blank stares that by the time the FBI fully showed up on the scene, Kaida, Keiko and the mysterious old woman had completely vanished. As it turned out, JD had not lost a critical amount of blood, but was in fact poisoned with a neurotoxin when the toxin-dipped star slashed his shoulder. The EMT informed him that one dose was not sufficient to cause death on its own, then added that two doses might have been a different story. JD, a bit dizzy and still seeing double, was currently receiving a liter of normal saline to replace his blood volume and flush the toxin from his system.

Bo arrived about midway through JD's fluid bolus and gave him a big hug.

"How is my indestructible hero?" she whispered into his ear.

"Feeling a little destroyed, but I still love you . . . both," he said with a smile.

"Funny. Don't get any ideas. You can only have one of me."

"I know there's only one of you, my love, no matter how many I see," JD said, then kissed her hand.

Just then Joker and Gerbil, draped in blankets, came up behind Bo to check on JD. Gerbil's forearm was wrapped tightly in a bandage, but other than being a little traumatized, they seemed fine.

"How are you, old man?" Joker asked.

"I believe I'm still half your age, though I don't feel like it at this moment," JD replied.

As the group was making small talk, Tom Wheeler came over to check on JD as well. He also took this opportunity to remind Joker and Gerbil to come by the FBI Field Office tomorrow morning to give their statements.

"JD, I have something here for you. When they took your dad to the hospital, he had this in his inside coat pocket."

Tom handed JD a blood-stained bundle of letters with a yellowed envelope addressed to him on top:

Jonathan

JD looked at Bo. "I don't think I can read it. My vision is still blurry."

"Let me," Bo gently took the old envelope from JD's hand, tore open the flap and removed a likewise yellowed letter. "It is dated August 16, 1977."

"That was my ninth birthday. The day he disappeared."

Bo began to read the letter.

Aug 16, 1977

Junior,

I don't know how to start or even how to explain this to a nine-year-old boy, but I'm hoping with time this will make sense and maybe by that time you will find it in your heart to forgive me. I guess I should explain where I've been before I can say where I'm going.

When I was 15, I was the quarterback of the Janesville High School football team and was going out with the head cheerleader. I didn't know how good I had it, but life would soon tell me. That fall there was a dance, the Harvest Dance to be specific, and I had just broken up with the cheerleader, so I ended up dancing with KK DuPree. Well, my cheerleader ex-girlfriend got mad and told me off some more, but then KK put her in her place and that made her even more furious. That night at the Hill, a place we went to drink and kiss girls at night, I spent the night with KK, then I went home.

Later that night when I was walking home down our driveway, I saw KK's ex-boyfriend with a torch trying to burn down our barn, so I ran after him. I fought with him to try to stop him, but he was able to start the barn on fire anyway. I thought this was the worst thing that could happen that night, but I was soon proven wrong when I watched a man and my half-dressed ex-girlfriend come running out of the burning barn. It got even worse when I went to confront the man, who I assumed was my brother, Arthur, but instead saw my father looking up as I walked toward him. I immediately turned and hid in the horse pen.

I was dumbstruck and didn't know what to do. I felt I couldn't go home, as I felt my father already treated me unfairly and now he possibly even thought that I set the fire because he was with my ex-girlfriend, so I ran away. I ended up in Lake Geneva and worked at a school and camp for girls run in what is now Stone Manor. I was fully settled when a girl I liked ran away and the camp administrator blamed me for her disappearance and even called the police. However, the other girls at the school warned me just in time and I ran away again. This time I felt I needed to be free of the Janesville area and decided to enlist in the Navy. A friend of mine was a recruiter and helped me forge my papers. Within 3 months I was a pharmacist's mate on the USS Indianapolis delivering part of the nuclear bomb that helped end World War II, and two weeks after that I was part of the worst sea disaster in U.S. naval history. The Indy was sunk by two Japanese torpedoes and the survivors were in the water and all but forgotten by the Navy for four days, all the while being attacked and eaten by sharks. Nearly 900 men died in those four days—they either went down with the ship or died in the water. I was lucky to survive. The experience still haunts me, but it also gave me some good friends that, as you will find, make life worth living.

Four years later, once I was done with

the Navy, I tried to go to college to become a pharmacist, but was expelled from school when the frat I was pledging set me and another pledge up to get arrested. They were trying to rid themselves of the other boy and I was just collateral damage. I left the next day after being expelled and the other boy, I'm assuming, burned down the frat that night. I was later questioned by the police and cleared of all involvement.

When I finally returned to Janesville, I discovered my ex-girlfriend had become pregnant and the whole town thought I ran away because I was the father. I also found that Guilford, the son of the newspaper editor, was in love with my ex and she agreed to marry him after I disappeared. However, he soon found out he wasn't the father of their first child and immediately assumed I was. After that, he dug up every one of the stories I've told you about and published them as if they were true: I burned down the family barn, I kidnapped that girl from Stone Manor, I was a bad apple and hated by my shipmates, and I was the father of my ex-girlfriend's baby. All these stories became common knowledge to those who didn't know me better or didn't know the truth and I was a pariah in my own home town until I decided to marry my ex-girlfriend to appear to make it right.

I assume you understand now that my cheerleader ex-girlfriend is your mother and your grandfather Jake is the father of your older brother, Joe.

Your mother and I have tried to make our marriage work, but her drinking and cheating led to my drinking and then to my further humiliation when I started to talk about meeting Elvis and my time in Montana. I've lived in Janesville, or Footville, nearly my entire life and since the barn fire have never been accepted or been comfortable in my own skin and haven't truly thought of myself as being home. I only have one true friend who believes in me, Riff, and only three remaining siblings that I can call family.

This brings us to today. Your birthday and also the day Elvis and Guilford died. I'm sorry I missed you at school today and couldn't take you to the batting cages. I'm sorry I have to be away on the road so much. I'm sorry for so many things, but most of all I'm sorry that today I found out about another death that made me reconsider my life. Today, I learned KK's husband died, then I also found out she was sent away by her parents after I ran away because she was pregnant at the same time your mother was. I know for certain I'm not Joe's father, but it is possible I am the father of KK's child and I need to find out—I need to know.

I need to save myself from the hole that

has become my life here in Janesville and Footville, and for this reason I need to say goodbye. This isn't forever—I hope—but it could be and I just wanted you to know how much I love you—more than I can say. I feel this will be best for both of us since if I stay, I fear I'll continue to wither into the man my father was and thus affect your well-being. I can't rename you "Sue" to help you become a man like the Johnny Cash song, but know my spirit is with you always and with me gone from your life you will have a better chance at becoming the good man that I believe I was when I started out my life.

Love always—your father,

Jonathan Edward Dearfield Jr.

Bo let a tear run down her cheek before continuing. "Then there is a note dated this week written below the original text."

JD—
It has been 30 years since I wrote this letter, then didn't have the opportunity

to leave it for you. I don't regret leaving when I did since I saved a woman in a world of hurt and now we've made a life together—the kind of life I dreamed of when I was 9 years old. I just want you to know there wasn't a day that went by where I didn't think of you and now that I've finally seen the man you've become and know in my heart you are my son, maybe leaving was the right thing to do for both of us. Imperfect people often choose imperfect solutions. I know I'm far from perfect, but I can honestly say I'm proud to be your father and I hope that one day you can forgive me and come to my home in Geneva to meet your stepmother, KK, your brother, John, and his family. They are your family too.

I know your mother returned the letters I sent you after I left, but I saved them all and now give them to you in hopes of building a bridge to heal any hurt you still feel.

Love, ~~Jack~~ Dad

Bo finished the letter with tears running down her cheeks and looked at JD to find his eyes filled with tears as well.

"I feel horrible. All this time I hated that man for ruining my childhood. I never went into the bars even when I was of age since there were some still around who would call me Elvis Jr. or Jonathan *Elvis* Dearfield . . . and then I believed all the lies—every one. What kind of man does that make me, to hate my own father because of the lies of others? And these . . ." JD said as he held up the bundle of letters marked *Return to Sender*, "these prove he was trying to be a good father while I was busy not being a good son. I don't know if I can ever forgive myself."

"I think this letter is telling you that he forgives you, so you should be able to do so as well . . . with time," Bo added.

Joker cleared his throat, then spoke.

"JD, I feel I have to tell you this since it seems to have affected your life as well as your father's. I'm sorry for getting Jack involved in project MK-Ultra. It was my job to bring targets to Montana and record their LSD trips to see if they revealed anything important to national security. I gave Jack the LSD out of friendship to help him deal with the trauma, what they call post-traumatic stress now, never thinking it would add to his distress. God, I'm so sorry."

"Joker," JD said, his voice a little gravelly, "I'm certain he would have forgiven you. As you can see from the letter, he was in a good place at the end of his life."

Gerbil suddenly broke into tears and Joker placed an arm on his shoulder to comfort him.

"You're all acting like Jack is dead?" Tom said with some surprise in his voice.

"What?" JD said, likewise surprised.

"All of the injured taken to the hospital are still alive from my last report. I can't swear they all will live, but I would not give up hope just yet."

"Gabby?" JD asked.

"Yes, she lost a lot of blood, but is still with us, as is your dad."

"How?"

"Well, from the sound of the letter, I don't know who raised who, but at this point in his life he was smart enough to wear one of your old vests. The bullet knocked him out cold, but the wound was only superficial."

"What about the blood . . . on the letters?"

"Oh, that's Gerbil's blood—from his arm wound. Jack should certainly make it unless there are complications."

"My father has faced more than a few complications thus far in his life, so I bet he can handle one more. Thanks, Tom."

"Thank you, JD. Without you and your partner's insightful detective work, I don't know where we would be. We still haven't heard back from the Air Force, but that bomb has a definite radioactive signature. We don't know if it's due to a fully intact nuclear core or just residual readings. If it is fully intact with an active nuclear capsule, it could have taken out the better part of the city."

"But if the core was removed, then it was just a dud, right?" Joker stated, more than asked.

"Well, yes and no. Even if the capsule and the core were removed, the bomb still contained a good amount of conventional high explosives that could have leveled the building. If the core was still present with no capsule, there would not have been a nuclear explosion, but it would have spread radioactive uranium all over the city. They call that a dirty bomb."

JD looked up at Joker to see the color wash from his face and his eyes roll up in his head as he slowly fell backwards, taking Gerbil to the ground with him.

"Medic!" Tom yelled.

* * *

Bo, Joker and Gerbil all gathered around Jack's hospital bed and waited for him to wake from the sedative he was initially given when they treated him in the emergency department.

"I can't believe it. I thought he was a goner. I was sitting right next to him and saw the blood. I had no idea it was mine from when Banzan cut my arm. Think of it. Then everything happened so fast after that—with all the shooting and flying stars—it was hard to know for certain," Gerbil said to the group.

"Gerbil, there was nothing you could have done. It was a melee from what I hear. You are all lucky to be alive and you should all be proud of the lives you saved—maybe even the whole city," Bo responded.

"Bo?" Jack moaned.

"Yes," Bo said, then scooched her chair closer to the bedside. "How are you feeling?"

"Like a truck punched me in the chest," Jack said, then opened his eyes.

Bo could see Jack's brow furrow and immediately assessed it was because he did not see JD waiting with the others in his room.

"JD is looking in on his partner, Gabby. She's in the ICU, but expected to make it."

"Oh. Thanks, Bo," Jack said, then rubbed his eye and tried to sit up. "Whoa! Well, that's not going to happen any day soon."

"Here. Tell me when to stop," Bo said as she pushed the button to raise the head of the bed.

"Oh, that's good. So, what happened to you, Joker? Did you get shot too?"

"No, he fainted," Gerbil answered before Joker could formulate a response.

"Fainted? Joker?"

"Yep. I have to be honest. Last night was a little too much for a retired top spy like myself."

"It's good to be honest," Jack answered.

"Yes, it is. And I'm honestly glad to see you were smart enough to wear a vest to a gun and knife fight," JD said as he entered the room.

"Me too. Who said old dogs can't learn new tricks?" Jack answered.

"Excuse me. Time for Mr. Dearfield's vitals," a young nurse said as she approached the bedside.

"Do we have to leave?" Bo asked.

"No, this should be quick and easy. Unless you want me to get the special thermometer, Mr. Dearfield?" the nurse said with a smile.

"No. I'm OK with the standard vitals, but thanks for the offer."

The nurse finished up her tasks, then said her goodbyes. On her way out she brushed up against JD, who thought nothing of it in the crowded hospital room, but then looked down to find a piece of paper between the fingers of his left hand. He opened the note and read it to himself while the others continued to talk.

JD, please meet us at the Lou Malnati's Pizzeria on N Wells St. We would like to extend an invitation to you and your group for aiding in thwarting the evil plans of Rai Mizushima and his pet monster, Jiji. Reservations this Sunday at 7 p.m. under Sado. With honor, Kaida

"Sorry for interrupting. I'm Leah, Mr. Dearfield's nurse, and I need to take his vitals."

Everyone in the room just stared at Leah for a long moment until Jack finally broke the silence.

"It's OK, Leah, but I could save us both some time and just tell you what they are."

"Is the patient trying to do the nurse's job? This girl still needs her paycheck," Leah responded.

"Test away, Leah. Test away."

As the group gave Leah room to work, Bo looked up to see JD holding the note and asked, "JD, what do you have there?"

"A note from Kaida. She wants to meet us."

"I thought that last nurse looked familiar," Gerbil noted.

"I'm all for it. She's definitely a big reason I'm still alive," Joker claimed.

"I don't disagree. I have some thanks of my own to convey," JD said, then put the note in his pocket as the group huddled back around his father's bed.

"Jack, I was surprised when you insulted Leslie so blatantly. That's not like you," Joker mockingly chided Jack.

"Well, it was difficult to insult him more than comes natural to you, but I knew I had a vest on and you did not."

Joker turned a bit pale again, then said, "Yes, there is that."

* * *

Lou Malnati's is a true Chicago classic and home to one of the most popular Chicago-style deep dish pizzas on the planet. Lou Malnati started out working in Chicago's first deep dish pizzeria in the 1940s and went on to open his own pizzeria in 1971. Today, a Malnati's pizza can be mail-ordered and shipped to almost anywhere, which is an impressive delivery zone for a local pizza parlor.

JD, Bo, Jack, Joker and Gerbil entered the dark pizzeria and asked for the Sado party. The hostess led the group to a back corner table already occupied by three women.

"Hello, to our American friends. I am Mirai and these are my granddaughters, Kaida and Keiko. Please sit and enjoy a celebratory feast with us. We have much to be thankful for."

The group sat down and Mirai continued, "I am sure you have many questions, but let us order first so we do not starve in our curiosity."

After the group ordered, Mirai asked the waitress to bring eight small empty glasses to the table. Once they were delivered, she continued.

"I would like to commemorate the trauma we have endured and the success we have enjoyed with some sake. This is Junmai Daiginjō-shu sake to be used only for the very noblest of celebrations."

Mirai poured out eight glasses of sake and then raised her glass for a toast. "I wish us all many happy years ahead and behind."

"Cheers," Joker added and then they all drank.

Gerbil made a face, but the others complimented Mirai on how delicate the sake tasted.

"Yes, in Japan we call this seishu, or clear wine, but it is a closer relative to your American beer than wine, as the alcohol comes from the starches of polished rice and not the sugars of a fruit like grapes."

"That was an interesting toast. Is it traditional Japanese?" JD asked Mirai.

"No, it is my own. My name, Mirai, means future and now that I am an old woman, I also represent the past, so my wish is that we do deeds that will create a better future and not actions that will condemn our past."

"That is very perceptive," Bo complimented.

Mirai bowed her head in appreciation, then said, "So, I can guess you all have many questions. Why don't we start the evening with those?"

"Are you the woman who shot the arrow?" Gerbil blurted out quickly.

"Yes, Chester, I am. I do not usually go on such trips, but this was a special favor to a new friend on Sado and my granddaughters. You see Kaida is the essence and Keiko is the shadow, while I am the guardian."

"For what?"

"For the Temple of Ai."

Keiko pulled on her grandmother's sleeve and whispered into her ear in Japanese, *"Gran, are you not telling them too much?"*

"Hush, my shadow. They do not know our ways—that women are not allowed in the temples—but now that they know of us, we must be clever to meld our essence back into the society they perceive."

"Yes, gran. I see," Keiko acknowledged, bowing her head slightly as she pulled away from her gran's ear.

"We learned of Rai's plot at the temple and knew we had to stop it, for America's sake, for Japan's sake and for the world."

Keiko then spoke directly to the group for the first time.

"Joker, I wish to tell you how clever you were to signal

SOS in that way. You connected the dots for us and helped us to bring in Special Agent Dearfield."

"So, you're the one who saw my SOS. How did you know to contact JD?" Joker asked a little befuddled.

"The caller said you gave my phone number along with your message," JD interjected.

"Phone number? Message? I was lucky to spell SOS correctly," Joker admitted, then JD and Joker both looked at Keiko.

"I used what Americans call poetic license? I believed this was the message you intended, no?"

"Well, you got me there. Thank you. I have never been so understood by a woman in my life," Joker said with a big smile on his face and the table laughed, while Keiko blushed and lowered her eyes in embarrassment.

"But how did you know where Joker was? I thought you lost him when Kaida saved Gerb—Chester," JD queried.

"I did lose Rai and Jiji when I saved Chester, but my sister did not. She was in the shadows following their every move," Kaida confessed, then added after looking at Gerbil. "In fact, it was fortunate we were together for this part of the . . . trip since if Keiko was alone, she would have had to decide whether to save Chester or follow Rai and Jiji. Being present with her allowed me to intervene and save Chester without compromising our intent to follow Rai and Jiji."

Gerbil looked over at Keiko and swallowed hard, then looked to Kaida and said, "Thank you again for saving me."

"It was my honor," Kaida replied.

JD also looked over at Keiko, her jade eyes again catching the light, then said, "So, you were the girl on the bike and that's when you placed the tracker—clever. I think the FBI could use a team like you two."

"That is related to what we would like to talk to you

about," Mirai admitted.

"You want your granddaughters to join the FBI?" Jack asked, finally finding the energy to fully join the discussion.

"No, we are happy at the Temple of Ai, but it is the history of the temple I wish to tell you about. Do you know what day this last Friday was?" Mirai asked the group.

"The worst day of my life?" Joker answered, then was immediately met with cold stares from Jack and Gerbil. "OK, maybe the *fifth* worst day?" he hedged.

"Possibly, but it was also Friday the Thirteenth. Is this not also the day The Unfathomable Ones left the Great Naval Academy?"

Jack, Joker and Gerbil all stared at each other a bit wide-eyed, then Jack asked, "We haven't heard that term since the war. How did you know about it?"

"Remember, in the shadows all is brought to light."

The trio turned their attention to Keiko who returned their glance with bright jade eyes and a warm, confident smile.

"So, do you know the significance of this date?" Mirai asked the group again.

"I know it's bad luck, or gives you bad luck on that day, or something like that," Gerbil answered.

"Yes, and I think we proved that as factual," Joker added.

"But why is it bad luck?" Mirai pressed.

"I believe it has to do with the history of the Knights Templar . . . the night their leader and other members were arrested in France," Bo answered.

"You are correct. King Philip IV of France was in deep financial debt to the Templars, who were bankers as well as holy soldiers. The king decided to get out of his debt by persecuting the Templars with false claims from heresy and idol worship to fraud and homosexual practices.

Confessions to these crimes, even though obtained during extreme torture, caused a public uproar which the king used to turn the very people the Templars protected against them. Even though Pope Clement V, a relative of the king, absolved the Templars of all crimes, King Philip still went forth with his false prosecution. Six years after the knights were absolved by the pope and 2 years after the organization had been officially disbanded, over 50 Knights were burned at the stake for crimes they did not commit. In Japan this date is only significant on Sado and only in the Temple of Ai. This is because in 1308 a Templar ship, the *Liberté*, was shipwrecked on Sado with only one surviving Knight. William Fraser—or Kumakichi as our ancestors called him, which means Fortunate Bear—lived among us for many years and eventually married Aika from our village and together with Aika's sister, Asa, they started the Temple of Ai."

"What does Ai mean in Japanese?" Bo asked.

"Love. Simply, love," Mirai answered, then continued. "It is for this reason we wish to extend an invitation to you all to come visit France."

"To celebrate the Templars, right? Not to be burned at the stake?" Joker clarified.

"Who knows what the celebration may hold for you," Mirai said deadpan, then smiled. "No, not just to celebrate the Templars, but to celebrate the Templars' legacy. You see this October 13 will be the 700-year anniversary of the Templar arrests and the Temple of Ai has protected the cargo of the shipwrecked *Liberté* for nearly as long. Now as our ancestors swore to Kumakichi, we will tell the truth to the world to set things right. For you see, the *Liberté* contained half of everything the Templars owned at their headquarters on the island of Cyprus. These possessions included valuable jewels and gold, but also contained documents—the actual history of the Templars and historical proof of their actions and accounts. These documents are treasures beyond the value of jewels and gold, and will be on display in the Louvre in France starting with the French opening on Friday, July 13. We would love to have you as our special guests at this this time if Bo can travel with the baby so close, of course. Then on October 13 at the international opening—700 years to the day after the false arrests of the Knights—the whole world will learn of these treasures and of the treachery of those who sought to destroy the Templars for their own ambition and greed."

Epilogue

October 31, 2007

A man and woman walked, pushing a stroller along the sidewalk, watching children run up to house after house and calling out, *Trick or Treat*. They both looked at each other, knowing this harried day of costumes and candy consumption was soon to be their future. They then looked down at their newborn twin girls and knew deep in their hearts that they had made the right choice to become a family. The twins had been born on October 13, which only seemed right.

One of the twins fussed and the woman said to the man, "Do you remember the statue of the man holding the baby in his arms at the Louvre?"

"Yes, I get the hint," the man said as he stopped to scoop up the crying child.

"This one seems to be the fussy one. Certainly not the shadow of the two," the man said with a smirk.

"How do you know I am not switching their hair ribbons on you?" the woman questioned.

"How do you know I'm not switching them back?"

They hugged and the woman took over pushing the stroller as they walked to the park at the end of the block. It was a gloriously warm fall day and the Halloween trick or treaters were out in force, swarming from house to house like schools of fish. The air was filled with screeches and giggles, and the sound of running feet.

"How do you think your dad and stepmother are faring?" the woman asked.

The man, feeling it strange to hear the term stepmother after so many years without a father or mother, felt a warm feeling inside that was so involuntary and made him smile so widely that his face hurt in the warm, but crisp fall air.

"I believe if they don't run out of candy, they may survive," he responded.

The two entered the park and after the woman took the remaining child in her arms, they both sat on a swing and gently rocked the babies.

As the man gently swung his fussing baby back and forth, he thought about what they had experienced in France. The Louvre, the world's most visited museum, was initially a fortress and served as a royal residence before being converted to a museum in 1793 after the French Revolution. The glass pyramid which sits atop the Louvre's underground lobby is in scale with the Great Pyramid of Giza and contains 673 panes of specially created glass.

The Knights Templar exhibition was wildly popular and if his group had not been on the special guest list, they would likely still be waiting in line for tickets. The exhibition consisted of illuminated glass panels that formed a maze to lead the visitors through a timeline of documents and artifacts along the way. Documents from each of the Crusades, bank records, ceremonial records and more all pointed to the devout Holy warriors the Templars claimed to be. Artifacts, including crowns and jewelry, gold bars and loose jewels, bones and works of art were abundant and contained in glass cases along the timeline trail.

However, the exhibition did not contain the one artifact that nearly every visitor hoped to see—the Holy Grail. But this did not stop them from coming as documents along the way verified that another ship, the *Warhorse*, set sail for Greenland just as the *Liberté* set sail for the source of the Silk Road. This revelation would launch more than just imaginations—the hunt for the Grail was on once more.

Also missing were documents that cast light on any of the false claims made by King Philip IV. This was further reinforced by a copy of the Chinon Parchment dated 17–20 August 1308, which proved Pope Clement V officially absolved the Templars of all heresies in 1308. Because of the Temple of Ai and their willingness to share these long-kept secrets, the Knights Templar were alive in the public eye again and receiving the honor they had earned and long deserved.

The woman, slowly twisting in her swing, said, "They just love this. We may have to get another rocking chair. Sharing one will just not cut it, especially when their teeth start coming in."

"Well, you know what grandpa says. *If rocking the baby doesn't work, just use bigger rocks.*"

"That's terrible. How long do you expect they will stay?"

"As long as you need help and longer. Their farm is well-maintained by their son and grandson, so they're under no pressure to return. I would like for them to stay through Thanksgiving if they feel they can be away for that long. I know they will want to have Christmas at home with their family and as you know we will have three new guests this Christmas. It was bold of you to ask Mirai, Kaida and Keiko to come to Chicago for an American Christmas. I believe it will be an experience they will treasure for years to come."

"Yes, I agree. And if your father and stepmother do stay through Thanksgiving, I would like to invite two other close friends in secret. I know we were all together in France just this last July, but having family and friends in our lives is a blessing neither of us could have even imagined before and Thanksgiving is the perfect time to bring us all together."

"I agree," the man said, then squeezed the woman's shoulder. "Life is so unpredictable, but when you take the time to understand it's all about love and family and friends, even the worst of times can be overcome."

"And celebrating the good times should never be neglected or taken for granted since they are not promised but earned."

"Yes. I agree. Let's get home and save grandpa and grandma before they run out of candy. We wouldn't want them to be eaten by zombies."

The woman looked over at the house across the street from the park and watched as three zombies and a witch ran down the front lawn toward the house next door and said, "Yes, eaten or turned into toads. We should go."

The pair placed the children back in the stroller and started their trek home. Home to a family they did not have even just six months ago. A family they planned to enjoy for years to come. The man thought about the insightful words he had heard about wishing for happy years ahead and behind and he knew he was heading to a home that planned just that—if he could get there before the candy ran out!

The End

About the Author

Scott Lothian is a clinical pharmacist and lives in the Chicagoland area with his family. He has practiced for over 40 years concentrating in solid organ transplant, oncology and pain management, but for the past decade has been on the clinical IT side of healthcare. This is his second novel. You can find his first—*Perfect Posture*—on Amazon.

www.facebook.com/ScottLothianBooks

3 1125 01133 8553

Made in the USA
Monee, IL
06 October 2021